Quinn

THIRST FOR JUSTICE

By Joe McCoubrey

Dedication & Thanks

This one is for Sam Quinn.

He was my great grandfather, an interesting man who lived in interesting times. A humble, hard-working soul who toiled to make ends meet in the poverty-ridden Ireland of the turn of the twentieth century. A proud individual, he worked as yard foreman at the local Rea's bottling plant, a job that was physically demanding during every minute of the 12-hours a day he was tethered to it across a 6-day working week.

He lived through two world wars and witnessed the birth of a new Irish nation in the wake of the Easter Rising, an event that gladdened his old republican heart. Sadly, he never really had the opportunity to see much of what lay beyond the boundaries of his birthplace in Downpatrick. He missed a lot, but achieved much more. I got to know him a little bit, but not nearly enough. He died when I was ten. I would've liked the idea of sitting down with him and hearing his full life story.

He was known simply as Da Sam, an endearing and apt moniker for the patriarch of what would become a dynasty. His direct descendants can now be counted in the many hundreds spread across Ireland and beyond.

He gave his name to those who came immediately afterwards. Quinn rolled into Fitzsimons and Smyth and Oakes, and then Jennings and Cunliffe and Ennis and McNeilly and McAlister and Dobbin and McCoubrey. Next came the Breens, Murphys, Grahams, Masons, Rosses, Currans and Galbraiths. The branches reach farther down to the Boltons, McMahons, Dohertys, Sharvins, Cheadles, Moores, Rhodes, Bradys, Savages, Neesons, Molloys, Bells, Casements, McGarrys and the

Tates.

There's a genealogical rollcall of Ireland, right there!

But that's not all! Many of Sam's lineage moved to England and became Millwards, Dockers, Hollicks, Whitehouses, Dalys, Selvesters, Robeys, Wilkins, Meakins, Edwards and Coscos.

And all that within four generations!

Old Sam didn't have an offspring named Francis Xavier Quinn, but I like to think he'd approve of my choice for the lead role in this new series of thrillers. I see them both as hard, unflappable characters in their own ways. Men of honour, principle and fortitude. Men of whom Downpatrick should be proud.

I've drilled this dedication down to the present day, to my grandsons – old Sam's great, great, great grandsons – Alfie, Rory, Ellis, and our new edition, Michael. I hope one day they will get to read this and be as proud of their heritage as I am.

Among other things, Sam was a chivalrous man, so he'd want me to mention the women in my life. I do so with true gratitude. My love and thanks to Teresa, Brenda, Lynda, and Lisa.

A final thanks and dedication to my editing team who are the go-to guys for wake-up calls when bad habits or poor research creep into my work. Without the blandishments of Brad Fleming, Mick Keane, and Martin Graham this manuscript would not be as polished as it should be. I thank them for their patience and for the little bits that make me better.

About the Author

Joe McCoubrey is a former journalist who reported first-hand during the height of the Northern Ireland "Troubles" throughout the 1970's and 1980's, firstly as a local newspaper editor, and then as a partner in an agency supplying copy to national newspapers and broadcasters. He switched careers to help start a Local Enterprise Agency, providing advice and support to budding entrepreneurs in his native town, and became its full-time CEO. He retired to concentrate on his long-time ambition to be a full-time writer. His previous novels have all been published to critical acclaim.

He lives in Downpatrick, County Down, and is proud of its historic connections to Saint Patrick, Ireland's Patron Saint.

You can visit Joe at: www.joemccoubrey.com

Also by Joe McCoubrey:

Exposure to Truth
No Margin for Error
Spent Force
Absence of Rules
Absence of Mercy
Someone Has To Pay
Death by Licence.

QUINN

Copyright © Joe McCoubrey 2018
ISBN: 978-0-9954687-5-7
Publisher: Inishfree Communications

CHAPTER 1

THEY CAME FOR him at seven o'clock in the evening. Not exactly the ideal time for what they had in mind.

Eight hours later in the dead of night would have been much better. But planning and circumspection meant little to the six men who stepped out of a rented minibus onto the grounds of the expensive detached residence on the edge of the city.

They cared little about factors outside their control. People walking their dogs or driving home from work or calling at the house for a neighbourly chat had an annoying habit of coming forward as witnesses in the aftermath of a murder. So what?

These were not the type of men to bother about detail. If they wanted to do something, they simply went out and did it. It was the way they'd always gone about their business, knowing that no matter what went wrong it could be fixed later by their usual methods of buying silence. It had worked before, so why not now?

They got lucky, in one sense. The region was being hit by a vicious snowstorm which all but eliminated the possibility of dog walkers, or house callers, or motorists seeing anything beyond the frantic sweep of their windscreen wipers. Which meant the murderers were left with a clear run at their target without realising the importance played by the weather in their grand scheme of things. Perhaps, therefore, if they had sat down and worked it out in advance, and worried about witnesses, and taken the snow into consideration, they'd have concluded that seven o'clock in the evening was just as good as three o'clock in the morning.

Luck? Maybe it would have been if they hadn't overlooked one other important benefit of engaging in a little pre-killing research.

They might have paid more attention to finding out who else was already in the house.

Ten-year-old Charlie McAndrew was at that moment playing in an upstairs room with Sophie, two years his junior and under Charlie's protective wing the way big brothers tended to do with their only sibling.

At face value the children were pampered by wealthy parents. But that masked the real truth of two independent souls, nurtured lovingly in a way that avoided fencing them in with boundaries which might stunt a natural urge to express their personalities. If that meant frequent bursts of playful yelling, screaming, and turning their den into a mess of upended furniture and toys strewn everywhere, then so be it. Their parents were big on the adage of letting kids be kids.

Charlie and Sophie were doing that now. Engaged in a pillow fight, running around the large games room, clambering over obstacles, and pushing aside chairs and tables in an attempt to ward off each other's blows. Charlie always held back, not quite putting full force behind his strikes, and careful to ensure Sophie landed her fair share of hits.

The staccato crash of breaking glass stopped the children in their tracks. Even from their room on the upper floor to the rear of the house they could hear the sound of voices raised in anger. They were the voices of strangers. Charlie realised instinctively that something bad was happening. He touched Sophie on the shoulder and held a finger to his mouth in a silent instruction to be quiet. Not sure what to do, Charlie was rooted to the spot. The shouting continued, and then he heard the plaintive cries of his mother. He had to find out what was going on.

He motioned Sophie to stay in the room as he tiptoed nervously to the door and stepped out onto a large hallway. He got down on his belly and crawled towards a bannister that overlooked the open-plan lounge where his parents spent most of their evenings. He peered between ornate wooden spindles to gaze down at a scene of destruction.

The large glass-topped coffee table which was a centrepiece feature of the lounge was lopsided against an overturned bookcase. Shards of glass sparkled across the beechwood flooring, now almost covered in smashed ornaments, most of which Charlie knew were priceless antiques gathered over a lifetime by his father and grandfather.

His mum and dad were sitting on the only piece of furniture still in its accustomed place. It was a six-seater angled sofa, although they barely filled one of the seats, so closely tangled were they as they cowered below the menacing figures of six men ringed in front of them.

The man in the centre of the group was wearing a long black overcoat with his neck encased in a multi-coloured scarf because of the sub-zero temperatures that had settled into the east coast of Maine shortly before teatime, a presage to predicted heavier snow showers due to batter the region later in the evening. The other five men were more lightly attired in identical dark-blue suits, white shirts and thin ties. Charlie saw that all of them were holding guns, and all of the guns were pointed at his mum and dad.

"So, McAndrew, you just thought it was your civic duty to run to the Feds with tall tales about how we do business?" The voice belonged to the man in the middle.

"It was not like that," Mark McAndrew shouted. "I keep telling you that they approached me. They wanted to know anything I could tell them about your dealings, particularly from the legal side of things. I only told them what were already matters of public record. For Chrissakes, I'm just a corporate lawyer who had the misfortune of representing a firm which was suing one of your companies. Everything was, and still is, subject to attorney-client privilege."

The man smiled. "If only that were true. The fact is that you've been feeding a lot of information to the Feds, particularly pre-trial discovery information. That was strategy stuff, not the kind that was used in public, but some of it was, shall we say, commercially-sensitive."

"No, no, I acted in good faith to all parties. I tried to...."

"Enough of this bullshit!" The man moved menacingly closer to McAndrew. "I know you've been spending a lot of time with Special Agent Carl Freeman and between the two of you a full schematic of all our interlinked businesses has been constructed. You've even gone as far as offering your assistance in helping to track offshore bank accounts, property deeds, and contracts with a number of shipping companies. This is not something we can tolerate."

McAndrew's eyes bulged. "How did you....how could you possibly know this?"

"Ah, there we have it finally! An admission, straight from your very lips. You do know there is only one way this can end? We can't afford loose lips and busybodies."

"Please, not in front of my wife."

The man roared with laughter. "You don't get it, do you? Before you die, you'll know it was your stupidity that caused her demise. You should have thought about that before running off at the mouth."

Without another word, the man raised his pistol and fired a single shot into the centre of Ruth McAndrew's forehead.

Upstairs, little Charlie bit down hard on his fist and watched as the man's gun swivelled towards his father. There was another loud shot, followed by his father contorting on the sofa before slumping across his wife's lap.

That was followed by a loud, piercing scream.

Charlie turned in horror to see Sophie standing

11

over the handrail, gazing down at the bloody scene below. He hadn't heard her approach or take up station beside him.

Everything seemed to happen at once.

"There's kids up there!"

"They must have seen what happened."

"Get them and silence them."

Charlie broke free from his trance and yanked at Sophie's hand as he raced for their games room. He was aware that at least two of the men were running up the stairs, but he didn't stop to look back. Inside the room he threw a bolt across the door and had the presence of mind to grab two coats, before scrambling into a closet. He opened a small hatch to reveal an enclosed canvas spiral chute that was bolted to the outer wall of the house and was meant as a fun slide leading to a large paddling pool during the balmy days of summer. The pool had been stored away, but Charlie knew the drop from the end of the chute was only a few feet. He urged Sophie into the opening and pushed her hard, jumping in as soon as she cleared the first bend.

Charlie knew how to arrest his momentum and easily stepped out at the end of the chute to find Sophie lying on the ground crying. He whispered to her to be quiet and quickly wrapped her in one of the coats he'd pulled from the wall rack in the room. He put on the other coat, lifted Sophie to her feet, and raced with her to a large clump of trees that led to a laneway about a mile from the nearby town centre.

He knew the men would eventually find their footprints in the light dusting of snow that covered the rear garden. By then he hoped to be far enough away to find help.

"What do you mean you lost them!"

"The little devils had some kind of escape hatch to the outside. Who would think of such a thing? It was too small for Jim and me to get into, but it must lead to the back of the house."

The group leader snorted. "Remind me to book you a place on Mensa's advanced IQ test. With that kind of brain, you're sure to ace it."

The man looked bewildered. "You want us to go out on the grounds and find them?"

"Yes, you idiot, I want you to find them, and I want you to kill them. And don't come back until you've done it."

CHAPTER 2

FRANCIS XAVIER QUINN stepped off Delta flight 8169 from Mexico City and hurried towards the warmth of the terminal at Boston Logan International. He had slept through most of the five-hour trip from Benito Juarez airport and was eager to keep on the move. He intended taking an Amtrak to Portland where he'd overnight before continuing to his next stop at Bangor, Maine. He was, as always, covering his tracks, using different IDs from a multi-wallet collection that had served him well in his chosen profession. The constant switching of venues and personas kept him one step ahead of his enemies, affording greater opportunities to spot any tails he might pick up on the way.

When he arrived at North Station, part of the confusing sprawl of real estate that took in South Station, the Back Bay Station, Boston Landing Station, Yawkey Station, and others, he was not sure why he suddenly decided to change his plans. Instead of overnighting in Portland, he'd go directly to Bangor, some 240 miles and three hours down the line.

After three weeks away on assignment, he simply craved for home, although in truth his destination was little more than a base. He didn't have a bricks-and-mortar dwelling there, nor did he spend more than one night at a time in a city with less than two hundred thousand souls. And frankly it was a place with little going for it, unless you happened to be endeared by its history or arts or its surrounding parks and forests. Quinn scored low on all three counts.

The only attraction for Quinn was its name. It shared the moniker with a seaside resort in Northern Ireland, barely twenty miles from the town of Downpatrick where Quinn was born and lived until he was sixteen. He no longer had any affinity with either location, or Northern Ireland in general, but one place was as good as another, so why not Bangor, albeit on the other side of the Atlantic?

At sixteen years of age, Quinn had crossed the border from Northern Ireland to the Republic of Ireland to take up temporary lodgings with an ageing uncle, an IRA veteran who'd long since hung up his gun, but not his hatred for the English. A few weeks after his arrival, Quinn became a bonafide, passport-carrying citizen of the Irish Free State, as his uncle continued to call it. It was the right of anyone born anywhere on the island of Ireland to be citizens of either jurisdiction, or both if they had a mind to. Quinn was having none of that. He was Irish through and through, his "Britishness" wiped out by a stroke of a pen.

On the morning of his seventeenth birthday he'd walked into the recruiting office at the Cathal Brugha Barracks at Rathmines to the south of Dublin city centre and joined the Irish Rangers, the country's elite special forces group. The Sergeant manning the front desk had tried to persuade Quinn to take a more conventional route into the armed services, pointing out that less than five per cent of cadets actually made it through the first four weeks with the Rangers. Quinn was having none of it. It was either the Rangers or nothing. Unbeknown to Quinn, the Sergeant had actually signed him up only to a taster Ranger session, with a 'return-to-unit' fallback in the event of failing to make the grade. He was now locked into the army, one way or another.

It took less than the usual four weeks for Quinn's instructors to recognise they had a real diamond on their hands. It would need a lot of polishing and maybe some remedial work around the edges, but nothing could take away from Quinn's natural aptitude for his new-found life. He craved extra sessions in martial arts, weapons training, parachuting and, most significant of all, in sniper school where he finished top of his class in each of nine tests held over a two-year period. He graduated from one-hundred per cent accuracy at five-hundred yards in all conditions, to one thousand, and then two thousand yards, a feat achieved only once before by a seasoned expert.

Over the course of the next five years he honed his skills in postings across the world, most notably in the jungles of Belize and the sands of the Sahara Desert. He'd risen to the rank of Captain, the youngest ever to serve in that capacity, an honour earned not only by his skills and his ability to follow orders without reservation, but also because the men around him began to look up at the six-foot-three, dark-haired youth with increasing awe and respect.

He'd quickly dropped his annoying first names. From day one at Ranger camp he'd insisted on being called just Quinn, a throwback to his teenage angst at the plethora of annoying shortcuts taken by those around him. He'd lost count of the number of times he'd got into quarrels over being called Frank, or Frankie, or Francie, or – most annoying of all – FX, which represented his first-name initials. The Rangers had no issues with his preference and from that moment he simply became known as Quinn. It was to stick with him, except of course when he used aliases, as he often did.

Midway through his second stint with the Rangers, he began to fall out of love with regimented life. The opportunities for action, and subsequent adrenaline rushes, became fewer and fewer. There had to be more to life than this, and Quinn set a course on finding out what was on the other side of the hill in civvy street.

At the end of eight years, he mustered out of the Rangers and headed for America. He had been a fastidious saver, putting away a tidy nest egg that would see him through at least a year without having to worry about taking the first job that came along. As it turned out, however, that's precisely what he did.

He was drinking in an Irish bar in Lower Manhattan when a fight broke out between two sets of drinkers seated at adjoining tables. There were six men in total, all stockily built and looking like guys who knew how to handle themselves. They held nothing back, throwing punches and chairs at each other in a frenzied attack that made the other patrons run for the exit doors.

Quinn sat on. He was at the opposite end of the room, well away from the melee, but with a good vantage point to see everything that went on. Not his fight. No reason for him to get involved. Until one of the men back-handed a barmaid who got too close to the action.

That was a no-no in Quinn's book.

He pushed back his chair, strode across the floor, and singled out the culprit. He tapped the man on the shoulder and waited until his target half-turned. No sense in waiting for a full-turn; the greatest damage could be done to the side of the face – and that's where Quinn planted a vicious right-handed jab that took the man off his feet and sent him sprawling against the other combatants.

Suddenly, their personal vendetta came to a stop. The five remaining warriors now had a common enemy. Quinn.

He watched them exchange glances and come to a decision.

"Take my advice," Quinn told them in a soft voice, "and walk away. There's no sense in any more of you having to be carted off to hospital. Let me finish my drink in peace and we'll call it quits."

Even as he spoke he knew it was futile. As they used to say back home in Ireland, their *dander* was up, and they were spoiling for a fight. It wasn't an ideal location for a five-on-one shakedown, but the cramped area would work in Quinn's favour. As usual, there had to be a ringleader, a guy who always had to show his macho side by being first into action. Quinn waited for him to step forward and when he did he walked straight into a piledriver that he never saw coming, mainly because Quinn had closed the distance the instant the man moved.

Quinn didn't wait for the unconscious man to drop to the floor. He pivoted on his left foot and delivered a high kick to the first man on his right, the boot landing at chest height and resulting in the sound of a couple of ribs cracking under the force. He pushed aside the wheezing fighter in time to block a downward punch from his mate, countering with a stiff uppercut that put the lights out for his latest assailant.

He was not so lucky with an attack from his left side. One of the two remaining heavyweights swung a chair that was calculated to smash into the side of Quinn's head. But the shadow of movement provided Quinn with a millisecond in which to adjust his body, taking the full force of the attack on his shoulder blades. Pain jolted through his entire body as he dropped to his knees, fighting to refill empty lungs.

It would have been a crippling blow for most men, but the Rangers had taught him well. Block out the pain, use the flush of adrenaline, and channel your remaining energy into one good targeted blow. In this case, he balled his fist and smashed it into the side of the man's exposed knee, making the leg turn at an angle it was not supposed to turn. The brute screamed in agony and fell to the floor.

Quinn leapt to his feet, ready for the last man standing. But the fight was over. The man stepped back with his palms raised and spoke in a plaintive voice. "Jeez, we've had enough. I don't want any more trouble."

The familiar brogue brought back memories. "I'm guessing," Quinn told him, "that you're from the North of Ireland, somewhere around Belfast, if I'm not mistaken." Quinn's own accent had been neutralised by exposure to the various regional dialects of his Ranger colleagues, so much so that it would have been difficult for anyone to place his origins, other than concluding he was from a generalised European descent.

"Yeah, that's right," the man answered, hoping to garner favour with what was obviously a dangerous individual. "Are you from the oul' country yourself, only you don't sound like it?"

"I'm not from anywhere," Quinn said in a tone of finality. "If I were you and your mates I'd keep my nose out of things. It's not nice making nuisances of yourselves by smashing up respectable places and generally making people want to puke at the sight of the lot of you. I suggest you gather up your friends and get them to the nearest hospital, but not before you dig into their pockets and pay for the damage. About five-hundred dollars ought to be enough."

The man was in no mood to argue. He bent down and startled rifling through his mates' pockets. "One more thing," Quinn told him, "make sure you all suffer a bout of amnesia about this little confrontation. I wouldn't want to have to hunt you down if you do talk."

"No worries there, mate. We don't go in for talking to the police; it's something we learned from back home."

Four days later, Quinn was back in the bar. He wasn't looking for trouble, but he'd be damned if he'd let a bunch of thugs keep him away from what was the nearest drinking establishment to the bedsit he'd rented. He had spent the intervening days exploring New York with typical visitor gusto, taking in all the landmarks via river cruising or just walking from one place to another. He spent a lot of time in Central Park, enjoying the mixture of solitude and bustle that seemed to be part of the park's unique make-up. He'd drank copious amounts of coffee at a number of Starbucks premises and dined at a wide selection of bistros and cafeterias. There was a lot to be said for this civvy street lark.

He was back in the bar, not for any alcohol craving, just merely the socialising. He had never been a great drinker; he could nurse a few bottles of Bud for an entire afternoon. He found establishments like these acted as a window to the world, and the world was what he wanted to see.

"Welcome back, stranger."

He glanced up to look at the smiling face of the waitress who'd been clobbered during the fist fight. She still sported the remnants of a black eye, but he'd have recognised the short-cropped blonde hair anywhere. She was a looker all right.

"I never got the chance to thank you," she purred. "What you did was freakin' awesome. I mean one man against six. Who are you anyway?"

"Just someone looking for a bit of solitude."

"It sure didn't seem that way! My boss, Mr Lonegan, wants to see you."

Quinn frowned. "Like I said, I don't want any

trouble, so if you don't mind I'll pass."

"No, it's not like that. He wants to thank you and offer you a job."

This time Quinn smiled. "Look, tell Mr Lonegan no thanks are necessary and I'm not looking for a job."

CHAPTER 3

QUINN SETTLED into the generously-upholstered Amtrak seat, staring out the window at a whitening world as snow flurries continued to blanket the countryside. For some reason, his mind wandered back ten years to that first meeting with Patrick Lonegan, a kind-hearted octogenarian who was easy to like and hard to say no to.

Lonegan owned a string of properties, mainly bars and restaurants, though he dabbled in low-cost rental accommodation as his way of distributing part of his vast wealth to those less fortunate. His tenants, mostly young families struggling to make ends meet, were often told to forego their rents to pay for food and clothing. They worshipped the old man and never tried to take advantage of his generosity.

Unfortunately, there were others with a lot less scruples.

Protection racketeering blighted the boroughs in those days, so much so that Lonegan was forced to cough up more than twenty thousand a week for his many enterprises. In his younger days he would have taken on the gangs and drop-outs who were strangling his businesses, but he had a large family of children and grandchildren to worry about, particularly when some of the threats were targeted their way.

He made a simple request of Quinn. Help me get rid of the gangsters and pocket ten thousand a week, in cash, for your trouble. Quinn relished the challenge, and within six months the protection payments had dwindled to a trickle. The old man was as good as his word, pushing more money Quinn's way than he'd ever thought possible of earning in a lifetime.

Then one night everything came crashing down.

Patrick Lonegan locked the rear door of his premises for the last time. As he turned to head for his car, he was cut down by a hail of bullets, fired from three semi-automatic pistols held by the Kelly brothers, formerly of Wexford and now trying to make a name for themselves in the dark underbelly of Manhattan's mean streets. They were nothing more than punks; cheap low-life immigrants out for a fast buck and to hell with whoever stood in their way.

Quinn blamed himself for Lonegan's death. Maybe he had pushed the rival gangs too hard. Maybe he was not as smart as he'd thought. At the very least, he should have been with Lonegan when the old man was at his most vulnerable. He should have seen this coming.

He went after the Kellys with a dark heart. There was to be no mercy. Less than twenty-four hours after Lonegan's funeral, the three siblings met a sorry end, one with a broken neck, another with a single stab wound to the heart, and the eldest brother, undoubtedly the ringleader, was found in an alleyway with a full magazine of 9mm bullets stitched across his torso.

Quinn left New York a changed man. Gone was the altruistic youth who'd pledged to serve and protect. In its place was a cold-blooded killer who intended to profit from his unique skills-set.

At first, he'd had to tout for work, selling his services cheaply until his reputation grew. He knew how to use modern technology, particularly the Dark Web, where he announced himself as *The Solutionist*, a gun for hire with no questions asked. His standard fee was one-million dollars, plus expenses. There was no shortage of takers. The money was payable up front into a Swiss bank account, where it usually disappeared without trace within hours of a lodgement being made. He never asked for the identities of his assorted employers, nor did they ever learn who they were dealing with. He had only one rule about his targets: no women, children or priests.

His wealth was spread over numerous bank accounts and safety deposit boxes in a dozen cities in various countries. At the last count, he'd calculated it to be well north of twenty-five million dollars. Quinn was now approaching his thirty-sixth birthday. Another four years of this and he would retire to the South of France. Even earlier, if he could find more assignments to match the five-mill fee he'd earned for killing two prominent members of a drugs cartel in Juarez, Mexico.

Quinn arrived in Bangor, Maine shortly after seven in the evening. He took a taxi across the city to a large industrial site where he had the driver drop him off at the front entrance. He walked for more than twenty minutes through the sprawl of buildings, finally stopping at a row of lock-up garages. He punched in a seven-digit number on a security plate fixed against the wall of a unit marked number twenty-three. The up-and-over door recoiled silently on well-oiled tracks and he stepped inside, waiting until the shutter returned to its closed position before he hit the light switch.

The entire space was taken up by a luxury Entegra coach, a dazzling silver and black RV that had set him back more than one-hundred thousand dollars, after taking in the fees paid to a master carpenter for a range of "extras" that were peculiar to Quinn's profession.

This was how he got around the country. This was how he stayed anonymous, away from the prying eyes of hotel clerks or sleazy landlords. It fitted his credo of never leaving an easy trail to follow.

The Cummins 15-litre ISX turbocharged 605HP engine whispered into life as soon as Quinn depressed the consul-mounted start button. He knew there was a full tank of diesel, something he always made sure of before returning the motorhome to its hideaway. Now, all he needed was to restock the kitchen and fridge and he was good to go. He checked his watch to be certain the small convenience store at Greenbush on the I-95 was still open. He had plenty of time.

He eased the Entegra out into the open for the first time in several months. After closing the unit shutter and resetting the alarm and entrance code, he climbed into the rear of the rig switched on the interior lights, and folded away a half-dozen dustsheets The gleaming mahogany surfaces encasing delicate patterned upholstery always brought a smile to his face. There was ample berthing for six adults, a fully-fitted kitchen, built-in wardrobes, a walk-in toilet and shower, and a multitude of drawers and cabinets. He had a breakfast/dinner area and a writing bureau on which sat a laptop, complete with mobile wi-fi to maintain his links to the world around him. This was where he logged onto the Dark Net looking for bids for his services.

The smoky-black windows kept him hidden from preying eyes, not that anyone would be stumbling around the area at this time of the evening. He sat on the edge of a bunk bed and pushed against a wooden panel, twisting it first to the right, followed by two turns to the left. He could hear the sprockets and pulleys working their magic from the innards of the woodwork, and suddenly a large shelf eased out from below his knees to reveal a gun rack.

There were eight pistols, complete with matching spare magazines, a waist utility belt and an assortment of small combat knives. He chose a silver-plated Sig Sauer P226, two magazines and a Tanto knife. He checked the pistol to make sure it was working smoothly, released and re-inserted the magazine, and chambered a round. Then he fitted the small arsenal into the appropriate utility belt compartments. The moment he wrapped the belt around his waist he felt complete. There was a feeling of nakedness when he had to leave stuff behind because of security screening in airports.

He reset the drawer mechanism and watched it retreat into the secret recess before moving across to the other side of the saloon to open another hidden cache. This one contained eight separate identification wallets, complete with driving licences, social security cards, passports, credit cards and a wad of cash. He chose one at random, looked at the details, and immediately slipped into his new persona. The wallet he'd used in Mexico was returned to the drawer. The stash had set him back a pretty penny at a master forger's office in Amsterdam, but it had been the best investment he'd ever made.

He closed the drawer and changed quickly into fresh clothes, opting for a turtle-neck sweater, a pair of black denims, and a black leather bomber jacket. He could already feel the warmth kicking in from the rig's hydronic water system, which delivered in-floor heating throughout the vehicle. Time to get on the move.

He drove sedately through the gates of the complex, already planning his onward journey. The snow would curtail his choices over the coming days, but he would find a trailer park somewhere and lie low until the roads cleared.

The streets close to the convenience store were packed bumper-to-bumper with vehicles belonging to local residents, most of whom seemed to be heeding the advice of TV weathermen to stay indoors. Quinn was forced to park in a side street about a half-mile from the shop. He welcomed a good stretch of the legs, particularly after almost twelve hours stuck in either a plane or a train.

He sucked in the frosty air, grateful for the way it helped to clear his lungs. Perhaps, however, it was time for a vacation in more sunny climes. Florida was a definite possibility. He needed time to recharge the body's batteries before looking for more work.

CHAPTER 4

THE STORE OWNER stood beside the aluminium console ready to attack the buttons. The clock dial moved to its ten-to-nine position and he immediately pressed every fourth button. The interior lighting dimmed in a signal to shoppers that it was closing time. With only a half-dozen souls left in the building, it shouldn't be much trouble to clear the decks and head home. Never mind these open-all-hours marts, he reckoned nine in the morning till nine at night was convenience enough for anybody. His head-count of stragglers had failed to take in the two waifs who'd slipped in unnoticed and were hiding in a small recess, sandwiched between the deli counter and the racks of fresh vegetables.

Charlie and Sophie McAndrew were scared witless. More than that, they were shivering with cold, trying to block out the early-evening horrors that had visited their home. After walking the deserted streets for more than an hour, Charlie had guided Sophie into the store in search of warmth. He had known they couldn't stay exposed to the elements for much longer.

He had searched desperately for a policeman, or anyone they could tell their story to. But they never met a soul, nor did any passing cars slow down to investigate why two youngsters were out alone in weather that was challenging for even the most heavily-dressed nocturnal pedestrians. The flimsy coats that Charlie had grabbed on their mad dash from the house were little more than rain jackets, hardly a match for the easterly wind that roared between the tall buildings.

Charlie had started to think the bad men were responsible for everyone else staying indoors. Perhaps they all realised they could be hurt if they tried to help. That's why nobody was around. They were scared, just like he was. He was all alone. No, he had Sophie, and it was his job to look after her.

He fought back the tears, put his arm around Sophie, and settled into their hide.

The store's automatic doors swished open and two men stepped inside. They were dressed in identical blue suits, white shirts, and thin ties.

The owner threw them a sigh of frustration. "Sorry gents, we're about to close."

One of the men turned sharply. The look on his face and the tone of his voice sucked the heat from the building. "Shove it up your ass! We'll take as long as we like."

The man walked to his left and nodded to his companion who moved towards the aisle on the far right. The store owner slumped in his seat, hoping whatever they needed was easily to hand. These were not two individuals he wanted to mess with.

The first man walked around the corner past the deli counter. Something caught his attention. "Well, well, what have we here?"

He reached into the recess and grabbed Charlie roughly by the coat collar, yanking him free. He did the same with the little girl, holding the squirming brats like a puppeteer just before the start of a show. He wanted to wring their little necks there and then, but there were too many preying eyes. This needed to be done discreetly. He would take them to the forest on the edge of town and make sure they disappeared permanently.

Charlie recognised the man as one of the group who were at his house earlier. He kicked the man's legs and started screaming. "Let us go! Leave us alone!"

The noise reached Quinn's ears in the next aisle. He dropped a can of beans into his basket and strode towards the commotion. The sight of two children being manhandled didn't sit well with him. It could be a parent, but that hardly mattered. Abuse was abuse.

He closed the gap within a few strides. "Mind telling me what's going on here?"

The man looked unconcerned by the interruption. "What's going on here is none of your business. This is a family matter, so I suggest you keep your nose out unless you want me to rearrange it on your face."

Charlie kicked out again and screamed. "He's a big, fat liar. He murdered my mom and dad. There were six of them. They are going to kill us too."

Quinn watched a shadow fall across the man's eyes. He'd seen that look too often not to realise what it meant. A bad situation was about to get a whole lot worse. The man let go of the children and swept his hand towards a pistol tucked into the front of his waistband. Quinn beat him to it, grabbing the man's wrist in a vice-like grip, while easing his own Sig from the utility belt. He pressed the nozzle against the man's forehead.

"Suppose we start over, and you tell me what's really going on?"

"You're making a big mistake, mister, probably the last one you'll ever make."

"Yeah, I've heard that one before, and from better men that you."

As he spoke, Quinn noticed the boy grab the girl and make a dash for the front door. He couldn't give chase, not with a pistol still stuck in the trousers of his captive. His back would be too much of a target. With his left hand he eased the gun out, holding it at his side while his right hand kept a steady aim at the man's forehead.

The man's eyes moved ever so slightly. Not enough to get the attention of most people, but a heck of a lot to a trained operative. It was that movement, plus the sensation of a rush of air against the nape of his neck, that made Quinn realise something was behind him. He tried to react. But this time he was a millisecond too slow. Sparks danced against a sudden blackness in his head. He registered pain. And then there was nothing,

Quinn woke up to a kaleidoscope of colours. He had no way of knowing how long he'd been out, and it took several seconds to focus his eyes on the blurs around him. He sat up, reaching to feel the back of his head, and coming away with the knowledge that there was a large bump, but no blood. Whoever had hit him must have used a cosh of some kind, not a wooden club, probably a leather pouch stuffed with sand. The butt of a gun, or a sharp metallic implement, would have broken the skin.

His Sig was nowhere to be found. No doubt a trophy for his assailants.

The shop owner, who he'd acknowledged when he'd first entered the store, was standing over him. Quinn rose to his feet and said: "How long have I been out?"

"Just a few minutes. Mind telling me what the hell was going on here?"

Quinn ignored the question. "Where are the kids? Where are the men who were in here?"

"All gone. Look, I'd better call the cops."

"No need," Quinn told him. "Just a misunderstanding. Can you tell me about the men?"

The shopkeeper gave a full description. "Yeah, there were two of them. Dressed like identical twins, though there was nothing twinsy about them, if you get my meaning. Sour-looking bastards, I can tell you. Say, where did those kids come from anyway?"

"That's what I intend to find out."

Quinn strode out into the street, looking both ways before deciding the best thing to do was to head back to the RV and start a search from the comfort of concealment. His head ached, he felt nauseous, but he quickened his stride, determined to get to the bottom of what was a strange encounter. Something about what the kid screamed was gnawing at his insides. *He murdered my mom and dad.*

This could be a long night. The kids could have run in any direction. The two goons could have caught up with them by now. What if the kid was right? *They are going to kill us too.*

Twenty yards from the parked RV, Quinn heard a soft plaintive moan. It was coming from the shadows under an apartment block porch. He moved forward for a better look, surprised to find the huddled figures of the two kids from the store.

"Hi there, are you kids alright?"

The boy pushed his sister behind him. "Go away! We just want to be left alone."

"I want to help you, if I can," Quinn told him.

"We don't need any help." The voice was cracking with emotion. He was a tough little beggar, and no mistake. He reminded Quinn a lot of what he was like himself at that age; independent, argumentative, and sometimes a downright handful. He knew if he moved any closer, or tried to force the lad to move away, the outcome would be a shouting match, which would only succeed in drawing attention that neither side needed.

"Okay, you kids know best."

"We're not kids. I'm Charlie and this is Sophie. We can manage on our own."

Quinn decided to change tack. "No problem, Charlie. You look like the kind of man who knows how to look after himself. I'll bet you want to make sure Sophie is safe. She'll want you to speak for her, but from where I'm standing she's already showing the first stages of hypothermia. You know what that is, Charlie?"

He didn't wait for an answer. "Hypothermia is bad, Charlie. It's caused by the cold and it shuts down a person's body before they can do anything about it. Pretty soon, Sophie won't be able to tell you what she wants, or what's wrong with her. She's relying on you to get her help. Without it, she could die in a matter of a few hours. I know you don't want that to happen."

The boy sniffled and pulled his sister closer. "She's all I got left. What can I do to save her?"

Quinn felt a surge of relief. He turned and pointed towards the RV. "See that big black and silver rig? That's mine. It's got beds and blankets and central heating. Why don't we take Sophie there and get her warmed up? I think she would want you to do that for her."

Charlie looked at the RV, then at his sister, and back again to the RV. "Can you help me to carry her? I don't think she can walk any more."

Quinn smiled and bent to scoop the girl up into his arms. She was in a bad way, her eyes glazed over and her little body shaking uncontrollably. This would be touch and go.

CHAPTER 5

FBI SPECIAL AGENT Carl Freeman slammed the phone hard into its cradle. He was still at his Albany New York Field Office, catching up with paperwork on three separate cases, and looking forward to a break after yet another twelve-hour shift. It always seemed to be like that around this place these days. Too much to do, and no time in which to do it. The call Freeman had just taken was the last thing he needed right now.

He pulled open the top drawer of his desk, flipped the lid on a plastic container, and dry-swallowed three Tylenol. Guilt always brought on a rapid migraine attack. One of his agents had just picked up a radio message from Bangor Maine Police Department. It was short, and anything but sweet. *City lawyer Mark McAndrew and his wife Ruth have been found shot to death in what appears to be a home invasion.*

"Home invasion, my ass," Freeman muttered. He knew what had gone down. This was a pre-meditated hit, ordered by or carried out by Devlin Montgomery, the subject of a two-year investigation into organised crime and corporate fraud on a gigantic scale. The case had been going nowhere until Freeman had enlisted the help of McAndrew, who'd unearthed some telling insights into the mysterious corporation that Montgomery hid behind. In particular, for the first time, Montgomery's name had been linked to several deals, each of which had resulted in the deaths of rival businessmen.

Freeman had spent weeks trying to bring McAndrew on board. He'd used every trick in the book, appealing first to the man's conscience and civic responsibilities. He'd tried a mixture of coercion, arm-twisting, and shovel-loads of flattery. He'd promised anonymity, witness relocation, anything to help persuade McAndrew to play ball. The lawyer had been an innocent pawn. Just a case of being in the wrong place at the wrong time, although back then, Freeman saw it as being in the right place at the right time.

It was why he'd pushed so hard at McAndrew, finally getting through after offering cast-iron guarantees that the lawyer and his family would be protected.

Hence the guilt. He deserved the migraine.

What Freeman couldn't fathom was how Montgomery got wind of McAndrew's involvement in such a relatively short space of time. Everything had been kept under tight wrapping, even to the extent that the Executive Assistant Director in charge of the Criminal Investigation Division at the Hoover Building in Washington wasn't told the name of the individual concerned. It was what Freeman had insisted upon, and the EAD had agreed to a *John Doe* designation, at least until some positive results started to come in.

Now Freeman would have to come clean. It was not a call he was keen to make, more so because he was about to spend a sizeable chunk of his Field

Office budget.

First, he had to contact a man who would be even more difficult to deal with than his superiors. All Washington could do was fire him. This guy could have him sent to Leavenworth, staring at the sky through a small window for the next twenty years. He was the children's grandfather. And there was only one person he'd blame for what had befallen his family.

Freeman was right on all scores.

It took him the better part of ten minutes to recover from the ear-splitting tirade. After another dose of Tylenol, he got back on the phone, but none of his next calls were directed to the EAD. He wanted to be in the air before he pressed that particular button. His first contact was second-in-command Drew Eisler, a buddy from way back to training days, and a man to be counted on when the going got tough. He outlined what he knew - which was precious little - and ordered Eisler to put together a full team for immediate assignment in Maine. Next, he called his contact at the Department of Justice Office to clear immediate transportation to Bangor International Airport. A Gulfstream V jet was put at his disposal, with a flight time of less than two hours, even allowing for the rapidly-deteriorating weather.

His final call was to the Bangor Maine Police Department and was patched through to the detective in charge of the McAndrew "Home Invasion." It took almost five minutes for a gruff voice to break the static. "Tell me this is a joke and that the FBI aren't really interested in one of our little cases."

"Who's speaking?"

"This is Detective Steve Burnett. What can I do for you, Special Agent Freeman?" Sarcasm dripped from every word.

"You can cut the crap for a start, Burnett. Unless you've got your finger up your ass, you're sitting on something that can hardly be described as a *little* case. We both know this was a professional hit, something I suspect you're already aware of, but for some reason you think it's appropriate to play silly buggers."

"Yeah, that's as maybe, but what's it got to do with the FBI?"

Freeman wasn't in the mood for foreplay. "This is now our case. Secure the scene, stand down your men, and wait for our arrival. We should be there in several hours. Is that plain enough for you, Detective?"

"The hell you say. You're just thinking of waltzing in here with your alphabet windbreakers and your shiny shields and expect us to roll over? What's this guy McAndrew to you anyway?"

"That's a need to know, and you can guess the rest."

The line went silent for several seconds before Burnett spoke again. "I'm going nowhere until I get orders from downtown. I'll be here when you arrive, and I expect some better answers than you're giving me right now."

"Something I look forward to." Freeman was about to cut the call when he remembered something. "What about the McAndrew children? There was no mention of them in the initial reports."

"No sign of them in the house, although we just had a report coming in about a fracas in a convenience store involving two kids who match their description."

"What kind of fracas?" Freeman wasn't aware he was shouting.

"Whoa there, Special Agent, don't go getting your girdle in a twist. It's a bit sketchy at the moment, might not even be them, but we're checking it out."

"Those kids have to be found! They could be in grave danger, if they're not dead already. Have you tried contacting friends in the area?"

It was Burnett's turn to shout. "We all might seem like Hicksville to you big boys, but we know how to do our jobs. I have a team checking on their schoolfriends in case they're involved in one of those sleepover fads, and I'm trying to track down any immediate family. No luck there, so far."

"Skip the family," Freeman said sharply. "I've already spoken to the kids' grandfather to see if by chance they were with him. Not an easy conversation, I can tell you, what with his daughter and son-in-law being wiped out, and the children gone missing. The bottom line is that he hasn't seen the kids since their last visit several months ago. Right now, I'm relying on you to find them and keep them safe. Start an immediate inch-by-inch search of the grounds and surrounding areas. If you need additional resources, including the National Guard, you just let me know."

"Phew," Burnett sighed, "this really must be a big one."

"They don't come any bigger, Detective."

Less than five miles from where Detective Burnett was standing, Devlin Montgomery was pacing a room in a suburban mansion. What should have been a simple matter of tidying up loose ends had turned into a complication he could do without. He fought to keep his anger in check as he looked across the room at two members of his travelling party. "So, let me get this right. You had the kids, and then you let them go?"

Bob Thornton and Jim Prudow shifted uncomfortably on their feet. Neither wanted to speak.

"Spit it out!" Montgomery roared.

Thornton jumped right in. "An interfering busybody got in the way. He had a pistol drawn on Jim before I cold-cocked him from behind. That put his lights out, big time."

"You want a medal for that?"

"Just saying, boss. We could do nothing about the kids. They ran away during the altercation with the stranger. We chased outside, but there was no sign of them. They can't have gone very far."

"Tell me about this stranger. Was he a cop or something? Where did he get the pistol?"

Prudow was quick to interject. "Man, he moved like lightning. I never saw anything so fast. One second, I was going for my gun, the next I was staring down the barrel of a Sig. The guy sure seemed to know how to handle it. Didn't look like a cop to me, but he could have been some kind of Special Forces shit. I mean, you don't expect to run into that sort in a convenience store."

Montgomery threw his hands in the air. "That's just great. By now, half the cops in the city are out looking for those kids, and here we have some vigilante do-gooder throwing in his five-cent's-worth. What the fuck am I paying you guys to do? Why didn't you just plug the brats the moment you found them?"

"Aw, boss, it was too public. I mean there were people there and the store probably had cameras. We'd have been made in a heartbeat, isn't that right, Jim."

Thornton's sidekick didn't have time to respond. Montgomery waved away the protests. "So, now you're telling me that your mugs were caught on CCTV? This keeps getting messier and messier. You'd better pray we find those eye-witness kids before anyone else, otherwise you two will be poured into the foundation cement of the next building erected anywhere in the country. Am I making myself clear?"

"What do you want us to do, boss?"

"I want you back out on the streets. The rest of the team are wearing down shoe leather because you fuck-ups couldn't do your jobs. I've had to send for more men, but it's going to be hours before reinforcements arrive. We need to cover cop precinct houses and any public spaces, such as shopping malls, in case those brats wander in out of the cold. There are just too many places they could surface in."

Prudow and Thornton exchanged nervous glances, each unsure how to proceed. Finally, Thornton broke the silence. "Any suggestions where we should go, boss?"

Montgomery smiled. "As a matter of fact, a thought has just occurred to me. Check the local hospitals. It's pretty rough out there, so maybe someone finds those kids and takes them for treatment."

CHAPTER 6

"WE HAVE TO take her to a hospital."

Quinn looked from Sophie to Charlie. They were lying on adjoining beds, wrapped in blankets, and showing renewed colour on their cheeks, thanks to the full kick-in of the RV's central heating system. The vehicle hadn't moved in almost two hours, with Quinn thankful for an improvement in the girl's condition. Nonetheless, he reckoned she needed better treatment than he could provide.

Her shaking had quelled to mild shivers, and she'd managed to take a few sips of water he'd heated from his stash of bottles on a shelf in an otherwise empty fridge, but she was drifting in and out of consciousness. Shock had to be settling in. Not something to be messed around with.

Charlie was faring much better. It had taken all Quinn's coaxing to get the little guy to remain under the blankets, but now he was sitting up, ready to spit at the world again. Quinn had taken a major shine to the boy.

He'd pushed slowly at Charlie to find out what had happened earlier in the evening. He needed the boy to tell things in his own time, but when it finally managed to come out, there was a rush of words and tears and sadness. Quinn couldn't believe the story that unfolded. The sheer callousness of the double murder, and the pursuit of the children, made him realise Charlie had been right. *They are going to kill us too.*

Yeah, they'll have to come through me first!

He hadn't intended to get involved. It was not the kind of thing he did, not when he'd spent the best part of ten years staying under the radar. In all that time he'd never drawn attention to himself. Slip in, get the job done, and slip out. No trails. No clues. No Quinn. This time he couldn't just walk away.

"Did you hear me, Charlie? We have to take Sophie to hospital. I did a bit of field-medic training in the Army, but nothing like this. The Army prepares you to dress wounds, but not to know what's happening on the inside of somebody. That internal stuff is for the experts. Best we get her checked out."

"Will you stay with us?" Charlie pleaded. "We have to go back home later. I want to talk to my grandpa. He'll know what to do. He'll get the police to find those bad men and put them in jail."

And there it was. Quinn's worst nightmare. Hardly the time to tell Charlie he couldn't ever go back home, or that there was probably little his grandfather could do about what had happened there. Worse still, the cops were involved by now, the place probably crawling with them. And APBs out for two missing kids. And Quinn caught in the middle.

He pushed aside a mounting feeling of disquiet and moved to the desk. He fired up the laptop, did a Google search for the nearest hospital, and memorised the zip code. The Eastern Maine Medical Centre on State Street, beside the

Pemobscot River, was three miles away, according to the Satnav screen when Quinn climbed into the cab and started the engine.

He resisted the temptation to replace the Sig with one of his other pistols. Quite apart from not wanting to alert Charlie to his cache of weaponry, there was a gnawing feeling that where he was going was too public to be walking around armed to the teeth. At some point, the cops would have to get involved, and the last thing he needed was having to explain why he was kitted out like Rambo. He started to construct his story about an innocent tourist who just happened to find two kids in need of medical treatment. It was flimsy, but it would have to do.

He slipped the utility belt from his waist and forced it into a hidden compartment under his feet.

Jim Prudow drew the short straw. Actually, more a case that he called heads when he should have called tails in a coin-toss, meaning his sidekick, Bob Thornton, got to keep the hire-car while Prudow was left with the prospect of using taxis to get to three local hospitals. The pair had consulted a city map for all health facilities and agreed to stay southside within a reasonable radius of the McAndrew house. There was only so much distance the brats could have travelled before being rescued. However, to cover the ground, they needed to split up.

At least Prudow got to return to his low-rent hotel to grab a parka, one of those waxed jobs with a lot of padding. The hired help didn't get to stay with their boss in a fancy five-star, nor was there any chance of being reimbursed for cab rides. Despite all the money and swagger, Prudow knew that Montgomery could be a mean sonofabitch.

Prudow stood outside the entrance to the downtown fleapit, waiting for a cab that had been ordered ten minutes ago by a surly receptionist, who seemed to triple up as a bellboy, waiter and general factotum. No chance of a concierge service in a dump like this.

The snow was getting heavier, making Prudow wonder if the cab companies had called it a night. Another two minutes of foot-stamping and he'd retire to the warmth of the hotel bar. Just then, a yellow cab pulled across two lanes and drew to a halt beside him.

"You the guy who called for a ride?"

Prudow climbed into the back without a word.

The driver swivelled to stare at him. "You going to tell me where you want to go? Only I can't start if I don't know where I'm aiming to finish. We call it logistics in the trade."

"That so," Prudow snorted. "Why don't you keep your witticisms for them that gave a fuck? Just drive."

"Not until you tell me where we're going."

"The Eastern Maine Medical Centre."

Quinn carried Sophie, wrapped in a blanket, through the hospital outer doors and across to a nursing station, which took up most of one side and was busy with people clamouring for attention from three blue-coated staff. Quinn barged through the throng and held Sophie up for one of the nurses to see.

"She needs immediate attention," he said brusquely.

The nurse looked with sympathy at his package but tried to maintain a professional response for the benefit of the rest of the queue. "Unfortunately, so do a lot of other people, as you can see. Is it an emergency, or just a broken limb? Did she fall in the snow? We seem to be getting a lot of that tonight."

"No, this is a real emergency."

"What's wrong with her."

"She's suffering from hypothermia and is undergoing traumatic-event shock."

The nurse raised her eyebrows. "You a doctor?"

"No, ma'am."

"Then how can you tell?"

Quinn leaned across the counter and beckoned the woman forward, until she was close enough to whisper in her ear. "These kids witnessed their parents being murdered, they've been chased by men determined to kill them too, and they've been stumbling around in the snow looking for help. I guess even a layman could add two and two and come up with a hypothesis for hypothermia and shock. How about you get a doctor now?"

"Omygod," the woman said. She reached under the counter. There was obviously a button of some kind down there. The next moment a sharp alarm sounded across the building, doors opened, and a group of medicos raced to the station, pulling a gurney and an emergency trolley. One man lifted Sophie from Quinn's arms and placed her on the bed. Stethoscopes, temperature gauges, and IV drip arms seem to appear from nowhere.

A white-coated woman grabbed Quinn by the arm. "Tell me what you know."

"Hypothermia and shock," Quinn repeated. "I'm guessing the boy is suffering from similar problems, but he's a tough little cookie." Quinn smiled at Charlie and ran a hand through the youngster's hair.

The doctor turned immediately to her team. "Room 4 now! Prep both children. I want full warm packs, 10cc of saline flushing, and broad-spectrum antibiotics. Test for cardiac dysrhythmia and prepare humidified oxygen."

While the doctor was talking, Charlie tugged at Quinn's coat. "I'm alright. I don't need anything."

Quinn knelt down. "They're just being careful, Charlie. You need to stay strong for Sophie's sake. Can you do that?"

"Will you stay with us?"

"Don't worry, I'm not going anywhere. You go with Sophie and I'll see you when it's finished."

As Charlie walked away, holding on to Sophie's gurney, the doctor turned to Quinn. "I recognised those kids from the TV news. They're the McAndrew children, aren't they? Considering the ordeal they've gone through, they're not actually in bad shape. What did you do, what did you give them?"

"Just kept them warm and gave them a warm drink. I was as much worried about dehydration as the effects of the cold."

"Good call," the doctor told him. "We'll get more warm fluids into them now. Seems to me, you just might have saved that little girl's life."

Quinn brushed aside the comment. "How long will it be before they're ok?"

"After we get them stabilised, I'll give them a sedative that'll keep them out for twelve hours. They'll need a good rest while the body plays catch-up. I don't think you have any need to worry. By the way, are you a relative?"

"No, ma'am, just happened to be passing."

"Good job you were, Mister......?"

"Quinn, ma'am." He had the word out before he realised. It was the first time he'd ever slipped out of character. Charlie and Sophie had thrown his world out of kilter.

A hospital security guard ambled over to Quinn. He looked a capable individual. Big and well-muscled, and a hand over the butt of a holstered pistol, he approached with a mixture of alertness and wariness that told Quinn this was no rentacop. Far from being concerned about the man's interest, Quinn rejoiced in the prospect of enlisting some much-needed support.

"Mind telling me what's going on here?" It was inquisitive, challenging, and placatory all in one sentence.

"Don't have time for all the details," Quinn responded. "It's enough to know that those kids who went in there are the McAndrew children. Their life is in danger and we need to protect them until the police arrive. Can you get a call into the nearest precinct and let them know what's happening?"

"Already done," the guard said. "Knew it was

them the moment you pushed across the nursing station. The city's in a bit of a flap over those kids. What's this about someone trying to kill them?"

"The men who killed their parents are after them. Apparently the children witnessed everything, and now someone wants to shut them up. How long before the police arrive?"

"Hard to tell. Could be anything up to ten minutes because of this blasted weather. When they do come, they'll come in force, probably dozens of them. I hear the FBI is even involved."

Which was a good thing, Quinn thought. Charlie and Sophie will get wall-to-wall protection.

Which was a bad thing, because he'd have to stay around to answer questions, sign a statement, and have lights shining into his dark places.

But he couldn't walk away. He asked the guard. "How many of you are on security duty this evening?"

"Four every shift."

"Can you radio the others and get them here fast? We need to throw a cordon around that treatment room until the cops get here."

"You really think someone will come for the children?"

"Hope for the best, plan for the worst" Quinn said.

CHAPTER 7

JIM PRUDOW paid the minimum fare and told the cabbie not to stay. The guy's rates were extortionate. Talk about price-hiking because of a little snow! Well, they could whistle Dixie before he'd even think of adding a tip and running up a wait-fare bill, just so some flunky could make hay out of the misery of others. This was going to be one of those nights.

Prudow knew he couldn't just walk into the hospital and ask if two kids had been brought in. This would require a bit of tact and patience. Maybe he could grab a coffee while he moseyed about looking for info.

The moment he stepped through the doors, he knew his plan was shot to hell. There was a larger crowd than expected milling about the foyer. They seemed to be gathered in lots of small groups, everyone talking at once, and most eyes turned upwards towards a wall-mounted television. It was a CNN bulletin screen, with live pictures streaming from the outside of the McAndrew house.

Prudow pasted on his best smile and joined one of the groups. "Hey, what's going on?"

A small, white-haired woman, probably in her seventies, and looking every inch the town gossip, took it upon herself to fill him in. "Those poor people who were killed and those poor children."

"What about them?" Prudow couldn't keep the urgency from his voice.

"Well, dear, they're here, aren't they?"

"Who's here?"

"The children. They were brought in a while ago. The doctors are with them now. I hear it's touch and go. Somebody said they'd been shot."

"Now, Edna, that's not right and you know it." A man stepped forward. "My aunt tends to listen to too much gossip. The kids are gonna be fine. They weren't shot. Just a touch of exposure."

Prudow tried for a sincere face. "That's great news. Where are the kids now?"

"Down the corridor and around the first bend. There's a whole team working on them, but I think it's just precautionary."

Prudow looked over the heads of the group. "Why aren't there any cops about? I thought the whole city was out looking for those children?"

The man shrugged his shoulders. "This is Bangor. When do you ever get a cop when you need one? No doubt they'll get here eventually. Just as well that big fella brought the youngsters in, otherwise God knows what would have happened to them."

"Big fella?"

"Yeah, ask me he's a hero for what he did."

Prudow's mind swept back to the convenience store. "Was he by chance wearing a black leather jacket?"

"Matter of fact, he was. You know him?"

"Yes, as a matter of fact, I do."

Quinn brought the hospital security team together and set about their deployment. He wanted a man at each end of the secondary corridor and two outside the treatment room door. He was used to tactics and giving orders, something the guards must have recognised. They followed his instructions without comment.

Quinn nodded at the guard he'd met in the foyer and told him: "I got a look at one of the pursuers earlier this evening, so I'll head for the entrance and see if I spot anything. It'll give us a heads-up if something's going to go down."

"Don't worry about us," the man said. "Nothing's getting past here that don't have a right to get past."

All well and good, Quinn thought, but bravery and determination wouldn't get them beyond first base if a team of professional hit-men came marching around the corner. He pushed aside the negativity and headed for the main corridor.

He had gone barely two paces around the corner when his heart missed a beat. He tucked back into cover and pushed his head slowly forward. No doubt about it! The guy was wearing a new overcoat, but it didn't cover the full head of unkempt black hair, or the hooked nose set against flabby cheeks. It was the gunman from the convenience store.

Quinn watched the man detach himself from a group of visitors. He was heading for the door and had a cellphone pressed against his right ear. Quinn bounded from his hide, crossing the floor in a series of long strides that were dulled by his rubber-soled boots. Wouldn't have mattered anyway. There was too much ambient chatter to alert the gunman.

It was obvious the guy was calling in to report. Maybe even whistling up reinforcements.

Which meant he was probably alone.

Which meant Quinn had to keep it that way.

He raced through the automatic doors less than two seconds after his quarry. The man was standing off to the left, speaking urgently, his back to Quinn. "I tell you, they're here. I'm at the....."

He never got to finish. Quinn hit him hard, just below the right ear, at the point of the temporal bone. He dropped like a sack of potatoes. Quinn shut down the phone, grabbed the unconscious man by the coat collar and dragged the deadweight around a corner into the shadows of the L-shaped building.

It took several minutes of cheek-slapping for Quinn to revive his victim. He hadn't hit him hard enough to crush the bone, though the man's lower jaw would be on fire from a knock-on effect to the temporo-mandibular joint. If he couldn't speak, he could nod. Either way, Quinn intended to get answers.

Quinn walked behind and bent to wrap his arm around the man's throat. He spoke urgently, knowing time was not on his side.

"I'm going to ask some questions. You answer truthfully, or you die. It's that simple."

The man croaked. "Fuck off!"

Quinn squeezed tighter. "How many of you are there?"

"To many for you, you bastard." The words were barely audible.

"Who's your boss?"

"Fuck off!"

"I guess we're done here, tough guy."

"What are you going to do?"

"Making sure there's one less of you bastards to harm those kids."

Quinn squeezed hard on the man's throat. At the same time, he placed his left arm against the side of the exposed head and pushed violently. At least two of the seven cervical vertebrae bones in Prudow's neck snapped. He died instantly.

Quinn pulled the corpse behind a large evergreen bush. He worked quickly, retrieving his stolen Sig, and pocketing the man's phone and wallet. There was no time now to start searching through them.

Keeping in the shadows, Quinn edged out to the end of the building and scanned the car park. It was about two-thirds full, and other cars were arriving in a steady stream. Most likely night-shift workers. No sign yet of any cops.

Satisfied the dead man had acted alone, probably as some sort of forward scout, Quinn decided not to go back inside the hospital. The security guards should be enough to keep an eye on Charlie and Sophie, while he kept watch from the outside. He moved away from the building on a circuitous route that brought him to the rear of the RV. He climbed in, moved to the front, and settled in for what he hoped would be a short wait.

It took less than two minutes for the first vehicles to arrive. Three Ford Crown Victorias, with the familiar police department black-and-white design, screeched to a halt at the entrance. Officers were still piling out when a convoy of Ford

Expedition SUVs rolled up beside them. The big boys had arrived.

There was nothing more that Quinn could do. He needed to put distance between himself and what would soon become a lock-down area. He started the engine and moved slowly away from the commotion, exiting the park via a slip road. His job was done. Charlie and Sophie were now in capable hands.

Why then, did he suddenly develop a cold sense of foreboding?

The detective and the FBI man met in an empty hospital administrator's office. There was no handshake. No pleasantries. Straight down to business. Burnett and Freeman were cut from the same cloth, strong independent types who expected others to follow their example and step up to the plate. Put your life on hold, skip sleep, and get the job done.

"You're satisfied the area's locked down tight?"

Burnett blew out his cheeks. "You saw for yourself when you got here. Nobody's getting in or out without being put through the ringer. Your own men are already out there checking the perimeter. Why don't you cut the crap and tell me what's really going on?"

Freeman ignored the question. "Tell me about this Good Samaritan, the guy who dropped the kids off?"

"Seems he done a runner shortly afterwards. We got a name from one of the doctors and a good description from everyone who was here at the time. It matches in with that convenience store incident I was telling you about. Same kids, same guy, but nobody knows where the hell he came from or where he went. I had a look at the hospital camera recordings, but it's as if the guy knew where to stand or where to turn to avoid any full-on view. All we've got is his back or partial sides."

"You don't find that strange?"

"Of course, I find it strange! Your ordinary Joe Public wouldn't know about these things. He's either got something to hide, or he just wants to keep out of the limelight. Either way, he's left us with a load of questions. What sort of person has these skills? Is he really on the side of the angels, or is there another agenda we're not seeing?"

"That's what I intend to find out, Detective. Any better luck with the convenience store cameras?"

"Zilch. The owner claims the system was knocked off during a power surge a few days ago. He forgot to reset the recording device."

"Any joy from the kids in getting some info about their saviour?"

"Another blank, I'm afraid," Burnett said. "They're still sedated, and the doctor won't let us talk to them for at least another twelve hours, and even then, she's insisting on a child psychologist sitting in. Says they've been through a lot and doesn't want us clodhoppers stomping in with our size tens. Her words, not mine."

"Seems like a smart lady. We'll be moving the children into federal custody as soon as they're able to travel. The plan is to get them to Washington to be with their grandfather, if this wretched weather allows. They'll be the responsibility of the Secret

Service from that point onwards."

Burnett looked lost for words. He pulled a chair from beside the administrator's desk and slumped down. "I know I've asked this before, but just what is going on?"

Freeman held the other man's stare for several seconds before responding. "Guess it'll come out sooner rather than later. Those kids in there are the grandchildren of the Chief Justice of the Supreme Court of the United States."

CHAPTER 8

CHIEF JUSTICE Thomas Jefferson Fleming was a man who knew how to get things done. And right now, he needed things doing.

It helped, of course, that he was head of the Supreme Court. It helped even more when the top men in the Department of Justice, and the myriad agencies under its wingspan, were all on his speed-dial buttons. To be more precise, they were on the speed-dial buttons of his Counselor, the name designated by Congress to act as Fleming's personal aide. The poor man was having a busy morning.

First, he had to set aside the Chief Justice's calendar for the day, moving a clutch of appeal hearings back by as much as six weeks. But what was six weeks when most of the appellants were waiting for anything up to six years to present their cases? The trickledown affected the eight Associate Justices, whose plans for the next few days included personal meetings with the great man in the hope of attracting his support for some of their causes. The Court worked like that. Deals behind deals, behind closed doors.

None of that mattered to Fleming this morning. His daughter and son-in-law were dead. His grandchildren were missing. He wanted answers, and he wanted them fast.

The Special Agent in charge had given him

diddly-squat. This Freeman guy was covering his ass. Justice Fleming didn't buy the line that his son-in-law had been somehow caught up in an ongoing federal investigation that might have something to do with the murders. Too early to say. Hard to see how it could have led to this. Probably just a coincidence. Yackety-yak, yackety-yak.

Something was badly off, and Fleming was determined to get to the bottom of it.

And so, his personal aide had tracked down the Director of the FBI, the Director of Homeland Security, the Director of Alcohol, Tobacco, Firearms and Explosives, uncle Tom Cobley, and anyone else who could move the mountain quicker than appeared to be the case at the moment. Chief Justice Thomas Jefferson Fleming was not a patient man.

The White House had been his first call. He didn't ask, or plead, or beg for help. He told the President what he needed. He got it in a heartbeat.

His daughter Ruth had married Mark McAndrew away from the glare of Washington, and against Fleming's wishes. It was not that he disliked the man. It was just that he was a mild-mannered soul who lacked ambition. I mean, who the hell plumps for corporate lawyering? And to cap it off, he takes Ruth away from her family to the wilds of Maine! Not so bad at the beginning, but later when the kids came along, the separation seemed even more acute. When Fleming's wife had died after a prolonged illness, he craved the attention of his grandchildren, but three or four short visits a year was hardly attention.

There was no way of knowing what McAndrew

had been up to. What could possibly have led to these seemingly senseless killings? He'd find out in double-quick time, although his priority now was locating Charlie and Sophie. Nothing else mattered. He would move heaven and earth to bring them under his protective wing. That's what the phone calls were all about. If there was a law enforcement officer currently in his bed instead of up in Maine tracking down those kids, he'd find his career coming to an abrupt halt.

The office of Chief Justice wielded awesome power and influence. Six years into the job, Fleming knew all the tricks and shortcuts. He was virtually a law unto himself, as decreed by Act of Congress. His appointment was a lifetime one. *Justices shall hold their Offices during good behaviour*, meaning that only impeachment could result in removal. Right now, however, Fleming didn't feel all-powerful. At seventy-eight, he was in great physical shape but the pain of what was happening was almost too much to bear.

He looked across his desk at a framed photograph of two children playing in a paddling pool beside a wall chute at their home. Fleming then did something he hadn't done since childhood. He began to cry.

Quinn's struggle against controlling the RV was starting to become a losing one. The roads had slushed up under the constant barrage of snow, with only single lanes navigable, even along major city streets. The gritters had been out for several hours, but they too were fighting a hopeless battle.

Any hopes of leaving Bangor were dissipating fast.

He had a decision to make.

Parking at a trailer site was no longer an option. The chances of his rig being picked up on cameras near the convenience store, or the hospital, or anywhere in between, were not odds he liked. At some point, little Charlie would provide a description of the vehicle. It would be the first thing they asked, and the kid would see no reason not to tell them. The doctor had said she would sedate the children for up to twelve hours, so he still had time on his side. There was really only one thing left to do.

He needed to return to the lock-up garage.

He kept his speed below twenty, allowing the big six-wheeler with twin driveshafts to plough a steady furrow through the blanketed asphalt. The outlying streets en route to the lock-up were the heaviest going, and it took the best part of an hour before he finally rolled up to the shuttered doors.

Quinn pulled the doors closed behind him and cut the engine. He threw a secondary switch that maintained the rig's central heating and lighting systems, courtesy of a bank of ten underfloor nickel lithium batteries, with enough capacity to last forty-eight hours. A thirty-minute boost from the vehicle's engine would restore full functionality, although at some point he'd need to open the garage doors for ventilation.

He quickly threw off his clothes and stepped into the shower cubicle, spending more time than usual in washing away the day's accumulated grime. He towelled dry, dressed in football shorts and t-shirt, and attacked his facial stubble with a plug-in trimmer. Back in the main cabin, he brewed an instant coffee from the last remnants of a jar that stood alone on what should have been a well-stocked shelf of provisions. He'd had to leave his shopping at the convenience store and had resisted the temptation to call in at an all-night forecourt on his return journey. Too risky to leave a trail.

It was something he'd have to sort out tomorrow. He rummaged in kitchen drawers and found two peanut-and-fruit power bars, which were still good, according to the sell-by dates. He washed them down with the bitter coffee, climbed into a generously-sized bed, pulled down from a wall recess, and buried himself beneath a mountain of blankets.

He knocked off the heat and lights, wondering what the next few days would bring. As always, sleep overtook his thoughts within a matter of minutes.

Jim Prudow's body was found shortly after midnight. The discovery was made by one of the uniformed police responders who'd sneaked behind the bushes for a quick smoke. His report sent the Eastern Maine Medical Centre into a renewed bout of frenzy.

A new room in an unused wing was set up for the transfer of the McAndrew children. It was chosen because there were no exterior windows to the rooms or corridors, and no lifts leading to the area. Just two sets of stairwells, each crammed with a dozen heavily-armed men, an eclectic mix of Bangor SWAT, FBI, and local detectives. Fuming hospital staff were forced to relocate patients from nearby wards, and all personnel underwent an immediate body search, carried out with a roughness borne out of the naked suspicion of anyone not carrying a badge or shield.

Outside, the grounds were turned into a surreal scene, the glistening snow and parked cars spread out in an eerie silence below the glare of enough arc lights to power an event at the nearby J. Henry Cameron Stadium. A five-block perimeter leading to the hospital was cordoned off, with strict instructions that no-one, including local residents, was permitted entry.

Carl Freeman assembled his FBI team in an empty ward close to where the children were being kept under sedation. The speed with which events were unfolding was almost unnerving, but Freeman was a consummate professional. This was a time for cool heads.

"We've got to assume this body is connected to everything that's happened in Bangor tonight. Best guess is that the victim was in pursuit of the children and could be one of the men seen earlier at the convenience store. Any id yet?"

"Nothing," Drew Eisler, his second-in-command, told him. "No wallet, no passport, nada. Whoever did this, was making it hard for us to know anything. Maybe it was a falling out among thieves. Maybe he was done by one of his partners."

"Don't buy it, Drew," Freeman said with conviction. "Doesn't make sense. If more than one man came here to kill the McAndrew children, they'd get the job done and sort out their differences later. No, the only thing that makes any sense is that our mystery Good Samaritan took care of this the same way he took care of the incident at the store. Who the fuck is this guy?"

Eisler shrugged his shoulders. "Let's take baby steps. First, we ID the body, then we go looking for the stranger. The stiff is probably linked in some way to Devlin Montgomery, and that's why we're here. Make the connection and bring down this mother. Then, we look for the Samaritan."

"So, where do we start?" The question came from one of four agents hustled over from the Bangor Field Office at Harlow Street.

Freeman shot him a withering look. "We're the fucking FBI! Where the hell do you think we start? Get a slab photo of the body and take it to the store owner for confirmation. If he's in bed, kick him out, and don't leave until you have an answer. The rest of you from Harlow Street, get back to the office and start running the databases. Use facial rec, known acquaintances of Montgomery, employees of all his companies, and even check his wife's cousin, twice-removed, if you have to. Get the local PD to take the photo to every hotel, motel, inn and doss house around the city. I want to know everything about this guy and I want it within three hours. Let's move, the clock's ticking."

Just then the door to the ward opened and Detective Steve Burnett strode in.

"Not now!" Freeman yelled.

"Suits me fine," Burnett said. "Whenever you get a minute and you want to know something interesting, just look me up at the hospital canteen. I'll be in there with my team, twiddling my thumbs, and waiting for you and your suits to get the finger out of your asses."

Freeman wanted badly to punch Burnett in the face. Instead, he smiled benignly. "I'm guessing you've got something you feel is worth sharing? Why don't you draw up a seat?"

Burnett remained at the door. "Nah, I'm good. Wouldn't want to get in the way. Thought you'd like to know that we've had another run through the hospital camera footage and found our dead guy talking on a cellphone before exiting the lobby in a hurry."

"And this is interesting, how?"

"He was followed from the building by the guy who brought in the children. Looks like he was in a hurry to have a quiet word with our deceased friend."

"What makes you say that?"

Burnett smiled. "Maybe it was the way he tore across the lobby, pushing people away. That's usually a dead giveaway for someone in a hurry. Then again, there's another good reason for suggesting haste by our elusive friend"

"Stop playing games, Detective. Spit it out."

"It's just that I find it odd that a guy who had gone out of his way to steer clear of the cameras, suddenly seemed to have forgotten all about them. We only missed this earlier because the sequence we're now looking at came much later than the footage of the children being carried forward to the nursing station when the mystery man first arrived."

Freeman felt a surge of anticipation. "Please tell me we now have a full facial?"

"That we do, Agent. That we do."

CHAPTER 9

THE COFFEE was great. Freshly made and in copious supply. Quinn took advantage of the free-refill policy, starting on his third mugful as he mopped up the last dregs of a mountainous breakfast and gazed out the diner window at the city of Bangor, coming to life under a bright early morning sky.

It's easy to tune into the heartbeat of a place just by sitting still and letting it drift past. Its beat and nuances give off signals, if you know what you're looking for. Pedestrians fighting for sidewalk space on their rush to work, or traffic snarled at junctions, or sirens providing a background symphony are obvious telltale signs of hustle, bustle, and maybe something out of the ordinary. Like a double homicide or concern for two missing kids.

There was nothing like that outside the window of *Jenny's Downtown Diner*. Traffic was thin and office workers light on the ground. The normal urban sounds of a busy city were muted to the kind of peacefulness more akin to a holiday weekend. No doubt the snow had helped grind the place to a slow crawl, but even that couldn't account for the lack of action and urgency.

Maybe the discovery of the missing children had taken the FBI and BPD defcon scale down a notch or two.

Which suited Quinn.

Having the Feds and Bangor Police Department running around like headless chickens was keeping him boxed in. At this rate, he could move on as soon as there was a break in the weather.

He was five miles and a ninety-minute trudge away from the lock-up. He'd stirred just after eight o'clock, grateful for a solid ten-hour sleep, and the fact that the garage was not blocked by snowdrifts. He'd been pleasantly surprised to see little more than a thin blanket of white when he'd opened the shutters. The flurries had stopped and windspeeds had dropped below a modest ten-mile-per-hour breeze. No room for celebration yet. Main roads would still be dodgy. He was stuck here for at least another day, maybe two.

He'd kept the doors open to vent the unit while he ran the RV's engine, turning the heating to full blast and recharging the back-up batteries. He needed food. His last decent meal was in Juarez, Mexico, if refried beans and tacos could be called a decent meal. His fridge and food cupboards also cried out for restocking. It was time to venture out.

A one-piece neoprene body suit provided a go-to foundation to ward off the cold. From there, he layered up with woollens, tucking a t-shirt and polo under a dark blue Aran sweater. Jeans, socks and laced-up combat boots completed the ensemble. He pushed his Sig into an inside pocket of a knee-length overcoat, added a scarf and beanie, and rummaged for the wallet and phone he'd stolen from the dead guy at the hospital. He'd check the contents later.

He wandered unnoticed through the industrial site and out to the main road. He didn't want the attention of hailing a taxi. Besides, a good walk was just the ticket to get his inner juices flowing. The roads were slushed, the sidewalks carpeted and icy. But he got into a steady rhythm, enjoying the challenge and solitude. In many ways, these were what defined his life.

He pushed the empty plate across the table and fished out the stolen wallet. It was a double billfold, with all the usual windows for cards and photos. There was a lot of cards, but no pictures. A faded driving licence and a familiar blue and white social security ID showed the deceased as James Prudow, with a resident address in New York. There was nothing much more to tell about the man's life, other than he seemed to like escort agencies, judging by the number of dog-eared adverts taking up half the wallet's window spaces. He was also a member of a gymnasium, had shopped in Macy's Herald Square store a few times, and had racked up three rows of stickers on the way to getting a free Starbucks.

The rear compartments held about three-hundred dollars in various denominations. Tucked between the bills was an hotel swipe card for somewhere called *The Jutland*, on Fairmount. At least he knew now where the rats were staying.

Quinn looked at the breakfast bill squeezed under a saucer. He'd had the ten-buck special, the best bargain meal he'd ever eaten. Figuring it was worth a lot more than that, he withdrew three twenty-dollar bills from Prudow's wallet and laid them across the saucer.

He was about to leave when he remembered the dead man's cellphone. It was one of those old-fashioned flip-tops, although it looked brand new and seemed to have all the bells and whistles. He hit the power button. The screen defaulted to a password request. That was that. Quinn knew his way around most electronic gadgets, but circumventing encryption was not one of his skills. He knew a few guys who could bust this piece of junk wide open in a matter of seconds, though it hardly mattered at this stage.

Maybe, with hindsight, the best option would have been to leave the phone at the scene for the Feds to do their work. Then again, they should've been able to ID the guy by now, which meant they could find out from the cell companies about his phone usage and history. If it was a burner, the very nature of caution in using such a set probably meant it was unlikely to have anything of value on it. Either way, it was a dead end.

There and then, Quinn decided he'd poked his nose in for the last time. Two days holed up with the RV should see him clear. As soon as he roads were free, he'd stick to his original plan and head for Florida. Charlie and Sophie were safe. That's all that mattered.

He headed out to the street. Two Crown Vics swept past him, the occupants stern-faced and glass-eyed. Eight suits, eight troubled souls. Maybe this thing wasn't over yet. Or maybe the feds were simply wrapping up and heading for home. Their problem, not his.

He spotted a man squatting on a makeshift cardboard mattress in a doorway wedged between two retail units. A notice, scrawled in charcoal, lay across his knees. *Help a Homeless Veteran.* Quinn opened Prudow's wallet, removed the remaining cash, and pressed it into the man's hand.

"Get yourself a hot meal and a room for a few days."

The man blinked in disbelief. "God bless you son. God bless you."

Quinn didn't hear the words. He'd already turned a corner, dumping the wallet and phone in a trash can as he went in search of a grocery store.

Twenty minutes after returning to the garage unit, Quinn had stored away his purchases. There was enough ready-meals, bottled water, snacks and coffee to keep him going for at least a week. He moved behind the small writing bureau and powered up the laptop. His cheerful mood changed in a heartbeat.

The default screen took him straight to the CNN International website. The headline article was like a punch to the gut.

Daughter and son-in-law of Supreme Court Chief Justice named as victims of Bangor slayings

A secondary strapline heading read:

Missing children found alive and well.

Quinn raced his eyes down the screen in a frantic speed-read of the salient facts. There was a lot of speculation, and a bit of what reporters refer to as *colour*, but precious little to add to the screaming banners. *Too early to say if there are links to any of Justice Fleming's legal caseloads.*

The FBI and local police studying whether this was a burglary-gone-wrong, or a pre-meditated double homicide. Did the intruders intend to kill the children? How did they escape from the house and end up in one of the city's hospitals? There were quotes from an unnamed FBI spokesman who stated, rather unnecessarily, that this was an ongoing investigation, blah, blah, blah.

As the column inches continued to expand across the screen, Quinn realised he was reading dross. What *was* clear was that this was no ordinary homicide, not with the close links to the Chief Justice. Nobody goes around killing the family of one of America's most influential figures without serious ramifications. This thing was about to be pitched into the stratosphere.

And that was worrying from two points of view.

First, just how safe were Charlie and Sophie? They were witnesses to an act that was bound to shake the country to the core. Anyone ruthless enough to bump off such prominent citizens would hardly baulk at shutting up two kids. Despite the protective glove of federal and local law enforcement agencies, these children were not safe. And Quinn should know. It's what he did for a living.

Second, Quinn's own situation was now perilous. Any hopes of his involvement being overlooked had just gone out the window. The FBI would be looking for him even harder than he'd thought possible. They'd want to shake his tree, find out where he'd come from, how he'd got mixed up in this. Was he part of the crew? Had he a late attack of conscience when it came to murdering children?

They had a lovely catch-all credo for this type of situation – eliminate from enquiries or throw the book at him. Either way, the alternatives probably involved an unpleasant sojourn in Guantanamo Bay.

He needed to get out in front of this.

He delved into his jeans pockets and came out with Prudow's hotel pass key. Maybe some of the answers were waiting for him at the *Jutland*?

Before that, he had one more website to visit. He rebooted the laptop, interrupting the start sequence to switch to the root directory. He keyed in a series of commands and waited for the screen to display what looked like a chat room. This was the Dark Web, home to *The Solutionist* and other nefarious activists. His private message board contained a series of new entries from his last visit. They all came from someone called Pontius666.

He read through the lines, converting and translating the odd language into meaningful script. The Dark Web had a syntax all its own.

Pontius666: ( ) 2pm off. 11111 for ii.

Quinn's blood boiled as he translated. *Limited time offer – five big ones (five million) for two little ones.*

There was a second line posted three hours later.

Pontius666: R u wit us r is this a Khyber?

The translation was fairly obvious. *Are you with us, or do you want to pass?*

A third more desperate message appeared an hour later.

Pontius666: DL is here. Erect or clam - meaning deadline is here. Put up or shut up.

Quinn checked his watch and attacked the keyboard.

In all the way. Details to be sent to POURL. ZIP on confirmation.

Translation: *I'm in. Send details to a Post Office URL, the code for which will be forwarded on your confirmation.*

Quinn sat back and waited. Nothing happened. He spent thirty minutes pacing the RV, stopping every few seconds to glance at the laptop screen. Thirty minutes stretched to an hour. Then the computer dinged an incoming message.

Pontius666: 2 late. Job awarded elsewhere. Your loss.

Quinn thumped the desk in anger. There was no doubt in his mind that the "two little ones" were Charlie and Sophie, and that somebody had just agreed a contract to kill them. He cursed himself for not checking the site earlier. When he'd placed his own message on the board there had been no question of taking on the contract. At the very least he'd hoped to muddy the waters and buy some time for Charlie and Sophie.

Now, the only way to save them was to find the mystery hitman before the children were caught in the crosshairs.

CHAPTER 10

THE JUTLAND HOTEL didn't have a lot going for it. On the outside at least. Maybe the interior had undergone more investment, though there was no reason for optimism on that score.

The outer walls of the six-floor building were grey, dirty and flaking. The aluminium sign, pitted with rust and layers of grime, was way past redemption, as were the narrow windows, ten to a floor, sixty in total, and all fitted sometime in the last century when native spruce hardwood must have been the rage. Now, it was cracked, bleached, and probably fused into the concrete lintels.

As far as Quinn was concerned, they might as well hang a sign over the entrance advertising a pukka, honest-to-goodness dive. He'd stayed in some lowdown places in his time, but this had them beat for decrepitness six ways from Sunday.

He was standing under the afternoon shadow of a large oak, directly across from the Jutland's entrance, with a clear view of a right-side alley, which was there as a service road. It looked every bit as unappetising as the main entrance.

The clock in his head ticked past the ten-minute mark. He'd spent the time, as he always did, getting a feel for the lie of the land, looking for escape routes and possible bottlenecks. An iron fire stairway was bolted to the building at the same side as the service alley. Presumably there was also a side exit door. Maybe even a rear exit, though he couldn't determine that from where he was standing.

The wait also gave him time to ponder how to handle the situation. He couldn't just walk in and ask for Jim Prudow's room, or the room of any of his friends. He also had to consider that some of Prudow's friends, particularly the guy who'd coshed him from behind at the convenience store, might recognise him if he wandered aimlessly around the foyer or bar areas, provided of course a dump like this had a foyer or bars.

On second thoughts, what did it matter if he was recognised? The whole point of being here was to ferret out the other members of the team who'd done for the McAndrews and gone after their children. He could handle men like this. He'd been doing it for most of his life.

In the end, the decision was taken away from him. Tyre screeches off to his left heralded the arrival of a new dynamic. Three overstated Ford Expeditions, with blacked-out windows and flapping antennae, braked to a halt directly in front of the Jutland. The Feds had arrived.

Quinn watched as ten agents poured from the vehicles. There were seven men and three women in FBI windcheaters, all carrying new-generation Glocks, the result of an eighty-five-million-dollar overhaul of its armoury. Even from his position, thirty yards away, Quinn could see these were not the familiar Glock 17s, the Bureau's previous weapon-of-choice. These looked to have a tinge of blue throughout the black polymer frame, and there was a sleekness to them that the old stock didn't have. The finger grooves on the Glock 17 were gone, and there was a new under-barrel slot for affixing a tactical light. What was still the same was that the barrels were five inches in length and the magazines held 17 rounds of 9mm stopping power.

Quinn knew what he was looking at because he'd acquired one shortly after their release. No-one outside the Bureau was supposed to have access to them, but Quinn had his contacts. He'd trained on it, got familiar with its idiosyncrasies, and promptly discarded it. He preferred the Sig Sauer P226.

It was easy to spot the group leader. Not simply because he stood alone whilst the others fanned around him in a semi-circle. No, this guy oozed authority and confidence. He stood about six-one, with a head of hair that had more greys than blacks. He looked in his mid-fifties, with a trim athletic body that showcased a healthy lifestyle, which probably included a lot of gym time. A man to be reckoned with.

Quinn watched as the agent gesticulated to his team. Two suits broke off and headed for the alley, two more climbed the hotel porch steps to stand sentry outside the doors. Another pair wheeled away to the left of the building, no doubt in search of a possible rear exit. This guy knew what he was doing.

As soon as his team were in place, the leader nodded at his three remaining members and disappeared inside the hotel. There would be a lot of badge-flashing, a degree of menace and urgency, and a swift direction towards Prudow's room and those of any associates. Quinn's window of opportunity had just been firmly shut.

The commotion outside the hotel caused the usual interest from passers-by. Within a few minutes of the FBI team's arrival a small group of people huddled on the sidewalk, some with arms pointing at the building, others nodding at the speculation being offered by their fellow travellers. It was a typical group psyche, leaders and followers. Mouthpieces and sheep.

Quinn perked up as he studied the small crowd. Most people fight to get a ringside seat. Others stand back out of the limelight. And then there are those with something to hide. One guy, hovering around the back of the huddle, definitely had something to hide. It was partly the way he kept the other bodies in front of him. It was mostly that he only sneaked glimpses at the hotel through small gaps, rather than expose himself in the open.

The blue suit, white shirt and thin tie was a clincher for Quinn. He'd seen a similar outfit on the thug he'd got the drop on at the convenience store. They were a matching pair. There was no such thing as coincidence.

Quinn retreated from his vantage point, careful to keep the big oak between himself and any preying eyes from across the street. He was in a semi waste area, with lots of trees and bushes to provide cover as he made his way to the left side of the hotel. He used a wide arc to come back behind a tree about fifty yards from where the subject of his attention was standing.

The man peeled away from the group and headed face-down towards a stretch of commercial premises, mainly low-end shops and offices that stretched several hundred yards on either side of a busy street. There were enough parked cars for Quinn to follow at a discreet distance.

This guy would either take him back to others in the hit team, or he would answer a few questions that Quinn intended to ask him.

The single bed shifted off its spot and flew across the room to hit a wall with a deafening crack. Carl Freeman's FBI boot was responsible for its rapid change in position. He was inside an empty hotel room, one of three booked at the Jutland by Jim Prudow and four colleagues, but all were empty. The birds had flown the coop and Freeman was not a happy bunny.

"Why are we always behind the eight ball on this case?" It was a rhetorical outburst, so no-one replied.

Freeman sat on the only chair in the room and gathered his thoughts. They'd got lucky with identifying Prudow's stay at the hotel, thanks to a beat cop showing the morgue photo around more than a dozen establishments before he'd hit paydirt. The only mistake made was that full surveillance was not put in place before Freeman and his team raced across town. The uniformed officer could have been spotted by one of the men, or a hotel staff member might have tipped them the wink. Too many exits for the policeman to cover. No use crying over spilt milk.

"Okay, it is what it is," Freeman said. "I want full forensics in each of the rooms. Pull the hotel registrations, room records, and any camera footage within the hotel, or from premises within a three-block radius. Get them coming or going. I want their full identities and histories posted at every rail station, bus terminal, and taxi rank throughout the city. Get photos and splash them across the media. I want these rats trapped in Bangor. Most of all, I want connections to Devlin Montgomery."

Drew Eisler detached himself from the other agents. "Do you think Montgomery is in Bangor? Not his usual style to get his hands dirty?"

"Assume nothing, Drew. Make sure the search for Montgomery is kept at full pace. Where are we with that?"

"The police department is continuing with its trawl of hotels. There are a lot to get around and this weather isn't helping. Plus, we have a team back at the Field Office making calls to every establishment to see if Montgomery is a resident. The big worry is that if he's here and staying somewhere private, we're pretty much snookered. We'll keep the foot to the floor and pray for a break."

"I don't intend to be just reactive," Freeman said. "This is now a three-part investigation. Drew, you take point on finding Prudow's associates. Nominate a separate team to hunt down Montgomery. I'll take charge of the third leg to this stool."

"Which is?"

"Which is finding our mystery man. I can't shake the notion that this guy is going to be central to whatever is going on here."

"What about the kids?"

"No longer our problem. Apparently, the phones in Washington have been red-hot over the past few hours. I'm hearing the Secretary of Defense, the Chairman of the Joint Chiefs, and every director of every agency has had to listen to an earful from Chief Justice Fleming. Say what you want about the old boy, but he sure knows how to shake trees."

"So, why are we losing custody of the children?"

Freeman smiled. "For once, I'm glad about that. We've enough to occupy ourselves without worrying about their safety. I've just heard that a team of US Marshalls is on its way. Get this: they're trying to get a bird in the air, or failing that, they're insisting on a rail track clearance operation to commandeer their own train. I was even told they have a vehicle convoy headed our way behind a snowplough."

"You're kidding!"

"Like hell, I am. Apparently two separate teams of Marshalls left New York in the middle of the night. One group is already on the I-95 and should be with us within the next few hours. The other left Penn Station on the first available train, but they're gonna be several hours behind, depending on the state of the track."

"What's the idea?"

"A typical belt-and-braces approach. The weathermen are expecting this break in the storm to last until the afternoon before the next front moves in. The plan is to get the McAndrew children on a flight to Washington to be with their grandfather. Bangor International is still closed to all traffic, but they're anticipating clearance for a flight sometime soon."

Eisler studied his boss. "Thought you said you'd be happy to get the kids off our hands?"

"Yeah, I will be."

"Then why do I get the impression you're not too thrilled about the airport re-opening?"

"Because," Freeman said, "I've been ordered outta here to answer some awkward questions back at Washington. Justice Fleming wants to know how we managed to get his family caught in the middle of a bunch of murdering maniacs. Right now, I don't have the answers."

CHAPTER 11

A LOGGING TRUCK stacked with freshly-milled timber crawled down the street. It was one of those two-part vehicles, the forty-foot front end towing a trailer of equal length in an exercise of freight cost-cutting. It took about four seconds for the rig to clear Quinn's line of sight to the opposite sidewalk. That was about two seconds longer than desirable.

When Quinn managed to get a look at where his target was meant to be, the man had vanished. Several side streets branched off from the main route and at least eight shops offered an escape route. The guy could have nipped in for a packet of smokes, or maybe just to get the morning paper. The only problem was that neither commodity was likely to be found in a hairdressing salon, a fashion store, or a shoe shop, which were the buildings directly in front of the spot where the man had last been seen.

Judging his quarry had likely turned into the first side street, Quinn crossed the road, careful to maintain an easy pace rather than risk drawing attention to himself. The secondary street was mainly residential with high-rise apartment blocks and a confusion of haphazard kerb parking, which left many vehicles with their wheels on the sidewalk. There was a row of dustbins, a few prams, a scattered collection of bicycles, and even the odd clothes-drying stand perched precariously on steps. Children were playing street games, moms were catching up on over-the-fence gossip, and stray dogs added their monotonous yelping as background music to a typical scene of urban domesticity.

There was a lot to take in. What wasn't there was any sight of the man Quinn had been following.

He walked forward on full alert, checking in particular the numerous recessed doorways and small walled areas that offered crude demarcation for bitsy gardens. His eyes darted left and right, up and down, forwards and backwards. Nothing.

He had just decided to retrace his steps to check the next street when a soft, chilling voice brought him to a standstill.

"Don't move, don't say anything."

He sensed a blur behind him. It rose from between two parked cars where the guy must have crawled as he awaited Quinn's arrival. Fair play. Nice move.

Quinn didn't turn his head, mostly because he could feel a pistol muzzle against his neck, but also because he couldn't judge how twitchy his assailant was. Any move could be misinterpreted. So, he stayed still. The gunman had the initiative for now. It was his show.

"Can I ask what this is about?" Quinn said in a manner intended to start a dialogue. He needed to buy time and an inane comment was as good a way as any to start.

"Cut the crap, asshole! I know when I'm being followed and now that I see you from behind I know exactly who you are. Should've finished you off at the convenience store. How's the head, by the way?"

Two birds with the one stone, Quinn thought. Not only had he got the guy talking, he now knew who he was. "You hit like a cissy, just the same as your mate Prudow. I guess a couple of kids are about all the both of you could manage. Even then, you didn't do much of a job, did you?"

Quinn felt the muzzle shake against his skin. It was a calculated risk to antagonise a gunman. Their little scene hadn't attracted any attention, meaning there was every chance the finger on the trigger would squeeze through the final half-inch of pressure. Quinn gambled on his attacker not being able to leave the matter without a few answers. He was right.

"You fucking bastard! You killed Jim? What the fuck do those kids mean to you anyway?"

"It's like this," Quinn said. "Charlie and Sophie are......"

The gunman had made two crucial mistakes. For a start, he'd pressed the muzzle tight against Quinn's neck. He should have stood off, made Quinn wonder where the weapon was. Hard to take evasive action when you can't judge your first point of contact. The second mistake was that he waited for Quinn to finish his sentence.

Quinn had already torqued his body to the left. A fast swivel of the hips, a raised elbow to dislodge the weapon, and it was over before the assailant registered what had happened. The gun flew over the bonnet of a car and skidded across the asphalt road.

The attacker stepped back. Quinn stepped back. It was the way he liked it.

Bob Thornton knew he'd underestimated this man. The same thing had probably got Jim Prudow killed. He too would end up in a box unless he came up with something special. He decided now was the time to deliver the best punch of his life.

Everything was open for a shoulder-height powerhouse, delivered right-handed into the left side of this smug fucker's face. Let's see how he likes a depressed cheekbone, a few teeth dislodged, and maybe even some catastrophic brain damage. Fuck the brain damage! This guy wouldn't get to live long after he was brought to his knees.

The only problem with Thornton's plan was that he started his attack in the wrong way. After that, it went downhill fast.

What should have been a fluid, instinctive thing turned into a textbook example of how not to do it. The punch began in his eyes, which took on a feral glinty look that betrayed his intention. He might have got away with it if he hadn't stacked one signal on top of the other. The balling of his right fist, the small, but noticeable inching backwards on his feet to create a launchpad, and then there was the merest twitch in his shoulders. One mistake piled on top of another.

They all happened in a concurrent motion that might have been missed by an amateur street fighter. But not so a skilled boxer. Or a martial arts expert. Or a special forces operative. Too many telegraphed signals to overlook.

The mistakes provided Quinn with more than a half-second warning. By the time the fist started its travel towards his face, he had already ducked below its path. No depressed cheekbone, no dislodged teeth, no brain damage. Instead, Quinn's own right-handed response, delivered with minimum backlift and full force, drove hard into Thornton's groin.

The man dropped to his knees like the proverbial sack of spuds, his coughing and wheezing adding to the background of street noises. Quinn chopped his victim hard to the side of the face and dragged the semi-conscious body between parked cars. He stood up, his right boot wedged against the man's throat, and looked around. Still no signs that the altercation had been noticed. People here were either blind or this was a neighbourhood that minded its own business.

"Who do you work for?"

"You'll get nothing from me," the man spluttered.

"That's what Prudow said and look where it got him."

Thornton's eyes widened. "Alright, alright. It was meant to be a simple job. Nobody told us about the kids. I've got nothing against them, but he wanted them silenced."

"Who?"

"He'll kill me if I talk."

Quinn's boot bit deeper into Thornton's neck. "And I'll kill you if you don't. You do the maths."

"All right it was...it was Montgomery."

"Montgomery who?"

"Devlin Montgomery."

"Where can I find him?"

"He's holed up in a big house. I don't know the address."

Quinn applied more pressure with his boot.

"You'll have to do better than that."

"I swear, I don't know. We were driven there, somewhere on the southside of the city. I don't know the area, but it's a big place with a ten-foot white wall running around the perimeter. There's an intersection with an Amoco gas station close by. That's all I know, you gotta believe me."

"I do," Quinn said.

It was twenty seconds before Thornton died. During that time, Quinn looked nonchalantly around as he applied foot pressure.

He ignored the temptation to search the dead man's pockets. This time, he'd leave the wallet and phone for the cops or the FBI. He already knew what his next move was.

It took surprisingly little time to find the location. In Quinn's opinion, Google Maps and Street Views were one of the wonders of the technological age. His internet search started with a city map, enlarged to the southside, with its handy little symbols for churches, railways, historical sites, hotels and gas stations. He hovered over the red teardrop shapes with inset outlines of black gas pumps and made a note of all Amoco listings. There were six.

The Street View app found the location on a search of the third address on his Amoco list. Starting at the gas station, he'd rolled the mouse across the screen until he spotted a white wall perimeter, less than two hundred yards from the station forecourt. Beyond the wall were generously-sized gardens encircling a three-floor mansion, a striking building full of ornate architectural features with lots of spiral columns, cornices and a wraparound portico above the ground floor.

Quinn was back in his storage unit. Taking stock. Chilling out. Staying patient. What he planned next was best done under the cover of darkness, which meant he had about eight hours to kill. He made cheese sandwiches and opened a can of potato and leek soup. After that, he intended to sleep for a few hours, take a shower, and get ready for whatever the evening threw at him.

He kept the laptop open at the Street View page. He would study the grounds of the mansion in more detail for at least an hour before leaving. He looked forward to meeting Devlin Montgomery. Looked forward to seeing what kind of man thought little of murdering two innocent children.

He pulled the blankets up to his chin and fell fast asleep.

CHAPTER 12

CARL FREEMAN figured he had three hours, maybe four tops, to catch a break. Which meant that somewhere between one-eighty and two-forty minutes from now they would clear the runway at Bangor and he would be climbing the steps up to an FBI Lear on his way back to Washington. After that, he'd be lucky to salvage his career.

He knew how the D.C. *Beltway Jungle* operated. It was more than survival of the fittest; it was a perpetual, finger-pointing, cover-your-ass chess match that had seen a lot of good people swept off the board to protect the careers of those above them. It suited the scenario that this new President seemed to fire people for fun.

Looking at his predicament objectively made Freeman realise just how precarious his position was becoming. At the end of the day, the son-in-law of the Chief Justice of the Supreme Court had been inveigled in an investigation that carried high-risk for all the players. He had not been put under FBI close-quarter protection, nor was his home kept under watch. He had been a tethered goat. The outcome was inevitable.

No, dammit, Freeman cursed, it was *not* inevitable. The involvement of McAndrew was under the tightest wrapping he'd ever devised for an investigation. His assistance and identity was known to only three other people, all of whom Freeman would have trusted with his life. Putting McAndrew under protective custody would have been counter-productive. It would have created unnecessary attention.

Maybe McAndrew himself had blown his own cover? Had he talked too much, was he unguarded at the wrong moment in the wrong company? Did he tell his wife, who told her book-reading club? No, the guy was too smart for that. So was his wife, who'd spent her life around the secrecy and protocols that go with being the daughter of one of the country's most-protected figures.

What it boiled down to, Freeman realised, was that McAndrew *should* have had an FBI surveillance screen from day one. We're the best in the business, he muttered to himself. We could have thrown an invisible blanket over the man and his family, and nobody would have been any the wiser. It just didn't seem necessary at the time. Whatever happened from here in, it was a decision he knew would haunt him for the rest of his days.

The clock was ticking on Freeman's three, or maybe four-hour window. He got lucky on two major fronts within the first twenty minutes.

A still, taken from the hospital footage of the mystery man who'd saved the McAndrew children, had been run through every database available to the FBI. Which meant every database that existed in the United States, plus those of its allies dotted around the globe. So far, the search had drawn a blank.

The name Quinn, reported by the hospital doctor, was also checked thoroughly. Another blank. A team back in the New York Field Office had run down more than eight-hundred Quinns, but none matched the description of the man they were looking for. An obvious alias. Which in itself added an extra dimension to the man's legend. Who goes around with assumed names? Who has the fieldcraft to avoid cameras, disappear into thin air, and re-emerge to take down a would-be assassin in the shape of this Prudow character found in the bushes outside the hospital entrance?

A dangerous, resourceful individual, that's who, Freeman concluded. Maybe ex-military, maybe an ex-intelligence agent. What about MI6, or Mossad, or the French DGSE? They'd all been shown the photo, but all denied any knowledge of the man. Then again, they'd do that, as a matter of course. Protect their people at all costs. Particularly if their man was in-country doing something they didn't want the Americans to know about. Everyone played that game. It was frustrating. But it was par for the course.

Freeman had also asked for the photo to be matched against all incoming international flights over the past seven days. It was a long shot, but it had to be checked. And there he was! Walking through the gates at Boston Logan International, off a flight from Benito Juarez airport in Mexico two days ago. The booking and passport details showed his name as William Peterson, a native of Sweden on a twenty-one-day tourist visa to visit the Americas.

Two things struck Freeman. His subject was not Swedish, and he was certainly no tourist.

On a whim, Freeman got the NY agents to check

for any unusual incidents in the Juarez region in the days preceding Peterson's departure. The return phone call came less than five minutes later.

"There's a stand-out incident at the top of the list," the agent in charge of the search told him. "Two drug lords, from rival families, were murdered within three hours of each other, one at Las Cruces, the other at Puerto Palomas. According to the Federales, these were professional hits. The Las Cruces incident was a sniper shot from over a thousand yards into a desert compound which belonged to Jorge Hernandez. The second murder was more up close and personal. Raul Rodriguez and three of his bodyguards were gunned down in the middle of an orchard on his estate. The Federales suspect a third crime family was behind the assassinations, but they're speculating a specialist was brought in from the outside."

The agent paused in his summary to go through notes. "There are a few other minor incidents showing up."

"No," Freeman said in a tone that didn't leave room for doubt. "Concentrate on this one. Get me a full file, ballistics, crime scene photos, the works. Feed the Mexicans a bullshit line about trying to help them by checking similar MO's on this side of the border. Lie through your teeth, promise them the stars, but get me that file."

Freeman sat back on a recliner desk chair and blew a short whistle. *Christ! Our mister Peterson, or Quinn, or whoever, is the new Carlos the Jackal! Talk about a turn-up? What if this guy had been sent to assassinate McAndrew and another crew got in the way? Professional pride would make him want to clean up the opposition.*

His thoughts were interrupted by Drew Eisler, who burst into the room at the Harlow Street Field Office. "You're never gonna believe this. We've got another stiff. Close to the Jutland Hotel. Doesn't that just beat a no-such-thing-as-a-coincidence drum?"

Freeman smiled. His second lucky break in under twenty minutes.

"This is, or was, Bob Thornton, one of Prudow's associates, according to the registry at the Jutland." Eisler stood over the body wedged between parked cars. "Middle of the day, and no eye-witnesses. However, this time we've got a wallet and a cellphone, so maybe our mystery man is getting sloppy."

Freeman shook his head. "This guy doesn't do sloppy, Drew. If he didn't sanitise the scene it was for a reason. Maybe he's throwing us a few crumbs. Probably thinks we need a bit of help or could be he just wants us chasing someone else instead of him. Any luck with the wallet or phone?"

"The phone's got password protection. Already sent over to the tech guy in Harlow Street. He should be able to break it in no time."

"Let's hope it gives us a line on the other members of the gang. There are still four out there from the original six who hit the McAndrew house. The little lad Charlie was adamant about the head count, so this thing isn't over yet, not by a long way. What about the wallet?"

"Nothing of interest. Everything's in

Thornton's name. These guys certainly weren't trying to cover their tracks."

"No reason for them to do so," Freeman replied. "They would have been long gone by now, if it hadn't been for the kids escaping, and our vigilante deciding to queer their pitch."

"What do we do now?"

"We wait for the tech guy to break the phone. And a little prayer wouldn't go amiss."

Charles Petrie, Thomas Sullivan and John 'Duke' Carter sat at the farthest end of a downtown pub lounge. A gallon pitcher of Bud, their second of the afternoon, was disappearing fast. The more beer they downed, the darker their moods became.

"Something must have happened."

"For Chrissakes, Duke, will you stop rattling on about it? We heard you the first dozen times. We've already agreed Thornton's either copped it or he's done a runner. Ask me, that's exactly what we all should be doing. The net's closing in and sitting around here with our thumbs up our asses isn't helping. We might as well hang a sign out telling them to come get us."

Duke Carter curled his bottom lip and snarled at his two companions. He was the most senior, taking account of both age and length of service, and was determined to show leadership, if only to mitigate his own personal failure when he next confronted Devlin Montgomery. He was a short, stocky individual whose pockmarked face and white scar lines were a window into a career spent as a brawler and all-round badass. He was used to getting his own way, but here was a situation spiralling out of control. And right now, Carter didn't know how to put a lid on it.

He was sitting with his back to the wall, scanning faces around the room and keeping a close eye on the door. There were fifteen other people in the lounge, six perched on bar stools at the counter, the rest gathered in groups of two and three seated at tables. None looked any threat. They had the aura of regular patrons, all talking animatedly and ignoring Carter and his friends.

The outer door opened and two workmen trudged into the lounge. Judging by the stained jackets and muddy boots they were fresh off a building site. They seemed more concerned about muscling their way into a space at the counter than about any of the assembled crowd. Carter watched them for a few moments before turning his attention back to his colleagues.

"Alright," he said in a pleading tone, "I admit Thornton has probably met the same fate as Prudow. Chances are we're next unless we do something about it. We know the kids are under protective custody with no hope of getting to them, so our options are limited. We tell Montgomery we need to leave town and regroup. We get him to accept that it's better to let things cool down before we try again. The roads aren't as bad as last night, so we take our chances and head for New York."

Sullivan frowned. "You think he'll just accept that? The bastard doesn't care about us. Far as he's concerned, we're expendable. I for one don't fancy heading back to the house to listen to him ranting and raving."

"We're not heading back to the house," Carter said. "We'll call him and see what he has to say. If he agrees to come with us, we'll swing by and pick him up, but if he insists that we stay and finish the job, we light out and don't look back. Are you with me?"

"That's what I've been trying to tell you for the past hour," Sullivan said.

"Suits me fine," Petrie chorused.

Carter lifted his cellphone and flipped the top. Almost immediately it chirped with the sound of an incoming call. He looked at the window.

"You're never gonna believe it. It's Thornton."

CHAPTER 13

THEY WERE WRONG about the FBI tech guy needing a few minutes to crack Thornton's cellphone password. It took barely ten seconds. Most of that time was taken up by a quick study of the set before hooking it up to an algorithmic console. Instead of switching on the sophisticated decoder, he first tried a default *Password1234* manufacturer's setting, and watched with a smile as the machine lit up. It never ceased to amaze how lazy some people were when it came to gadgetry.

The log history showed a list of just twenty outgoing calls, involving the same five recurring numbers, and twenty-four outgoing text messages, this time involving seven different numbers, five of which mirrored the call list. The incoming call and text logs were busier. In a thirty-minute window after the estimated time of Thornton's demise, more than fifty items were displayed.

The messages were particularly revealing, if only for the incremental rise in frantic tones.

What's happening?"
Call back immediately
This is getting beyond a joke
Where the fuck are you?
If you've done a runner you're a dead man.

Carl Freeman scanned the list and knew they'd hit paydirt. "I take it that it's safe to assume these recurring numbers are those belonging to the other members of the gang?"

"That's the assumption I've been working on," the tech guy responded. His name was Gary Harte, a twenty-something with shoulder-length black hair, diamond-studded pierced ears, and bleached denims with holes where the knees were supposed to be covered.

Freeman shook his head. The FBI was really going with the times. "Have you been able to ping their whereabouts?"

"Does a fox know how to get inside a chicken coop?"

On another occasion Freeman might've smiled. "We don't need levity, just the essential details."

If Harte was fazed by the mild rebuke he didn't show it. "You gotta bear in mind most of these are off-the-shelf numbers common to burner phones, so there are no registrations and no way of knowing who owns them. However, two of the sets are currently on, giving us a pinpoint GPS location in downtown Bangor."

"Show me," Freeman urged.

Harte hit a few buttons on a desktop keyboard. Behind him, a whiteboard lit up with a street map of the city. Two small lights blinked side by side. "As you can see, the two cellphone owners are together. I've got the precise address. It's a bar which advertises itself as *The Ponderosa*. That's where you'll find Big Hoss and Little Joe.

This time Freeman smiled. "Good work, Agent. You mentioned that most of the numbers were off-the-shelf. What about the others?"

"I traced one to New York. It's registered to a

Mrs Jacqueline Carter. Isn't that the surname of one of our suspects from the registrations at the Jutland Hotel?"

"Yep, could be the wife of John Carter. What about the others?"

"There's a number listed to an address in Boston. Seems to be a dead end, likely a postbox drop. It's under the name of Smith, so I wouldn't get up any hopes of progressing much further."

"Okay, stick with the burner numbers and let us know the moment any of the others are activated. Don't leave your desk. If you need the toilet, use the wastepaper basket."

"I do happen to have a smartphone app which I can carry with me, but I get the picture. As soon as there's any activity, you'll be the first to know."

Freeman was beginning to like this kid a lot. He slapped him on the shoulder and turned to face Drew Eisler. "Round up a full team. We're heading to The Ponderosa."

Eisler smirked. "Thought we'd dispensed with levity?"

"You're never gonna believe it. It's Thornton."

Duke Carter hit the answer button and spoke urgently. "About time! Where the fuck are you?"

Instead of Bob Thornton's usual nasal drawl he got a voice he didn't recognise. "I'm sorry, Bob can't come to the phone just now. He's having an argument with Saint Peter about not having the right credentials to pass through the Pearly Gates. Seems like he's headed in the other direction."

"Who the fuck is this?"

"This is Special Agent Carl Freeman of the FBI. I suggest you sit tight because you're under arrest."

It took Carter a full second to register what had been said. It was almost as long as it took him to realise that the two workmen he'd noticed entering the bar earlier were now standing beside his table. They both held bluish-coloured Glocks. Both weapons were aimed directly at him.

The *workmen* stood three feet apart. They both shouted at the same time.

"FBI! You're all under arrest."

Sullivan and Petrie threw their arms in the air. This was not a situation for heroics. They'd been caught cold, and they knew it. They used their eyes to try to transmit the same thought process to Carter. But they both knew it wasn't working.

Carter reached below the table and pushed up with all his strength, sending drinks glasses tumbling to the tiled floor. The trajectory of the upended table sent one of the FBI men stumbling backwards, his feet slipping on the beer-drenched surface. It was all the opening Carter needed.

His right hand fumbled for a pistol tucked into his waistband. He brought it clear and raised it towards the second FBI agent. The manoeuvre got barely halfway to where he needed it to be.

The agent fired twice, a double-tap just as he was trained to do. The bullets hit Carter on the left side of his chest, finding the centre of his heart. From a range of no more than three yards, the 9mm parabellums tore through the body and buried themselves into the stucco wall.

By that time Carter was already dead. It took a moment for his brain to switch off its neural signals, a brief period in which the body stayed upright before folding to the floor like a rag doll.

Five minutes later, out in the street, Freeman watched the two prisoners being loaded into the rear of a Crown Vic under the watchful gaze of five agents. "All in all, that went pretty well. At least we've got two live ones to get to work on. Put them in separate holding cells at Harlow Street and let them sweat for a few hours."

Eisler turned to meet his boss's stare. "You sure we can afford to wait? Seems like these bozos might help us clear up a few loose ends."

"Better to go with the tried and trusted methods. Their initial reaction will be to clam up. If we go in after a few hours we can convince one that the other is singing like a canary. The offer of a deal for the first to turn turtle usually works."

"A thought just struck me," Eisler said. "We've now accounted for five of the six assailants at the McAndrew House. That just leaves Montgomery, assuming he was the sixth man. Suddenly it's become very important to get a GPS location on those other numbers we grabbed from Thornton's phone."

Freeman was already punching a number into his smartphone. "Let's see where our tech genius has got to."

His call was answered immediately. He spoke for several seconds, nodded his head, and then turned to Eisler with a thumb raised. He powered the phone off and stared at the screen.

"What is it," Eisler said.

"Another burner just activated. I'm waiting for the location address to come through in a text."

Quinn stood alongside the white perimeter wall. His journey to the mansion house involved a lot of walking, a Hampden Route community connector bus, which was still running despite the sudden increase in snow showers, and a lot more walking. The promised new storm front had moved in, bringing with it a sharp plunge in temperatures and a dramatic escalation in wind speeds.

It had to be around minus five or six, not a welcome prospect if the buses were grounded and he had to make his way ten miles across town to get back to the lock-up. He'd briefly considered taking the RV but dismissed the idea almost immediately. It was a sure way of drawing attention, particularly if as he expected, there was a BOLO alert out on the vehicle.

He'd checked his Google maps and studied several possible entry points. Ordinarily, he would have brought a rubber-tipped grappling hook to scale the outer wall, but he was already bulked out with clothing and his utility belt. There were two possible entry points, both at spots in the wall which were overhung by street trees.

What he hadn't reckoned on, and what Google maps couldn't show him, was that the large gates at the front entrance would be open. And yet there they were, both sides pulled back to rest against the driveway kerbs. Either the owner wasn't worried about security, or he was too lazy to venture out.

Either way was good for Quinn.

He stepped through the gates and slipped into the interior shadows of the wall. The house was about a hundred yards away, the lights from a sprinkling of rooms not enough to cut through the gloom all the way to the perimeter.

Quinn skipped across a snow-covered lawn and approached a row of garages at the right side of the main building. There were no guards, no dogs, nothing to impede his progress. He headed for a side door, grateful for the absence of motion lights, another sign that security was lax.

He pressed against the wall and listened. Somewhere in the background he could hear the faint strains of concert music, a strange mix of jazz and orchestral gusto, perhaps coming from a television or a surround-sound stereo system. He stood stock still for several minutes but could detect no other noises.

He pulled the glove from his right hand and tried the door handle. It gave way. The door moved back on silent, well-oiled hinges. He walked inside, closing the door behind him, and opening his coat to retrieve the Sig Sauer from his utility belt.

Cooking smells told him he was in the kitchen area. There was just enough light to make out a fridge, built-in wall cupboards, and a central food-prep island counter that took up most of the floor.

He tiptoed across the wooden surface and eased his ear against an inner door. Still no voices. Maybe the owner had retired to bed early.

This was becoming a lot easier than he thought it would be.

Maybe too easy.

CHAPTER 14

THE WIPERS FOUGHT gallantly against the constant barrage of snow on the windscreen of the point car in the FBI convoy. Visibility was down to forty yards, leaving Carl Freeman to curse at the crawl speed of the Ford Expedition. It was a big, boxy SUV with four-wheel drive, an anti-lock brake system, and all the usual top-of-the-range bells and whistles that came with its fifty-thousand-dollar price tag. Not much good when you can barely see what's ahead.

The needle on the speedometer had flickered on the thirty-mph mark for most of the journey since the three-vehicle convoy had left *The Ponderosa* bar on its route across the city. The address pinpointed by the activated cellphone showed a location fourteen miles away. At a rate of one mile every two minutes, they were looking at a minimum of twenty-eight minutes before arriving on site. Factor in at least another four minutes for traffic-light stops. A lot can change in thirty-two minutes.

The phone's GPS location signal had lasted just fifteen seconds before the handset had been turned off. The Sim card had probably been removed along with the battery. The user could be anywhere by now. Freeman was experienced enough not to overthink the situation. Turning off the phone after a brief period could be simply a case of someone playing it safe, checking only periodically for incoming calls or messages. The weather conditions probably meant the phone owner was staying put. Which meant it was more likely than not that they would find him there. If not, they would uncover some clues as to his new whereabouts. No sense worrying about it yet.

What had really got Freeman on edge was the thought that the cellphone most likely belonged to Devlin Montgomery. The idea of tying Montgomery directly to the McAndrew shooting was almost too good to be true. *Stay put, you bastard, and you're all mine.*

Freeman kept his eyes on the car's Sat Nav signal showing their progress towards the target address. They couldn't be more than five minutes away. Maybe things were starting to fall his way. The new storm had moved in quicker than predicted, meaning the runways at Bangor International were still closed. Which meant his summons to Washington had been cancelled. Which meant he had at least another twenty-four hours to wrap this up in a way that just might save his neck from the chopping block.

The storm had also put paid to plans to transport the McAndrew children back to their grandfather. The US Marshalls, a team of four hard-looking bastards, had taken charge of the children and moved them to a new location. Typical of the USM Service, they refused to share where they were taking the kids. It had to be one of the city's luxury hotels, since they had no active safe houses in Maine. At least as far as Freeman was aware of.

He had been relieved to transfer responsibility. He was even more heartened by the fact that the Marshalls had thought to bring a child psychologist along with them. Those children would need all the help they could get. It was probably their grandfather who'd thought of that one.

"Heads up," Drew Eisler said from the driver's seat. "We're here."

Freeman peered through a white blanket at a large perimeter wall. The gates to a mansion house beyond were folded back in an invitation to enter. The three Expeditions swept through the opening, crunched the virgin snow on the driveway, and rolled to a stop beside an illuminated porch.

Quinn faced a long, wide hallway running from the kitchen to the far right of the building. He counted off five doorways, three on the left, two on the right. Five doorways meant five rooms, all of which had to be cleared. There was no quick or easy way of doing it. Unless, of course, this was a television show, where they kicked down doors, windmilled their weapons in frantic sweeps of the area, and then carried on to the next room. Five rooms, a minute per room, the ground floor cleared in less time than it took to brew a coffee.

It didn't work like that. Not if you didn't want to alert someone to your presence. That kind of racket would get anyone's attention. Even if they were on the upper floors. Which was a worst-case scenario. Having someone shoot down at you from a concealed vantage point was no way to survive in the room-clearing business.

And so, Quinn advanced slowly and carefully. He moved against the wall at the hinged-side of the first door and gently nudged it open with his foot. That gave him three distinct advantages. The first was that bullets from inside the room couldn't pierce the walls where most of his body was shielded. As the door moved inwards he would get a clear view of one side of the room without exposing himself. Another distinctive plus point. When the door was pushed to its full ninety-degree angle he could peer quickly between the hinged cracks to ascertain if there were any nasty shocks on the other side of the room. Advantage number three.

He saw nothing to concern him. He stepped quickly into the room, moving his Sig in a slow traverse across the tops of an upholstered settee and two matching armchairs. If anyone suddenly popped up behind any item of furniture they did so at the risk of losing parts of their heads. No-one popped up.

He moved slowly, manoeuvring to find angles that allowed him to see behind the seating. The room was empty. Judging by the large bookcases, which filled one wall, and a pedestal desk positioned in front of a big bay window, this was some kind of library, or reading room, or a gentleman's den. The smell of pipe tobacco and furniture polish hung in the air.

He moved back into the hallway. It had taken almost five minutes to satisfy himself there was no threat there. That was five times longer than his television counterparts. But at least he was still standing.

Ten minutes later, he was done with another two rooms. One was a dining room, with eight chairs standing sentry either side of an elliptic walnut table, the other room was little more than a storage space, with a smorgasbord of boxes, discarded furniture, and old kitchen appliances. This was a house that was well lived-in. The sort associated with a large family, with a maid and a butler thrown in for good measure. The place cried out with all the characteristics of old money. It had the feel of a pre-war upstairs-downstairs era.

So where was everybody?

Room number four provided a partial answer.

Quinn finished his usual ritual of nudging the door open with his foot, peering through the crack, and stepping into what he thought was another empty space. It was a room not unlike the first one he'd checked. There was a wall-to-wall bookcase, an upholstered settee and chairs in a similar floral pattern, and a large-screen flat TV mounted on a wall above a fancy stone fireplace. Instead of tobacco, there were the sweet aromas of jasmine and lavender. Rooms one and four looked like expensive examples of his and her private getaway retreats. Her Yin to his Yang.

The fireplace and television were additional accessories.

So, too, was the bloodstained body sprawled behind one of the armchairs.

Quinn knelt beside the body, placing the back of his left hand against the victim's cheek. Even through the thin covering of his latex gloves, he could feel warmth on the skin. Quinn knew that rigor mortis usually set in somewhere between three and four hours after death, depending on ambient temperature. The absence of rigor, and the residual heat of the skin, told him this unfortunate had meet a grisly end within the last two hours, more likely closer to one hour than two.

The corpse was that of a man in his early forties. There were enough wrinkles and grey hairs to suggest that was the case, although copious amounts of drying blood over the head and face made it difficult to be certain. There were puncture holes in his forehead, below his right eye, on his chin and at several points on his chest. It looked as if someone had emptied a full magazine of point-twenty-twos into him.

Even at close range, a .22 bullet is not designed to tear through a body. Its purpose is to expand and fragment on impact. Quinn rolled the corpse and checked for signs of exit wounds. As expected, there were none. This guy was facing his killer when he got the full count.

A search of the deceased's pockets yielded a helpful wallet. According to a driving licence, complete with a grainy photo, this was not Devin Montgomery, the man Quinn had come to find. Maybe he'd been sold a pup by Bob Thornton before he choked to death under Quinn's boot.

The body was that of a New Yorker by the name of James Vicenti. There was nothing else in the wallet to explain anything about the man, or what he was doing at an address that belonged to Devlin Montgomery. An acquaintance? A rival? An unlucky door-to-door salesman? None of the above?

Quinn rose and gripped the Sig tighter. Clearing the rest of the house had just become a whole lot harder, especially with the prospect of a trigger-happy gunman on the loose.

It took him an hour to reach the third floor. Unlike the other two floors, this one was in darkness. He'd found little of note in the second floor, other than signs that someone had either ransacked the master bedroom or had flung open drawers and wardrobes in a rush to pack and flee the scene.

He was standing in the second of what appeared to be six rooms at this level when he heard the sounds of vehicles and saw headlights dance around the gloom. He moved carefully to a window, cracked an opening in the heavy curtains and looked down at three SUVs sliding to a halt at the front door. He'd seen these vehicles before outside the Jutland Hotel.

And there was no mistaking the tall, grey-haired man who climbed out of one of the units. The FBI had arrived. And Quinn was boxed in.

He watched the man deploy his team in much the same way as he'd done at the hotel. This time, one figure ran off to the left of the building, another took the right. Quinn pondered the rationale behind the leader's thinking. The only way to cover both flanks and the rear was for the men to take up positions at the corners of the back of the building, thereby allowing each of them to watch their respective sides whilst also scanning across the rear. Neat.

That left the leader plus seven others in the group. They all headed under the porch and were lost to sight. Once again Quinn put himself in their shoes. He'd leave at least two agents inside the door to guard against someone coming down the central staircase and disappearing into the night while a necessary room-searching operation was underway. Split the remaining agents into two groups of three to search the east and west wings, starting on the ground floor. No sense doing more than one level at a time. The exits were covered, leaving the emphasis on caution and patience.

Quinn figured he had no more than twenty minutes before the inside group reached the third level. Six agents could clear rooms up to eight times faster than he did. It wasn't a simple case of multiplication. Their movements in triplicate would save time on an exponential basis, meaning they could work more a heck of a lot faster than he did. Hell, his twenty-minute guess could be undercut by another five minutes.

He couldn't let the FBI take him in. Too many questions. Too much exposure to a raft of possible charges, including murder, interfering with a federal investigation, false documentation, illegal immigration, and generally making a nuisance of himself. There were no upsides.

As much as he was determined not to be arrested, he was equally sure he would not fight it out. Killing scumbags who needed killing was one thing. Shooting at the FBI was a whole different ballgame. He'd never attacked a law enforcer at any time, in any country, and he was not about to start now.

He was quickly running out of options.

CHAPTER 15

QUINN LEFT the room and hurried to the end of the hall, the farthest point from the large circular stairwell, the only access he could see to this level of the building. A small gable window allowed him to look out at the grounds, which at this side of the site were covered in show-topped shrubs and bushes. In any other circumstance they would afford solid cover for an escape towards the perimeter wall.

Except for the FBI man he spotted standing on a broad pathway at the rear corner. He'd been right about the leader's deployment tactic.

He glanced up at a small hatch in the ceiling. It looked like a typical attic opening, the kind that probably had a pull-down ladder. He couldn't see a pole or hook and guessed it was an automatic unit operated by a switch. He fumbled on the wall and found two square plastic blocks, both of which had familiar central push buttons.

He paused his thumb over one of them. Even if he got into the attic unnoticed what would be the point? There was a dead body downstairs and because of it the FBI weren't going anywhere in a hurry. The house could be locked down for days while forensic teams combed every part of it. Eventually, they would get around to the roofspace.

He walked back to the gable window. It had eight panes set into a wood frame that was split in the middle and held shut by a simple brass arm. He moved the arm cautiously, keeping his eyes on the sentry below. The guy's attention was on the ground floor windows. He waited for a minute before inching the bottom half of the window upwards.

Thankfully, there were no moans or creaks. He brought it all the way to its optimum point and fixed it in place by tying off a small pulley rope built into the side of the frame. The gap was big enough for him to squeeze through, but first he had to figure out how to get to the ground below.

He moved his head slowly through the opening. The guard was still huddled against the building, his head bowed against the driving snow. A solid-looking drainpipe was fixed to the wall on the right of the window. It was ideal for a quick getaway, if only it were about six feet closer.

The left side wall promised a better route. Thick ivy snaked its way from the roof to the path below. It should hold his weight and could be easily reached. The only problem remaining was getting rid of the guard.

Quinn left the window open and moved as fast he could back down the hallway. He heard doors slamming on the ground floor. The FBI boys were using the noisy television version of room-clearing. That allowed him to track their progress while he put the next phase of his plan in motion.

He chose a door that he knew must lead to a room at the rear of the building. It was a disused bedroom, judging by the musty smells and the dust-sheets covering most of the furniture. He lifted a heavy chair and flung it against a large window, before dropping to his knees, pulling the Sig from his belt, and firing six rounds into the air through the gap.

He immediately raced out of the room and headed for the gable window.

Quinn was betting all his experience on two crucial things happening. The guys at the rear of the building would figure they were under attack. A smashed window, crashing furniture and a volley of shots would be a no-brainer assumption on their part. Their best bet would be to hug the rear wall, probably on bended knees, and train all their attention on a possible escape attempt from one of the upstairs windows.

Quinn waited a moment beside the gable window. Then he pushed his head out in time to watch the FBI man at his side of the building do exactly what Quinn reckoned he'd do. For all intents and purposes, the coast was clear. Quinn holstered the Sig and reached out to grab the ivy stalks. Twenty seconds to reach the ground, twice that to get to the perimeter wall. If there were no buses or taxis operating in the deteriorating weather, he was resigned to the fact that it might be hours before he got back to the lock-up. He shivered in the sub-zero temperature, knowing he faced a long trip of hopping from one cafeteria or bar to the next one in order to stay warm and out of the clutches of the FBI.

He pulled his body clear of the window and began a fast descent, his hands and feet groping for purchase against the slick surface. He lost his grip twice but recovered to continue downwards until he was ten feet from the bottom. That's when disaster struck.

The ivy roots were not as strong as he'd reckoned. The entire bottom section of the structure pulled away from the wall, sending Quinn backwards in a freefall towards the path below. The layer of snow provided only a token cushion against what was to come. He hit the ground hard, his shoulders and lower back taking the brunt of the impact, although he also felt his head crack against the surface. Air was forced from his lungs as pain exploded in sharp needles across his torso. Before passing out he had a weird thought that this must be what it's like to be kicked by mule. Magnified by a factor of ten.

Carl Freeman heard the shots and the frantic radio message from one of his agents. "We're taking fire, we're taking fire! They're trying to escape through the rear."

He knew the shots had come from above, although it was difficult to judge if the shooters were on the second or third floor. Just moments before, he'd come across the dead body in one of the ground-floor rooms and was about to call his team together when he'd heard the sound of breaking glass followed by a salvo from a semi-automatic. He had to consider that the killer or killers were still on site. He intended to trap them, no matter what.

"Listen up everyone," he snapped into his throat mic. "Hold your positions. I say again, hold your positions. No heroics. Inside teams to meet me at the central stairwell."

Freeman strode out into the hall and joined with Drew Eisler and the remaining agents as arranged. He nodded at Jan Moseley, a ten-year veteran who somehow balanced the rigours of the job with being a single mother to a young daughter. "Jan, go to the other end of this hallway and check for another staircase, or an elevator or a laundry chute. Sweep around until you're certain the only way down here is via these stairs."

Rory Cheadle was the next to fall under Freeman's gaze. "The same goes for you on the west wing."

Two other agents were despatched under the stairs towards the rear of the building. "There's likely a kitchen or dining area in that direction. Check for dummy waiter shafts and stay down there in case we need to support the guys on the exterior."

Cheadle raised an eyebrow. "I take it you're not expecting whoever's up there to surrender. What's our ROE?"

Freeman patted him on the shoulder. "Your rules of engagement are not to get killed. The rest of us are heading outside to cover the grounds."

Eisler looked quizzically at Freeman. "Do you think it's Montgomery and some of his other cronies still on the loose?"

"To tell the truth, Drew, I haven't the foggiest. Something doesn't add up. I thought we'd accounted for the rest of the gang, unless Montgomery had a back-up crew stashed away here. But why the body inside? Is he the homeowner or one of Montgomery's lot?"

"We'll find out soon enough," Eisler deadpanned.

"Until then we need to lock this place down tighter than your wallet. Get us some back-up."

"You want to bring in the boys in blue?"

"Hell no. Get some of our own people here."

"We've stripped the Field Office bare. There's nobody left except the tech geek and a few admin staff. None of them's gonna be any use."

Freeman frowned. "Forgot about that. Looks like we've no choice. But I want SWAT people here."

"Copy that. I'll get BDP to set up a ten-block cordon. Do we wait for SWAT before moving in?"

"No, we'll start putting the squeeze on, but on a slow-slow basis. Our first priority is to make sure nobody is going anywhere."

Outside on the porch, Eisler nodded. "How do you want to work this?"

"You split left with two of the team. I'll take the other two and go right."

At the right side of the building Quinn suddenly sat up. There was no way of knowing how long he'd passed out, although he guessed it could only have been seconds. He glanced around. No sign of the two FBI men who'd been guarding this side of the building.

And then the pain started up again. It was a continuous, all-over assault that made him bite his bottom lip to stop squealing. He could have a few broken ribs, or at the very least dislocated his shoulder. He pressed his palms against the path and hauled himself to his feet. A wave of nausea swept over him, and for a moment he thought he was going to pass out again.

He shook his head, gulped in a few deep breaths, and studied the terrain. Two large bushes swayed about fifteen yards in front of him. Behind those, he could see a sprinkling of trees and more bushes. Behind that, was the perimeter wall. And freedom.

He moved forward cautiously, keeping his eyes pinned to the rear of the building. Once behind the first bushes he should be safe for the rest of the way. Fresh snow was already covering his tracks. His legs felt like lead weights. This was taking too much time.

Halfway to the bushes the stillness of the air crackled with a booming voice.

"FBI! Don't move a muscle."

Quinn was still staring at the rear of the building. There was no-one there. That's because the voice was coming from behind him. He cursed himself for his stupidity.

"Hands in the air where I can see them. If you do not do exactly as I say, I will shoot. Is that understood?"

Quinn raised his arms slowly. No sense giving this guy the opportunity to over-react. "I surrender. I know the drill."

"All the way up," the voice said.

"I think I've dislocated a shoulder. This is about as high as I can reach."

"Cut the bullshit, asshole, I've heard it all before."

Quinn didn't bother responding. He put his hands behind his head and interlinked the fingers. Then he sagged to his knees. He heard the crunch of footsteps coming towards him. At any other time, he would already be working on a strategy to turn the tables, take down his captor, and head for the wall. Not this time. He was not about to use a lethal counter-thrust against the FBI. Not that any of that mattered. He simply didn't have the energy to move.

A shadow fell across Quinn's face and he glanced up to see a Glock pointed steady at the centre of his forehead. Behind the weapon was a white-haired man who was instantly recognisable. "I see I get the head honcho himself."

Carl Freeman looked down in shock. "You! What the hell are you doing here? You've got a lot of explaining to do, mister whoever-you-are."

Quinn smiled. "Would you believe I was just out for a walk and stopped to ask for directions to the nearest coffee house?"

Then a black cloud seemed to envelop Quinn and he pitched forward onto the snow-covered lawn.

CHAPTER 16

AN ARROW-SHAPED neon sign cut through the gloom of the I-95 thirty miles south east of Bangor. It was impossible to see the lettering, much of which was covered by snow clamped to the plastic surface. What mattered was that it represented a diversion, a way off the perilous four-lane carriageway that was becoming almost impassable.

Devlin Montgomery gratefully accepted the gift. He nudged his Mercedes hire car across the road and entered a large service area, brightly-lit with a filling station, a coffee house, a cafeteria and, most importantly, a motel. He'd found a bolthole, at least until this weather released its grip.

He crawled the vehicle into a spot close to the motel entrance and grabbed his suitcase from the trunk. The place was busy. A small queue had formed at the receptionist counter, which was little more than a hinged shelf outside a door that seemed to lead to the owner's private area. People were clamouring for the attention of a young lady, barely out of her teens, and finding it difficult to deal with the demands being placed upon her.

Ordinarily, Montgomery would have marched to the head of the throng, slapped a wad of cash in front of the receptionist, and insisted on being immediately shown to a room. Not this time. He needed to keep a low profile. More than anything, he needed time to think. Not being in control was something Devlin Montgomery was not used to.

He listened intently to the conversations ahead of him. The motel had twenty-two rooms, all with their own exterior access around a rectangular block that offered little by the way of privacy or comfort. He imagined paper-thin walls, threadbare carpets, lumpy mattresses, and a toilet-cum-shower space with hardly any room to turn sideways. Right now, it sounded like the Ritz Carlton.

He heard the girl say they had only four rooms left. A head-count showed six people ahead of him. Maybe it was time to flash the cash. The thought quickly dissipated as the next in line asked for a single room with four beds for a husband, wife and two sons. The man agreed to take a pair of fold-up cots for a discount on a price that had probably gone up by three times the normal rate because of demand over the last few hours. Entrepreneurship was alive and kicking on the I-95.

Montgomery got a key for number eighteen at the farthest end of the rectangle. There was no porter, no food-ordering service, and no in-house coffee-making facilities, so he trudged to the room, dumped his suitcase and trudged all the way back, walking past the receptionist block towards the separately-franchised cafeteria.

He hadn't eaten all day, largely because his appetite had taken a massive downwards hit shortly after receiving an early-morning phone call from someone he hadn't wanted to speak to. At least until he could plead his case in person.

Montgomery had risen through the ranks of the

conglomerate in a little under five years. He was a streetwise mover and shaker, with a ruthless streak that was guaranteed to see him slide up the ladder over the backs of others. He was a figures man, at home with spreadsheets, mergers and acquisitions, the kind of acquisitions often conducted through blackmail or at the point of a gun. The violence, however, was left to others. Montgomery was squeamish about those things, particularly if he had to be up close and personal when they were happening. His job was to figure out what needed doing, and then send someone else in to get the job done.

The hit on Mark McAndrew was different. He'd taken it too personal. This was one trigger he'd wanted to pull himself. The lawyer had betrayed him and had left him exposed to the wrath of his superiors.

Montgomery was at the organisation's top table. But there were still a few tiers above him. It was one of those tiers who'd made the breakfast-time call. The conversation, mostly one-sided, had sent shivers through Montgomery's normally-calm disposition.

"You made just about every mistake it was possible to make," the voice said. "You decided to take out the son-in-law of the Chief Justice of the Supreme Court, a gentleman who can call on the full resources of every known law enforcement agency in the country, and probably a few that are off-the-books, and won't mind what it takes to get answers. They're gonna come looking for you, which means they're gonna come looking for us, which means we need to get this situation under control."

Montgomery tried to cut in. "I didn't know McAndrew was married to the Chief Justice's daughter. How could I know? She'd been estranged from the family and had changed her name before she met McAndrew. I found all this out only after the news broke on television."

"It was your job to know, you fucking cretin! You should have checked and double-checked. It's what we do. It's how we stay in business. Now, thanks to you, we'll be lucky to have anything left when this shitstorm finally blows out."

"I'll make it right," Montgomery pleaded.

"And I'm supposed to be heartened by that? Not only did you order this hit without our authorisation, but you actually participated in it. Then you sent a bunch of idiots to deal with two children in full view of a media spotlight, thereby piling one catastrophe on top of another. Frankly, there's no way you can make this right."

"What do you want me to do?"

"I want you to disappear."

The phone line had promptly gone dead. Montgomery had known at that second what was meant by *disappear*. They didn't want him to lie low. They wanted him out of the picture. Permanently.

It was why he'd sat alone all day in the big house trying to work out his next moves. He'd spent the first few hours in front of his laptop, moving part of the organisation's huge cash reserves around several offshore accounts. He'd known he had to leave the country and for that he needed a nest egg. Twenty million should be enough to give him a head start. If only this fucking weather would relent!

He'd packed a suitcase, taking little care about flinging together the bare essentials. Where he was going he would get a new wardrobe, a new face, and new papers. He'd learned a long time ago that nothing was impossible if you had money for a companion. Sure, he'd be a fugitive, but the heat would eventually die down.

The smile that had played across his face disappeared when a man stepped into his study and levelled a suppressed pistol at his head.

How the fuck could they have got someone here so fast through this weather?

The gunman eyed Montgomery's suitcase. "Going somewhere?"

Devlin Montgomery was nothing if not a survivor. All those boardroom skills and instincts had immediately kicked in. He knew the score. More than that, he knew if he couldn't overturn the dynamics of this confrontation, he would not be leaving Bangor, except in a body bag. He needed one of his famed stratagems. And he needed it now.

He wore a frown when he looked up to face the gunman. "It's about time. I've been waiting for you for hours. Your orders are changed. You're to accompany me to New York and make sure I get safely to the chairman before the net closes in."

"What the fuck are you talking about?"

"See for yourself," Montgomery had replied, stepping back from the laptop and inviting the gunman to look at the screen. "I got an email to confirm the new arrangements. Apparently, they've been trying to get through to you but you're not answering your cellphone."

The gunman was torn between looking at the laptop and reaching for his phone. Montgomery had moved farther away from the desk, turning sideways to hide his hand disappearing into his coat pocket. "We don't have all day," he'd yelled. "Read the fucking message and let's get out of here."

The gunman's eyes had dropped to the laptop. It was the opening Montgomery had been waiting for. His hand was now filled with a Beretta Jaguar 71, a short-barrelled semi-automatic with an 8-round magazine of .22 ammunition. Montgomery used them all. It had not been a pretty sight. There had been no finesse, no applied marksmanship. He'd just fired and kept firing, the bullets penetrating the gunman's face, chest and arms in a frenzied kill.

Afterwards, Montgomery had bolted for the door, dragging his suitcase, and praying the gunman hadn't disabled the Mercedes before entering the house. He was in luck. The big German engine purred on the first turn of the key. He was out of the grounds and onto the snow-covered roads within a matter of seconds.

But his luck hadn't held. The blizzards had intensified, making it impossible to get to New York. Both figuratively and literally, the neon sign had proved to be the one bright light in an otherwise shitty day.

Now, as Montgomery sat hunched over the best steak the cafeteria had to offer, he wondered if his luck would continue to hold.

Four hundred and forty miles away, a stern-faced

woman walked into a mahogany-panelled boardroom overlooking the Manhattan skyline. Her white hair was parcelled into a bun at the top of her head and her eyes were framed by red glasses that were much too big for her elfin face. She glanced from a handheld iPad to a man seated at the top of a large table.

"You were right, Mr Chairman. He did try to manipulate our funds, but we managed to piggyback all his transactions, which have now been fully reversed. As of this moment, Mr Montgomery has nothing on his credit or debit cards, nothing in his bank accounts, and has been frozen out of all password entries onto our systems. All he's got left is whatever cash he has in his wallet"

The baritone voice that resonated across the room was the same that had droned into Montgomery's phone a few hours earlier. "Well done, Clarissa, though by now it should be a moot point. Have we heard anything back from Vicenti?"

"Nothing yet, Mr Chairman, though I'm bound to say we were rather limited in our options there. Vicenti's little more than a bagman, hardly the sort we'd normally engage for such an important job."

"Quite so, Clarissa, but he was the only available asset we could find in the Bangor area at such short notice. Perhaps after this we should consider setting up better-equipped regional offices to take care of eventualities such as this."

"That would cost a fortune, Mr Chairman."

"Unfortunately, Clarissa, there's a lot more than fortunes at stake here. This is a massive damage-limitation exercise. We have to distance ourselves from Montgomery, write him out of our history, so to speak. I want backdated notes on file and revised board minutes to show we sacked the man for gross incompetency months ago. We have to demonstrate that whatever he was doing was not on behalf of this company. How's that coming along?"

The woman smiled conspiratorially. "We got quite creative with that one, Mr Chairman. Our email server has been wiped clean of all transactions involving Montgomery, as has our door-entry passkey system, which shows it has been months since he was last in the building. I created internal memos demanding the return of his company car, and our payroll folder now contains a final severance payment dated six months ago."

"You seem to have thought of everything, Clarissa. Now tell me, have you been able to raise Vicenti?"

"No sir, he's not answering his cellphone."

"Then we must plan for the worst. If Montgomery has managed to escape I want a full alert sent to all our people. Get men stationed along every possible route out of Bangor. Put the squeeze on. He must be found and eliminated at all costs."

CHAPTER 17

A BRIGHT LIGHT helped Quinn reach for the surface. It was just beyond his grasp but getting closer as he clawed against the black morass. His arms and legs felt as if they were wrapped in treacle, sucking him back into the abyss each time he seemed to be making progress. He concentrated on the light and finally broke free.

"Good to have you back with us, Mr Quinn."

The voice triggered a memory. It was a female voice, caramel-coated with a twang of Texas. He couldn't place it, couldn't see the face behind it because of the fog that covered his eyes. He shook his head and the blur began to fade, leaving him with partial focus, enough to make out the white coat and the outline shape of the doctor he'd met when he'd brought Charlie and Sophie into the hospital. He had the sensation of being hogtied into a straightjacket, his shoulders, arms and chest tightly bound, his right wrist cinched by a pair of handcuffs that jangled against the metal arm of his bed.

"What's happening here, Doc?"

The answer came from a new voice, somewhere across the room. "What's happening is that you're under arrest. Don't ask me about the charges; there are too many of them to run through. We'll deal with all that as soon as we get you outta here."

The FBI team leader stepped into view, positioning himself between the doctor and Quinn. It was a bad mistake on his part.

The doctor placed a hand on Carl Freeman's shoulder and pushed him hard. "Not so fast, mister. This man is going nowhere until I say so. He has suffered a traumatic brain injury, which means he could lose full functionality if he's moved, or worse still he could slip into an irreversible coma. Either way, you won't be taking him anywhere, not until I've finished what I need to do."

"I don't think you understand, doctor, this man is highly dangerous and could be the key to solving a number of murders. It's imperative we start questioning him immediately."

"It's you who doesn't understand," the doctor said with quiet authority. "I'm telling you now that it is my qualified opinion this man could die unless my instructions are followed to the letter."

"C'mon, doctor, let's not get melodramatic about this."

The doctor's nostrils flared in anger. "How's this for melodrama? If anything happens to my patient, I will see to it that you face charges because of your callous disregard for expert medical advice. Now, I want you and your agents to leave this room."

"Not gonna happen, doctor."

"I will give you precisely ten seconds, after which I will summon hospital security, after which I will have our administrator call the FBI Director, and our Congressman, and our Senator, and whoever the hell it takes to get you to listen. The countdown starts now."

Freeman glanced around the room at several other agents, then down at Quinn, then at the doctor. "Okay, it's your show for now. But we'll be right outside the door."

When the room cleared, the doctor bent over Quinn and whispered. "Now we get the chance to talk freely. I'm Dr Andrea Flint and I'm pleased to see you again, even in these circumstances."

Quinn was puzzled by the change in mood. "Thank you for giving me some space. How are the McAndrew children?"

"They're doing fine, thanks to you."

"So, am I really going to die?"

She smiled. "Around here traumatic brain injury is a rather glorified and exaggerated terminology for simple concussion. In your case it's a mild form, although we do like to take precautions. It certainly won't kill you, but you need to take it easy for a while."

Quinn looked down the bed. "What's with all the bandages?"

"You dislocated a shoulder, which has been reset, and you have heavy bruising on a number of ribs. The shoulder straps can come off, but not the chest bandages. Ribs need a bit of time to cure themselves. I've given you pain killers and I want to continue to monitor your vitals to judge the effects of concussion. How is your head? Do you feel nauseous? Can you focus in on certain things, such as the picture on the far wall?"

"Is that a poster encouraging mothers to eat healthily throughout pregnancy?"

"Nothing wrong with your focus then."

"Why so blunt with the FBI, doc? They could be

right about me being a dangerous killer."

"From what I've seen, Mr Quinn, you are not the man they're painting you out to be. What you did for those kids deserves better than being railroaded by people who seem to be looking for a scapegoat for their own shortcomings. If you ask me, I think for all their swagger they know, deep down, that they've a lot to be grateful to you for."

"Not sure they'd agree with you, doc, but thanks for the endorsement. What happens now?"

"First, I'm going to remove the shoulder straps, run a few more tests, and see what we need to do to get you up and about. I'm afraid that FBI man, Freeman, is right about one thing. Within a few hours I'll have to agree to release you into his custody."

"Don't sweat it, doc. There is one more thing you could do for me."

"Name it."

"Any chance of coffee and something to eat."

Two hours later Carl Freeman, Drew Eisler and two other agents stood in a semi-circle around Quinn's bed. An empty mug and sandwich wrappers littered the top of the roll-in bedside tray, which Freeman wheeled away towards a window.

"Let's start with the basics," Freeman said. "You gave your name as Quinn when you met the doctor earlier, yet according to the papers in your wallet your name is Michael Tate. Care to explain that?"

"It's a nickname."

"What is?

"Quinn."

"You trying to tell me you have a nickname that sounds like a surname? Isn't it more likely that Quinn is in fact your real name and that the driving licence and social security card in the name of Tate are fakes?"

"It comes from my great-grandfather."

"What are you talking about?"

"My nickname. My ancestor, on my mother's side, was Sam Quinn, a fine upstanding County Down man who managed a local brewery, lived to be a ripe old age and started a dynasty that runs into hundreds, maybe even thousands. Apparently, when I was younger I bore a striking resemblance to the old man, so everybody started to call me Quinn."

"Bullshit!"

"What, you don't believe he could have had that many descendants?"

"You know well enough what I'm talking about. Might as well come clean. We'll run these papers through everything we've got. If they're bogus, we'll know about it soon enough."

"Be my guest." Quinn had paid over the odds for what was his US-resident ID. There are top-notch forgers who can turn out passports, driving licences, social security documents, birth certificates, college papers, marriage licences, fake doctorates, job references, and just about anything produced on paper and ink, or the latter-day laser and digital equivalents, complete with bar codes and holograms. Ten-thousand-dollars a pop buys state-of-the-art paperwork that would fool the most sophisticated of scanners. That's what Quinn had done with most of his fake IDs. But not with the

Michael Tate alias.

He'd decided from an early stage that he needed a solid USA legend, one that he could use with impunity whilst in-country. He'd paid over ten times the going rate for that one. The paperwork was exceptional, produced by a craftsman in Cincinnati who had access to places he shouldn't have had access to. That meant he worked with original materials, a bit like a counterfeiter getting his hands on the US Bureau of Engraving and Printing's bespoke plates and cotton fibre papers to produce dollar bills. This particular forger was also a cyber buff, meaning he accessed official government databases and implanted his legends as if they were real people, with family backgrounds, school attendances, sporting achievements and job histories. The only thing missing was an IRS file, which required annual tax returns, which was no biggy, since more than seven million Americans failed to do so each year.

Quinn was confident his Michael Tate alias would stand up to FBI scrutiny. So what if someone, somewhere down the line decided he owed Uncle Sam some tax dollars?

"Tell me about the RV you used to transport the children to the hospital."

It was a neat switch in direction by Freeman. "Nothing to tell," Quinn said. "It just happened to be nearby and I hotwired it. Figured time was of the essence. Don't tell me you're going to charge me with grand theft auto?"

"Where's the RV now?"

"Left it at the hospital. Guess it must still be there." Quinn knew the agent wasn't buying his feeble explanation. At the very least, they would have spent a lot of time and resources looking for the RV, which was not abandoned within the hospital grounds or, for that matter, anywhere else in the city.

Freeman again ignored the response and moved quickly to his next line of attack. "Where are you staying in Bangor?"

"I'd only just got off the train and was looking for an hotel when I ran into the children."

"Why were you in the convenience store if you were looking for an hotel?"

"Needed some toiletries and other things."

"Why did you interfere with the men who were trying to snatch the kids?"

"Would you have stood back and let two apes manhandle children?"

"Why did you kill the man at the hospital? Why did you kill the man near the Jutland Hotel?"

And there it was. The FBI man was finally getting around to the pertinent questions.

Quinn looked vacantly at Freeman. "Don't know what you're talking about."

"We know that you organised the security guards at the hospital and warned them about an imminent threat against the children. You knew someone was coming and we have you on CCTV following the man out of the hospital. Quite a neat kill. You broke his neck in a way that suggests you knew exactly what you were doing."

"Pure coincidence that I might have left at the same time as this man you're talking about. Yes, I made sure the guards were looking after the children, but I figured I'd done enough for the night. I just needed to find an hotel."

"Bullshit!"

"You need to enlarge your dictionary. You seem to use that word a lot. The CCTV will show that I had nothing to do with this man's death."

"Bull.....you know very well there were no outside cameras. "

"How could I possibly know that? I've never been to that hospital before."

Freeman sighed and pulled up a chair beside the top of Quinn's bed. "Let's skip the other guy who died near the Jutland Hotel. What were you doing at the house where we arrested you? Why kill the man we found in one of the downstairs rooms?"

"That guy was dead at least an hour before I got there. As I said, I was looking for an hotel and got lost, so I decided to call at that house to ask for directions. The front door was lying open so I walked in. Then I heard your posse arrive and decided it was time to make myself scarce. I knew you wouldn't believe me, and I guess I'm being proved right."

Freeman rose from the chair and kicked it behind him. "Alright, tough guy, have it your own way. We're taking you outta here back to our offices where we can get a little cosier, if you know what I mean?"

"I gotta tell you, Agent Freeman, if you're thinking of resorting to violence it won't end happily. Maybe we should just stay here and save you the journey back for treatment. And that goes for your three pussy friends."

Two of the agents moved forward. Freeman held up his hand. "Not now, boys, Mr Quinn or Mr

Tate will change his attitude soon enough."

"I think we're done talking," Quinn announced.

Freeman smiled. "I don't think so. We still haven't covered all those shenanigans you got up to in Suarez, Mexico."

CHAPTER 18

QUINN WAS fully dressed, sitting on a chair bolted to a floor. He leaned across a table, also bolted to the floor, and scanned his new surroundings. It was a small, windowless room, the walls and ceiling painted in a drab military grey that looked more like a primer coat than the finished article. The place could do with a spring clean to remove water stains, layers of dust, and a few well-developed cobwebs. It was a cross between an interview room, except there was no two-way mirror, and a holding cell, except there was no bed or urinal.

The table was a sturdy four-leg solid wood affair. Quinn sat on a single chair facing two others. No room on his side for an attorney. The FBI were not big on suspects having access to legal representation. The Patriot Act afforded them a lot of leeway, something Quinn suspected they were going to use to the full.

He had been transported out of the hospital shortly after six o'clock in the evening. The journey across town was surprisingly quick, with streets and pavements rapidly clearing, thanks to another sudden shift in weather patterns. It had been twenty hours since his arrest at Montgomery's house and outside temperatures had risen dramatically.

It took less that thirty minutes to reach the FBI

Field Office, a monstrous old building hidden behind high walls and a solid roll-back gate leading to a tarmacked car park in a generous compound that took up several acres of city-centre real estate. It looked as if it could double as an under-siege foreign embassy, the sort where you'd expect insurgents to attack at any moment, or at the very least to mount demonstrations against the incumbents.

There was of course none of that. The area around the compound was deserted, the whole place looked bland and innocuous, just another piece of New England garish architecture. No FBI lettering, no nameplate on the wall, no public access from the street. A private residence? An office block? Somehow it didn't seem to matter. It was not a place that people took a second look at.

Quinn had been ushered through a rear entrance and down several flights of stairs before being locked into the room with the bolted chairs, and bolted table, and stains, and dust, and cobwebs.

That was two hours ago.

It was a classic case of letting him sweat. Some psychiatrist or behavioural science boffin must have figured out yonks ago that suspects left alone were more likely to resort to letting their imaginations run riot. Initial confidence slowly eroded by doubt. Alibis choked by overthinking details. Determination replaced by indecision.

Quinn was never one to worry about things outside his control. Whatever they had would be revealed soon enough. He did admit that his connection to events in Mexico was not something he would have seen coming in a million years. He narrowed it down to facial recognition software at the airport. They had his photo which probably popped up on one of their database searches. Apart from using another of his false aliases, they had nothing of substance to charge him with. They'd probably threaten to turn him over to the Mexican authorities, warn him about the notorious state prison in Ciudad Juarez, then offer to make it all go away in return for full disclosure.

He pushed the thoughts away and let his mind wander back to Ireland. It was twenty years since he'd left Downpatrick. He remembered the familiar townscape, dominated by the Church of Ireland's Down Cathedral on one of the highest of many mounds which characterised the geography of the region. A big granite stone, hewn from the nearby Mountains of Mourne, lay in the shadows of the Cathedral's south-west approach and marked the gravesite of Saint Patrick, Ireland's Patron Saint. Below it, less than eight-hundred-yards away on a smaller mound, was the equally imposing Saint Patrick's Catholic Church, built seven hundred years after its more illustrious neighbour. Two religions, two traditions, two diverse and opposing histories. Which just about summed up Northern Ireland and was one of the reasons he'd left the place.

But he'd always retained an affection for the small market town with its history dating back to AD497. It was the chosen place of residence of many of the early Kings of Ulster and at its core was a convolution of four roads that hadn't changed much down the ages. He remembered the main street with the Northern Bank at one end, the Ulster

Bank at the other, and familiar family businesses in between. Hanlon's Greengrocery, McCartan's Shoe Shop, Breen's Grand Cinema, Kelly's Hardware, Coburn's Menswear, and Rea's Emporium.

He thought of the local schools and public playing fields and all the other places where he'd hung out with his friends. He recalled watching gaelic football at a bumpy field a mile outside town and his early trips to the local horse racetrack. Soccer played at Dunleath Park and cricket at Strangford Road. Catching fish on the Quoile River and going to dances at the Canon's Hall. Maybe it wasn't such a bad childhood after all.

He smiled, folded his arms on the table, and rested his head. He was asleep within two minutes.

Carl Freeman and Drew Eisler watched Quinn from a monitor linked to a small camera in a ceiling light.

"Can you believe this guy?"

"I've gotta admit, Drew, he's one cool customer. We have to find a way to rattle his cage. An educated guess tells us he's got history, probably in the military, and that there's a dark side to him. Just look at the skills he used to take out two of Montgomery's men, and then there's that nonsense in Mexico. Too much of a coincidence him being there around the time those two cartel leaders were snuffed out."

"You thinking he's a gun for hire?"

"Everything points that way. But why would somebody like that get mixed up with Montgomery's hit on the McAndrew family? Why not just walk away? Why risk the exposure?"

"Wrong time, wrong place. Maybe he just couldn't stand by and watch the kids being manhandled in the convenience store."

Freeman rubbed his chin. "But it didn't end there. He killed the guy at the hospital and then another near the Jutland Hotel. And don't forget, we found him at Montgomery's place. That had to be premeditated. He was searching for answers."

"So, you're putting him in the frame for the body we found at the Montgomery house?"

"No, the timeline doesn't fit. He was right about that. Besides, that was a messy, frenzied attack. Someone just lifted a pistol and emptied it into the dead man without finesse or professionalism. Not what someone like Quinn or Tate would do. We've already seen his other handiwork and I gotta say it's as clean and competent as I've ever come across."

Eisler continued to watch the monitor as he spoke. "How do we get him to give up what he knows?"

"We can tie him to at least two murders here and two more on the other side of the border. Whatever way he looks at it, he's going down hard. Maybe he doesn't know that much about Montgomery. Maybe he's just a do-gooder. Bottom line, however, is that he won't get to walk away. We have laws in this country. I want to know this guy's entire history. Who he works for, who he's killed as part of his duties. Unless he cuts a deal, he'll end up doing a lot of time."

"Isn't it a bit of a stretch to say we can tie him to all four murders?"

"I'm not worried about Mexico, but by the time our forensic boys finish with the scenes here in

Bangor, we'll have something. A shoeprint, a hair, a partial print. If it's there, we'll find it."

"How do you want to play it?"

"Let's get started with the cage-rattling."

Quinn woke instantly at the sound of the door opening. He sat upright and watched the two FBI men cross the floor and take up station on the chairs opposite his.

"Sorry to keep you waiting, Mr Tate. I've had the devil of a time keeping the Federales from hopping on a plane and hauling your ass back to Mexico. Seems they're anxious to speak with you about several murders. I've held them off for now, but that can only last for so long. How about giving me a reason for extending your stay here?"

"Please, Agent Freeman, just call me Quinn. All my friends do and I feel like we're getting to know each other so well."

"You think?"

"Yessir. For example. We both know you haven't spoken to anyone in Mexico about me. It's not how you do business. You guys like to play the cards close to your chests. Nothing, or nobody, trumps the FBI, particularly not a bunch of corrupt brown-shirted Mexican Joes from the other side of the border. Either pack me off or let's just forget about Suarez. I'm good either way."

Freeman kept his composure. "You really think you've got all the answers, don't you? How about we just charge you with double homicide here in Bangor and ship you off to a holding block in Leavenworth? Those murders were part of a federal case, which means we can tie you up in all sorts of paperwork, which means it will probably take a year, or maybe two, before we even proceed to trial. Are you good to go that way?"

Quinn leaned back in his chair and held Freeman's stern gaze. He didn't doubt for a moment that the FBI man could do exactly as threatened. Short of someone, somewhere invoking *Habeas Corpus*, he could indeed disappear behind the walls of the notorious federal prison. The big problem was that he had no someone, somewhere who would stand up and issue a *you may have the body* writ on his behalf. At the moment, Freeman was holding all the aces.

"I don't think I'd like that," Quinn said. "But I get the sense it wouldn't suit your purpose either. So, what exactly are you looking for from me?"

"I want everything. I want to know all about you, from the cradle to where we are now. I want to know who you're working for and why you got mixed up in this Montgomery affair. Why do the McAndrew children mean so much to you?"

Quinn bolted upright. "Shit! I'd forgotten about the children. Where are they now? Are they safe? How many people are guarding them?"

Freeman frowned in surprise at the outburst. "See, that's what I'm talking about it. Why the big interest? For your information, they're being well looked after and as we speak they're on their way to Washington under the protection of US Marshals."

"Christ! How are they travelling? Those kids are in danger, the kind of danger that US Marshals won't see coming. You need to get off your backside and issue an immediate lockdown order. Do it now!"

"Whoa there, buddy. The immediate threat is over. Montgomery is on the run and all his crew have been accounted for. I think we can assume the Marshals can take it from here and deliver the children safely back to their grandfather."

Quinn's eyes bulged and his face reddened in anger. "Listen to me, you idiot, there's a five-million-dollar contract out on those kids. That kind of money buys the best in the business. I'm talking about someone who'll need only a window of a few inches from a mile away. The children could already be in his crosshairs."

CHAPTER 19

THE STERN-FACED woman with the iPad and the red glasses and white hair tied into a bun once again crossed the mahogany-panelled boardroom overlooking the Manhattan skyline and looked sheepishly at the man seated at the head of the large table.

"What is it, Clarissa?"

"I have bad news, Mr Chairman."

"Your face already told me that. Spit it out, my dear."

"We've just found a five-million transfer that Montgomery made the day before his abortive attempts to pilfer other funds."

"So, what's the problem? Reverse-engineer the transaction, or whatever you people do, to bring the money back where it belongs."

Clarissa's eyes dropped to her iPad. "I'm afraid we can't. It's already disappeared into thin air. It was transferred originally into an escrow account in the Cayman's but was immediately rerouted. It's probably bounced around a few other places and now it's gone."

The man behind the table frowned. Then he smiled. "Not to worry, Clarissa. It's not as if Montgomery will get the time to spend it. We can always write it off against taxes."

"I wish that were the case, Mr Chairman. We

don't think this money was for Montgomery himself. It looks rather like it was an advance payment to someone who used a similar Cayman's account before. It was something we authorised several years ago."

"Well, who was it?"

"We don't know, Mr Chairman. This particular person remained anonymous, which suited both parties. The money was paid, the work was done, and everyone was happy."

"What work was that?"

"It's a bit delicate, Mr Chairman. I think the parlance is that it was a hitman or hitwoman. We requested an assassination and that's what we got."

The man behind the table lapsed into silence and stared out at the light clouds and strengthening sunlight. He held the pose for several minutes before he spoke. "So, Montgomery engaged an assassin. We know it wasn't for the McAndrew hit because the stupid bastard decided to do that for himself so, what was the purpose?"

"It was paid a day after the attack on the McAndrew home."

"Motherfucker! He put out a contract on the kids after he let them get away. We have to stop this. How do we get in touch with the assassin? Tell him or her to keep the money but at all costs they must stand down."

"It's a convoluted process, Mr Chairman. There's a message board on the Dark Web, but once a contract has been taken out the board is deleted. There's no reason for the contractor to check for new messages. We can always try, but I think it will be a dead end."

"Have you any idea what will happen if those kids are murdered? If you think we're trying to ride out a storm now, just wait for the fallout from an incident like that."

"But surely, Mr Chairman, we've already distanced ourselves enough from Montgomery not to suffer too much of a backlash."

"Don't be naïve, Clarissa. This kind of thing will utterly ruin us. They'll crawl over everything we do, and that's after they've shut us down permanently. Put out new orders on Montgomery. I want him taken alive. Maybe he knows how to contact the assassin. Get everyone out looking and tell them there's five million for the man who brings him in."

"Anything else, Mr Chairman?"

"Pray to God we get some answers before the assassin fulfils the contract."

Devlin Montgomery checked out of the motel shortly after lunchtime. The four lanes of the I-95 heading towards New York were choked with traffic; everyone it seemed was taking advantage of the improving weather and clear roads. It suited Montgomery to be hemmed in by the hustle and bustle. With luck, he'd stay anonymous until he reached Newark International. He'd thought about getting a flight out of JFK, but it would be too obvious. Better to go against the flow. Besides, all he wanted to do was reach Canada. Take his time to figure out his next moves. Disappear.

He could have backtracked and crossed the border into Montreal using I-95 north and autoroute 10E. Six hours tops, but probably the first place they'd look for him. Going in the opposite direction would add a few extra driving hours, which was worth it because of the busier roads.

In the event, it took him ten hours, including a few rest stops, to reach New Jersey. He ditched the Mercedes in the long-stay car park and used the shuttle bus to get to the terminal. He glanced at the large flight information board dominating the main concourse. He was in luck. There was a flight to Edmonton leaving in less than thirty minutes.

Then his luck ran out.

"I'm sorry, sir, your card has been declined."

Montgomery's face reddened. "Are you sure there isn't something wrong with your machine? Please try again."

The girl behind the Westjet counter smiled and pushed the American Express card back into the reader. "I'm sorry, sir, your card is not being accepted."

Montgomery fumbled through his wallet and took out a Mastercard. "Please try this one."

Back came the same answer. Montgomery was aware of people whispering in the queue behind him. He grabbed the cards from the check-in girl and stormed away, looking for an ATM. He spend ten minutes going through each of his cards, taking it in turn to attempt cash withdrawals and check balances. The answer was the same each time. He had zero balances.

Bastards. They've cleaned me out. He checked his wallet again. There was less than two hundred in cash, barely enough for a room for the night. And then what? *Think. Think.*

The answer when it came was blindingly

obvious.

Montgomery stormed away from the ATM and crossed to a quiet corner of the concourse. He flopped on to a padded seat, fished out his cellphone, and pressed a stored number.

The white-haired bun, red glasses and iPad were back in the boardroom with the skyline view of Manhattan. "Mr Chairman, I have Devlin Montgomery on the line. He insists on talking to you. Said he didn't call you direct because he thought you wouldn't take it, and besides he wanted a witness."

A witness to what, Clarissa?"

"Better you talk to him directly, Mr Chairman." She handed over her phone and stood to attention at the top of the table.

The chairman waited a few seconds to compose himself. When he spoke, it was with as much indifference as he could muster. "I must say, Devlin, you have a nerve to contact us. To what do I owe the dubious pleasure?"

"You can start by dropping that smug tone. You tried to have me killed, you bastard, and then you emptied my accounts. You didn't honestly believe I would take that lying down, did you?"

"And what is it you think you can do about it?"

"How about I hand over a little back-up USB stick to the Feds? I'm sure they'd be interested in what they'd find there. All those juicy transactions, all those scams and criminality, all those names and dates. I'm sure they'd be particularly interested in what's on there about you."

"You're bluffing."

"About what? About handing it over or about having it in the first place? You don't really think I'd work for a person like you for all these years and not protect myself? I started virtually from day one, recording and storing anything relevant, knowing there'd be a rainy day when I'd need it. Looks like it's just arrived."

Montgomery was bluffing to an extent. He did have a USB copy of various transactions, but at that moment it was stored away in a safety deposit box in a Manhattan bank. He couldn't get access to it for at least another two days. It was Saturday and the bank was closed until Monday. He needed to stay alive until then.

The response to his threat had taken on a new edge. "You can't go to the feds. They'd lock you up and throw away the key for what you did to McAndrew and his wife."

"And just how am I supposed to survive with no money and a pack of your wolves on my tail? The feds look like my only option to stay alive. I'll cut a deal with what I have."

"So, what precisely are you proposing?"

"Call off your bloodhounds and deposit twenty million in one of my accounts. This time I'll make sure you can't retrieve it."

The chairman bit down on his lip. "That's not going to happen. Too many variables. What's to stop you from repeating this little threat in the future? No, I need to see that USB, which means you need to come in so that we can clear up this mess once and for all."

"You must really think I'm a sucker. As soon as

I step forward you'll have me taken out. We both know I need to disappear, so give me the twenty mill and I'll get out of your hair for good."

"No, I need you to hand over the data stick and then I need you to call off the assassin you set on the youngsters. That's the only way you'll get a deal. Take it or leave it."

Montgomery had reckoned the old bastard would be a hard nut to crack. The revelation that he knew about the assassin shouldn't have come as a shock, although it was one more reminder that he was dealing with someone who probably invented the rules, never mind knowing how to play the game. He couldn't call off the assassin, but he was not about to tell the chairman that. He decided to take a leaf out of the old man's book on brinkmanship.

"Then I guess I'll have to leave it. No money, no deal."

Silence. Then an unexpected offer. "I'll tell you what," the chairman said. "I know you need a bit of walking-around money so I'll agree to top up your AmEx with ten thousand to help you get from wherever you are to here. We meet at a location of your choice, do an exchange and you walk away free with twenty mill."

"Make it a top-up of one million. Let's call it a good-faith payment."

"Done."

There were five possible locations, all under a mile. The man had spent two hours at each site, ticking off his usual checklist, weighing up the pros and cons, getting a feel for the heartbeats of the various areas. Traffic, both vehicular and pedestrian, was critical. Were the chosen spots in busy precincts? How well were they screened from activities around them? Were they near jogging or walking routes? Were people likely to stumble across them whilst gaining access to nearby fields and properties?

In the end, he decided on two prime vantage points, one to the west of the estate, one to the south. Lines of sight form both were excellent and the surrounding terrain offered easy getaways, something the man always scoped out before deciding to proceed.

It was one of the reasons he'd spurned the airport. Even if he'd figured which one they would use, there was the problem of not guaranteeing an escape. Too many houses and office blocks and motorists and pedestrians and traffic cams. Altogether too risky.

Instead of wasting time, he'd spent two full days on location. It was obvious they'd have to transfer the kids to the grandfather's Washington estate at some point. Didn't matter if the snow kept them in Bangor for a day or a week. Sooner or later they'd have to come to Washington.

Just a matter of patience.

For five million, he could be as patient as the next man.

CHAPTER 20

QUINN PACED the empty room for twenty minutes before the FBI men returned. He had no choice but to tell them about the Dark Web contract on the McAndrew children. He'd kept back some pertinent details but fed them enough to make sure they took the threat seriously. Charlie and Sophie deserved nothing less, particularly with him out of the picture and powerless to help.

Freeman and Eisler stormed back into the room and ordered Quinn to sit down. It was obvious from their demeanour that they had spent the interval either chewing out somebody or getting chewed out themselves. Probably a bit of both, Quinn guessed. It was obvious they wanted more information. And they didn't look like men who were prepared to suffer any more stonewalling.

"Here's how this is gonna go," Freeman said. "I've stuck my neck way out on your say-so and I want some answers. I'm done dancing around. You need to tell me everything, or I swear to God I'll stick you in a hole and forget you ever existed."

Quinn leaned across the table. "You go first, Agent. What exactly have you done since we last spoke. Did you follow my instructions?"

Freeman turned to Eisler. "Can you believe the gall of this bastard? He thinks he's running the show."

"Looks that way to me," Eisler said. "Maybe we'll convince him otherwise when he hears what we have in store for him."

"Enough with the tough guys act!" Quinn snarled contemptuously. "The lives of those children are at stake while you two bozos pump up the testosterone. Just tell me what's been done, so that we can move forward."

There was a long pause while Freeman tried to get his emotions together. Finally, he spoke in a measured tone. "We got the message to the US Marshals about a viable assassination threat. They were still in the air and acknowledged the plane would taxi into a hangar before the children would be allowed to leave. There will be a minimum of a three-vehicle convoy from the airport to the grandfather's home, and they will take the most circuitous route possible. We've also contacted the Secret Service team at the Chief Justice's residence and advised that a canvas tunnel be erected to funnel the children from their vehicle to the back door of the house. Oh, and they will draw the curtains throughout the house and make sure the children don't leave the premises until this thing is over."

"I'm guessing you got a bit of a lecture about over-reaction?" Quinn said.

"And then some," Freeman responded. "These are professional agents. They know how to protect and defend. Don't like being told to do the obvious. They know how to screen a subject from possible attack, besides which I was reminded that all windows in the Chief Justice's house are already bulletproof."

"No such thing, Agent. A 7.62mm bullet will go through just about anything. Ever seen an armour-piercing round in action? From the right distance it will tear through several heavy layers of reinforced metals as easy as a hot knife through butter. Give the right person the sniff of a target and he'll take it down, ten times out of ten. That's why I insisted on the tunnel and getting the curtains drawn. No visual, no target."

"I think they would have figured that out for themselves."

"No, Agent, there's a lot they wouldn't figure out. They'd do the same as you'd do. You all look at these issues in a one-dimensional way. You channel your energies to just one part of the equation, which is the standpoint of your protectee. You try to cover the bases from your side of the fence, but you never once look at the angles the assassin sees. You never put yourselves in his shoes. You don't seem to grasp that he's every bit as professional, dedicated and determined as you are. The assassin by nature lives to get the job done, by whatever means, and against what often appears to be insurmountable odds. The history books will tell you who comes out on top. Think JFK and the Texas School Book Depository, or Martin Luther King and the Lorraine Motel in Memphis. Hell, this goes all the way back to the assassination of William McKinley in 1901 when Congress requested presidential protection, although many argue the protocols were already in place after Lincoln's assassination thirty-six years earlier. The rest of the world started to cotton on to the need to guard against the skills of assassins after the killing of Archduke Franz Ferdinand in 1914 in

Sarajevo. It's been a cat-and-mouse game down through the ages, and the one who blinks, the one who makes the smallest mistake, is the loser."

Freeman threw his hands in the air. "Please, spare me the history lesson. There are a lot of good agents out there putting their lives on the line against people like you. I'm not going to take a lecture on how they go about things."

Quinn ignored the accusation. "This isn't about getting personal. It's about getting real. Ever seen what an IED can do?"

"Yeah, yeah, I know all about Improvised Explosive Devices. Don't tell me you're an expert on those too?"

"It would take a lot for someone to be an expert," Quinn snapped. "There's nothing improvisational about these types of devices. The term implies something that's makeshift or impromptu, but there's nothing spontaneous about them. People think of IEDs as a crude piece of ordnance stuck under the sand in a road in Iraq, but they've come a long way since then.

"They're usually highly-sophisticated, most often than not disguised as everyday items, and are capable of taking out even the most well-guarded fortification. That's why they've become a weapon of choice for your run-of-the-mill assassin. When he can't get a shot away, he adapts, he improvises, he gets the job done. I've seen IEDs disguised as milk bottles and I've heard about limpets with shaped charges which are magnetised against the side of a vehicle by a passing motorcyclist."

"Is that how you'd do it? Do you think an attempt will be made between the airport and the residence?"

"No, I don't," Quinn replied. "Too many variables to work out. OK if you've been watching a pattern of journeys over a period of a week, but useless to attempt on a whim."

"Then why mention it if you're ruling it out?"

"It's better to cover all the bases. We could also talk about poisons. These guys have ways of finding out what you buy, where you shop, what foods are likely to be used by kids. It's easy to inject something into any product, including canned soups. They could also contaminate water supplies, taint medicines, or spray play equipment with any manner of instant-death substances. Just look what happened with the former Russian spy Sergei Skripal and his daughter, Yulia, in Salisbury in England - their front door handle was coated with the Novichok nerve agent for Chrissakes! No-one is untouchable and no method can be ruled out."

"But you're still saying any attack will be at the house?"

"That's my best guess. Whoever the assassin is he couldn't have made it to Bangor because of the weather. Let's assume he's a native of Washington, or at least within easy commuting distance to the capital. Which means he's had a few days to study the lie of the land around Chief Justice Fleming's house. He'll have spent that time wisely, getting to know the rhythms of the area and mapping the weak spots. He'll have his distances measured, his weapon calibrated, and be good to go as soon as he's offered a chance. He'll have a choice of locations, a Plan A and a Plan B. He's in this for the long haul."

"How do we catch him?"

"You won't. But I can."

"Just what are you suggesting?"

Quinn smiled. "Take me to the residence and leave me alone to figure out how and where he's going to do it."

Freeman stared in disbelief, after which he banged his fist on the bolted-down table. "Not going to happen, not in a million years. You'll be going to Washington alright, but your final destination won't be within the same zip code as the Fleming estate."

"That's a helluva head-in-the-sand attitude to take, Agent, but have it your own way."

"I intend to," Freeman told him sternly. "Now, I want those answers. Tell me about your life as a gun for hire."

"Think I'll take the Fifth on that one."

The flurry of activity to the rear and west-facing sides of the house brought the assassin fully alert in his heavily-concealed hide, eight-hundred and forty-two yards away on the slope of a hillside. He'd guessed right about them using the back entrance. However, he'd never have guessed that they would do what they were doing now.

Four Secret Service agents – they couldn't be anything else with their coiled-wire earpieces disappearing under the lapels of matching black suits – were rolling out a polytunnel, the kind of ten-foot high contraption used at football matches to shield players leaving the field. It was also seen more and more as the best possible choice for guarding high-ranking politicians entering exposed public buildings. Most used to shun the notion of hiding from their supporters; now it was seen as a measure of importance, *de rigueur* for the self-important, more so even than for genuine high-threat individuals.

Whatever! It spelt a nuisance the assassin could have done without.

The significance, however, went way beyond throwing his plan into a temporary tailspin. It was clear from the appearance of the tunnel that the children were on their way to the house. It was also clear that those in charge were taking no chances. But what he was witnessing below was not merely a precautionary exercise.

Which meant that someone had figured there would be an assassination attempt at this location. Which meant it wouldn't be long before they came looking for him. Did they have the manpower and expertise to flush him out? Yes, to the first question, probably no to the second. There weren't that many people around with the skills equal to or better than his own. He'd spot them coming. He'd take them out. Then he'd regroup and go again.

Chief Justice Thomas Jefferson Fleming watched from an upper floor window as the men secured the tunnel in readiness for his grandchildren. He'd listened in disbelief when lead Secret Service agent Sheridan Smith told him about the five-million-dollar contract and the need for exceptional security arrangements. He'd agreed, albeit reluctantly, to let them do what was necessary, but had been determined this would not be a long-drawn-out affair. This was no way for his grandkids to live!

Fleming had built the family home on an estate near Bailey's Crossroads, a rural expanse of farmland on the west bank of the Potomac River. It was barely a twenty-five-minute drive to the Supreme Court offices at First Street Northeast, although most evenings - particularly since his wife's passing - he had chosen to stay in official rooms within the court complex.

All that would change with the arrival of Charlie and Sophie. Henceforth he'd stay at home. He'd cut back on his schedule. He'd give those kids the care and devotion they deserved. He'd make up for all the lost times with his wife and daughter.

And no fucking assassin's going to stand in the way of that happening!

He stepped back from the window and moved behind a large desk, a faithful reproduction of the Resolute Desk, that was gifted to President Rutherford B Hayes by Queen Victoria in 1880 and was still a focal point in the Oval Office. The original was made from the oak timbers of the British ship *HMS Resolute*. Having a facsimile always reminded Fleming of the historical importance and significance of his own role. It brought with it a level of power and influence he was playing to the full.

He lifted an ornate marble and gold phone handset and placed the first of what would be many calls to the man sitting behind the original desk in the West Wing of the White House. One resolute man to another.

CHAPTER 21

CHILD PSYCHOLOGIST Maria Zeigler had studied Charlie McAndrew for more than thirty hours. She was in awe of what she'd witnessed. No ten-year-old should have that much maturity and calmness and inner stoicism. Sure, there'd been moments when the veil had slipped and Charlie had shown his vulnerability. But he'd somehow sucked it up, placed a reassuring arm around his sister, and helped bring her back from the darkness she'd retreated into.

Sophie had resisted all Zeigler's attempts to get through. But when Charlie spoke to her, or offered her a drink, or made her eat her food, Sophie reluctantly shrugged her shoulders and acquiesced. Despite twenty years of training, Zeigler knew it was Charlie and not her who offered the best possible chance for the young girl to climb out of the abyss. It would need patience, but with Charlie's help, Zeigler would see it through to the end. These kids were no longer part of her job. They'd got under her maternal skin.

Ten minutes before touchdown at the Ronald Reagan International, Charlie had slipped away from his sleeping sister and moved across the aisle to sit with Zeigler. "Are we going straight to our grandfather's house?"

"Yes, we are, Charlie. He's looking forward to

seeing you both."

"What about our parents? Will there be a funeral? Why didn't you bring them with us?"

Zeigler gulped down the shock of the direct question. "I think your grandfather will want to make all the arrangements. I guess he needs to speak with you first before deciding what to do."

"What will he want to ask me?"

"There's the big question of where your parents should be buried. Should it be in Bangor or in Washington?"

"That's easy," Charlie said. "We're not going back to Bangor. We're going to live with grandpa, so we'll all want mom and dad to be near us."

The journey from Ronald Reagan to Bailey's Crossroads was uneventful, save for the constant shifting of lanes and the irksome leapfrogging of the three armoured and blacked out SUVs. It was also about forty minutes longer than it needed to be. The US Marshals were sticking to the script of avoiding obvious routes, sometimes even doubling back to ensure they weren't being tailed.

Fleming greeted the children from inside the polytunnel, which had been rolled forward to the rear door of the middle SUV. He was almost knocked off his feet by their forward rush and the arms wrapped around the tops of his thigh.

"Grandpa!"

"Grandpa!"

The old man fought back a tear and scooped the youngsters into his arms. He turned, marched up the tunnel and carried his grandkids through the kitchen and into a large drawing room. A roaring fire threw shadows across the dimly-lit space, a needless precaution given that the windows in the room were fitted with newly-installed blackout curtains.

Fleming dropped cautiously onto a wide settee with Charlie and Sophie still clutching tightly to his neck. The group of Secret Service and US Marshals filed quietly into the study and stood to attention.

The old man gently prised away the children's arms and addressed the agents. "Ladies and gentlemen, I thank you for what you've already done, and continue to do, for my grandchildren. Now, however, I would like to be left alone. We have a lot of family catching up to do."

"Of course, sir," Sheridan Smith said on behalf of the group. "We'll be right outside the door, if you need us."

Charlie turned to watch the men and women file out of the room. "Why so many people here, grandpa? Are we still in danger?"

"We have to take every precaution, Charlie, but only for a while longer. I promise you things will get a lot better."

"But, grandpa, if we're in danger why isn't Mr Quinn here to help us?"

Fleming nodded at Charlie. "That's a name I've been hearing a lot recently. Why don't you tell me all about him?"

Eight-hundred and forty-two yards away, the man in the green combat suit stirred beneath a netting cover and came to a decision.

He unrolled a large canvas pouch, dismantled his Barrett M107 shoulder-mounted 50-cal rifle, and began a meticulous packing-up procedure. He uncoupled the Picatinny rail, folded the stock, and removed five separate pieces, including the magazine housing, the forward v-shaped legs, and the Nightforce NXS 25X scope. There were special compartments within the pouch for each item.

He'd stayed on site long enough to witness the arrival of the three SUVs. He'd known there was no chance of an opening, but he wanted to judge the strengths and weaknesses of the enemy. Another four agents had alighted from the vehicles, making a total presence of eight bodies, assuming there were no others unaccounted for inside. They all looked like they knew what they were doing, which was an obvious strength. However, no-one had ventured outside the estate grounds for a recce of the surrounding area. Which was a weakness.

Nightfall was fast approaching and he didn't expect anything to change. No point hanging around. He'd get a good night's sleep and return in the morning. First, he wanted to check on his secondary position.

He left the camouflaged netting in position and belly-crawled away from the hide. He waited until he reached the other side of the rise before getting to his feet and double-timing in a wide arc on a southeast bearing. He used the generous cover of several small forest areas to mask his run, carefully picking his way over the uneven ground.

A hundred yards out from his alternative position he stopped and grabbed a small radio from one of his jacket's multi-pockets. "It's me. I'm coming in."

"I'll be waiting."

He allowed several seconds to elapse before dropping to the ground and crawling the rest of the way towards the location of the secondary vantage point. He lifted the netting and smiled at the hide's occupant. "Honey, I'm home."

A petite auburn-haired woman rolled onto her back and stretched out her arms. They fell into an embrace, kissing long and hard before surfacing for air.

She said: "I take it we're done for the day?"

"You saw for yourself. Nothing's going to happen here tonight. How about a hot bath, a hot meal and a hot session?"

"In what order?"

"Any order you like, honey."

Quinn was pushed roughly into one of the Gulfstream's rear seats. It was a generous, well-appointed jet, with ten large leather armchairs and enough leg room to guarantee a good sleep during the trip to Washington, even allowing for the manacles on his arms and legs.

The FBI team had given up on him. They were blanking him out, and he couldn't blame them. He'd stonewalled them for more than two hours before they'd finally threw in the towel, shortly after receiving a message that their ride back to Washington was fuelled up and ready to go.

Quinn would have liked to be there for Charlie and Sophie. He knew he could make a difference, maybe one that would save their lives. At least the people guarding the children seemed to be showing all the right moves. They'd listened to what he'd had to say and they'd acted on it right down the line. Couldn't ask for anything more.

Maybe it was time to start worrying about himself. One thing was for sure. He'd break the rule of a lifetime before he'd let them lock him up and throw away the key. Somewhere, somehow between here and his final destination he'd get a chance to make a break. If that meant busting a few FBI heads, so be it.

Yes, there'd be a massive fugitive search for him. But he'd spent a lifetime living in the shadows. He knew all the escape and evasion techniques. He'd disappear and resurface later to kickstart a new life, maybe back in Ireland. He never imagined he'd even think of such an eventuality, but right now it sounded as sweet as any other alternative.

He thought about Special Agent Freeman. He was a tough cookie, for sure, but also a first-rate professional. The guy was having to deal with all sorts of pressures - not least letting one of his star witnesses get gunned down - and was still unable to apprehend the culprit in the shape of Devlin Montgomery. He was coping better than most people would do in his position. He liked Freeman. In another time, they might even have been friends.

That wouldn't stop him from smashing a forearm into Freeman's nose or drilling a 9mm into soft shoulder or leg tissue. He hoped it wouldn't come to anything more than that. *I guess that's his choice.*

Quinn became aware of commotion at the head of the plane. He watched as Freeman stormed from the cockpit and headed his way, his right foot kicking out at imaginary obstacles on the carpeted aisle.

"Do you have a fucking guardian angel, or what?" Freeman yelled.

"What are you talking about."

"I've just come off the phone with the Director of the FBI, who'd just come off the phone with the Secretary of Defense, who'd just had his ear chewed by no less than the President. And do you know what the subject of all those calls was about?"

"I'm hanging on your every word, Agent Freeman."

"You!"

"Me? Now, why would I rate the attention of such prominent men?"

"My fucking sentiments exactly. It seems that Chief Justice Fleming wants to meet with you, and what Chief Justice Fleming wants, he gets. The silly old sod is even thinking of using you as a special consultant in the hunt for the assassin."

Quinn slumped back in his seat. He hadn't seen that one coming. This could be his way out, no doubt about it. He needed to milk it for all its worth. He'd stick around long enough to eliminate the threat to Charlie and Sophie, but after that, all bets were off. He'd simply disappear.

He raised his arms and spoke quietly to Freeman. "How about we get rid of the chains? Then I'd like some coffee and sandwiches. Can't meet the Chief Justice without looking and feeling my best."

Freeman clenched his fists and took a step forward. "I swear to God, I'll beat you to a pulp if you don't lose that attitude pretty damn quick. This isn't a get-out-of-jail card, so the chains stay and the coffee is on hold."

"I've just two things to say to you, Agent Freeman. First you couldn't take me down even with my hands tied behind my back. Second, coffee, sandwiches and no chains, or the deal is off."

"What the fuck are you talking about?"

"I refuse to meet with the Chief Justice unless my terms are met. You can tell that to your Director, who can call the Secretary of Defense, who in turn can call the President. Do you really want to go down that road?"

CHAPTER 22

THE POLYTUNNEL was still bridged between the rear door of the house and the curved driveway. It was concertinaed to half its length, leaving about ten yards of exposed walking space. Plenty of time for a sniper to zero in. Hardly likely, though. None of the six figures who emerged from two cars shortly before midnight were considered to be targets.

Quinn was in the middle of the group. He kept his head down, resisting a strong urge to look over the grounds to the open moonlit terrain beyond. They all wore trademark FBI windcheaters, at Quinn's insistence. A trained assassin, staring through high-powered night-vision lenses, would look for nuances, something that didn't fit, a figure that wasn't like one of the others. An expert, just like himself. No sense in Quinn advertising his presence just yet.

And so, he kept his head bowed, tried to look like a bored agent on a boring baby-sitting assignment, and disappeared into the tunnel. He was greeted by Sheridan Smith, though a surly look and a silent nod of the head towards the direction of the front of the building hardly constituted a greeting. Resentment hung in the air.

Smith pushed open a door and stood back to allow Quinn to pass. He crossed into a gloomy spacious lounge, noting the log fire and the bulk of a large man sitting in an armchair with its back at a slight angle towards the centre of the room.

The Secret Service man remained in the corridor, pulling the door shut in slightly theatrical fashion. Orders had obviously been given that this was to be strictly a one-to-one session.

Chief Justice Fleming rose from his chair and fixed Quinn with an icy stare. He was an immense figure, and not just because of his six-two, broad-shouldered frame. He radiated an aura of authority, laced with a menace that suggested he was not a man to be taken lightly. He wore a lengthy wool cardigan over an open-necked tartan shirt and completed the country-squire ensemble with blue corduroy trousers and matching blue loafers. A man who looked comfortable in his world, without even trying.

"So, you're Quinn?"

"Actually, sir, the name is Michael Tate, just as it says on the passport."

"Save the crap, son! I don't deal in fairy tales. We both know you have something of a chequered history, so why don't we cut to the chase and find out exactly who you are and what I should do about you."

Quinn wasn't sure what to make of the old man's statement. He decided on a stock-in-trade answer. "With the greatest respect to your position, sir, I've nothing further to add to what I've already said." As soon as he spoke the words, Quinn readied himself for another outburst.

What he got was the polar opposite.

Fleming crossed the distance between them

and held out his hand. "We'll get into that later," he said softly. "For now, I want to thank you for saving my grandchildren and for looking out for their welfare since you rescued them. Don't see how I'm able to repay you. Those kids mean the world to me. I'm not sure I'd want to keep going if something happened to them. Not after what happened to...to...Ruth..."

The words tailed off and Quinn saw tears beginning a sad journey down Fleming's cragged face. The Chief Justice wheeled away and beckoned Quinn to an armchair in front of the fire. The old man composed himself and flopped into the other chair, his knees almost touching Quinn's."

"The FBI say you killed two of the men who attacked my daughter and son-in-law. They also say you went hunting after the ringleader, this Devlin Montgomery, and that you're probably a professional assassin, which is why you know about the contract that's been taken out on Charlie and Sophie, and why you know which counter-measures should be used to avoid that contract being filled. How am I doing so far?"

Quinn said nothing.

"Very well, what say we look at this from another angle? Why did you help? It's something I need to know."

Quinn felt compelled to respond. "I don't like to see people being bullied, especially kids. It was easy to step in at the convenience store, plenty of others would have done the same. When I later heard Charlie's story on the way to the hospital I knew it wouldn't end there. I stuck around to make certain they'd be safe. That's really all there was to it."

"Not quite all, was it? You saw one of the gunmen at the hospital and decided to eliminate him. You did the same thing with another at the Jutland Hotel. You learned something from those men, didn't you? You got them to tell you about Montgomery and where he was holed up, and then you went after him. That's not something a lot of other people would do. So, tell me why?"

Quinn was treading on dangerous ground. He needed to establish a baseline. "You don't expect me to admit to anything you've just said. Like I told the FBI, I think I'll take the Fifth."

Fleming smiled benignly. "The Fifth Amendment is a fine upstanding piece of our Constitution, one I'd lay down my life to safeguard. However, what you need to understand is that it probably won't do you much good. Doesn't matter if you clam up from now to doomsday, the FBI is confident of making a solid case against you for at least two murders. On a first review of the facts, I'd say they're probably justified in that confidence. And I should know what I'm talking about; wouldn't you agree?"

"Doesn't change the fact, Judge, that I'm not going to incriminate myself."

"I'm not a Judge, I'm a Justice. There's a fine distinction, not that many people know or understand it. But we do like to preserve our little idiosyncrasies. I'm not asking you to incriminate yourself. You have my word that anything we talk about will never leave this room. This is strictly between us."

Quinn didn't doubt the sincerity of Fleming's words. They didn't, however, lessen his resolve to remain guarded. "With all due respect, sir, I'm not sure I want to go any further with this."

"Jesus Christ, son, do you know who I am? Do you really believe the Chief Justice of the Supreme Court of the United States would attempt to inveigle you by underhand chicanery? This is not about the law; it's about you, me and my grandchildren. I want to know what makes you tick. I want to know if you can help protect my family. Think of it as a plea bargain with the country's top law-maker. Convince me about your bona fides and then we'll talk about cutting a deal."

"I don't know what to say to that."

"You strike me as a smart young man. Don't look a gift horse in the mouth. Start talking."

Quinn's spirits soared. Was this really the get-out-of-jail card that FBI Agent Freeman was so sure he wouldn't get? "Where do you want me to start?"

"Let's go back to the beginning. I want it all. I want to know everything there is to know about you. I want to know if you're the sort of man I can trust with the lives of my grandchildren. I want to make a judgement based on a warts-and-all confession. But here's the kicker. I've been on the bench for over thirty-five years. I've heard and seen just about everything. I've listened to con artists, tricksters, serial liars, slick lawyers, smarmy so-called experts, and every manner of excuse and alibi dreamt up by man. I've learned to read people, to know when they're trying to pull a fast one. I think of it as an infallibility. You leave anything out or attempt to put a gloss on parts of your history I'll spot it. Then you'll really rue the day we crossed paths. Work with me here, son. I owe you that much. And I suspect you owe it to yourself."

Quinn spoke for more than a half hour. He started tentatively, before accelerating into a full dissertation of his life. He left nothing out. From Downpatrick in Northern Ireland to the Cathal Brugha Barracks in Dublin, from his life and missions with the Irish Rangers to meeting with Patrick Lonegan and the subsequent slaying of the Kelly brothers in revenge for Lonegan's murder. He explained about the Dark Web and listed the contracts he'd fulfilled, including the hits in Suarez, Mexico, prior to stumbling upon Charlie and Sophie at the convenience store.

He told Fleming about the document forgers and his RV hideout. He admitted to killing Montgomery's men, and about his intention to dispose of Montgomery himself. He wanted to make sure Charlie and Sophie would be safe, particularly when he'd learned about the contract on their lives. He wanted a chance to see the job through to the end.

When he finished, he slumped back in his seat. He'd undergone some kind of a catharsis and felt sweat on his palms. His hands were shaking. For the first time in his life he had a sensation of losing control, yet he'd somehow never felt more at ease. Shadows were dissipating from around him, an invisible weight seemed to be lifting from his shoulders, his lungs were filling with clean air. It was a new experience. He liked it.

Fleming said nothing. He rose from his seat and crossed to a drinks bar at the far corner of the room. He busied himself for several minutes before walking back with two cut-glass tumblers, handing one to Quinn and retaking his seat. "That's Irish Bushmills whiskey. I have it on good authority that the distillery is not too far from that town of yours, Downpatrick."

Quinn raised his eyebrows. "About eighty-five miles actually. But how would you know about something like that?"

"Like most Americans, I've a bit of Irish blood in me, though truth to tell, I've never set foot in the place. I did, however study Saint Patrick in my collegiate years, so I know about Downpatrick and where it lies roughly in relation to other major centres around it. Now, here's a toast to Francis Xavier Quinn, a proper name for a proper Irishman."

"Thank you, sir."

"Don't thank me yet, son. I can't condone the things you've done and the choices you've made. You're quite a remarkable young man, yet I can't help thinking you missed the boat somewhere along the line. After you left the Irish Rangers, you could have gotten a job in law enforcement. Your talents are ideally suited to all manner of agencies. They'd have been lucky to have you."

Quinn gulped down half the tumbler's contents. "I guess I just got caught up in things after what happened to Lonegan. In my own way, I like to think I helped mete out justice to those who deserved it."

"No, son, those were not your decisions to make. No-one can put himself above the law. It may not always get it right, it most certainly doesn't come close to justice in many cases where it should, but it's all we've got. Without it, we'd be back in the Dark Ages. You need to understand that from this point forward, you're done with that life, or at least you will be after you track down this assassin and put the Fleming orbit back on its axis."

Quinn looked puzzled. "I'm not sure I'm following what you're saying."

"Let me simplify things. I'm going to prepare a legal document that offers you a full pardon. You'll get citizenship papers in your proper name, and you'll start to make a positive and legal contribution to this country's way of life. That might mean working for the government from time to time, and I'm guessing if that happens, it will require you to put your life on the line. We can't let your talents be wasted, but this time you'll do things with legal authority and be subject to oversight."

"You can do that? Just make things go away?"

Fleming beamed. "Yes, I can do that. I can do a lot more besides, but the real point is what can *you* do? If anything happens to Charlie or Sophie, there's no deal. You go right back to square one. If you try to cross me or do a runner, I'll sweep you off the board like a discarded pawn. Do you accept the terms?"

"You don't leave much wiggle room, do you, sir?"

"This is not about stacking the chips. This is about finding the bastard who's trying to kill my grandchildren. Find him and do whatever you think is necessary to end this nightmare."

CHAPTER 23

EIGHT HOURS. An uninterrupted four-hundred and eighty minutes of dreamless sleep. Another thirty minutes planning his day. Time well spent, Quinn reckoned. There was much to do.

Deal with the FBI. Placate the Secret Service. Check the terrain and pinpoint the dangers. Take a shower. Get a change of clothes. Fetch his weapons. Oh, and a bit of breakfast wouldn't go amiss. Decisions made.

He was tempted to throw back the curtains in the small guestroom, one of a dozen in the Fleming household. Thought better of it. *Practice what you preach.*

The door flew open. He swivelled in a defensive mode, but immediately relaxed at the sight of Charlie sprinting across the room. At least somebody was glad to see him.

"Mr Quinn, Mr Quinn, I knew you'd come! Grandpa promised he'd get you. Are you here to help Sophie?"

Quinn melted at the boy's enthusiasm. It was great to see him again, especially in one piece. "Yes, Charlie, I'm here to help. I guess I have to thank you for my being here?"

"Sophie needs the best. That's what I told grandpa."

"And what about you? Do you think I can help

you too?"

Charlie gave him a mischievous grin. "Naw, I'll be alright. We have to worry about Sophie. But she'll be OK now, won't she?"

Before Quinn could answer, a second small figure appeared at the door. She was clutching a rag doll, probably one that once belonged to her mother. Quinn knew she'd taken nothing from her home in Maine, and it was doubtful if anyone had thought about grabbing some of the children's possessions before the trip to Washington. It's strange how generational playthings had a way of coming around full circle. Sophie had dark, haunted eyes, her shoulders drooped and she hung her head away from meeting his gaze. When she spoke, her voice barely rose above a plaintive whisper.

"Charlie, please come back to our room."

Charlie ran over beside her. "Sophie, this is Mr Quinn. Remember how he helped us and took us to hospital? He's here to help us again."

"Hello, Sophie," Quinn said. He was careful to stay in his spot. Didn't want to spook the girl. "How are you doing? Would you like me to stay around for a while?"

There was no response. Charlie prodded his sister. She kept her head tilted away from Quinn and began to back out of the room.

Charlie held on to her hand. "Don't go, Sophie. Tell Mr Quinn you're glad to see him. Ask him to stay."

Silence.

"I'll tell you what," Quinn said, "I'm starving. Could you tell me where I can get something to eat? Is there a restaurant in this big house?"

The chin came up and a hesitant smile flitted across her features. "No, silly, we have a kitchen, that's all."

Quinn caught his breath. The sound of her voice seemed like a reawakening. Don't push it. Take it slow. "Well, a kitchen would do if it has a coffee pot and ham and eggs and toast and jam and maybe some pancakes. Is it that kind of a kitchen?"

There was that smile again. "Of course, it is."

"Will you show me where it is?"

She turned away and squeezed Charlie's hand. The boy needed no encouragement. He skipped out of the room, dragging Sophie behind him. "Follow us."

Thora Brennan was the resident Fleming housekeeper. She was on the second go-around of breakfast for several shifts of agents when she saw the children enter the kitchen ahead of a new visitor. She'd heard about the stranger and was hoping to meet him. What she wasn't prepared for was the presence of Sophie. It was the first time the girl had ventured into Thora's domain.

There were five agents on this shift. All, bar one, glowered in Quinn's direction. Sophie stopped in her tracks and hid behind Charlie.

The housekeeper quickly grasped the situation. "All right, I'm sure you people have plenty to do. Everyone out except Charlie, Sophie and their guest. Time for me to prepare a special breakfast."

The child psychologist, Maria Zeigler, was the first to rise. "Great idea, Thora, although if you don't mind I would like to stay behind." Without waiting for an answer, she turned and used her arms to herd the other agents towards the door. They filed out without any backward glances.

Zeigler took Quinn aside and introduced herself. "I've heard a mixture of things about you, Mr Quinn, some good, some not so good. My only concern is Sophie, so while you seem to be working a bit of magic there, you won't get any hassle from me. You and Charlie are quite a double act."

"They're both great kids," Quinn said affably. "I'm glad they've someone with your expertise around. The next few days aren't going to be easy."

Quinn joined the FBI and Secret Service agents in Fleming's study an hour after breakfast finished. He walked in on a babble of voices, none of them friendly, and all with only one subject on their minds.

Freeman summarised for the group. "Just so you know, we've been telling Mr Justice Fleming that we don't need you around. If this sniper really is within a mile of the estate boundaries, we can have several hundred trained agents, including military support, blanket the area within ten minutes. If he's there, we'll flush him out and that'll be an end to it."

Quinn looked at Fleming. "Mind if I say something, sir?"

"Go right ahead, my boy, it's your show."

Quinn noticed grimaces on the agents' faces at the Chief Justice's comment. This was not going to be easy, but it needed to be said. Perhaps with a touch of honey. "I don't doubt for one moment that you could mount such an operation, and probably nobody could do it better. Consider this, though. What if the assassin sees it coming and ducks out? The use of draped windows and the polytunnel will have put him on notice that we know he's about. So, he's on full alert. He's watching for something like that. He's already prepared a back door and will execute his departure at the first sniff of danger."

"We could start a secondary cordon within a two-mile radius before we launch the primary search," Freeman responded stubbornly. That way, we increase the chances of grabbing him."

"The same thing applies to a fall-back perimeter. He'll have thought about it, planned for it, and know how to slip through the net."

"Christ!" Freeman exploded. "What is he, the fucking Scarlet Pimpernel?"

Fleming fixed him with a withering stare. "There'll be no blasphemy in this house."

"Sorry, sir. It's just that I don't see how anyone could be that good."

Quinn understood Freeman's scepticism. "Look, let's say that eight or nine times out of ten, your plan would work. But what about the other one or two times that it won't? The assassin will simply walk away, perhaps for as long as six months or a year. This is an open-ended contract. It has to be fulfilled, which means a long delay actually works in his favour. He gets to choose his moment farther down the line, when we've all let our guard slip, when we're least expecting it. And how are the children supposed to live with that kind of ongoing existence? They'll be like prisoners, with no fresh air, no sunshine, nothing to occupy their young minds except a constant reminder of the horrors of the past few days. They will get to visit and revisit it when they should be getting healed. Am I right, Agent Zeigler?"

The psychologist wasn't expecting to be dragged into the discussion but didn't let it show. "Don't ask me to pick the best option. What I will say is that this has to end as soon as possible, which means a matter of a few days, not weeks or months. Those children need normality. Without it, I can't guarantee their long-term state of mind. Despite the horrors they've already suffered, things are recoverable. However, it's not too melodramatic to state it might not be the case unless we can start a full healing process at the earliest opportunity."

Her words hit Fleming like a punch to the solar plexus. "Can't let that happen. We have to do something!"

"Consider this, sir," Quinn told him. "Give me forty-eight hours to find the assassin. Keep Charlie and Sophie under a strict quarantine until then."

"Can you guarantee you'll get him?"

"No, sir, I can't. The upside is that if I fail, you can go with Agent Freeman's suggestion. All we'll lose is a few days. Surely, it's worth that?"

"If we don't hear from you within two days, what do you propose we do?"

"If you don't hear from me, it means he'll have neutralised me. I'll be out of the picture. After that, it's Agent Freeman's show, or whoever else you bring in. Blanketing the area with troops is not a bad idea. No disrespect to anyone here, but I'd call in Delta. Those guys will know how to hit fast and hard."

Fleming got up from his seat and stilled a babble of voices. "I'm going with Quinn's suggestion. I want him to get full co-operation, is that understood?"

Freeman spoke. "Sir, what are we supposed to do while Quinn is off traipsing around the countryside. Do you really trust him to stay on mission?"

"That ground's already been covered," Fleming said testily. "Quinn has my full confidence."

The room fell silent

Quinn rose and moved to the centre of the circle of agents. "I need three things. One, the FBI is to retire from the estate. We need your energies concentrated on finding Devlin Montgomery to see if he can be persuaded to pull the contract. I doubt it, but it's worth a shot. Either way, he needs to be found. You also have to rule out the possibility of someone else involved with Montgomery, someone who can activate a new contract at a later date in the event that we succeed in getting the assassin this time. There's still too much that's not known about the attack on the McAndrew family. I'd say that's the job of the FBI."

Freeman looked surprisingly calm. "Can't say I disagree with that, but is it a good idea to deplete the protection around the children?"

"That's my second request," Quinn said. "The Secret Service are better than any of us in providing protection." He turned to Sheridan Smith. "There's no need to clutter the place, but if you feel you need more support call in some of your colleagues. Prepare your usual contingency plans, triple check them and factor in one thing above all else."

"And what would that be?" Smith asked.

"Kids are inquisitive. They don't follow rules. They like to explore and get up to mischief. They'd pull back a curtain in the blink of an eye or find a way to wander outside before you know they've gone. It won't be easy, Mr Smith, but you'll have to find a way of keeping them tied down, twenty-four seven, including posting someone in their room when they're sleeping."

Smith looked at Quinn with a new-found respect. "Consider it done."

Fleming raised his eyebrows. "You said there were three things?"

"Yes, I want my wallet, I want a car, and I need to be left alone for at least six hours before I scout the area. I'll return sometime late this afternoon."

"What are you up to?" This from Freeman.

"I need a shower and a change of clothes. Plus, I want to do some off-the-grid reconnaissance before actually venturing out there."

CHAPTER 24

WASHINGTON HAS a lot of things you won't find in Bangor, Maine. The two cities share the same Eastern Time zone, but with a 700-mile separation the difference in weather patterns can often be striking. Just like now. Mild, humid air, the odd glimpse of sunlight, and no snow.

Where Bangor is a bustling blue-collar town with functional shop fronts, enterprise zones, bricks-and-mortar office blocks and people without pretension, Washington is big and brassy, full of glass and open spaces and monuments and suits and briefcases. Self-importance oozes through the sidewalk cracks in every precinct.

The one thing Washington doesn't have is a lock-up garage with a fully-fitted RV, a change of clothes, a selection of armaments, and a freedom of choice. Quinn needed to balance the books with at least some of the missing items.

He eased the big SUV into light traffic on New York Avenue and found an open-air car park close to the Nike Factory Store. He reversed into a vacant spot, killed the engine, and lifted his wallet from the small tray beside the gear stick. The FBI had stripped out his ID papers, leaving him with only his debit and credit cards and a small stash of dollars. He grimaced, ruefully. Agent Freeman, it seemed, was still not prepared to take him on trust.

He spent an hour inside, buying a large sports bag and a selection of outfits. He concentrated on heavy-duty black and blue chinos, t-shirts, dark wool jumpers, hiking boots, socks and underwear. He blew through more than six-hundred dollars' worth of gear before realising his cards might have been messed with by the FBI. It would be like something Freeman would do.

He handed over a Mastercard and waited sheepishly while the small, electronic dispenser went through its connection sequence. The screen bleeped and prompted him for a pin number and he breathed a sigh of relief.

Back in the car park, he tossed the holdall into the SUV and walked away in search of a Walgreens drugstore. There was always one on any corner of any US city. This part of Washington seemed to buck the trend. It took forty minutes to find the familiar sign, and another twenty to stock up on toiletries.

Shortly after two o'clock in the afternoon he pulled up at the valet parking station outside the Washington Hilton on Connecticut Avenue. He paid for a suite for the night, checked in at the business lounge to confirm the availability of a workstation and internet, and headed for his room.

He went straight to the bathroom, stripped off and tackled two days beard growth. He double-showered, switching between hot and cold torrents, towelled dry and dressed in his new clobber. He was ready for the world again.

He ordered room service of coffee and sandwiches, after which he stretched on the bed and tried to assemble his thoughts against the backdrop of a cream-coloured papered ceiling.

Something was all wrong about the hit on the McAndrew family.

He'd come across enough deadbeats like Devlin Montgomery to know that rage and red mist can sometimes make people do the strangest things. But was it really worth killing a prominent lawyer just to cover up some shady business or property deal? Why expose a corporate giant for the sake of revenge or bloodlust? There had to be more than that. Something was missing from the equation.

This Montgomery guy seemed to have been a big wheel in an organisation with tentacles spread through numerous high-finance deals. So, why get involved in a Mickey-Mouse court case? What was the real exposure here? Was there a deal that needed safeguarding above all others? Was there something in the wind that needed to be protected at all costs? If there was, it had to be something capable of causing quite a stir. A major drugs or arms shipment? Government corruption? Terrorist-related? The top three worst-case scenarios for any law enforcement agency. Take your pick. Or maybe it was none of the above.

Too many imponderables. He gave up and headed for the business lounge on the ground floor, spending his first hour studying Google Earth images around the Fleming estate at Bailey's Crossroads. He panned out from the estate to memorise the general terrain on a three-mile radius. He'd do a thorough on-the-ground recce later for possible sniper vantage points, but for now he wanted to see what was beyond the immediate threat area. Escape roads, places to hole up, a base for planning the attack and lying low afterwards.

Chances were the sniper was from out of town. Which meant he had to travel by car to bring his gear with him. You can't carry a heavy-duty rifle on the Metro, or risk drawing attention because of backpacks or combat gear. He'd need somewhere to change. Somewhere far enough away from the target site, yet close enough to gain quick access by using a motorbike or rough-terrain vehicle.

Quinn studied hotels, motels, and ask-no-questions bedsit locations. Just too many of them. What if the sniper took a leaf from Quinn's own book and had an RV? No better way to stay hidden, yet mobile. He looked at trailer parks, campsites and large picnic areas. The choice here was more limited. At least three spots jumped out. There was also the possibility of trails and clearings in a forest site situated four miles from Bailey's Crossroads. Unfortunately, Google Earth was no help in drilling through the foliage for closer inspection.

He memorised the options and switched to the Dark Web, jumping in and out of more than a dozen message boards in the hope of finding something new, something with even the vaguest connection to the McAndrew contract. It was a long shot.

But it paid off.

Pontius666: Assignment cancelled. Keep the money and disappear.

It was the original signature of the paymaster. But who was it, and why cancel? The message was time-stamped less than two hours ago. There was no reply. No response. No follow-up. Which meant the contracted assassin either hadn't seen it or was ignoring it. Quinn could understand the first option, but not the second. Forget professional pride. If someone was offering you the chance to walk away with your reputation intact, you grabbed at it. Unless of course you were a psychopath who enjoyed the kill maybe even more so than the money.

Either way, it didn't make Charlie or Sophie any safer.

Devlin Montgomery chose the Lincoln Park on Capitol Hill as the venue for his meeting with the Chairman. It was three o'clock in the afternoon, with little more than an hour of February daylight left. Still, there were plenty of people about, enough certainly to guarantee the other side wouldn't try anything too dramatic.

Or so he hoped.

The Chairman was sitting on a bench overlooking the iconic statue depicting President Lincoln's Emancipation Proclamation. Beside him was the familiar figure of Clarissa, the white-haired, ever-present, irksome dogsbody. For all the world, they looked like an elderly retired couple enjoying the solitude of the great outdoors, though Montgomery knew they rarely spent time away from their Manhattan base of operations.

Montgomery switched his attention from the bench to a small group standing near the base of the statue. The two men he was scanning for were immediately recognisable. Bulky, menacing figures. Brothers in looks as well as character. The Chairman's personal rottweilers, cold-blooded killers who'd as soon strangle a man as eat a burger, a go-to diet that was usually laced with steroids. Their presence didn't change anything. It was what he'd expected.

"I see you've brought some company," Montgomery said as he took a seat and nudged Clarissa to the end of the bench. "I wanted this between you and me, but I guess you were never much for keeping your word."

"I'm not here for banalities," the Chairman intoned. "Convince me we can do business or this is the last you'll see of me. In which case, you won't be leaving this park alive."

"Come, come, Chairman, even you wouldn't be so foolish as to attempt anything, especially since I hold an ace up my sleeve. I take it you *do* want the memory stick?"

"Have you got it with you?"

"Do you take me for a compete idiot?" It's somewhere safe until I know you'll keep your end of the bargain."

"You got your one million dollars, didn't you?"

"Yes, and this time you won't get the chance to claw it back through your little electronic genius. I've already put it beyond Clarissa's reach, so what say we discuss the rest of the payment? Are you ready with the other nineteen million?"

The Chairman turned to Montgomery with a frosty stare. "Are you absolutely mad? I already told you on the phone that I want the stick, I want assurances there are no other copies, and I want you to call off the contract on the McAndrew children. All three of these conditions have to be fulfilled before you see another dime."

"I'll lay my cards on the table," Montgomery

replied. "There is only one copy, which is currently residing in a safe deposit box in Manhattan. You'll just have to take my word for it. You'll get full details on how to access the box, after I'm gone of course, and you already know from Clarissa that all my computer log-ins, including my personal laptop, have been frozen so there's no way I could retrieve anything from Cloud storage, or such like, even if I wanted to. In one sense, you hold all the aces, Mr Chairman."

"What about the contract?"

"That's a bit more problematical. As of three hours ago I posted a cancellation through the usual channels. There's no guarantee the contractor will see it, and since I have no other way of contacting him we will have to assume it will go ahead. I can see how this is an issue for you, but there's not much more I can do about it."

"So, you think I'll pay up and look happy? I expected arrogance from you, but not stupidity"

"I'm neither arrogant nor stupid, and you'd be wise to remember that. We either both wipe the slate clean and walk away, or things could get very messy."

The chairman threw back his head and roared with laughter. "You don't know the meaning of the word messy. How about I get the boys over there to take you for a little ride, somewhere nice and quiet in the countryside? Know what'll happen when they get you there? They'll start by peeling back your skin, every inch of it from your entire body, until pretty soon you'll beg them for mercy, even after you've given up all your little secrets. But they won't stop. They'll enjoy it too much. They've done it before. Their record is keeping a man alive in the most exquisite pain for five full days. Not something you should want to contemplate."

Montgomery shook his head ruefully. "That's why I knew I needed a few guarantees. You really are a contemptible bastard, but you're way too predictable."

"What guarantees are you talking about?"

"The kind that involves our friends from the Middle East. What do you think will happen when they realise you can't keep up your end of the bargain? What will they do when you don't deliver as requested? Suppose I showed them how you've been playing two ends off against each other? They've paid a lot of money for that shipment. Doesn't seem right it should blow up in their faces."

"You're stark raving mad!"

"What? For not letting you get things all your own way? I've set up a timed-forward email with attachments, from an untraceable ghost account. It's amazing what you can do from internet stations in cafes and libraries. It spells out the fine details for your Iranian friends. Clarissa here will tell you how it works. Pay up and you get access to stopping the email. Call it two-for-one, along with access to the safety deposit box. Now, do we have a deal?"

CHAPTER 25

QUINN DECIDED to skip his planned afternoon return to the Fleming estate. Instead, he called Agent Freeman and explained his change of mind, along with a demand for a meeting at the Washington Hilton. He also dictated a shopping list of items which he wanted Freeman to bring with him.

Two hours later the FBI man stormed in to the hotel lobby and marched straight to Quinn, who was seated in front of a television, his feet splayed under a glass-topped courtesy table covered with the remnants of an early-evening meal.

"Comfortable, are we?"

"As a matter of fact, yes, thanks for asking."

"Look, Quinn, I don't know what's going on, but we've wasted a day while you've been soaking up some luxury. Mind telling me what the hell you're doing here?"

"Fair enough." Quinn straightened in his seat and recounted his afternoon's activity, after which he explained how he was going to spend the next twenty-four hours. "Did you bring me what I asked for?"

"It's all in the car," Freeman said. "That was quite a shopping list. Sure you didn't miss anything out?"

"No, I think I've covered all the bases. There's

something I want to discuss with you before we leave."

"I'm all ears."

Quinn summarised his earlier thoughts. "So, you see, I'm sure there's more to this than just McAndrew being unlucky for getting on the wrong side of Montgomery. This has to be bigger than that."

"Give us some credit! Whataya think we do in the FBI? Sit on our thumbs while smart guys like you do the math for us? We've looked at all the angles. I started McAndrew on this investigation into Montgomery and his associates on the chance of bringing down a runaway train in the shape of this corporation. There's a lot going on there, most of it small, unrelated stuff, which doesn't amount to much in isolation, but taken together, probably represents corporate fraud on a gigantic scale. There's no single, seismic scenario that we can find. This is about joining the little dots to get the big picture."

"I'm not so sure," Quinn said. "Something spooked Montgomery, and it wasn't one of those little dots. Let's say for a moment that this organisation was somehow involved in a treasonous or terrorist act, would that set you off on a different path?"

"You know it would, but there's nothing in the past, or in anything McAndrew found, that would lead us even remotely to a conclusion like that. You're barking up the wrong tree."

"I hear you, but I can also see your mind whirring around. You can't rule it out, can you?"

Freeman looked around the lobby before

leaning closer to Quinn. "You know I can't ignore anything. I've been in this job long enough to understand there are no surprises. What we're missing here, however, is even the flimsiest of threads to pull on."

Quinn nodded in agreement. "What you need to do is go back to the start. Check the timeline from the first moment McAndrew got involved with the organisation. There might be something there."

"This whole thing blew up because of a minor wrangle over some real estate. A business tenant in an industrial complex sued the owners for tearing up a property lease on a warehouse he used in Virginia. Turned out the owners were a company linked to the corporation, which was how McAndrew made the connection and how Montgomery became embroiled in the dispute. It was nothing more than a hundred-thousand-dollar claim for loss of privileges. Chicken feed for the corporation."

"So why didn't they settle up and make it go away before the need for a court case?"

"Maybe somebody took their eye off the ball. Big corporations like this must find it hard to keep track of all their assets. A guy files a claim, the other side thinks it's frivolous and decides to put up a defence. The whole ball started rolling before someone realised it shouldn't have gotten that far. McAndrew did a great job representing the plaintiff. Got the guy his hundred thousand after filing for discovery and seeing the scope of the corporation's holdings. They did eventually settle out of court, but I guess Montgomery reckoned the damage in exposure was already done."

Quinn rubbed his chin in contemplation. "It's the level of exposure that bothers me. Forget companies and financial shenanigans. What was really at the bottom of the lawsuit?"

"Probably a labyrinth of shell companies packed on top of other shell companies. I can see why they'd want to keep it all hidden."

"No," Quinn said, "it's more basic than that. What was the plaintiff standing to lose?"

"I guess he wanted to hold onto his warehouse."

"So, why not let him? Is the location of any significance? Where is this industrial estate? What's around it? Why turf out a respectable business tenant?"

"Are you thinking they had something to hide and didn't want him to see things?"

"It's the only scenario that makes any sense. Might be worth your while taking a look around. Talk to other tenants, if they have any, though my guess is McAndrew's client was not the only one who suffered eviction. Makes you wonder, doesn't it?"

Freeman sagged back and stared at the muted television screen, without taking in any details. "Yes, it does give me pause for thought. You know, Quinn, I'm beginning to think there's more to you than I've been giving you credit for."

QUINN STARTED four miles from the estate perimeter. Darkness had settled by the time Freeman dropped him on a road running alongside a small forested area. They'd agreed to go in one vehicle – Freeman would arrange for the SUV

Quinn had used to be picked up from the Hilton hotel. Quinn wouldn't need transport, since he'd planned to make his way back to the Fleming house by foot sometime the following evening.

On the trip over, Quinn used the time to study the contents of the backpack he'd requested from Freeman.

All-purpose combat jacket. *Check.*

Glock 19 with suppressor and two spare ammo clips. *Check.*

Combat knife. *Check.*

Six-inch telescopic sight. *Check*

Night-vision goggles. *Check.*

Infrared heat detector unit. *Check.*

Pre-programmed satphone. *Check.*

Thermal blanket. *Check*

Bottled water and power bars. *Check.*

He familiarised himself with the gadgetry, setting a default GPS location, and twisting dials to ensure he had each unit's operational nuances firmly implanted in his brain. When he finished, he started over again, switching the gizmos on and off, until he was confident they wouldn't let him down.

He'd chosen the forest area, mainly because it was the farthest point in the imaginary circle he'd drawn around the estate perimeter, but also because he needed to rule it out as a possible base for the sniper's operation. If there was a vehicle within the woods he intended to find it and disable it.

He waited at the side of the road until Freeman's car disappeared from sight. Then he waited some more. The lights had impaired his night vision. He was allowing time for full restoration of ocular power.

He climbed a small stone wall and disappeared into thickly-clumped trees, most rising more than thirty feet and cutting off the faint support of the moonlight. He travelled lightly for the first few hundred yards, carefully placing his feet between fallen twigs before applying any pressure. He gradually built up into a steady rhythm, but a half-mile into the trek he was forced to don the night-vision goggles. The scene in front turned into an eerie green blanket, which allowed him to see obstacles, but didn't help with his footwork.

He used a zigzag pattern to try to cover as much ground as possible. It took him a while to adjust to the sounds of the forest and to recognise the muted wanderings of various animals. Those critters were way better than he was at masking their nocturnal forays, but such was the solitude of the place that even their cushioned tread pushed the decibel counter past zero. It reminded him to go slower.

After two hours he'd barely covered half the area closest to the Fleming estate. He sat down on the roots of a large tree and turned off the goggles to preserve power. He munched his way through an energy biscuit and downed a half-litre of water. This was a time for patience, something Quinn had shown in vast reservoirs on numerous occasions whilst stalking a target or an enemy.

He closed his eyes and tuned into his surroundings. He was in a state of near paralysis, yet fully alert. He caught the first whiff of a familiar smell and rose instantly to his feet, hiding his bulk behind the trunk of the large cedar, and carefully pulling the goggles back into place.

It was the smell of smoke. Not the nicotine variety, with which he was all too familiar, but the earthier aroma of an open fire fuelled by dry leaves and twigs, with probably a sizable log thrown in for good measure. It drifted towards him from the left side of his current location. The source was likely no more than a few hundred yards away.

He pulled the heat sensor unit from one of his jacket's multi-pockets and powered it up. It was no bigger than a cellphone with a one-inch-square window, showing a hazy cloud of blue and grey colours. He swept it slowly on a one-eighty traverse across the front of his face, stopping when it flared into two red blotches, close together, the signatures for heavy heat patterns.

The unit was switched off and returned to its pocket. Quinn eased the combat knife from its sheath, clamping it between his teeth, before dropping to his knees and starting a bellycrawl aimed at bringing him in on a gentle arc towards his target. He cinched the backpack around his shoulders and pushed the goggles onto his forehead. He wouldn't need them until the last twenty yards or so.

Within ten minutes the smell had intensified. He could now hear voices, one male, one female. They appeared so close it was as if he could reach out and touch them. He wriggled forward towards a clump of gorse, its thick cover masking him from what lay beyond.

He wouldn't need his goggles. The area in front of the gorse was a good-sized natural clearing, one of those curious traits of nature that went against uniformity. Moonlight spilled into the gap, highlighting a strongly-constructed canvas tent, a blazing open fire straddled by a makeshift spit-roast skewer, and two people with their heads folded into each other's shoulders.

He removed the knife and gently drew the suppressed Glock from a leather shoulder strap. He pointed the weapon at the couple and waited. One wrong move and it would be their last.

He listened to their chatter and their intimacies. There was talk of school books and football matches. Office gossip and fashion and food, the weather and holiday destinations, buying a new car, and maybe visiting their parents. It was the talk of ordinary nine-to-five people, enjoying a bit of escapism from humdrum lives. Maybe they weren't ordinary. Maybe they didn't lead humdrum lives.

But one thing was for certain. These were no assassins.

Quinn backtracked noiselessly, pulled down his goggles again, and gave the couple a wide berth.

CHAPTER 26

ANOTHER THREE hours took Quinn to the edge of the forest. It was four o'clock on a damp, freezing morning. The sweat of his exertions cooled against his skin, adding to a dramatic drop in body temperature, something that needed correcting before moving on. He found a small clearing surrounded by waist-high bushes, unpacked his rucksack, and rolled himself into the thermal blanket.

It served two purposes. The obvious one was to aid heat restoration; the bonus was that it masked telltale red blotches in case anyone had a thermal imaging unit pointed in his direction.

He was confident, however, that he was alone in the woods. He'd criss-crossed most of the area in a painstaking sweep that had yielded evidence of tracks, probably made by bicycle tyres; some old footprints, most likely put there more than a week ago; and a variety of surface scratches that were definitely created by the forest's furry denizens. No fresh indents made my humans. No signs that anyone had been in the area recently. Even the romantic campers mustn't have strayed beyond their own little private clearing.

There was a lot of forest he hadn't explored. Working on the assumption that four miles was the optimum range for a base, there didn't seem much point in going beyond his best guess. Yes, it was a notional demarcation, but experience had taught him the practicalities of field missions. An exfil point had to be manageable and accessible. Get in, get the job done, and get out fast. No point hanging about. And slogging beyond four miles definitely amounted to hanging about.

He was confident no-one was at the outer reaches. Confident too that if someone was using the inner forest as a launch base, he'd have found it.

That left open country on three sides of the Fleming estate. The frontage could be ruled out. It bordered the main road and was on flatter ground, offering little or no elevated points compared to the flanks and rear, which rose into steep mounds and chunky hills. Come first light, he'd start on the eastern segment, snaking his way along the higher ground where any self-respecting sniper would take up position. Tall grass and boulders would be helpful cover. Daylight would be a bummer, making progress even slower than it was through the dense forest.

He wolfed down another power biscuit and snuggled into the blanket.

Quinn's body clock woke him exactly two hours later. It was still dark and chilly, but full inner heat had been restored. Another quick stint on the infrared and thermal imaging handsets confirmed the world around his position was still green, with no hint of red. He gulped more water, packed his gear, and crawled out from cover, figuring he could do at least two miles before the skies brightened.

Shortly after nine o'clock, three hours into his journey, he decided on another rest stop. He was on the crest of a hill, overlooking a worn pathway, less than a mile from the Fleming house. It was a great vantage point, which he confirmed by using the telescopic sight to zoom in on the darkened windows, and below to three figures walking in the front garden. Sheridan Smith was instantly recognisable. Judging by his body language he was pointing out Secret Service assignments for the day.

Quinn wondered if anyone else was watching the little cameo below.

It was important for Smith to show his agents in operation. Stay by the house, make out as if this was a close-protection detail, and give no hint of being wary of a threat from much farther away. The sniper needed to believe he was under no immediate danger of discovery. He also needed to think that if he stayed on station, an opportunity to get at the kids might present itself.

Quinn wanted the assassin to hang around. It was the best chance of finding him in the short term. The alternative didn't bear thinking about. Scare the guy into running meant the prospect of a cold trail and endless weeks of watching over their shoulders. He owed it to Charlie and Sophie to make sure that didn't happen.

He lay for a long time, rubbing circulation into tired and cramped limbs. The slow, monotonous exertions on all fours was taking its toll. He'd developed a good rhythm and technique, but his body cried out for ten minutes of stretching, followed by a good pounding run to get some adrenaline flowing through his bloodstream. He couldn't risk it. He'd just have to soldier on.

He was suddenly alerted by a new sound mixed among the morning chorus of birds and distant livestock. It was coming from below and to his left, getting stronger, and taking on a familiar resonance. Footsteps! Someone was on the path and heading in his direction.

He lowered his head into the spindly reeds and trained his eyes on a sharp bend, less than fifty yards away. His right hand eased the Glock from its holster. He held the weapon across the crook of his arm and waited.

The slap, slap of feet intensified. Suddenly a figure appeared like an apparition, backlit by the morning sun, arms and legs swinging in a rhythmical choreography that somehow looked natural even in such a surprising environment.

It was a woman, dressed in mid-leg jogging pants, her auburn hair swinging on a ponytail. Chest out, shoulders back, knees up, a smile playing across a face that could adorn the front of any fashion magazine. She wore a tight-fitting t-shirt, shadowed here and there with perspiration spots, and carried a backpack that danced between her shoulders to the beat of her strides.

She loped gazelle-like on pink and white Nike trainers that were scuffed with age and use. Quinn smiled and drank in the full outline of her body. Curves in all the right places. Youth on her side, probably no more than twenty-five, with vitality seeping through the flawless bronzed skin. The kind of woman who would make you want to cross a crocodile-filled river just for the chance to say hello. He watched her pert backside disappear into the distance, and sighed. *Get back on focus!*

She was probably a local, although he couldn't remember any houses close by on the Google Maps screen. Maybe she came from one of the picnic areas or campsites farther down the line. The path looked like it was used frequently, not by farmers as a link to their fields, as Quinn had originally thought, but maybe for walking and jogging. He made a mental note to ask Fleming about his neighbours and the general land use of the region.

He shook his head, returned the Glock to the holster, and crawled onwards, his mood lightened considerably by the chance encounter. He stayed above the path for about a mile, stopping every so often to check through the telescope at the ground below and possible direct lines of sight to the house. In contrast to the bland one-dimensional views offered by Google, there were more distinctive possibilities from the 3D perspective. It was time to cut back. Which meant he had to cross the path and risk exposure. Which meant, in the words of one of his old instructors, it was *time to fish or cut bait*.

He waited at the side of the path for three minutes, not an arbitrary time plucked from the air, but one that had become a habit. He'd used it often while waiting for a sentry or look-out to move position or shift attention. Anything less than three minutes was risky, particularly if the subject was fidgety. Anything much more than that could cause the cycle of nervousness to kick off again. Give them time to settle, and then go. Three minutes was his favoured option. So, he went.

He folded back into the grass at the other side of the path, relieved there had been no gunfire or shouts or any indication that he'd been spotted. He resumed his slow, forward crawl.

Ten minutes later, he found what he was looking for.

Quinn had angled towards the spot on purpose. It was one of three possible locations he'd noted during the earlier sweep from higher ground. It was nestled against an overhanging rock with weeds and bushes pushing out at either side, a natural hide, about eight-hundred yards from the house.

He kept downwind and lay prone twenty feet away, giving him a direct view of the right side of the house. He didn't need the telescope to see the slight swaying of a camouflage net spread across the top and front of the hide. He'd found his mark.

He didn't move a muscle, not so much as a blink of an eye. Three minutes. Nothing. *Get on with it!*

The Glock appeared in his right fist at the same time as his left hand patted the ground gently for a small rock or pebble. No such luck. He switched attention to the combat knife, drawing it out slowly, and gripping it by the tip of the blade. He leapt to his feet, hurled the knife at the side of the netting, and tuck-rolled down six yards of rough terrain that brought him level with the front of the makeshift cavity. The Glock was on semi-auto mode, meaning Quinn's preferred control rate of four rounds would travel to target in less than a quarter of a second. The inside of the hide was therefore a total kill zone.

Except there was nothing there to kill. The hide was empty.

He spent several minutes doing a three-sixty of

the area around the boulder. Satisfied there were no surprises, he carried out a painstaking inspection of the interior. No cigarette butts, no empty water bottles, no detritus of any kind. He expected no less. The guy was a professional.

He did find two small indents in the ground. They were spaced roughly six inches apart, the telltale signs of a bipod used to support particular kinds of weapons. Heavy duty. Lots of firepower. Lethal.

But why had the assassin abandoned his lair? Why leave the netting? Was he coming back? Lots of questions, but the answers didn't make any sense.

You don't just up and leave the perfect platform for a spot of relaxation and return later for another stint. You find somewhere, you hole up, and you abandon only when the job's done. Was he spooked? Had he heard Quinn approach?

Quinn needed to regroup. He decided to spend another hour checking the higher reaches of the eastern flank before returning to the house. The closer he got to the estate, the less the level of attention. The sniper would not choose a spot within five-hundred yards. Too close. Too risky. But where the hell was he?

"I tell you, there was someone out there!"

"If you say there was, then I believe you, baby."

Karen Atwood pulled the elastic band from her ponytail and shook her hair free. "It's strange knowing someone is watching you instead of the other way around. Good job you insisted I dress as a jogger, otherwise whoever that was would have nabbed me."

Her husband John grabbed her by the waist and squeezed. "He'd have got a lot more than he bargained for, my sweet. Don't forget I've seen you in action."

She squirmed away and frowned. "It was still a big chance. Why did you get me to check the hides after we'd already decided to abandon them?"

"Just needed to know the lie of the land. I thought they'd bring in an expert tracker, but thinking and knowing are two different things. We might not be pressing ahead with the two sniper hides, but that doesn't mean this guy won't continue to track us. Knowing about him keeps us one step ahead."

"I get it that they've learned about the contract and I understand why we won't be able to get a shot off when the windows are blocked up and the kids are confined to the house. What I don't get is why you think this specialist can thwart our other plans."

John Atwood smiled. "Because they've set an assassin to catch an assassin. That's what I'd do in their place. Someone who thinks like us, someone who can look at all the angles and decide what works and what doesn't work. If we've thought of something, then chances are he'll think of it too. Now we know what we're up against, we can take some extra precautions."

"Shouldn't we just leave the area and try again at a later date?"

"What? And lose our advantages?"

"What advantages? Seems to me that if we stay here, we'll get squeezed."

"We have the edge of deciding what to do and when to do it. What I've planned will completely blindside them. They won't see it coming, not in a million years?"

Karen looked around the dirty interior of their fifteen-year-old camper van. "The sooner we get out of this fleapit the better. Why are you so confident we can pull this off now, instead of later?"

John wrapped his arms around his wife's waist again and whispered in her ear. "Because, my sweet, they don't know there's two of us!"

CHAPTER 27

QUINN USED THE satphone to warn the Secret Service team he was entering the estate from the rear garden. He'd waited for darkness before breaking cover and sprinting towards patio doors where Sheridan Smith stood behind partially-closed drapes.

"We've been tracking you on GPS all the way. Thought you were staying out for another night? What's changed?"

Quinn flopped on a seat beside the kitchen table. "Everything's changed. I need time to regroup. Something doesn't add up." He quickly recounted details of the abandoned hide, admitting that its significance had thrown him a curve ball. "I just don't get it. Why disappear and leave the evidence for us to find?"

"Maybe you spooked him, or maybe he's decided this location is a wash-out. Either way, we have to assume he's looking at other alternatives."

"You're right on at least one count," Quinn said. "He's definitely looking at alternatives, but not because he knew I was in the grounds hunting him down. The hide had been abandoned for hours, long before I got within two miles of it. Besides, he wouldn't have heard me coming anyway."

"Pretty sure of yourself," Smith said without any hint of rebuke.

"Sure enough to know he didn't get past me. Which means he'd already gone, even before I entered the four-mile perimeter. I get it that he probably figured out we'd send in a tracker, but why jump the gun so early? Guy like that would be confident enough to stick around for confirmation before upping stakes."

"So, where do you go from here?"

"Food, sleep, a shower, change of clothes, and then I'm heading back out. I'll leave sometime after midnight."

"Why bother, if the guy's skipped the area?"

"Belts and braces, Agent Smith. "Gotta check the western flank. Maybe there's a secondary hide. Maybe what I found was a decoy. It's a long shot, but we've got to know what else we're facing. First though, I need to speak to the old man."

"He's with the kids. Asked not to be disturbed."

"Can't be helped."

Quinn walked from the kitchen, down the long hall, and knocked on the lounge door. He didn't wait for an answer. Fleming looked surprised, but pleased to see him. "Back so soon?"

Before Quinn could answer, Charlie was on his feet and rushing towards him. Sophie held back, although there was a trace of a smile when she looked across the room.

"What kept you?" Charlie enthused. "Did you find the bad man?"

"Not yet, but I will. Mind if I talk to your grandpa for a while?"

Fleming took the hint. "Alright, children, go find Thora and tell her to give you some ice cream with chocolate sauce."

"That's quite a development," Fleming said after hearing Quinn's report. "Does it mean this thing will continue to drag out?"

"I'll know better by this time tomorrow. Tell me about your neighbours and the kinds of usual activities that go on around here."

"Not much to tell. There are only are a few scattered beef farms and the odd small horse ranch within about ten miles of here. We do get tourists to the trailer parks, but they never venture this far from the most popular sites."

"There's a path that's worn with use about a mile on the eastern side. Who uses it?"

"That'll be mostly old Chad Evans. He lives a good way inland and uses the path as a shortcut to the main road. He has a few grazing fields along the way, so I guess it helps him to kill two birds with one stone."

"It's not wide enough for a vehicle," Quinn said.

"That'd be right. Chad got himself one of those quad bikes a few years back. He's like a kid with a new toy. Goes out at every opportunity, just for the thrill of it. Surprised you didn't see him on your travels. Never known him to stay put for more than a few hours, even when the weather would keep a normal being indoors."

"No, never saw or heard him. What about joggers or walkers? Ever known the path to be used for that?"

"Can't say that I have, not with us being so far from the parks, and with no young 'uns that I know of still living around. Mostly elderly folk, like Chad, and I can't see him walking about on arthritic hips when he's got his nippy little four-wheeler to show off. Why do you ask?"

Quinn frowned. "I encountered a very attractive young lady. She was your typical athletic, outdoor type. Looked at home in her surroundings, as if she knew her way about the place. Does Chad have a granddaughter, or a niece? Could she be related to one of the other families about here?"

"Chad had no children. As for the other families, it's hard to say. Maybe one of the offspring who moved away has come back visiting with their own children. Is it important?"

"Just an anomaly," Quinn said. "A very pleasing, good looking one. But an anomaly nonetheless."

Devlin Montgomery visited six separate ATMs over the course of two hours. He maxed out his daily allowance of ten-thousand dollars, enough to do until he hit the cash machines again tomorrow. Using his cards for hotel registrations was out of the question, particularly because he knew the feds would just love to pinpoint his location. On the other hand, bouncing them around ATM machines was a risk worth taking.

The greenbacks would fund a nondescript room for a few nights, with plenty left to spare for a shopping list to help him get out of the country. He needed a new identity, not something he was particularly knowledgeable about. But he knew a man, who knew a man.

The Feds were the least of his problems. The

bank opened in two days, which was the deadline set for handing over the memory stick and email details to the Chairman. Two days to figure out what the old bastard would do once he got his hands on them. One thing was certain: he wouldn't just stand back and let Montgomery walk off into the sunset with another nineteen-million dollars. The Chairman was one of those people who needed to have everything his own way. The trick was to let him believe the transfer would achieve exactly that.

Montgomery thought about one of his favourite anecdotes from the writings of Sun Tzu, the old Chinese military strategist. *Hence that general is skilful in attack whose opponent does not know what to defend; and he is skilful in defence whose opponent does not know what to attack.*

The solution was obvious. Make sure the Chairman doesn't see what's coming. But first make sure he can do nothing about it.

Montgomery nipped into a hardware store and bought three burner phones, which he explained were for his nephews and nieces. Not that the young salesman seemed to give a toss about the reasons for his purchases. *Is it any wonder this country is in the mess it is?*

He found a seedy hotel on the Upper East Side, on the corner of Seventy-ninth, close enough to be within walking distance of Midtown, which is where he wanted to be shortly before midnight. He tore the packaging from the phones and made the first of three calls, using a different handset for each one. Two of the numbers were to recipients within five miles of his current location. The other was six-thousand miles farther afield. Each call lasted no more than twenty seconds. Curt, business-like, and to the point.

The warehouse estate sprawled across fifty acres of reclaimed marshland near the James River on Lynchburg City's south-east suburbs. It was a garden-variety place, with intersecting poured-concrete roadways, minimal landscaping, separate corrugated structures - each the size of aircraft hangars - and green PVC-coated, welded steel-wire fencing. Bland, functional, and uninviting. Not the sort of place to attract attention.

Except of course if someone was looking for something out of the ordinary.

Carl Freeman noted the incongruity of the place almost as soon as he assembled his FBI team at a raised point overlooking the site two hundred yards away.

There were four buildings, each sitting a considerable distance from its nearest neighbour. Three of them showed no signs of activity. No open-door views into scenes of industrial grafting, no vehicles entering or leaving, no parked cars for workers. Nothing. The fourth structure was different, but only just. It showed similar signs of inertia, except for two large commercial trucks standing sentry outside a shuttered door. Hardly evidence of much activity, but at least someone appeared to be home.

The real oddity about the place was the presence of a large guard hut, built on an old railway-sleepers base that dominated the main-gate area. Freeman counted three uniformed guards milling around the exterior of the hut, which meant there was most likely at least one or two more inside. Human nature. Someone close at hand to man the phones or operate the mechanised gate.

Why so many people to guard a derelict area?

Freeman turned to Drew Eisler. "Guess this wasn't such a wild-goose chase after all?"

Eisler nodded. "That's a lot of guards for a lot of emptiness. Must be something in there that someone doesn't want us to see. It'll be real interesting to take a look around."

"One step at a time, Drew. I want full reconnaissance before we move in. Whistle up some thermal-imaging and radiation-signature equipment. I want all four sides inspected and reported back on. Also, get one of our people to zoom in on those vehicle registration numbers. Find out who owns them and where they're usually parked up. Those addresses will become secondary surveillance targets, which means we need more people on the ground. You have my full authorisation to cut through the usual re-assignment bullshit."

Eisler whistled. "You really think it could be that big?"

"I really don't know what to make of it. All I'm saying is that we already missed this place first time around when McAndrew was involved in the court case over a lease, so there's no way I'm going to pass it by without making sure there's nothing for us to worry about."

"Yeah, boss, but ordering up radiation detection isn't exactly going to go unnoticed. Shouldn't we at least let Homeland know what we're doing? Those guys can raise quite a fuss if they're kept in the dark, particularly if there's even a hint of a dirty bomb on US soil."

"Do me a freaking favour! Those clodhoppers will stomp in here without a second thought. It'll be gung-ho, guns blazing and worry about piecing things together after the dust has settled and valuable intel is ruined. Don't forget, this thing could be linked to the assassination attempt on the McAndrew children, and while there's the remotest chance we might get a line on who's behind it, we'll play it my way. This is an FBI operation until I say otherwise."

CHAPTER 28

THE WESTERN boundary of the Fleming estate was going to be a doddle for Quinn. Compared to his exertions of the previous night, he calculated it would take no more than four hours to cover the area, or at least the parts he reckoned were the most vulnerable. He'd spent an hour in an upstairs room looking at the landscape through night-vision goggles, calculating potential sniper lines, looking for natural terrain cover, and finally zooming in on two preferred options.

He'd split the entire boundary into eight segments, immediately dismissing the outer stretches as impractical. No direct line of sight. Not enough cover. Another two segments were scratched off towards the centre. The land was too flat. He'd just cut his search grid by half.

Despite the nagging thought that the assassin was unlikely to be out there, he had no choice but to apply the same care and attention to detail as he had on the eastern boundary. That meant another four hours of stop-start crawling. More numbness. More fatigue. More aches and pains.

He pushed back the patio curtains and slipped into the darkness. He still had his backpack, and his gadgets, and his Glock, and his knife. He wouldn't do this in half measures. It owed it to Charlie and Sophie to deliver the best professional job he could muster. That's what the situation demanded, and that's what it would get.

It took him less than an hour to arrive at his first target location, a small plateau framed by gorse bushes that were thick with their evergreen prickly coats and yellow flowers. It was a rectangular area, stretching for about fifteen yards on its long sides and half that distance on its flanks. If someone hollowed out the centre, they could do pretty much what they wanted with little or no risk of being observed.

Quinn powered up the thermal-image intensifier and swept the ridge. Nothing except greens and greys. No reds. The place was deserted. He inched forward, straining to listen for any sounds that might signal the approach of an intruder. *Never assume – assumptions will get you killed.* An old training mantra, as fresh in his mind now as when he'd first heard it at the Cathal Brugha Barracks in Dublin all those years ago.

The plateau didn't have a clearing, either natural or man-made. It was wall-to-wall gorse, with no evidence of disturbance and no tracks leading to or from it. Quinn cursed. It would have been his primary choice, so maybe he was not as tuned in to the sniper's thinking as he'd hoped.

He wheeled away and headed for the secondary option, a rocky outcrop less than a half-mile to his right. If there was nothing there, he'd do a slow sweep back to the house, his tail firmly tucked between his legs. His confidence was ebbing fast. Maybe he wasn't the right man for the job after all?

It took him forty minutes to reach the outcrop. Considerably less than that to realise that maybe he still had his head in the game.

His gadgets told him no-one was in the area. A closer inspection told him otherwise. The same type of camouflage netting swayed between two boulders, enclosing a dark space that was unmistakeably a sniper's hide. The bastard *did* have a fall-back option! Quinn pulled the netting aside and stepped in to the makeshift den.

And that's when he realised he'd screwed up in just about every way it was possible to screw up. One stupid assumption after another. Mistakes heaped on top of a pile of mistakes that were already there. He'd looked at this thing all wrong from the start. He'd missed too many signs and ignored what should have been obvious. He'd put himself in the unforgiveable position of chasing shadows while the other side had watched him flounder. How the hell was he going to put this right?

"Perfume?"

Quinn threw up his arms in exasperation. "Yes, bloody perfume. I mightn't know my Diors from my Chanels but I can recognise the scent of a woman."

"So, our assassin is of the female variety?"

"Haven't you been listening to anything I've said? The perfume was present in only one of the two hides, which means we're dealing with a double act. A man and a woman, a two-for-the-price-of-one tag team, which is something I would have thought about if I hadn't kept my head buried up my ass."

They were in Chief Justice Fleming's lounge,

less than twenty minutes after Quinn had made the discovery of the second hide. He'd wasted little time returning to the house, most of the distance spent in an all-out sprint without the fear of running into his quarry. He'd known by then that the game had changed. There was nobody out here!

Fleming tried to cool Quinn's anger. "Come, come, son, don't beat yourself up. How could you possibly have foreseen something like this?"

Quinn threw his benefactor an apologetic look. "I'm sorry, sir, but that's simply not true. I sold you the idea that I knew what I was doing. Made you believe I could handle this. And what did I do? I started out from the wrong base, focussed on only one strategy, and left your grandchildren to be exposed by silly, fundamental mistakes that should not have been made."

"What mistakes?"

"This was all wrong from the start," Quinn said. "The Feds should have done a lot more to track down Montgomery, although I didn't help matters when I stole the wallet and cellphone from the guy at the hospital. Maybe they could've used that intel to get to Montgomery before he fled. They also should have looked closer at the court case your son-in-law was involved in. They couldn't see the wood for the trees, which has led to a catch-up situation that should have been dealt with from the start.

"Don't get me wrong. They weren't the only ones treading water. I ambled about like there was all the time in the world. I could've got to the guy at the Jutland Hotel quicker than I did. I was too worried about protecting my own back to see how important it was to tie up the loose ends. When I finally got a line on Montgomery, I spent too much time planning how to take him down instead of calling the Feds and letting them do their jobs. We missed Montgomery by no more than an hour. That one's down to me."

Fleming held up a hand. "All very noble, son, but aren't you being rather hard on yourself? My grandchildren are alive because of you. The precautions you've put in place here have probably kept them that way. I don't see how it changes anything just because we have two snipers instead of one."

"It changes everything," Quinn replied. "I admit it's a rarity. I've never before heard of assassin partnerships, although the idea is highly practical and is almost guaranteed to get results if you find a compatible pairing. Just think about it; two angles covered simultaneously. You can catch your target in a crossfire, or set up a plausible distraction by starting one thing in one place while something else happens in another location. One guy could fire heat-seeking missiles into a building from one direction while his partner waits patiently for people to flee into sniper fire coming from another position. It's a diversionary tactic as old as the hills. And I never once considered the possibility."

"Do you think that's what they were planning?"

"No," Quinn said emphatically. "Just an illustration. I think this duo was setting up to cover the best two angles should an opportunity arise. If one had a shot, they'd take it. Chances are they wouldn't have been able to kill both Charlie and

Sophie in one go, but that won't have mattered. Fifty per cent of the contract fulfilled. Less to complete later."

Quinn saw Fleming's eyes mist over. "I'm sorry for being so graphic, sir. The reality is that these kinds of killers don't see people, just targets. It's all about getting the job done, getting paid, and disappearing until the next assignment comes along. Life's cheap when measured against dollars and cents. Half the contract now and half later is way better than outright failure now."

Secret Service Agent Smith cut in. "What I don't get is why they've abandoned the hides. Have they given up on this location, or not?"

"What I can say," Quinn responded, "is that they won't be using the hides again, which can lead to only one conclusion."

"Which is?"

"They've ruled out the chance of using their rifles, at least from around the perimeter of the house. We've locked the place down too tight. Either they'll regroup and try again at another point in time, or they've thought of an alternative way of getting to the kids within the next forty-eight hours. Anything outside that timescale would leave them exposed. The question is: what's scheduled to change here over the next two days?"

Fleming leapt from his seat. "My God! It's the funerals. We're burying Ruth and Mark on Tuesday afternoon at the Glenwood Cemetery over on North Capitol Street. The kids will have to be there."

Quinn nodded. "That could be it. Have the funeral arrangements been made public?"

"Yes, it was on CNN last night, shortly after I

confirmed the arrangements with the undertakers. Maybe I should have insisted they keep things under wraps. Just never thought of the consequences."

"Wouldn't have mattered, sir, the news would have leaked, one way or another. We'll deal with it after we look at what to do about my other mistakes."

"There's more?"

Quinn got up and walked towards the drinks cabinet. He waited for Fleming to nod agreement before pouring three glasses of Bushmills. He brought them back to the desk and swallowed most of the contents of his own tumbler before continuing. "I know half the double act. I saw the woman."

"How? When?"

"It was the jogger," Quinn said. "Had to be. No other reason for her to be out there. It looked strange and it felt strange, but I let a pretty face and a tight body blind me from what I should have been seeing. You said yourself, sir, we're too far away from the trailer parks, and none of the families from around here have children to visit them, so where did she come from? The perfume in the sniper hide tells us there was at least one female in the area. What are the chances of two strangers turning up near this location at this time? The odds have got to be too long. The woman I saw in the pathway is the same one who set up the hide. It was staring me in the face and I ignored it."

"Nonsense! This is the breakthrough we've been waiting for," Agent Smith enthused. "We can put you with a photofit expert and have her image plastered everywhere within a matter of a few hours. We'll tie the net so tight, a cockroach couldn't crawl through."

"We'll get to that later. First, we have to deal with my biggest mistake."

Quinn finished the last of his whiskey. He was tempted to ask for another, but thought better of it. He needed his brain at full capacity. "My biggest blunder was setting the perimeter at four miles. I'd taken a good look at the countryside and decided it was the optimum range for an assassin to be comfortable with. I'd weighed up a lot of factors and came down on the side of four miles. It was always going to be a best guess, although I was convinced it was based on sound judgement. But I missed something. Perhaps the one thing that shouldn't have been missed."

"What are you talking about?" Fleming asked.

"I should have added another mile to the perimeter or, to be more precise, another mile and a quarter. The extended area would have taken in the place where Chad Evans lives. And that's where I believe the assassins are holed up."

Fleming looked bewildered. "What's old Chad got to do with it?"

"Everything, I'm afraid," Quinn responded. "I listened to you telling me about Chad and his quad bike and how he likes to run around on it every chance he gets. Well, I've been out there for the better part of two days and there's been no sign of Chad or his bike. He could have fallen and broken a leg, or taken suddenly ill with a winter fever, or ran out of gas for his bike, or a whole litany of other innocent reasons behind his sudden inactivity. But I don't buy any of them. It's another coincidence, another incongruity, and I'm done ignoring the obvious."

"You're saying Chad is in on this? I've known the old boy for most of my life and I have to tell you that's just not possible."

"I agree, sir. He's an innocent caught up in a sorry mess. Best bet is that he was taken hostage, or they've already killed him. Either way, his home is an ideal base for the assassins. He just happened to be in the wrong place at the wrong time."

"My God!" Fleming shouted. "We have to get over there."

CHAPTER 29

THE CHAIRMAN had three immediate problems to solve. They were all to do with damage limitation, which left him with little room to manoeuvre and a hefty price tag to be paid. But he prided himself on being a practical man. It wouldn't be the first time he'd cut his losses, regrouped, and came back stronger. The situation he faced demanded decisive action. And no-one could accuse Tyrell B Linkmeyer of not being decisive.

His primary concern was moving the goods and equipment stored in depots across the country. He'd always known that because of Devlin Montgomery's crass stupidity the Feds would eventually get their ducks in a row and come calling? The trail from that needless court case to one of his warehouses was so obvious that a child of ten could have made the connection.

He'd just received a phone call that confirmed his worst fears.

The warehouse has been made. Get everything out now!

The man on the other end of the line should know what he was talking about. He was Linkmeyer's inside track on the FBI.

Linkmeyer's options were limited. He decided to move what he could and destroy the rest. Several frantic calls later, three flat-bed trucks, capable of transporting large shipping containers, were already rolling before Linkmeyer got halfway through his to-do checklist. The plan was to store the containers in separate freight compounds along the eastern seaboard. They'd be hidden in plain sight, in massive holding yards, ostensibly waiting for final despatch papers that would never come through. An expensive leasing exercise, but one Linkmeyer could afford. Let the dust settle, maybe a year, then restart the operation.

One container would have to be treated differently. It represented another write-off, this time close to fifty-million dollars, the worst loss he'd ever suffered. Not a decision Linkmeyer took lightly, which meant that after examining the alternatives from every angle he was left with no choice. These were not clients to mess with, especially since Montgomery had threatened to blow the whistle on how the Corporation, or to be more exact, the Chairman, had been skimming off the top for years.

He'd already decided that Montgomery had to die. It was only a matter of timing. Despite not wanting to admit it, he had to concede that for now Montgomery held all the aces. The bastard would get his nineteen million in return for a memory stick and revealing the access password to stop a forward-dated email going to people that the Chairman would rather it didn't go to. It would buy some badly-needed time to put his house in order. After that, they'd track Montgomery and kill him. It would almost be worth a nineteen-million-dollar write off.

He couldn't trust Montgomery to keep schtum,

not even for the extortionate amount that was demanded. Somewhere down the line the bastard would tell the clients. He wouldn't be able to resist it, not if he wanted to cover his own back.

Devlin Montgomery was trying to solve some problems of his own.

The first had already been taken care of. He'd handed over a down payment of eight-thousand dollars for a new passport. Another eight was due on delivery, which was expected to be no earlier than Tuesday morning. It meant a day longer than he'd hoped to spend in Manhattan, but no amount of additional cash could prompt the forger to go any faster. This was an art that couldn't be rushed, he was told by a smug old codger operating out of an attic in the Bronx area.

To be fair, the guy seemed to know what he was doing, including a quick makeover session involving wigs and eyeglasses before taking Montgomery's head-and-shoulders photograph. It was a subtle, yet total transformation, certainly more than enough to fool any airport scanners.

Montgomery had thought long and hard about his next problem. Yes, the Chairman had been responsible for skimming millions from one particular client, but it was he, Montgomery, who'd been the director of operations. He was the man on the ground. He was the one who'd fiddled the books and provided assurances to the client. His neck was on the block every bit as much as the Chairman's.

And so he used the third of his burner phones to make another call.

He'd already made contact some six hours earlier to set up an appointment with a man who was usually hard to track down. Montgomery's cryptic message had made sure that wouldn't be the case this time.

"This is DM calling for Asif."

Six thousand miles away a voice responded. "You know I don't like phones. Make it quick."

Baghdad was seven hours ahead of New York. Asif Morani was getting ready to do a nightly tour of his nightclubs, one of a string of enterprises that almost rivalled those of the Corporation.

Montgomery knew he had to pitch this just right. He tried for a meek and frightened tone. "Praise be that I've reached you. I'm going out of my mind with worry. Something terrible has happened. I've just found out that you've been cheated on a massive scale. I think they know I've discovered what's been happening. My life is in danger."

"Calm down, Mr M. Tell me all about it and we'll see what we can do to help."

And so Montgomery laid it all out. The Chairman did this, the Chairman did that. The Chairman. The Chairman. The Chairman.

"That's grave news indeed," Morani said. "It seems to me that we have to do something about the Chairman. Can you let me have all the specific details? We need to take some action to recover our assets and I'm counting on you to help us."

Montgomery marvelled at the man's equilibrium. He'd expected a tirade of cursing and shouting and dire warnings. However, don't look a gift horse in the mouth. "Of course Mr Morani, I'll do anything to help. I have a full list of all transactions saved to a memory stick, which I will be able to retrieve from a bank within a few hours. I can email this to you."

"No, no. I will arrange for it to be collected. Where exactly is this bank?"

Asif Morani cut the call and turned to one of his most trusted lieutenants. "Two separate calls in less than two hours. It seems to me that the rats are jumping ship and blaming each other. The Chairman says Montgomery was behind the whole thing without his knowledge, yet Montgomery swears it was the Chairman. This is why I never trust Americans."

A tall, bearded man stood to attention in front of Morani's desk. "Which of them do you believe?"

Morani smiled. "It doesn't really matter, Ashwan. They're both greedy individuals who will have to pay for this insult. The Chairman promises the return of all our goods, which will not be enough to save his wretched skin. We've being doing business with this corporation for fifteen years, a lengthy period for them to have ripped us off. We will require not only the restoration of the full amount of our losses, but also interest and penalty charges, which I think will be as much as the original sums. It seems as if Allah has shown us a path to new wealth, so that we may continue to work in His Blessed Name."

Carl Freeman squeezed into the rear of a surveillance truck. Drew Eisler, Jan Moseley and Rory Cheadle already occupied three seats in front of a bank of monitors, which showed images from night-vision cameras placed strategically around the perimeter of the warehouse complex. The truck was parked a mile away, on the outer edge of a garage forecourt. It was eleven o'clock on Sunday evening.

"Full sit-rep, please, "Freeman said as he looked around for somewhere to rest.

Eisler toed a stool in his direction and told him: "We have eight agents still on site, two at each side of the compound. Our initial scouting trips confirm there are six people inside the warehouse and at least five at the guard hut. There's not a lot of activity that we can tell, although the place does seem to be crammed with machinery and storage boxes. Hard to know what's going on."

"Where are we with the radiation detection."

"Definitely no telltale signatures," Moseley responded. "We've swept the place front to back, side to side, and there's nothing."

"You sure?"

"Doubly so. We did it twice for good measure. Whatever's in there has nothing to do with dirty bombs."

"There is one thing," Cheadle chipped in. "Thermal imaging is picking up a large heat source in the centre of the building. Could be some kind of a boiler, or one of those industrial heating units. It's giving off a lot of therms or joules or whatever the correct expression is. All I know is that it's damned hot, right at the edge of what our machines can measure."

"We should maybe consider another alternative," Eisler said.

"Which is?"

"What if they've built a big fire pit and are disposing of evidence? Could be they're getting ready to abandon ship, so to speak. Maybe we should consider moving in now before they leave us with nothing to find."

Freeman shook his head. "Not yet. My gut tells me that whatever that heat signal is, it's got nothing to do with burning evidence. We hold back for now, but I want a detailed plan for getting in there as soon as I give the word. Drew, you're our master tactician so work out how we hit them before they know we're even there."

"One step ahead of you, boss. I've already sent for something that'll make the job easier. Should be with us in the next hour."

"Sounds good. Any word back from the addresses where those parked trucks are registered?"

Cheadle leaned across the console desk and lifted a single sheet of paper. "Two separate companies, one here in Lynchburg, the other headquartered in Richmond, no more than two hours away. Seems like they're both freight companies. We have agents keeping an eye on them, but they seem to be locked up for the weekend. There's a lot of trucks and containers parked around the sites, but other than a skeleton security crew there's nothing to report."

Alpha Three to base. Be advised. We have activity.

All eyes in the surveillance truck turned to the monitors. Headlights were sweeping across one of the screens.

"What have you got, Alpha Three?

Two flat-bed loaders, no, make that three heading in our direction.

"How far out?"

Hundred yards from the main gate. Looks like they were expected.

Freeman studied the monitor. The gates to the warehouse complex were swinging inwards. Then the first truck entered into the narrow camera lens. He noted a large shipping container belted into the truck's chassis. The same thing with the second truck, and then the third.

"Looks like they're getting prepared for deliveries, or could be they're getting ready to haul stuff outta there. We need that plan, Drew. We're going in a lot sooner that I thought we would."

CHAPTER 30

THE HOUSE WAS at the end of a narrow, pitted lane that stretched a mile inland from the main road. It was a single-story log-cabin, typical of the 1800's when poor dirt-farmers used what nature provided to create sturdy, practical homes that withstood harsh winters and unforgiving summers. It stood, like many others, as a testament to the resilience and ingenuity of craftsmen and women who carved out an existence and underscored a way of life that had long since faded from the American psyche.

Chad Evans had been born within the cabin's mixture of oaks and pines and native hardwoods that his parents had hewn from the surrounding forests. He had buried his folks in a small family plot, on a hillside that had once been their favourite picnic spot a hundred yards from the cabin. Chad's wife, Ethel, had joined them many years later. Chad had always known he would go there too, the last in the line of the Evans dynasty. The couple hadn't been blessed with children, which Chad reckoned was God's way of telling him this was no place for a modern family.

The old three-part fencing on either side of the approach road was now largely missing. Here and there a few broken strands of rotted wood and posts marked its route, though mostly it was lost to the tall grasses that stretched into stubbly, abandoned fields for as far as the eye could see.

Old Chad might have forsaken the fences, but he'd tended to the house with as much care as his frail body would allow. The exterior of the cabin was clean and showed evidence of regular scrubbing with wood oils and anti-fungal washes. There was a small flower garden to the front and one side, and heavy gravel had been placed around the perimeter to keep down dust from the soils and clays below the surface. A small extension had been added to the rear to create a new bedroom for Chad and his wife, and there was a barn, a more modern stand-alone structure, thirty yards from the cabin. It wasn't much to look at and had little practical purpose other than for the storage of small items of equipment and perhaps for a workshop retreat for Chad. It was made from eight-by-four lengths of milled timber, now cracked and faded by the sun, with gaps where there were once windows, and an old iron weathercock that was rusted into a permanent position atop the roof.

The barn doors were closed, as were the front and rear entrances to the cabin. Chad's quad bike was butted up against the flower bed. There were no interior lights blazing, and no smoke rose from a central chimney stack. The whole place had the look and feel of one of those old, deserted Pony Express relay stations.

It was an hour past daybreak on Monday morning, and Quinn had used the light to familiarise himself with the lay-out. He'd circled the perimeter on a radius of fifty yards from the central point of the cabin. His thermal-imaging handset showed no body-heat signatures, though there could be a cellar in either the cabin or the barn, which would not show up on his monitor. Only two choices. Either there was no-one there or someone was taking great pains to stay invisible.

Quinn was crouched behind an old headstone, one of three within a small hillside compound that was undoubtedly the Evans family's own private cemetery. Chad's mother, father and wife looking down on an idyllic rural tableau. Not a bad way to spend eternity. At that moment, Quinn fervently hoped Chad wouldn't be joining them any time soon.

Time to find out.

He hit a pre-dial button on his satphone. "This is Quinn. Move in." No need for the usual cryptic radio messages or call-sign slang. He was on a protected satellite circuit, not that he would have changed his approach in any case. He waited two minutes, as agreed, and crept closer to the barn. He'd have to clear this area before moving on the cabin, which was the most likely place for Chad to be held prisoner. *Always protect your six before advancing.*

He was on the ground below an open window at the side of the barn when he heard the approach of the FBI convoy. Old man Fleming had whistled up a tact team from the Washington office as soon as Quinn had offered his theory on where the assassins might be holed up.

"I need an hour on site before they move in," Quinn had insisted.

"Do you think that's wise? Why not let them deal with it?"

Quinn had held his ground. "There's nothing to beat real-time feedback. I can get in there unnoticed and I can help to protect Chad before the cavalry arrives."

Fleming had nodded his agreement. "Okay, my boy, I'll pass this along to whoever's in charge."

"Just make sure they know there's a friendly on site."

Quinn crouched below the window and counted off three minutes. The first of the FBI vehicles was sweeping into the last corner of the driveway when he sprang up and pointed his suppressed Glock through the gap where glass had once been. The interior of the barn was dusty and murky and smelly. There were sad fragments of old mowers and scythes and tractor parts strewn across a concrete floor, but mostly it was full of open spaces. There was no-one in there.

He climbed through the gap and moved stealthily across the interior, checking behind obstacles and testing the floor for any hint of trapdoors. Nothing. He made his way to the rear door, stepped outside and crossed the twenty-yard stretch to the rear of the cabin. Tyres squealed and car doors opened at the front of the building.

He trained his weapon on the exit, and knelt against the rough-log surface to create a narrow target in the event that someone suddenly decided to make a bolt for it. He heard the sounds of padded feet racing along the sides of the cabin. Knowing it was the FBI taking up positions, he sat his Glock on the ground and raised his arms as high as they would go.

Four black-suited figures emerged at the rear

corners of the building. They had gone for the full SWAT works. Heavy-duty Kevlar vests, visored helmets, knee pads, and MP10 automatic pistols. Adrenaline was pumping, nerves were on edge, and fingers were tight on triggers. They needed to be treated with respect.

"I'm Quinn. Everything's clear at this end."

One of the figures nodded in his direction. It was a silent signal for him to retrieve his gun and stand behind the uniformed group. The leader paused for a few seconds before kicking against the rear door. Quinn could hear a similar smashing of wood from the front of the cabin. Someone must have been counting down through ear mics.

It took less than five minutes to clear the buildings. There was no-one in either location.

Not strictly true. They found the body of old Chad Evans in a rear bedroom.

Quinn gazed down at the corpse. It wasn't difficult to figure out what had happened. The assassins had probably rolled up three or four days ago on the pretext of looking for camping sites. Then they'd forced the old boy into the house and tortured him for information. Three broken fingers on the body's right hand were evidence of that. They probably got him to describe the general terrain, and learned about the quad bike and the path that ran from Chad's place to within a mile of the Fleming estate. He'd have told them he lived alone, didn't get any visitors, and had no house telephone. A classic case of someone who wouldn't be missed for a few days.

Then they'd killed him. A single bullet drilled through the centre of his forehead. It would have been a relief to the old boy, judging by the painful facial contortions that were frozen by the onset of rigor mortis. They'd dragged the body across the wooden floors and dumped it unceremoniously on top of Chad's bed. It had bounced and fallen off and was wedged between the bed and a night locker that bore a picture of happier times. Chad and his wife in their wedding clothes, sitting on a small bench at the front of the cabin, and dreaming of an idyllic rural life together.

Quinn strode angrily from the bedroom. He shouldered aside several FBI men and careered off two armchairs as he made his way outside. He kicked the gravel with the toe of his boot and stared at the horizon and seethed. *Missed them a-fucking-gain!*

The FBI assault leader walked forward from the barn. "We've got fresh oil stains and tyre tracks from inside the barn. Looks like that's where they were parked up."

Quinn was in no mood for conversation. "Yeah, that'll get us closer to the perpetrators, won't it? While your team analyse the scene and dissect the clues and hypothesise on what happened here, these bastards are in the wind and free to do whatever they please. Standing around here talking about it won't stop an attack on the Fleming children, unless you're about to tell me you know who they are and where they've gone."

"I know you're angry," the FBI man responded, "but there are no shortcuts. We'll learn a lot from the tyre tracks, such as what sort of wheelbase the vehicle has, which will narrow the search down to particular makes and models. The oil will give us a clue to engine age, which will refine the search a bit more. We might even get lucky with fingerprints, given that they were bedded down here for at least two or three days. Add to that your photofit of the woman and I'd say we've got a lot going for us. I agree it's slow, methodical steps, but it's the only way to get the job done."

"No, Quinn yelled, "it's not the only bloody way to get the job done. You do what you gotta do, Agent, and good luck with it. I'm done sticking around. It's time to get out from under this security blanket. It's choking the life outta me. It's time I found these bastards my way."

Less than five miles away, as the crow flies, Karen and John Atwood were at that moment hunched over a map that was spread across their campervans's pull-down table.

"The funeral is the only chance we'll get. Nice of them to let us know the time and location. Now, all we've got to figure out is where to hit them from."

Karen nodded in agreement. "Promise me we'll only do this if everything is one-hundred per cent right. If it works in our favour, we'll take the shot, otherwise we'll walk away. I'm getting a bad feeling that we've outstayed our welcome in Washington."

"Agreed. Didn't I already listen to you about moving away from the Evans place? You were probably right that it was too risky to stay, and I promise we'll do the same here if things start to look dodgy."

She put an arm around his shoulder. "That's

why I love you, baby. You always know when to do the right thing."

He smiled. "I know when you're playing me, just as you are now. Let me concentrate and then maybe we'll talk about what we're gonna do for the rest of the day."

"Promises, promises."

He turned his head back to the map and started tracing lines with his finger. She left him to it. He was the planner. She was the doer. His expertise stopped at around six-hundred yards; hers was twice that.

"I think I've got it," he said. "We ignore the cemetery completely. They'll have it under wall-to-wall surveillance, and there are no long-range shooting options to fall back on. We could plant a few explosives around the grave plot, but they'll use sniffer dogs before locking down the area. Besides, bombs are messy, indiscriminate things. No guarantee we'd get the outcome we want."

"Are you thinking what I think you're thinking?"

"Yes, we'll hit them en route. There are a few roads they can take away from the judge's house, but ultimately they have to cross the Potomac, right here at the Fourteenth Street Bridge." He pointed at the map and moved his finger slowly to the left. "This looks like an ideal site. We can set up a crossfire, if we can find a nice tall building."

"Which side of the river?"

"Just as they get on the bridge. Doesn't matter if they use the I-395, or the George Washington Memorial Parkway, they'll have to get on the overpass to access the bridge."

"What if they decide to use a helicopter from Bailey's Crossroads?"

"Not an option. Nowhere to put down near the cemetery. It would still mean a car journey at one end or the other, which means they have to figure we'll know that."

"But what if they *do* use a chopper?"

"In that event, I guess you'll get that early vacation you've been pushing for."

CHAPTER 31

IT TURNED OUT to be a busy time for FBI teams that morning. Less than two-hundred miles from the Evans' property, Carl Freeman had assembled his own squad in preparation for a forced entry into the industrial compound at Lynchburg, Virginia. Freeman's group numbered more than thirty agents. He was going for shock and awe.

Three sides of the compound had already been breached during the night by six-person units, which were concealed as best they could behind a mixture of sparse undergrowth, discarded pallet stacks and rusting trailers. They felt vulnerable and exposed in the harsh daylight, each man and woman willing Freeman to transmit the go signal.

A mile from the compound Freeman waited patiently for the transport promised by Drew Eisler. It eventually lumbered into view shortly after ten o'clock. It was a six-wheel, thirty-ton Volvo dump truck commandeered from a municipal depot where it usually made twenty trips a day ferrying rock and soil to a landfill site. A big yellow monster, it had an open box-bed, enclosed by six-foot steel walls, and a cab that stood ten feet from the ground. All in all, an ideal ramming tool.

The municipal driver climbed down from the cab and handed Freeman two high-viz jackets. He was excited to be part of an FBI operation, but apprehensive about whether his vehicle would be returned in one piece. Hardly his concern, however, since he guessed his employers had already agreed a compensation deal with the Feds should anything go wrong.

Freeman and Eisler donned the jackets and motioned for ten more agents to scramble into the truck's box-bed. One look at the dust and grime told them their shiny black suits would need a visit to the drycleaners after this was over. They accepted the situation stoically and squatted below the rim, knowing they couldn't be seen by anyone at ground level.

Eisler took the wheel and Freeman climbed into the passenger seat. The cab stank of sand and cement, and stale smoke, and the remnants of too many fast-food packages. Freeman hit a door switch to depress his window while Eisler tried to familiarise himself with the surprisingly short gear lever.

The rev counter jumped to maximum, the gearbox grated, the types spun, and the municipal driver turned away in disgust.

Eisler settled into a steady thirty mph and centred the truck down the road leading to the industrial compound. Freeman found a clipboard and held it in front of his face, as if checking for an address. Two hundred yards from the compound's main entrance, he thumbed a comms mike and issued instructions. *Thirty seconds on my mark. Mark.*

The dump truck eased to a crawl in sight of the guard hut. Freeman pushed the clipboard in front of Eisler and gesticulated behind him in what he hoped was a clear indication to the sentries that they had taken the wrong road. Eisler nodded and swept the truck over to the left verge in preparation for what seemed to be a three-point turn. As soon as he was lined up with the main gate, Eisler slammed it into first gear and stomped on the accelerator to build up the giant machine's rev count. It shuddered and sprang forward as soon as Eisler eased off the clutch.

Three guards looked on, bemused by the scene. Attitudes changed dramatically when the big yellow torpedo headed straight for them. They were still jumping out of the way when the gates were torn open, a glancing blow from one end of the aluminium structure sending one of the men flying through the air.

Three other figures raced from the guard hut. One was carrying a Steyr bullpup assault rifle, which he aimed at the passenger side of the dump truck. Ten agents suddenly emerged above the rim of the box-bed, their Glocks scanning for threats. Three of them zeroed in on the gunman. They each unleashed three-round bursts, which almost cut the guard in two, before catapulting him back through the doorway.

Any fight that was left in the remaining guards quickly dissolved. They flung their arms in the air and dropped to their knees. Freeman shouted at four agents who disembarked to secure the area. As soon as they vaulted from the truck, Eisler again hit the accelerator and barrelled towards the front of the building.

The assault teams at the rear and sides of the

building used plastic explosives to gain entry. A small rear door was easily disposed of, though shaped charges had to be used on the side panels to create openings where none existed. The three pops were simultaneous. Automatic fire followed almost immediately.

At the front of the building, Eisler decided not to use the truck as a battering ram. The door was a heavy-duty affair, as tall as it was wide, and likely to cushion the impact sufficiently to snarl progress. As Freeman jumped from the cab he could hear the sound of gunfire from the interior of the warehouse. The guards in there seemed to be putting up stiffer resistance than their counterparts at the gate.

They quickly found a small wicket gate built into the mainframe. It wasn't locked. Freeman pulled it outwards, standing back to allow his team to race inside, in an alternate right-left fashion. By the time he stepped through the gap the shooting had stopped, partly because the agents who had breached from the rear had already accounted for three armed workers, but mostly because the remaining gunmen had surrendered at the sight of reinforcements from the front of the building.

There were eight men still standing. Not all were armed and most had hidden when the shooting started. They now stood in the centre of the vast space, their eyes switching nervously between the bodies of their buddies and the hard looks of their captors. These were no kind of professional gunmen. At best they were street-type brawlers who fancied themselves as hard men; at worst they were delusional amateurs.

Freeman waited until the men were zip-tied

before he allowed himself to gaze around the warehouse. He was not a man to shock or surprise easily. This, however, was definitely a jaw-dropping moment.

The three flat-bed trailers which had rumbled into the site the previous evening were parked to one side, their freight containers lying open and already half-filled with goods from the main factory floor. Beside each trailer stood portable stairs and winch cables that reached down from large ceiling beams. This was a slick well-rehearsed operation.

It was the contents of the containers which took Freeman's breath away.

The first one, especially so. The rear was filled with four high-stacked pallets of gold, silver and platinum ingot bars. They were standard-sized bars, each just over twenty-seven pounds in weight, or twelve-and-half kilograms in recognised international trading. At a rough count Freeman estimated sixty gold bars, which he knew from Bureau newsletters, were worth around half-a-million dollars per bar. Thirty million in total.

Alongside the gold ingots were twenty bars of platinum, often more expensive than gold, but lately trading at around eighty per cent of its more illustrious rival. Even at four-hundred thousand dollars apiece the haul came in somewhere around another eight-million dollars.

Freeman continued doing the mental arithmetic as his gaze moved across to the silver ingots, the poor relation of the precious metals on show. Thirty bars at roughly six thousand each added close to another couple of hundred thousand dollars to the total.

But this particular Aladdin's Cave was not done with yet. In front of the pallets were stacked cartons of good old Uncle Sam greenbacks, heavily encased in vacuum-packed polythene. The denominations were all *Benjamins*, the hundred-dollar variety named after Founding Father, Benjamin Franklin. They are issued by Federal Reserve Banks in blocks, or straps, of ten-thousand-dollars. Each of the polythene cartons comprised fifty blocks, or half-a-million dollars. There were twenty blocks in total.

Freeman peered closer. The dates on the top block of notes were from seven years ago. Several faded stickers on the outer casing revealed the lettering, *Iraq Funds*. These bills had been earmarked for a war zone to pay for restructuring, or security training, or bribes, or all manner of other spending that Capitol Hill would disavow in an instant. So these had either gone to Iraq and back, or maybe never left the USA in the first place.

The Iraq connection continued in the second freight container. Freeman didn't need a close inspection to conclude that the jumble of statues, ornaments, figurines, jewellery, carvings and paintings were looted artefacts from around the time of the American-led 2003 invasion. The distinctive Middle East designs and colours were a dead giveaway. He knew that the National Museum of Iraq, based in Baghdad, had been looted in the hours before the first USA troops rolled into the city. More than eight-thousand items were still unaccounted for. Not any longer.

Not much work had been done on filling the third container, the farthest away from the roller-shutter doors. There were four crates, each measuring three feet by two feet by eighteen inches, propped against the rear of the unit. Freeman found a crowbar, which he used to pry open the wooden lids, revealing stacked rows of Beretta M9s, still in their greaseproof wrappings and reeking of gun oil. These were the favoured American sidearm of the day, shipped across to support ground forces, and somehow shipped back without seeing the light of day. Or perhaps, like the Benjamins, they'd never even left USA soil?

The floor of the container was also littered with an eclectic assortment of other loose weaponry. There were a half-dozen Colt M16A assault rifles, a small stack of Colt M4 carbines, and a row of ten Barratt M82 anti-tank rifles. The haul was complemented by a mound of ammunition boxes, which according to their faded labels were a mixture of 9mms, 7.62s and 50 calibres. Enough to start, or end, a small war.

Freeman descended the portable stairs and hailed Eisler. "Find anything else?"

"We've just located the heat source that showed up on the thermal imaging. Can you believe this? It's a smelting furnace, built into the warehouse floor, and surrounded by boxes of loose jewellery and gold and silver coins, all from Iraq. It's like one of those *Cash for Gold* operations. Someone was making a lot of money from old Saddam Hussein's fall from grace."

"What the fuck have we stumbled into here?"

"Ask me," Eisler said, "this could be the biggest coup the Bureau's had for years. It's gonna take weeks, maybe even months to sift through the provenance of these items. The value must run into the tens of millions."

"Not even close, Drew. This operation has been going on for years, probably right back to 2003. What we have here could be only the tip of the iceberg. God alone knows what's already passed through this place."

"Why sit for so long on the cash bundles and the stolen artefacts? Surely these should have been disposed of before now?"

"No, just think about it. You can't suddenly flood the market. The cash alone needs careful laundering, which requires a big organisation to release the notes into its normal operations in a way that won't raise the suspicions of the Federal Banks. These are serial-marked bundles, so recirculation needs to be patient and methodical, probably involving scores of business transactions, both here and throughout the Middle East. Same goes for the artefacts. My guess is one item at a time inside the black market for dealers. The beauty about doing it this way is that the value keeps increasing the longer the item is sought after."

Eisler shook his head at the enormity of the situation. "The real good news is that the Director is gonna be mighty pleased. This'll be a big feather in his cap."

"I've gotta admit," Freeman responded, "we needed something like this to take the pressure off for the way we handled the McAndrew affair. Looks like I'll be holding onto my job for a while longer. I'm gonna head back to Washington to break the news in person. You're in charge here, so get these clowns off for interrogation and lock this place down tight until the forensic boys are let loose."

"Much as I hate to say it, Boss, but a large part of the credit has to go to Quinn. If he hadn't steered us in the right direction we might have missed this."

"I know, Drew. Time for me to eat some humble pie and see if I can't help him out a bit more."

CHAPTER 32

TWENTY-EIGHT HOURS. And every minute would be precious to Quinn. It was eleven o'clock on Monday morning, with the funerals scheduled for three o'clock on Tuesday afternoon. Sometime between now and then Quinn would have to find the assassins and eliminate them. Simple formula in theory, not so simple in practical terms.

Actually, his calculation was already out by at least an hour before he even got started. It was a notional allocation of time for a sit-down with Chief Justice Fleming. The old man needed to hear some blunt assessments, maybe a theory or two, and definitely some strong recommendations. Whatever time it took would be money in the bank for down the line.

There was another actuality Quinn had to factor in. He'd have to review by Google Maps the topography around the cemetery and all roads leading to it. He'd have to visit at least two key target areas, maybe more if his online research pointed to additional weak points. Total time required: at least another four hours. His twenty-eight had reduced suddenly to twenty-three.

No time to waste. So, when he faced Fleming across his desk study he launched straight into it. "I'm not going to beat about the bush, sir. I think there's more you could be doing, there's definitely more that the FBI and the Washington Metro Police could be doing, and don't get me started on the other agencies that are supposed to be lending a hand. We've spent two days looking for a camper van and we've had a photokit picture in circulation for the better part of twelve hours. And what have we turned up? Diddly squat. How hard can it be to lock down Washington with the kind of manpower that's supposed to be at your disposal?"

Fleming nostrils flared. "I'm told that everyone is giving this their priority attention. I have assurances direct from the White House that no stone is being left unturned. I'm as anxious as you are, in fact doubly so, but I fail to see where I've let the side down or where the fault lies with any of the agencies you mentioned. You've got a bee in your bonnet, son, and I'd rather you spit it out."

"Okay, try this for size. When was the last time you demanded an update? Who's co-ordinating the search and what have they been telling you? By my calculation there are only so many places you could hide a camper van, so you start by ticking off trailer sites and underground garages and shopping mall parks and visitor attractions and private rental storage units. Divide those by the right number of searchers and you get the ground covered in less than twenty-four hours. You add in traffic camera surveillance and beat patrols and helicopter flyovers and pretty soon you get a situation where a small bug couldn't crawl through the cracks. Yet that's not what's happening. Our assassins have shifted position more than once, and they appear to be doing so with impunity. Does that really add up in your book?"

Fleming's shoulders drooped. "I must admit when you put it that way we should have heard something by now. What do you suggest I do about it?"

"I'm not going to sugar-coat it, sir. You should get off your backside and start screaming down the phone. Every hour on the hour. These are your grandchildren we're talking about, but no-one else seems to be taking this as personal as they should. That's got to stop right now, and you're the only man who can fire a rocket up their asses. Tell the President you're not happy, tell him there's some sloppy work going on, and demand an immediate change of direction. Get him to agree the appointment of a new co-ordinator, someone with the experience and the knowledge and the directness to make a difference. Every moment from here on in is vital."

"I'm guessing," Fleming said, "you have someone in mind?"

"Yes, I do. The FBI lead agent in your son-in-law's case is the best man for the job."

"Hold on just a minute!" Fleming showed the first sign of anger. "This is the guy who put us in this position in the first place. If he hadn't botched the way in which my son-in-law was handled we wouldn't be here. For the first time, I'm beginning to doubt your grasp of the situation."

"Hear me out, sir. Yes, there's a lot of things Carl Freeman could have done differently. Personally, I think his strategy was okay except for the fact that he didn't take into consideration that someone from his own Bureau would rat him out."

"What are you talking about?"

"Someone had to tip the wink to Devlin Montgomery about your son's involvement in an ongoing FBI investigation. Freeman did his best to cover the tracks, but there's not much you can do when a suit in the same food chain decides to throw an unforeseen spanner into the works. It had to be someone in the FBI, nothing else makes any sense. Freeman was shafted and he doesn't deserve to carry the can. From what I've seen he's a top-notch agent with a lot already invested in how things go down. There's no-one more determined to put things right. One thing I know for sure is that he'd move mountains to protect Charlie and Sophie. That's the kind of guy I'd want front and centre."

Fleming shifted uncomfortably on his seat. "I'm not so sure I agree with you, although I can't fault your logic. Supposing I do bring Freeman into the equation, what then"?

"You bring him in all the way. No half-measures. You insist he has full autonomy, you make sure every agency jumps at his command, and you get him whatever he needs, whenever he needs it. Trust me, sir, I'm not wrong about this."

"I don't know why," Fleming said, "but I can't argue with anything you've said. I've known from the start that it was a blessing you became embroiled in this terrible business. I'll do what you say, but only if I have your assurance you'll work closely with Freeman to resolve the matter."

"Actually, sir, I think it's best that Freeman and I work this from two separate ends. I intend to leave here shortly and you won't see me again until it's all over."

"You're jumping ship?"

"Hardly, sir. I need to get out there. I'm sick of trying to second-guess my way around. I'll keep in touch with Freeman through the satphone he supplied, but I want to do things differently. I'll start by scoping out likely sniper attack spots, which I'll pass onto Freeman, but for the most part I intend to blend in on the ground. The best solution will be to stop an attack before it starts and the best way I can do that is by walking the walk, so to speak. I'm banking on Freeman getting to them before I do, but I want to be out there as a fall-back in case they somehow squeeze through."

Fleming rose and shook Quinn's hand. "Good luck, my boy."

Quinn gestured to the old man to sit down again. "There is one other thing I need to discuss with you. It's a bit delicate, and it's probably out of order, but I would like you to listen to what I have to say."

Fleming dropped back into his seat. "Fire away."

Quinn took the cue and started talking. He spoke for more than ten minutes and finished just within the overall hour he'd set for the meeting.

The twenty-eight hours, which had become twenty-three, had now become twenty-two. Quinn had remained at the Fleming house for just over fifty minutes, during which time he'd completed his internet searches and wolfed down a tray of Mrs Brennan's sandwiches before leaving in a commandeered Secret Service station wagon. It had taken just over four hours to visit two locations, measure the ground, check traffic flows, and estimate sight lines. It was an hour longer than he'd hoped, but it was time well spent.

He'd decided from an initial survey that there was no suitable sniper spot within range of the Glenwood Cemetery. Any attempted hit would therefore have to be made against a convoy en route from the Fleming estate. His preferred choice of location was at or near the Fourteenth Street Bridge, with a back-up point less than a mile away, among the buildings of suburban Washington.

He abandoned the station wagon at a car park near Columbia Heights. From here on in he'd walk or use taxis. He went into a cafeteria and took a seat by the window, trying to put himself into the mind of the assassin less than a day before a hit. What would he do? Where would he go? How would he pass the time? He suddenly remembered to stop using the singular. There were two of them, possibly an item, maybe even man and wife. Would a couple stay cooped up in a camper van? Would they go out for a meal, take in a show, try to look touristy?

In their minds they would feel untouchable. They were important people. They'd done this lots of times. They were well off. Why not splash out a bit? So where would they go? The fanciest, most expensive restaurant they could find, that's where.

Quinn jumped away from the table, planted a ten-dollar note for an untouched coffee, and headed out into the city's rush-hour traffic.

Carl Freeman was headed into that same traffic when his cellphone buzzed in its dashboard mount.

The small window announced the caller as William Perry, Director of the FBI. It was not a call Freeman cared to take right now. He wanted to face Perry across a table and size up the man's reaction to the successful raid at Lynchburg. If he was being honest, he wanted to show the smug bastard what real smugness really looked like.

He was headed into the Mount Vernon Square intersection, less than twenty minutes from the FBI offices at Eleventh Street. Maybe thirty minutes, given the way traffic was building up. Perry could wait that long.

Freeman ignored the call until it eventually rang off. Several minutes later the phone chirped again, this time with an incoming text message. He hit the open button. It was from Perry.

URGENT: Message from the White House. Pick up the phone!

Freeman couldn't believe what he was reading. What could the White House want with him? One thing was for sure; it couldn't be ignored. He fingered through the phone's log and hit redial on the last call. Perry answered immediately.

"So, you respond to mention of the White House, but ignore your own Director? Where the hell are you, Freeman?"

"Sorry, sir, I'm close to the office. Caught up in traffic. Should be there within twenty minutes or so."

"Just make sure you are. You're skating on thin ice as far as this Bureau is concerned, even if you have made some friends in high places. How come you're suddenly flavour of the month? Been doing a bit of brown-nosing, have we?"

"I don't quite follow, sir. What's this about a message from the White House?"

"Don't play the innocent with me, Freeman. I've just had the President himself on the line. They want you to take charge of the hunt for the assassins who've targeted the McAndrew children. For some reason they seem to think you're the best man for the job, and that the rest of us have to jump to your attention until this thing is over. How'd you wangle that one?"

Freeman was lost for words. He couldn't decide if this was a wind-up or somehow true. "I know nothing about this. What exactly are they asking me to do?"

"Apparently you've to become some sort of multi-agency czar. In the President's words, if you crack the whip people better start dancing. Just so we understand each other, I won't be putting myself under your spell. This is a time-limited deal, so when it comes out the other end I'll be waiting to bring you back down to earth."

Freeman was fed up with the bullshit. "Director Perry, I'm not sure I understand or merit your hostility. If what you say is true, and I've no reason to doubt it, then you'll do exactly what's required, which means anything I say is required, and you'll do it without your usual propensity for rudeness."

"Stop right there, mister. Do you know who you're talking to?"

Freeman ignored the question. He'd been handed a poison chalice, not least because his own Director was being sidelined, which in itself would have ramifications somewhere down the line. Perry was not the sort to take things like this on the chin.

He'd find a way to undermine and belittle Freeman's efforts, and then he'd look for payback when the dust settled. But all was not doom and gloom. Freeman was determined to make this work. And he still had an ace up his sleeve. It was for that reason that he chose to keep quiet about what happened in Lynchburg. It was also for that reason that he decided to go on the attack.

"I want you to listen carefully to what I have to say, Director Perry. If you don't feel up to obeying a direct order from the Commander-in-Chief, feel free to step down. I'll be there shortly and I expect a full and comprehensive briefing. In the meantime, make some calls and get me all available agents within two hours travel time to Washington. Rustle up the NYC Police Commissioner and the Metro Transit Police Chief, and have them in your office within thirty minutes. Also, tell the Mayor's office what we're up to and see if she wants to sit in."

Freeman paused a few beats before ending with: "Now, Director, do you know who you're talking to?"

CHAPTER 33

WHEN ONE PARTY has something it's willing to trade and another is willing to pay the price, that's commerce at work. Call it reciprocity or *quid pro quo*, or good old-fashioned capitalism. Except when the deal going down is of the nefarious kind – a category which almost always has one other intrinsic characteristic. Distrust.

Which was why Devlin Montgomery emerged from the Park Avenue branch of the Atlantic Bank of New York flanked by two recently-recruited minders.

Which was why the Chairman, Tyrell B Linkmeyer, was waiting in an underground car park two blocks away on East 53rd Street with his own version of protection.

Between the two groups there was enough concealed weaponry to deal with any eventuality. Not that anyone wanted the hassle. Make the switch, walk away, no hard feelings. But neither side really believed that was going to happen. And so they were ready for whatever came their way. One wrong move, an involuntary twitch, or even a disapproving look, could start a bulletfest.

Montgomery chose to walk. He wanted to take in the surroundings, maybe spot a tail or signs of danger lurking on the sidewalks. The pen drive, all two inches of fifty-gig storage, was in his trouser pocket. The password to the forward-dated email was in his head. The Chairman wouldn't settle for one without the other.

He also carried a smartphone, one he used only for emergencies. He'd no doubt the hawkish Clarissa would be at the meeting with her iPad, ready to validate the efficacy of the data unit and email access. While she was doing that he would be checking the money transfer and hitting a pre-set button to redirect it on its merry way. Job done, go their separate ways, no handshakes.

Montgomery's minders fell into a well-rehearsed routine. One in front, one behind, right hands hidden under their jackets. They were both ex-cops who'd transferred to the dark side many years previously, working for the highest bidder and not fussy what the assignment entailed. Despite only just getting out ahead of a number of disciplinary and Internal Affairs probes into their conduct while servants of the great New York public, they'd somehow managed to finagle private eye badges, together with permits for the concealed carrying of firearms. It leant a certain credibility to their new personae, but to those who knew them, they'd always be low-life, opportunistic thugs.

The trio paused on the sidewalk directly opposite the entrance to the underground car park. Montgomery scanned left and right, looking for something out of place, though he was well aware of his limitations in matters concerning fieldwork. He couldn't see or sense any dangers, which didn't mean there was nothing for him to worry about. Not worrying got you killed. He drew in a deep breath, stepped off the sidewalk, and crossed between two lanes of traffic on the one-way street. He took a pedestrian ramp to the lower level and stood for a moment to acclimatise to the gloomy exterior in contrast to the bright sunshine outside.

He spotted the Chairman perched against the bonnet of a Range Rover. As expected, Clarissa stood tightly to his elbow. As expected, Dumb and Dumber, the heavyweight muscle, lurked on either side.

Linkmeyer was seething with rage. Only seconds before, he'd received another call from his FBI contact.

You were too late. Everything in Lynchburg has been seized.

There was no discussion. The man on the other end always spent as little time as possible, even on a burner phone. He knew how things worked. Pass the message, cut the link, and bin the phone. He had a ready supply of burners, and knew how to use them.

The information brought Linkmeyer out in a sweat. The warehouse losses would all but bankrupt him, particularly since he was already committed to paying sizeable compensation to his Iraqi suppliers. There just wasn't enough left to go around. He might be able to do a long-term deal with Asif Morani by taking less commission against future transfers. Yes, that might work! But not if Montgomery's damning information found its way into Morani's hands. The deal he'd come here to transact would still need to be done – but with one important change.

Montgomery will die here today!

Linkmeyer whispered quickly to his entourage, just as footsteps echoed off the concrete floor. He looked up to see Montgomery and two other men walk forward.

"I see you brought company," the Chairman said. "Let's get this over with."

"Just wanted to play match-up with you," Montgomery responded. "Are you ready to make the money transfer?"

"Let's first see the storage pen. When Clarissa has verified it, you'll get your filthy reward."

"You know, we could play *you go first* all day, but I'm a reasonable man, so here's part of what you want." Montgomery smiled as he handed the data pen to Clarissa.

She immediately plugged the USB into a camera adapter dangling from the side of the iPad. Her fingers danced across the keyboard before switching to a screen scroll that went on for several minutes. Finally, she looked up at Linkmeyer and nodded.

"It seems you've actually kept your word, Montgomery. Now, what about the password for the email?"

"Not so fast, Mr Chairman. I think we can proceed with the money transfer before going any further." Montgomery lifted a piece of paper from the breast pocket of his jacket and pushed it across to Clarissa. "My bank details. Make the transfer."

She hesitated for a moment, waiting for a signal from Linkmeyer. His eyes flickered briefly and she went back to attacking the handheld keyboard. Montgomery turned on his smartphone and waited patiently for news of the transfer.

"Completed," Clarissa snarled.

"I'm not seeing anything," Montgomery responded. His two minders closed in. So too did Dumb and Dumber.

"It takes a few minutes for the transfer to go through," Linkmeyer told him. "While we wait, I want to see the email password."

"Not so fast, Mr Chairman. I prefer to wait."

"Don't be a bloody cretin," Linkmeyer exploded. "Thanks to you, our warehouse at Lynchburg was raided by the FBI this morning. They got everything, which means they're probably already closing in on us. We don't have fucking time to stand around here for longer than necessary. You're getting your money so give me the password. Now!"

Montgomery looked genuinely shocked at the news. He pulled another piece of paper from his jacket and handed it to Clarissa. "It's all there. Hurry up and get this over with."

As soon as the second piece of paper was safely in Clarissa's hands, Linkmeyer's minders pulled weapons from below their coats. Their actions were practiced and fluid. But so too were those of Montgomery's ex-cop bodyguards. Suddenly there were four guns in experienced hands, each seeking an individual target.

Before any of the group had a chance to fully understand what was going on, a strange voice echoed through the underground chamber. "Everyone stand perfectly still."

Five men emerged in a line from shadows at one end of the park. They all carried suppressed sub-machine pistols, grasped comfortably at waist height like men who knew how to use them. They were all dark-haired and dark-skinned, and wore sunglasses which looked strikingly incongruous in the gloomy surroundings. They walked forward with a swagger; some showing snarled lips and white teeth, in a display of superiority and disdain for the two groups in front of them.

Montgomery knew instantly who they were. So did Linkmeyer. This was no double-cross. A third party had just entered the equation, which would have been fine except the message couldn't be transmitted in time to their respective back-ups. Before anyone could speak, the two ex-cops turned their weapons towards the new threat. As far as they were concerned someone was interfering with their payday and they needed to do something about it.

They should have known better. Experience should have told them not to play heroes when the odds are stacked. But they'd grown complacent in the private sector; got things their own way for too long, perhaps even thought they were indestructible. They were quickly disabused of their beliefs.

They both died instantly. Bursts of 9mm parabellums from high-powered weapons at a distance of less than twenty feet will do a lot to a body in a blink of an eye. It was fortunate for the others that the two had been standing slightly detached from their companions, which meant the through-and-through rounds sailed into open space before their terminal velocity was arrested by contact with parked cars and a concrete wall. By then, of course, they'd already done the required damage to the two ex-cops whose vital organs were shredded by the blitz. What remained simply folded and crashed to the ground.

Montgomery squeezed his eyes closed, as if he could be saved from harm by the simple expedient of shutting out the danger.

Dumb and Dumber threw their arms in the air.

Clarissa screamed and dropped her precious iPad, which shattered on the concrete floor.

Linkmeyer alone maintained a modicum of calm, even though his heart was racing and he felt a sudden weakness in his legs. He pushed his palms towards the gunmen and somehow found an authoritative voice. "Stop this nonsense! Tell us what you want."

The man in the centre of the assault group stepped forward. His colleagues peeled off in pairs to stand either side of their targets. The leader removed his sunglasses, folded them into a breast pocket, and readjusted his machine pistol on his hip. A smile danced briefly across his cragged features.

"You know exactly what we want," Mr Chairman. "My principal is not pleased with the way in which you have stolen his money. We are here to get it back and to make sure you pay for your sins."

"I've already squared this with Asif," Linkmeyer responded. "There's no need for this violence. I have ensured him that full reparation will be made."

"But he cannot trust you. You have said the responsibility for this lies with your Mr

Montgomery here, yet he says it was you who dipped your fingers into our pockets. Perhaps it is best that you both pay the price."

Montgomery stumbled forward and glared into Linkmeyer's face. "You piece of shit! Don't think you can squirm out of this one. It was you who gave the orders and creamed off the top. You had a good thing going there, but nothing's ever enough, is it?"

"Come, come, Devlin, this is all too unseemly. I'm sure our friends here know exactly who to blame."

"I'm not taking the fall for you," Montgomery shouted and turned towards the lead gunman. "It's all on there," he said pointing at the broken iPad. "The pen drive has full details of everything that went down. When the chairman reported that he could only get forty cents on the dollar for washing the cash he was lying. He was getting seventy and eighty cents. There are also details of how artefacts were sold for up to three times the price that was quoted to Mr Morani. By my reckoning, he put away more than fifty million dollars on top of the agreed commission fees."

"Preposterous!" Linkmeyer roared.

The assault team leader watched the bickering with amusement. He bent down to lift the broken iPad and pulled the data pen from its docking. "Perhaps this will reveal all. Our people will analyse what is on here, although I suspect Montgomery's version is close to the truth, if only because such a snivelling coward will have made sure he covered his back. In any event, Mr Chairman, you have forty-eight hours to make an initial payment transfer to Mr Morani. Let's say thirty-million-dollars, which seems to be about half what is due after we account for interest charges."

Linkmeyer blanched. "I can't raise that kind of money in such a short space of time. Mr Morani has to be reasonable. We can continue to make profits together for years, so let's not spoil a good thing. I will arrange for a new monthly payment structure which will include restitution until everything has been settled in say a year from now."

"I'm afraid, Mr Chairman, you don't have a year. Forty-eight hours for the first payment, to be followed within seven days by whatever Mr Morani says is the final balance."

"That's unrealistic. It would put our little arrangement in jeopardy. We can still make a lot of money together."

"No. The operation has come to an end. It is time for compensation."

"What do you mean it has come to an end?" Linkmeyer asked. "We can go on for years. There are still places in the Middle East to exploit."

"Alas, no," the gunman said with finality. "I overheard your admission that the warehouse where you've been keeping our goods is now under the control of the FBI. So, it appears it really is all over. Perhaps we will find another broker who will handle our future transactions in an honourable way."

Linkmeyer slumped against his Range Rover. "Just a temporary setback," he lied. "I can deal with this. I just need some time."

"No more time! You will come with us until the payments have been made. Your secretary will come too. She appears to know all about bank transfers."

"Please, no," Clarissa whimpered.

The gunman swiped his left arm in a blur of motion. His knuckles caught the hapless Clarissa on the cheekbone, drawing blood and sending her spinning across the floor. At the same moment he flicked his eyes at one of his men, who depressed the trigger on his Heckler and Koch, and stitched holes in the breasts of Linkmeyer's minders. They died before they could understand what was happening.

"I don't like loose ends," the assault group's leader said. "Does anyone else want to argue with what I have asked you to do?"

"No, no," Linkmeyer responded feebly. "I'll come with you to help clear up this mess."

"I can help too," Montgomery pleaded.

"We shall see."

CHAPTER 34

THERE ARE ONLY so many cups of coffee a person can stomach in one day. Even for a prolific imbiber as Quinn was, the basic ingredients of an Americano, black, no sugar, which was the way he liked it, contained a mixture of ingredients that worked both for and against the body. Caffeine, which is basically a plant toxin, like nicotine and cocaine, is great for keeping people awake by blocking neuroceptors for the sleep chemical, Adenosine. And that suited Quinn just fine. Unfortunately, coffee is also a diuretic, which can bring on dehydration when consumed in large quantities, which conversely leads to people becoming abnormally tired. Which didn't suit Quinn.

And so, he pushed the silver-plated coffee pot to one side as he hunched over a table in the foyer of the Hay-Adams Hotel on 16th Street. It was his seventh hotel lobby and his seventh coffee pot in an afternoon of frustration. He'd flashed his temporary FBI badge and photofit image of the female jogger at managers, maître d's, concierges, and wait staff, none of whom had seen anyone resembling the image. He'd checked evening dinner reservations, scanning for bookings by couples who maybe stood out as last-minute, or were not regular patrons, or had an attitude problem, or who'd used a cash inducement to somehow secure them a corner table in a sold-out dining room. He was clutching at straws, but right now he had a bale-full to go around.

He'd told staff his target was a dangerous terrorist, any sighting of whom had to be reported immediately. He'd left copies of the photokit and his satphone number, not that he expected anything to come from it, though the bases had to be covered and he had to be sure there were as many eyes as he could recruit at the venues most likely to be visited by the assassins.

He walked out of the Hay-Adams and glanced at his wristwatch. It was almost five o'clock in the afternoon. Barely twenty-two hours until the funerals. Having dispensed with Washington's finest hotels it was now time to turn his attention to the next category; the best and most expensive restaurants the capital had to offer. He'd already decided against thumbing through directories or using his old friend Google. If you wanted to know where to go in any city, you asked the one group of people whose job it was to know. Taxi drivers.

Before that, there was had one thing needed doing. If he couldn't continue to use coffee to spike his adrenal glands, there was always the next best thing. It was ten years since he'd packed them in, but right now he craved a cigarette, those wonderfully-addictive, nerve-settling, four-inch sticks of magic that would help him through what was going to be a long night. He ducked into a small convenience store, located the tobacconist counter, and bought a pack of king-size filter-tips, plus a disposable lighter.

Seconds later he was sitting on a park bench, sucking in a lungful of nicotine and over two-hundred other harmful chemicals, and feeling the tension drain from his body. He ignored disdainful looks from passers-by and watched as the sun finally fell below the horizon. The city's street lights would be his friends for the next dozen or so hours.

He finished the cigarette, stubbed it under his heel, and walked to the kerbside. A yellow taxi appeared a few seconds after he raised his right arm. He smiled. *You gotta love the faultless radar of cab drivers.*

He climbed into the rear seat and nudged across to an opening in a metal guard rail that separated drivers from their fares. The meter was already running, showing a base charge of four dollars winking in the centre of the console. *You gotta love the way cab drivers make their money.*

Quinn peeled off three twenty-dollar notes and flashed them at the driver. "This is for you taking me to the best, most exclusive restaurant in town."

"That there's a sweeping statement," the driver replied. "Do you want Italian, Chinese, Indian, Irish, British, German, French, Russian......"

"Cut the geography lesson," Quinn interrupted with a hint of anger. "I want to go where the in-crowd go. If you don't know, just say so and we'll call it quits at four bucks."

The driver was not about to let a sizeable tip walk out the back door. He was a squat man, with thinning blond hair and a bushy moustache that blended into his pale features. He looked to be in his fifties and had the repartee of someone who'd done this job for a long time. "I gotcha, sir. Don't hold with all this foreign muck myself. Can't beat a bit of good old open-range Texas beef, marinated in those cheffy sauces, and served on proper plates with a charge that's probably more than the whole herd was worth to begin with. I know just the place, if you've got a stomach for their prices and a wallet that doesn't pay much mind to those kinds of things."

"Now you're talking," Quinn said. He'd suddenly warmed to the driver's rapid and undisguised change of tone. "I tell you what; how do you fancy making a night of it?"

"You mean, you've more than one place to go and you want to hire me for the night?"

Quinn glanced across at the driver's badge clipped to the passenger-seat window visor. It identified him as Ernest Valverde. "Here's the deal, Ernest. I need a chauffeur for the next eight or nine hours. I don't mind paying your company, but I'd rather give the cash to you. How does a thousand bucks sound for your exclusive time and knowledge?"

"What's the catch, mister? Are you into something shady? I can't be involved in anything like that, not with a wife, eight kids and a mortgage to worry about."

Quinn flashed the FBI badge. "I'm looking for someone who might be visiting top-end restaurants this evening. It's a long shot, but that's what they pay us Feds to do. Have we got a deal?"

"Yes sirree, you bet. Only thing is I can't use the company cab. I knock off in about thirty minutes. If you have time to wait for me, I'll leave the cab at the depot and use my own car. It's not exactly a limousine, but it'll get us around. Please say yes. I could do with the money."

"Don't sweat it, Ernest. Drop me off at this first location and come back when you're ready. It should only take me twenty minutes, so don't dawdle. I've a lot to get through."

Ernest swivelled in his seat and pushed his hand through the grill opening. "Thanks, mister. I've suddenly developed this bad tummy ache, which means I'll have to knock off earlier than usual. I'll be waiting outside the restaurant ten minutes after you go inside. Do you mind me asking who you're looking for?"

Quinn was about to ignore the question before remembering he needed whatever support he could get. "As a matter of fact, I'm looking for two people, probably a husband and wife, although as yet I only know what the woman looks like."

Ernest reached across his seat and lifted a piece of paper which he flashed at Quinn. "Don't suppose it's her, is it?"

Quinn recognised the photofit. "Yes, it is. Where did you get that?"

"Every driver got one today. The city's awash with these flyers. They say she's some kind of terrorist."

This time Quinn didn't respond. He knew the blanket circulation of the photofit was down to Carl Freeman. He thumped the seat. He'd forgotten to check in with Freeman about the best possible locations for a sniper attack.

At that moment Carl Freeman was in a makeshift control room at the FBI's 11th Street headquarters.

It had been the longest afternoon of his career, sometimes fraught with emotion and tension, other times lightened by a sense that he had ticked all the boxes and done everything he could to find the assassins. Now it was down to the hard part. Waiting.

The meeting with agency heads had gone better than he'd hoped for. The Director had done what was asked by bringing the key players together. He'd disappeared after that, which was a relief to Freeman, mainly because he didn't want to deal with the man's interruptions and inflated sense of his own importance.

Not that there weren't other egos in the room. Freeman dealt with them at the outset. "I'm glad everyone who should be here is here. Not that any of you had any choice in the matter. This comes direct from the White House, which means we demand full co-operation and the Sunday-best management of all your resources. You people deserve the utmost respect for the jobs you do and the time you've put in to get where you are, but know this: for the next twenty-four hours I couldn't give a rat's ass for all that. I'll be making demands, I'll probably be blunter that I ought to be, and I'll run the risk of alienating some, if not all, of you. Get over it. Give this two hundred per cent, or leave now and send your deputies, or your deputy-deputies, or whoever is prepared to do what has to be done. I won't stand for anything less that total commitment."

If there was going to be a challenge to Freeman's authority he knew it would come from the NYC Police Commissioner. Here was a guy ten years into one of the toughest public posts in America yet somehow, he continued to bat successfully through City Hall and Capitol Hill politics while retaining the grassroots support of his men. Not an easy balancing act, and certainly not one for the fainthearted.

"I want to say something, Agent Freeman."

"Please, feel free, Commissioner."

"Right, here it is. I've been around a few rum things in my time, some of them little more than cockamamie interferences from just about everyone in this town who thinks they've got a right to oversight, including whatever incumbent happens to be in 1600 Pennsylvania Avenue. Sometimes I go with the flow, most times I don't. I use a simple measurement for our political masters; do they really want something done the right way and for the right reasons, or are they just vote-buying. When it's the latter, I tend to rail against their ambitions."

"Not for me to comment on the politics or otherwise," Freeman interjected.

"Not asking you to do so, Agent. My point is that we all know what's going down here. We know whose grandkids' lives are at stake and who has been rattling the White House sabres. Can't fault Chief Justice Fleming for using all the clout he's got at his disposal. I'd do the same thing in his situation, although I'm left to wonder whether we would all be here if this was the grandchildren of Joe Public. I'd like to think so, and maybe when the dust settles we all should use what we're doing here as a yardstick for going forward."

The Commissioner paused and looked around

the table before pointing at Freeman. "This young man has come among us with fire in his belly and a fuck-you-all attitude that I've found quite refreshing. Has he been disrespectful? Hell, yes. Has he said some things we're not used to hearing? That's a given. Maybe he thinks this is a great career move. Maybe he believes he'll get all the kudos if this works out. Time will be the judge of that. But for now we listen to what he has to say. I for one will be standing four-square behind his temporary authority. So, Special Agent Freeman what do you want us to do that we've not already been doing?"

Freeman could have hugged the man. In one simple, heartfelt speech the Commissioner had cleared the path for action. Now it was time for Freeman to step up.

"Let me first say," Freeman began, "this should not be a matter of resources. Don't worry about your budgets, Federal dollars will meet all your expenses, including overtime, use of helicopters, or anything you need to get the job done. I'm going to run through what I think should happen, which means I expect it to happen, but the implementation is down to you. All reporting is through your usual chains of command, although I need each of you to provide me with hourly updates."

He held up a copy of the photokit. "I know your people have already been issued with these, but I've taken the liberty of having another twenty-thousand printed up. I want them to cover the city like a tsunami. I want everyone with a uniform to hand them out in every public place, particularly rail and bus depots, hotels and guesthouses, and make sure every cabbie in Washington has one. This woman and her partner should have nowhere to hide."

Freeman quickly changed tack. "We know this couple were travelling in some kind of campervan. We need to find it. Underground and overground car parks, trailer parks, airports and private garages. We need at least twenty mobile units tasked with this one specific job, while at the same time we need to redouble our surveillance of traffic and CCTV outlets. My guess is that this campervan won't be on the move. They've holed up somewhere and won't resurface until they're ready to carry out their executions. But that doesn't mean we stop doing the surveillance."

Everyone in the room seemed to squirm at Freeman's terminology. He wanted them to. "I have tasked FBI units with checking hotels just in case our couple have permanently ditched the campervan. Don't worry about duplication of effort. I'd rather we visit a place twice than not at all. Is there anything I've missed?"

"Yes," said the Commissioner. "We need to go public with this. Stick with the story about a terrorist-related manhunt, or in this case womanhunt. Get her face out there in every news channel and social media outlet at our disposal. The public don't like this sort of thing, so let's enlist as many of the seven-hundred-thousand people who live in the DC area as possible."

Freeman nodded. "I agree entirely, Commissioner. In fact, I want you to call a press conference and be the public face on this."

CHAPTER 35

THERE WERE SEVEN restaurants on the cabbie's list of important places to eat in Washington. It was not that Ernest Valverde had frequented any of the establishments personally, certainly not at around two-hundred-dollars a plate in some cases. He'd put the compilation together based on his experiences of driving high-rollers around the capital, and listening to their pretend knowledge of all things culinary. Most times he'd smiled at their choices, fully aware that people like those usually put more store on high prices as a measure of quality rather than what was actually served up to them.

Quinn sat in the front passenger seat of Valverde's ancient Volkswagen as it nosed against the kerb on the corner of Pierce and First Street NE. In front of him was a garishly-lit building which housed the sixth restaurant on Ernest's list. The owners hadn't gone for understatement. Flags of as many nations as they could fit on the frontage waved above a sign that read *La Culinaire Extraordinaire*. As if to emphasise the point, a montage of colour photographs depicting various menu concoctions adorned the gable wall in a twenty-by-twenty square-foot advertising board. Not the sort of place that could be missed on a drive-by.

"I'll be the usual twenty or thirty minutes," Quinn told Ernest as he climbed from the vehicle and headed for the front door. He heard the sounds of animated voices, and through the window saw what looked like a packed house of patrons. He pushed through the door and came up against a strategically-placed counter which barred further progress. A tall man, overdressed in a blue suit with gold braiding, flashed Quinn a condescending smile. No doubt the blue jeans and windbreaker was not the customary garb for *La Culinaire Extraordinaire*.

A sign in front of the guardian read *Phillippe Rousseau, Maître d'hôtel*. "Bon soir, Monsieur, may I 'elp you?"

Quinn almost laughed at the phoney French accent, but decided against it. "Reservations," he said simply.

"C'est impossible. We are fully booked."

Quinn shook his head and flashed the borrowed FBI badge. "I'm not here to dine, just to check your bookings for tonight. And do me a favour; drop the phony French accent. I'm guessing your real name is Phillip or Phil, so what do you say we hurry this along?"

The man looked around before bending forward towards Quinn. "Please, keep your voice down. I'm Phillip Ross, but they demand that I act as if I'm from Paris. Seems to keep the patrons happy.

"Needs a bit of working on."

"Yeah, I guess it does. Why do you want to see our reservations?"

Quinn give him the well-rehearsed explanation of looking for terrorists and showing the photofit. "Have you seen this woman?"

"Non, I mean no, there's nobody here who looks like that."

"The restaurant seems pretty full. How can you be sure?"

"I admit I can't be certain. This is our second block of the day. We go through about eighty diners each sitting. This is the seven-thirty intake; the next is the late-night shift starting at ten o'clock."

Quinn looked over the Maître d's shoulder at the seated diners. "I'm going to take a look around. When I come back I want to see a list of the ten o'clock bookings."

The young man was about to protest, but thought better of it. He lifted a section of the counter and admitted Quinn into the inner sanctum. From his new position, Quinn could see most of the faces in front of him. He stood for a while scanning the younger females, hoping to catch sight of a ponytail, although he conceded she had probably changed her appearance with a wig. It didn't matter. He'd pick out her gorgeous features in a heartbeat.

There were parts of the room he couldn't see, so he moved forward between tables, aware of the glances he was getting from diners. There was one table in the farthest corner which was dimly-lit with an ornate candle centrepiece. He could make out a man, probably in his thirties, sitting opposite a short-haired brunette whose back was all that was offered to Quinn.

He needed a closer inspection. He angled in on

the table from one side, concentrating on the parts of the woman's face that began to emerge as he drew closer. Her profile showed youthful skin, lightly dusted with make-up and pink lipstick which complemented a one-piece maroon leather catsuit that clung to a lithe body. She was ticking enough boxes for him to make an even closer examination.

He walked straight to the table. "Pardon the interruption. I'm searching for my sister and from a distance you looked remarkably like her."

The woman turned to give him a full view. It was not her. "Have you seen enough," she asked with a hint of annoyance.

Quinn realised he'd been staring at the woman, allowing his eyes to roam over her body. "Forgive me, it's just that you look so much like her and I'm frantic to find her. She's run away from home and our parents are anxious to get her back."

It was a bit over the top. Ordinarily he would have shrugged aside hurt feelings, but this was not an occasion to draw unnecessary attention. Unfortunately, that's what he got.

The woman's companion rose from his seat and pushed his hand firmly against Quinn's chest. "Why don't you get the hell out of here, you pervert?"

Quinn grabbed the man's hand, twisting his thumb in a particularly painful *Krav Maga* martial arts hold that rendered the recipient helpless. Quinn pushed backwards and eased the diner into his chair. "Don't say a word and don't make a fuss, otherwise I might have to break a few bones. Let's put this down to a misunderstanding and leave it at that."

Quinn released his grip, smiled at the woman

and walked away, ignoring the murmuring of voices from surrounding tables. He found the Maître d' hunched over the bookings register, pretending he hadn't seen the commotion. "This is our list for the rest of the evening."

It took Quinn only a few moments to scan down the registry He was looking for parties of two. There were four listed, each with a scribbled note beside their names. He couldn't make out the scratchy writing, most of which seemed to be in coded shorthand.

CD entered/accepted.

FB by Metro.

RC.

SO priority.

"What do these mean?"

Ross, aka Rousseau, followed Quinn's finger down the list. "The first means that Card Details were entered in advance and accepted. We insist on this in cases where we don't know the client. If they don't show up we take the full booking fee of fifty dollars."

"What about the others?"

"Forward booking by the Metro Hotel. We have a commission arrangement with all the top hotels.

"The next is Regular Client. This means we trust the booking without prepayment.

"Lastly, this was a Senator Office booking, which gets priority."

Quinn nodded. Nice arrangements. He went back to the first entry. "How do you record the entry and acceptance of the credit or debit cards?"

"Simple really," Ross responded. "We take the card number and security number and pre-book the required fee. This is held in our name until such time as we process the completed transaction."

"Is the fee always fifty dollars?"

"No. That's a minimum. Usually we ask for fifty per cent upfront for the anticipated costs of the meal?"

"Which is?"

"Allowing for wines and other drinks, a table for two usually costs about three-hundred dollars."

Quinn shook his head in amazement. He hadn't come across these pre-booking requirements at any of the other establishments. Maybe there was something *extraordinaire* about this place after all. "Do you have the card details for this transaction?"

"I don't think I can give those out. You'll need to speak to the owner when he comes in at ten o'clock."

"I don't have time to wait," Quinn grated. "Get me the details or I'll close the place down. This is a federal terrorist investigation and we don't take kindly to anyone who stands in our way."

"Sure, sure. Look mister I only work here. I'll get you what you need." He bent below the counter and removed a filofax-type folder, bending pages against the ring binder until he found what he was looking for. "Here it is. The booking came in at three o'clock this afternoon. It was a Mastercard in the name of a Mr John Atwood. The expiry date is...."

"I don't need that. Write down the full card number for me."

Back in the Volkswagen, Quinn turned to Ernest. "All these smells have made me hungry. What say we grab a burger and fries somewhere?"

"Now you're talking my language. I take it a

plain old diner will do instead of these fancy joints?"

"Works for me, Ernest."

"About time you checked in," Freeman snorted when he heard Quinn's voice. "Where are you? There's a lot going on here and I haven't heard your report about possible sniper locations."

Quinn had finished his snack before making the call. It was eight o'clock on Monday evening. Nineteen hours until the funerals.

"Sorry about that, Agent Freeman, but I've had a lot going on here too." Quinn quickly brought him up to speed on his afternoon exertions, including mapping out two potential danger points for the funeral cortège. "I picked out a number of high-rise buildings that overlook the areas. You need to blanket these points with agents, particularly by putting men on several rooftops and posting look-outs at all entrances."

"Ordinarily, Quinn, I would tell you in no uncertain terms that we know how to do our jobs, but I guess I owe you one for what you've done so far. What I don't get is how these snipers will be able to take long-range shots at blacked-out vehicles without knowing which car their targets are travelling in. I just don't see the logic."

"They're a tag team, which means one will try to disable the convoy while the other will be at ground level at the ambush site to apply the coup de grâce."

"That could be messy. They've got to figure we'll have an armed escort ready for such an eventuality."

"I agree," Quinn said. "Depends how desperate they are to complete the contract. They won't worry about collateral damage, that's for sure. The one on the ground could sprint from cover using an automatic weapon, maybe even attach limpet mines to each of the convoy vehicles, and be outta there before your agents know what hit them. If any of your men do manage to get out of the vehicles to repel the attacker, the sniper will take them out. It won't be pretty, and it's not what professionals like these are used to doing but, like I said, it depends on how desperate they are."

"Do you really see it going down that way?"

"To be honest, Agent Freeman, "there's no other way it can be done. What we need to do is make it impossible for them to execute their plan. Flood the two potential target areas with agents, be obvious and upfront about it too, and make them think twice about proceeding."

"Are you banking on them aborting."

"No. I'm banking on catching them before then."

"Let's hope you're right. Anything else for me?"

Quinn dug a piece of paper from a pocket in his jacket. "Run a search on a John Atwood. It's a bit of a stretch, but worth a full press at your end. Start with details held by Mastercard." He read out the card number and explained where he'd got the information. "Don't ask me to go through my reasoning for this because frankly I wouldn't know where to start. I just think it could be important."

"Already on it."

CHAPTER 36

THE FINAL RESTAURANT on the makeshift list proved to be a washout. Unlike the previous establishment it didn't require upfront booking fees, which meant there were no card details to track. It hardly mattered, as Quinn quickly discovered. All the evening diners were already in situ when he'd arrived, so all he had to do was take a look around the sea of faces. His photofit female was not among them.

He slumped back in the Volkswagen seat, rubbed tired eyes, and stared through the windscreen, wondering what to do next. What had started out as a long-shot exercise was proving to be just that. He'd wanted to be proactive, and had even nursed a forlorn hope that he'd somehow stumble across the assassins. Who was he kidding in a city which stretched across sixty-eight square miles? But what else could he do?

"Is that us finished?" Ernest's voice cut through Quinn's growing despair.

"Let me think," Quinn said with more harshness than he intended. There could still be other restaurants to visit, perhaps every bit as swanky as those Ernest had come up with in his own partisan fashion. And what about theatres and cinemas? Would it really be practical to sit outside these kinds of venues and watch people coming and going? What were the chances of actually seeing his targets? Talk about the proverbial needle in a haystack!

He looked at the dashboard clock. It was now nine in the evening. Eighteen hours to go.

"Drive around for a bit," he ordered Ernest. "I want to kill a bit of time before we head back to *La Culinaire Extraordinaire*. Show me some sights, take me to where people go for walks, let me see the public face of Washington. You never know; we might get lucky."

Ernest sensed Quinn's despondency. "You know, my old pappy used to say that when things look bleak and there seems to be no answers, you should chill out and stop over-reaching. Empty your mind, think positive thoughts, and the sun will eventually shine through."

"Did it work for him?" Quinn asked.

"Well, he reared ten children on a dirt farm back in Mexico with hardly two pesos to rub together and lived to the ripe old age of ninety. Must have been something in it, but I just thought it was an easy way of getting out of actually doing something about his predicament. Don't get me wrong; I loved the old fella even if he was a bit of a dreamer. One thing's for sure, the sun didn't do a blind bit of good when it came to putting food on the table or shoes on our feet. That's why I crossed the border looking for a better life."

"And have you found it?"

"Naw. Leastways, not until I ran into you."

"How the hell have they got my image splashed all across the city?"

John Atwood squeezed his wife's hand and whispered. "Keep your voice down. It must have been the guy whose presence you sensed on the final jog around the Fleming estate. There's can be no doubt now that he was their spotter and somehow he connected the dots after seeing you."

"But how?" Karen Atwood asked in exasperation. For the first time in her life she was genuinely frightened.

"Doesn't matter, babe. It is what it is. Good job you thought about using one of your many disguises. That picture in circulation bears no resemblance to who you are now. The fact that we've been freely walking around all day tells us the cops and Feds won't make the connection. Let's relax and enjoy the film. Afterwards, we'll have a great meal and an early night."

The couple were seated in the back row of a cinema, which had fewer than twenty customers in an auditorium that could have accommodated ten times the number. Earlier, they'd gone for a walk in one of the local parks, after which they'd spent a few hours of window-shopping in the Georgetown area. That's when they'd noticed the posters and the unusually-high numbers of police on foot patrols. One officer had even stopped them to ask if they had seen the woman in the photofit!

Before setting out on their downtime, Karen had tied her hair into a bun, fitted a red-coloured wig that reached to the back of her neck, and donned large white-rimmed glasses. She'd used foundation creams and blushes to dull her bright skin, and wore a stylish knee-length patterned dress below a cream designer raincoat. The final look was a million miles away from the athletic model Quinn had spotted on old Chad Evans's pathway.

"You can't be serious? We have to leave Washington tonight. We can't go ahead with our plans, not now. Be reasonable, John."

"I'm being practical, babe. Just look at you. Would you recognise yourself? Nothing's changed. We saw the mini digger preparing the grave at the Glenwood Cemetery, so we know they're going ahead with the funerals as planned. We've picked out our spots, we'll do a final check on the area in the morning, and if anything is out of place, we'll pack it in. If not, we proceed as agreed. Come on, it's not like you to get cold feet."

She snuggled into his shoulder. "Maybe you're right. Maybe I just want this over with so that we can head to the Bahamas for a month of doing nothing except working on our tans."

"We'll be there before you know it."

Quinn's satphone thrilled on the seat beside him. He snatched it up and hit the answer button. "What've you got for me?"

"Quite a lot, as it turns out," Carl Freeman responded.

"I could do with some good news for a change."

"How about three pieces of good news?"

"I'm all ears."

"We've found the campervan."

Quinn shot up on his seat. "What? Where?"

"Thought that'd get your attention. It was parked in a shopping mall complex over at Georgetown. We'd intended keeping it under surveillance, but a quick check of security cameras showed it's been there for over twelve hours. Looks like it's been ditched."

"So did you move in?"

"Sure did. Our techies found all kinds of interesting things, including partial prints, a few discarded wigs, and print-out maps of the area around the Fleming estate. Looks like you were right again about their choice of transport."

"What about the partials? Did you get a hit on them?"

"That's the second piece of good news I was going to tell you about. We got a trace print for a guy who was in the system for a felony in Wyoming fifteen years ago. Seems he jacked a car belonging to a neighbour and pleaded out for six months with a follow-on two-year probation. Hasn't been heard of since."

"What's the name?"

"None other than John Atwood."

Quinn blew hard on his cheeks. "You know what this means, don't you?"

"Yep," Freeman said. "It seems your restaurant hunt has paid dividends. We know where this guy will be about thirty minutes from now. I'm assembling a team and will be there quicker than you can say....whatever it is you were about to say."

"I was about to say, hold the fort. I want in on this. In fact, I want to take the lead. Don't try to freeze me out."

"You're welcome to tag along, but this is an FBI takedown and we'll do it my way. Don't think I'm not grateful to you for getting us to this point, but it's now our show. Too much at stake for it to be otherwise. That's how the game's played, Quinn, so don't get all belligerent on me."

Quinn said nothing. He let the silence stretch into more than ten seconds while he thought through his next move. Finally he spoke. "Okay, I'll agree to work with you on two conditions."

"Thought we'd done with ultimatums."

"Hear me out. If you go into the restaurant I want to be beside you. We do this together, or I'll jump the gun on you. I'm closer to the location than you are, so there's nothing you can do to stop me. I'm going to take these people down, with or without you. I'm not looking for glory, just the satisfaction of knowing that two great kids won't have to worry again about someone trying to kill them."

"For Chrissakes, Quinn, don't you think that's what I want too. We stand a better chance of getting these fuckers if I can get a cordon in place to make sure there's no possibility of escape. I'm not going to let you put that in jeopardy. We can't afford to make any mistakes."

"I don't intend to make mistakes. I intend to kill them."

"I'll pretend I didn't hear that! This is not an execution operation. I want to avoid gunfire, if at all possible. Best case scenario is that they give themselves up and co-operate in a full investigation into how this all came about."

Quinn allowed his anger to bubble to the surface. "Don't be so fucking naïve, Freeman. We know how this came about; we know it was Devlin Montgomery who set it up, so don't let Atwood and his partner plead their way out by providing information we've already got. Someone in the Justice Department will dream up a mishmash of conspiracy charges which will let these people walk free after five years, maybe less. Who's to say they won't go after Charlie and Sophie once they get out, or take out some other family just for a payday?"

"Don't forget that's what you also do for a living, Quinn."

"Cheap shot, even for you, Freeman. It's water off a duck's back, as far as I'm concerned. No matter what you say it doesn't mean I'm wrong."

"You're right about one thing; it was cheap, and I apologise. You've done a lot for this operation since the get-go, and don't think I'm not grateful. I also know it was you who helped put me in control of the hunt, so I owe you double-thanks for the opportunity to put things right. All I'm asking is that you work with us and see how the chips fall."

Quinn mulled over Freeman's plea. He'd no doubt the FBI man was genuine. "Okay, we'll do it your way to start with, but there's something else that needs to be factored in."

"Is this your other condition?"

"Let's just call it a fallback situation. What if, for any reason, Atwood doesn't show up at the restaurant? He might lose his appetite or simply decide not to go. Where would we be then?"

"I agree we have to take it into consideration. We've got his picture from updated social security paperwork, so we'll be able to issue these along with his wife's ID. I forgot to tell you, the pretty young jogger *was* Karen Atwood. They were married in Tennessee five years ago."

"Great work," Quinn said, "but we need to do

more. If Atwood used his credit card to book a restaurant, the chances are he might also have used it to book an hotel room. We now know he's abandoned the campervan, which means he needs somewhere to put his head down until tomorrow afternoon. Worth getting your people to check registrations against the Atwood name."

"I'm not going to say I'd already put this into action because frankly I haven't. It should have been the first thing that occurred to me, but the restaurant booking got my full attention. I'll put a team on it now. What's your take on them carrying sniper rifles around? Would these not stand out, even in well-concealed bags or cases?"

"Not at all," Quinn replied. "They'd go for a weapon that would easily strip down to fit in a normal suitcase or holdall. Something like a Barrett M99 or a Heckler and Koch PSG. There are plenty of others on the market, although those two would be my best guess. They'd want to keep their rifles with them at all times, which means I don't think they'd use a luggage locker at train station. However, might be worth putting a second team on possible locker-space provisions around the city."

"I know, belt and braces," Freeman laughed down the phone. "I'm beginning to learn how your mind works, Quinn. I'll meet you at a side road leading to the restaurant in let's say twenty minutes."

"Wait, wait," Quinn shouted before the connection was ended. "You said you had three pieces of news?"

"Yes, almost forgot. There was a shoot-out in New York this afternoon. Four dead, two with links to Devlin Montgomery. We're still working on identifying the other bodies. It looks like the rats are turning on each other."

"Sure hope so."

"I've despatched Drew Eisler from Lynchburg to take charge of the investigation. Good man, so we should know a lot more about what went down when he's had a chance to take stock. That reminds me, there is actually a fourth piece of good news that had slipped my mind when I was last talking to you. The tip-off on the property search that started the McAndrew court case paid dividends. We've hauled in millions in stolen cash, gold and ancient artefacts. But don't go looking for a finder's fee!"

"Just knowing I've helped is reward enough, Agent Freeman. Never know, it might even lead to another thank-you."

"You've got it," Freeman laughed. "Seriously though, forget the harsh words I tend to come out with now and again. I've come to respect your intuition, which is almost on a par with Eisler's, and that's saying something."

CHAPTER 37

THE COUPLE DIDN'T pay much attention to the latest in the long list of *Star Wars* sequels. It was either number nine or ten, but keeping track was one for devoted fans, which John and Karen Atwood were not. To them, it was just another film, a means to pass a few hours in the sanctuary of a darkened cinema. They'd always found it difficult to relax on the eve of a big score.

John's increasing restlessness finally boiled over. "Fuck this, how about some fresh air?"

"You took the words right out of my mouth."

They pushed back their hinged seats and shuffled towards the central aisle, not bothering to take a last look at the big screen where Daisy Ridley was standing back-to-back with John Boyega, wielding Lightsabers in readiness to repel an impossible number of Stormtroopers. It was the kind of action that kept true *Warriors* glued to the edge of their seats. The Atwoods were totally disinterested.

A slight drizzle greeted their emergence onto the sidewalk outside the Cinemark Theatre building. The area was busy with pedestrians heading for the many bars and bistros which dotted the landscape around the nearby Capital One indoor arena. Shania Twain concerts had been headlining there for the past week.

"We've got an hour until our dinner reservation. Want to take a walk or grab a drink?"

In response, Karen pulled the raincoat lapels around her neck. "We've done enough walking for one day. How about a few glasses of wine? I know we're only about ten minutes away from the restaurant, but we'll get a taxi after we finish our drinks."

"Sounds good to me."

The argument started as soon as Freeman finished briefing his men. He had more than fifty agents in position, most of them stationed along an inner cordon which circled the restaurant. A dozen were despatched to an outer ring at a distance of one hundred yards. Quinn was impressed by the deployment.

What he wasn't impressed with was Freeman's insistence on the Atwoods being taken down before they entered *La Culinaire Extraordinaire*. Quinn wanted all bases covered, which meant getting someone inside in case their targets were disguised enough to fool the watchers. And he wanted that someone to be him.

"We've already gone over that ground, Quinn. I'm trying to avoid a shoot-out in a packed restaurant. Even if we miss the targets going into the restaurant, the Maître d' has my number to call as soon as the Atwoods arrive and ask for their table. In that event we'll wait for them to leave."

"Doesn't have to be a shoot-out. I could disable the pair before they get a chance to reach for their weapons. The best they can take in there are handguns, which have to be concealed in a holster or a handbag, which gives me a big head-start, seconds-wise, while they reach for the weapons. I can pass off as a diner minding my own business until I see an opening."

Freeman scoffed. "You'd need a change of wardrobe and some female company to stop them making you in a heartbeat. All due respects, but you look exactly like the kind of person the Atwoods would be watching for. I'm not risking it, and that's final."

Quinn had to admit his size and looks would work against him. He slumped back in the passenger seat of Freeman's Ford Expedition and balled his fists in frustration.

"You don't do the waiting game very well," Freeman quipped.

"Normally I'd tell you it's what I'm best at. This time is different. I just want this to be over with."

"Still thinking about Charlie and Sophie?"

"Nothing else to think about. It's why we're here."

The Ford Expedition's digital clock flashed 10:30, the time booked by the Atwoods. Quinn had watched it creep forward minute by minute, passing the time wondering about Ernest Valverde and his newly-acquired fortune. Before dispensing with Ernest's services, Quinn had walked to an ATM and withdrew two-thousand dollars, twice the agreed fee. The smile on the cabbie's face was worth every cent.

"Don't forget to wait for the sun," Ernest had said as he pumped Quinn's hand.

"Make sure you use that money for your family. Don't repeat your father's mistake of living in a dream world."

Ernest's parting shot had been delivered humorously in a stereotypical Mexican accent. "Si, senor Quinn, I will tell my bambinos they are getting ze new shoes because a crazy gringo has more money than sense. Also I will pray that you see more sunshine than rain. *Gracias, muy amable.*"

No hay de qué, had been Quinn's response. The literal translation was *nothing to thank for*.

Valverde's wide-eyed reaction had been almost as precious as when he'd received his cash reward.

Quinn shook the memory away and looked again at the clock.

10:34.

Where the hell are the Atwoods?

10:40.

Something's gone wrong.

10.48.

Quinn fidgeted in the seat. "I don't like this. They're not coming."

Freeman nodded in agreement. "It's not as if they could have been held up in traffic. There's hardly anything moving on the main thoroughfares. Maybe they're just a couple who like to keep people waiting."

"Not the type," Quinn responded. "They live by the clock. Timing is everything. It becomes second nature, even down to routines such as getting up in the mornings, or taking a shower or buying a newspaper. It's a matter of developing an ability to break their days down into segments. I've known some who don't have a wristwatch yet can tell the time with uncanny accuracy. If these people are late, it's because they're not coming."

"We'll give it another ten minutes."

10.58.

"That's it," Quinn said. "We need to move to Plan B. Anything back from checking hotel registrations against their name?"

"We'd have heard by now."

"Get on the blower and ask for updates. We can't keep sitting around here."

Five minutes later, Freeman ended his tenth check-in call. "Nothing. They've covered more than thirty hotels, but there's no registrations in the name of Atwood."

Quinn grabbed the car door handle. "Think I'll do some checking of my own."

"Where are you going?"

"We have to narrow the search. We know the Atwoods are not using the campervan, so they had to have found an hotel or boarding house without using their personal credit cards. Maybe they used bogus cards, or paid in cash. I'm still banking on them being a lot closer than we think."

"How does that help?"

"Remember those high-rise areas I identified as possible sniper locations? We need to see if there are hotels or rooms to let within those buildings. I should have thought about it earlier, but I was concentrating on rooftops without paying enough attention to the bigger picture."

"To be fair," Freeman offered, "until a few

hours ago we thought the Atwoods were still using the campervan."

"Doesn't mean we shouldn't have considered the what-if scenarios. That was a mistake, one that needs to be put right."

Freeman lifted his phone. "Might as well get some of these agents to help with the search."

Quinn grabbed the FBI man's wrist. "No, this is a one-man job. Those suits out there will be spotted a mile away. Better that I poke around for a few hours on my own. We've still got plenty of time."

"Maybe you're right, but I'm coming with you."

It was the third Ford Expedition that made the hairs stand on the back of John Atwood's head. Bulky, blacked-out SUVs were a common enough sight in Washington, the home of more alphabet agencies than just about any other city in America. If it wasn't the Secret Service or the FBI, it was most likely Homeland Security, or ATF, or the DEA. Hell, even the Bureau of Prisons had started using them.

Citizens usually paid no heed to the comings and goings. Late-night convoys were a different matter though. Certainly enough to get Atwood's attention as he sat at a bar window and gazed across the three-lane that led to the Georgetown area. His interest was more than piqued when a fourth, fifth and sixth SUV blurred across his vision. Someone was in a hurry to get somewhere.

And Atwood was beginning to think the unthinkable.

It has to be the restaurant! How did they know about it? Fuck, he'd used his own personal credit card instead of one of his aliases. It was the first one to hand, and it was not as if he needed to worry about it, especially since his identity was well off the radars of law enforcement agencies. So how could they know? A glance at a wall-mounted television provided the answer.

The sound was turned low, but the pictures painted the full story. The centre of the screen was taken up by images of white-suited men emerging with bags from his abandoned campervan. A rolling information bar filled in the gaps: *FBI agents locate vehicle belonging to suspected terrorists. Arrests imminent.*

Atwood nudged his wife and flicked his eyes towards the television. The face of Police Commissioner Irving Greenway now filled the screen, the lower part of his body hidden by a lectern cluttered with a bank of microphones. It was obvious from the smug smile that the Commissioner was delighted at whatever information he was imparting to the assembled members of the media.

Atwood fought a temptation to ask the bartender to turn up the volume, but thought better of it. Moments later, he was relieved he hadn't done so.

The Commissioner was suddenly replaced on screen by two photographs. The rolling information bar changed to a new announcement: *Husband and wife, John and Karen Atwood, on the run as the net closes in.*

How was this possible? What had they found in the campervan? He was certain he'd scrubbed the vehicle clean, but had he? He knew all about fingerprints and DNA. It came with the territory. In his line of work nothing was left to chance, which was why he always wore surgical gloves and rubbed down surfaces before abandoning equipment. Sure, there were times when it was impractical to keep the damn things on, but that's why a final scrub-down was used. Did Karen mess up? She hadn't used any of the wigs they'd left behind, so there was no chance of getting a DNA sample from loose hairs. She'd taken one from a new collection and left the rest to save space in their holdalls. And anyway, Karen was never in trouble before.

Christ, it's me! That fucking car theft from way back had resulted in his prints getting into the system. It was so long ago he'd forgotten all about it. *What a fucking idiot!*

He could feel Karen's body shaking beside him. He leaned across and whispered, "we have to get away from here. We'll leave separately and meet outside. I'll go first."

He kept his head bowed and inched away from the table, careful to avoid eye contact with other customers, most of whom were standing in small groups around a packed counter, and paying no attention to the television. He made it to the street and walked quickly to the corner of an alley that was shadowed from the glow of streetlights. Two minutes later, Karen emerged and looked around. She spotted him, almost running to his side as the headlights from a passing car illuminated the sidewalk.

"What do we do, John? They have us cornered."

"I should have listened to you, babe. We should have blown this town twelve hours ago. Now, I'm not so sure we can."

"There's always a way. If anyone can find it, it's you."

"You saw what's happening. They're painting this as a terrorist alert, the smart bastards. The place is crawling with cops and Feds, and they have our faces. We'll be lucky to last an hour unless we duck out of sight and lie low."

"What are you suggesting?"

"We don't have many options. Return to base, wait things out for twenty-four hours, and then steal a getaway vehicle. We can't use taxis or trains, not until we put D.C. behind us. Your disguise will get you through, but you'll have to help me change appearance before we split up."

"I'm not leaving you!"

"Be sensible, babe, they'll be looking for a couple. I reckon you can grab a bus into Virginia. I'll hotwire a car and meet you there. After that, we'll be able to head just about anywhere we please. The problem is that we're done in America, so we cross the border and see where we go from there."

"So, we call off the hit?"

"Nothing else we can do."

CHAPTER 38

THE BUILDINGS LOOKED a lot differently at night. Quinn had scanned them in daylight from a reverse perspective near the Fourteenth Street Bridge. He had nothing to go on, except some distinguishing rooftop features, such as multiple chimney stacks or clusters of telecommunications dishes. The problem was that he couldn't spot these from ground level.

"Is this the right area I reported to you earlier," he asked Freeman.

"Yep, you mapped out four possible locations. I have two teams nested on the roofs here and there," he pointed to two buildings. "They have coverage of the four sites."

"What about ground-level surveillance?"

"We have three teams in tricked-up works vehicles dotted around the vicinity."

"Can we risk keeping them there, bearing in mind the Atwoods will check for any ambiguities? Remember, these guys will have a vantage point using high-powered scopes to sweep around the buildings close to where they're holed up."

"We can't just sanitise the area, Quinn. I'm confident my agents know how to blend in."

"Alright, but do me a favour and let them know we're here. I don't want any of them breaking cover for the wrong reasons."

Freeman smiled. "See, you can work with a team when you put your mind to it."

They covered five blocks over the next thirty minutes. No hotels, no guesthouses, nothing to suggest there was a way for the Atwoods to put their heads down for the night. This was one of Washington's business areas. Street-level premises were the usual mix of fast-food outlets, dry-cleaners, small grocery stores, a print shop, a florist, a betting shop, and a liquor store. All were closed and shuttered for the night.

Above the retail frontages were storeys of offices, most of which seemed to be tied to the financial sector, judging by the rows of nameplates, announcing the homes of insurance brokers, investment bankers and mortgage lenders. There was also a smattering of law offices and real estate brokerages. But no nameplate for *J & K Atwood, Assassins for Hire.*

Freeman looked across at Quinn. "What are you smiling at?"

"Nothing, just a silly thought that crossed my mind."

Quinn walked to the centre of the road and looked again at the buildings that had a view to the Fourteenth Street Bridge. He couldn't have been wrong about this! The sniper point had to be somewhere within this location, which meant the Atwoods had to be find shelter here. They needed time to set up their nest, and they had to ensure they wouldn't be disturbed. Nothing else made any sense.

But there were no hotels, no abandoned buildings, no empty warehouses. Nothing but office blocks. Short of breaking in and gagging staff, there didn't seem to be any options. Too messy. Too many things to go wrong. What about callers to the office, or routine deliveries, or families worried about the absence of loved ones? The chances of discovery over a minimum 24-hour siege were simply too great.

So what did that leave them with? His mind whirred and clicked through a sequence of alternatives, all of which were dismissed immediately as either impractical or fanciful. For the first time in his life Quinn had to admit he was stumped.

But suddenly a new thought came charging through the morass of negativity. He sprinted back to the sidewalk and marched purposefully down the row of buildings, stopping to check each office doorway.

Freeman fell into step beside him. "What's going on? What are you looking for?"

Quinn didn't respond. He kept walking. He kept walking and checking. And then he stopped.

"What is it?" Freeman asked.

Quinn pointed at a door which had the usual festoon of individual push-buttons and names on a wall plaque beside it. His finger rested midway down the plaque where one of the name-spaces had a different kind of message: *OFFICES TO LET. THIRD FLOOR.*

Freeman looked, quickly plugging into his partner's reasoning. "Why not? Could account for us drawing a blank with hotel registrations. Wonder how many of these other buildings have redundant offices waiting patiently for temporary tenants?"

"We'll check them all after we get through with this one."

"What? We're gonna just waltz in there?"

Quinn ignored the question and withdrew a silver-plated gadget from one of his trouser pockets. It resembled a bottle-opener, though no bottle-opener Freeman had ever seen had curious-looking antennae and a protrusion that resembled a drill bit. He watched as Quinn inserted the piece into the lock and depressed a button that activated an almost noiseless motor. The door clicked open.

"What is that thing?"

Quinn quickly pushed the lock-pick back into his pocket. "The FBI really has to get up to speed with the latest technologies. Guess that's why you need the private sector."

"Smartass."

Both men drew Glock pistols and tiptoed into the building. Ahead lay a dozen stairs within a narrow well that led to some sort of landing area. Quinn took point and edged upwards, keeping to the sides of the stairs to avoid squeaky floorboards. As it turned out, the stairs were of the concrete variety, but old habits die hard.

He reached the top and scanned around. It was some kind of foyer, with small groups of armchairs and coffee tables dotted around the generously-sized room. Two elevator doors were set into the main wall, and another stairwell could be seen in the farthest corner.

"Looks like some sort of breakout space or reception facility for tenants," Freeman offered.

"How do you want to play this?"

"We take the stairs. No sense announcing our arrival by using an elevator. One of us will have to stay here while the other heads for the third floor."

"Let me guess," Freeman chided, "you take the stairs and I stay put?"

"Just long enough for me to reach the right level and keep anyone from using the elevator. Give it five minutes and follow me up."

Karen Atwood stood behind her husband and checked her handiwork. The blonde dye and new middle parting had worked wonders on John's hair, although it was her make-up skills and the addition of thin-wire reading glasses that produced the real transformation. Quite simply, his own mother wouldn't be able to identify him.

"Great job, babe. I'm beginning to believe we'll get out of this mess after all."

"We've still a long way to go, but I'm suddenly more confident than before."

"Attagirl! You'll be sipping Margaritas before you know it."

She walked across the room and looked through lace curtains towards the Fourteenth Street bridge in the distance. Not that distant actually. She'd already calibrated it at 852 yards through the Leupold Mark 4 telescopic sight. Pity she wouldn't get to take the shots.

The plan had been simple. Yet, if everything went their way, it would have been highly effective. They'd run through it a dozen times, tweaking and buffing the edges, making allowances for the unforeseen, trying to second-guess the reactions of what would be a large contingent of FBI and Secret Service agents.

She would be the one to stay behind in the rented office. The Barrett M82 would be mounted in place behind the lace curtains from no earlier than two o'clock. No sense taking the risk of being seen by spotters on nearby roofs. Since there was no way of knowing precisely when the convoy with the McAndrew children aboard would set out on its journey to the Glenwood Cemetery, she couldn't leave it later than an hour before the appointed time of the funerals. They could be unusually early, or fashionably late. She'd be prepared either way.

That danger would come when she opened the window and created a tiny space in the curtains. The barrel would protrude no less than two inches beyond the curtains, a virtually invisible anomaly, provided there was no wind to billow the lace apart. Which was why she'd wait until the last possible moment.

She had three 10-round detachable box magazines for the rifle. The success or failure of the mission depended on how she used the first one. The lead vehicle had to be disabled immediately, stopped in such a way that it blocked the progress of those travelling behind. She'd place a 50-cal bullet directly into the quadrant of the windscreen where the driver sat, and follow-up with two rounds poured into the engine block. These were anti-material ordinance, designed to stop a tank. It wouldn't matter about armour-plating or bulletproof glass; these babies would make mincemeat of SUVs.

As soon as the initial shots were made, the plan was to fire two additional rounds into the windscreens of each of the other vehicles in the convoy. No way of knowing how many vehicles had to be dealt with, but she was ready for whatever confronted her. As soon as the initial action was over, she'd swop out the magazine for a fresh unit and get ready to provide cover support for John.

He had delegated himself to take the greater risk. He'd be on the ground, at the edge of a small copse of trees twenty yards behind the precise spot where the first car was to be disabled. That would put him in line with the follow-on vehicles, ready to break cover and pour a withering barrage of 7.62 hollow-points into the side windows. He'd be carrying four fragmentation grenades to hurl through the shattered glass while Karen kept the protection agents pinned down.

He'd calculated the action to last no longer than three minutes. No chance of staying around to confirm the kills. If the McAndrew children survived the assault, so be it. The odds, however, would not be in their favour.

He had an exit route already mapped out and he intended sticking to it. He'd ditch his weapons and holdall of grenades and spare magazines, dash across a small park, and disappear inside a shopping mall. Karen would leave everything at the office and join him there. Then they'd simply get a taxi to the train station and disappear.

That had been the plan, and it had been a good one, with every chance of working. The events of the last few hours had put paid to everything. Karen stood at the office window and shrugged her shoulders. Probably for the best. She had no compunction about killing children, but it was always going to be a high-tariff operation. At least now she'd get to enjoy a vacation. She turned back towards her husband. "Any regrets, John?"

"No babe, you know me; never look back. Good job we got these offices. No-one will bother us until it's time to leave. As far as anyone knows, we're a legit small business setting up secretarial and bookkeeping services. We're supposed to be redecorating the place before opening, which means it won't look strange that we keep the door locked. Not bad for a five-hundred-dollar deposit."

"Still think we should hang here until tomorrow night?"

"It's our best chance of avoiding detection. This part of the city will be manic until after the funerals. When nothing happens, they'll pat themselves on the backs, reel in the troops, and leave us with a clear run to Virginia and then Mexico."

"What will we do with ourselves when we get across the border? I'm going to miss America, although if I'm honest, I'll miss our assignments even more."

"We've got enough money put away to do whatever we want. I'm thinking of Europe. There are always lots of customers willing to pay for the kind of services we have on offer."

He looked across the room at two holdalls. "It's a pity to leave our rifles behind, but it'll be easy to pick up top-quality gear, particularly in Hungary, which has become an international market for under-the-counter stuff. We'll take our pistols, however. I'd feel naked without them. Give me a hand to clean them, and then we'll turn in for the night."

CHAPTER 39

QUINN LAY PRONE at the top of the stairs and looked down the length of the corridor. On his right was the wall that housed the elevator shafts and some small utility rooms, indicating that the four doors on the left were the only rooms to worry about. A faint glow emanated through frosted glass beside the third door. Either someone was in there, or the tenants had left on a nightime security light. The other rooms were in darkness.

He retrieved the thermal imaging unit from the inside pocket of his windbreaker and pointed it down the corridor. It immediately showed two red spots close together at the right side of the room. It was people, no question about it.

He heard Freeman's footsteps on the stairs behind him and turned, putting a finger against his lips in the universal signal for quiet. Freeman nodded and slithered to Quinn's side.

"What have we got?" Freeman whispered.

"Two tangos, though it could just be cleaning staff, or the boss playing footsie with his secretary."

"You don't really believe that, do you?"

"No, we gotta work on the assumption it's the Atwoods. I say we go in hard and fast, ready for the worse-case scenario. If we find a guy with his trousers around his ankles, we apologise and leave.

No harm. No foul."

"And if it *is* the Atwoods?"

"Silly question, Agent Freeman. We react to whatever confronts us."

"Okay, but I want your word we'll try to take them alive, if possible."

Quinn frowned. "We'll play it your way. What's the gameplan?"

"I'm thinking kick and rush."

"Who's doing the kicking and who's doing the rushing?"

"You're younger than me so you do the kicking. I guess after that, we'll both rush in, but be careful we don't snag each other in the doorway. After you apply the kick, stand aside and let me through. I'll take the left, you cover the right."

"So you're hellbent on going first?"

"Yep. It's my show."

"I guess it is," Quinn conceded.

They belly-crawled side-by-side down the wide corridor. It was slow-going, inch by inch, using elbows and knees while keeping wary eyes on the door ahead of them. They stopped against the wall opposite the door, and rose slowly to their feet. Freeman used his left hand to count off silently with three fingers. As soon as the last one folded, Quinn sprang forward and smashed the sole of his boot against the flimsy lock. As the door burst open, he stood aside to let Freeman rush into the room.

Karen Atwood was the first to react, mainly because she'd finished cleaning her Smith and Wesson 3.6 Compact ahead of her husband. She twisted on the floor and fired twice into Freeman's chest. The FBI man stumbled backwards and let loose a single shot before collapsing to the ground.

The round hit the woman on the side of the neck, causing her to drop the weapon and roll across the floor.

John Atwood threw his half-assembled weapon to one side and dived across to his wife's side. It wasn't clear whether he was reaching to comfort her or was making a grab for her pistol. It didn't matter to Quinn, who had quickly assessed the situation. He went for what he was trained to do. A double-tap that exploded John Atwood's head, sending a shower of blood and pieces of bone across Karen's face. Her husband's lifeless body crushed down on top of her.

Quinn knelt beside Freeman and felt for a pulse. There wasn't one. But neither was there any blood. He ripped open the FBI man's windcheater and saw the Kevlar body vest with two misshapen bullets lodged in the folds. He breathed a sigh of relief and squatted on the floor. He'd seen this kind of thing before. The impact of the bullets had temporarily stopped the heart; at least he hoped it was temporary. He decided to wait ten seconds before applying CPR.

Freeman suddenly coughed and sat upright. "Jeez, that hurt."

"Welcome back to the land of the living."

The FBI man glanced at his partner who was sitting cross-legged with his back against the wall. "Yeah, I can see you were worried."

"I knew a tough nut like you would make it. Just glad it wasn't me who insisted on going first through the door...."

"Watch out!"

Quinn followed Freeman's gaze towards Karen Atwood. She'd squirmed from below her husband, struggling to bring her weapon to bear. It was a slow, painful exercise, one that Quinn could have stopped by getting up, ambling across the room, and kicking the gun from her hand.

Why bother? He lowered his usual head-shot aim and fired without mercy or regret, the bullet tearing a chunk out of the woman's throat.

The smoke billowed upwards, contorted by a slight breeze that quickly dissipated the trail before it had a chance to reach more than twenty feet. The area was crammed with SUVs, ambulances and two Coroner Office station wagons as Quinn sat on the edge of a step outside a nearby office block.

"You should give those things up," Freeman said with feeling.

"Thought I already had. Maybe I'll quit again after I finish this pack." Quinn laughed and dragged deep on the cigarette, feeling the weight of the world fall off his shoulders for the first time in over a week. Was it only nine days ago that he'd interrupted the assault on Charlie and Sophie?

"You know," Freeman said, "I've crashed some rooms in my time, but that was a first for me. It was dumb bad luck that we chose the moment they had weapons in hand."

"Maybe it was for the best."

Freeman rubbed his chest. "Easy for you to say. If that bitch had gone for my head I'd be toast."

"Can't think that way. Wasn't your time; it was her's."

"Speaking of which, you could have disabled her. That pistol must have felt like a ton weight. No way she'd have been able to lift it high enough, let alone squeeze the trigger."

"Couldn't take the chance," Quinn said, wondering where the conversation was leading to.

Freeman sighed. "There'll be a lot of paperwork about this one, probably even an internal Bureau enquiry, if Director Perry has his way."

"So, what are you going to report?"

"Like you said, you had to take the shot. She was getting ready to fire on us."

Quinn flicked away the cigarette and watched it spark across the sidewalk. He shook his head a few times before turning to Freeman. "You were right about one thing."

"What was that?"

"There's a lot to be said for this teamwork lark."

They both burst out laughing, which drew the attention of a group of agents standing nearby. "They probably think we're undergoing some sort of post-action release," Quinn said."

"I guess in a way we are. What will you do next?"

"Gonna find me a hotel, take a long hot shower and sleep for twelve hours. After that, I'll pay my respects at the McAndrews funeral before disappearing. No disrespect, Agent Freeman, but much as I like your company it'll suit just fine if I never see you again."

"Whoa there! Thought you had some sort of agreement with old man Fleming?"

"Exigent circumstances. That was then, this is now. It suited him to be grandiose when things looked bleak, but now he's got a whole lot of other things to worry about."

"Such as?"

"Charlie and Sophie. They'll need all his energies. I was just a passing ship. Better this way."

"Don't be too sure," Freeman responded as he glanced at his watch. "It's just gone past midnight."

"Yeah, we did it with fifteen hours to spare."

"Not what I meant. Fleming will still be up and around. I think you should give him a call. He deserves to hear it's all over."

"I'll leave that to you."

"No, you deserve to take the honours. We only got this wrapped up because you led us here."

Quinn rose and stretched. "Not my scene. Besides, as you pointed out earlier, it's your show."

The five Iraqis split into two vehicles when they exited the underground car park. Linkmeyer and his secretary were forced into the rear of the Chairman's Mercedes with the group leader and one other gunman for company. Montgomery was put in the back of a Lincoln Continental, which had been used by the assailants to ferry them to the rendezvous.

As the cars made their way through light traffic, Montgomery knew it was a one-way trip. They had the pen drive containing the trail of deceit and embezzlement. What did they need him for? He'd heard stories about how these bastards liked to take their time over extracting revenge, usually with knives, and always with the intent of inflicting as much pain as possible.

He had nothing left to bargain with. Linkmeyer had reneged on the money transfer, which left him with a mere million, less recent expenses, with which to bargain for his freedom. Wasn't going to happen. It was chump change to these bozos. Even if they did agree to a deal, they'd start in on him as soon as they had the money.

The car slowed and came to a stop at traffic lights. The Mercedes ahead had already pulled through on the red light, but the Lincoln driver braked to a halt. It was now or never!

He hadn't heard the car's central locking feature being activated at the start of the journey. It didn't matter; neither did the fact that his backseat co-passenger had a gun casually trained across the gap between them. Better to die quickly than wait to be carved up like some turkey.

Montgomery hit the door-release handle. To his amazement it opened. He fell out, waiting for a bullet that didn't come. He stumbled to his feet and started running, finding a well of energy he never knew he had. He dashed across three lanes of traffic before reaching the sidewalk, pushing aside pedestrians and running like a man whose life depended on getting as far away from this place as he could.

Daring not to look behind, he maintained an awkward, loping stride until finally his legs began to seize. He fell against a store front and slid to the ground, expecting to see the gunman emerge at any second. Nothing. There was no pursuit!

It took several minutes for Montgomery to

recover his breathing. He eventually stood up with a new look of determination on his face. His whole being was now occupied with one thought. *Find the bastard who interfered in the events at Bangor. Find him and kill him!*

CHAPTER 40

TWO HEARSES ROLLED to a stop outside the country house at precisely eleven o'clock on a dank Tuesday morning. Chief Justice Thomas Jefferson Fleming put protective arms around his grandchildren, his heart torn asunder by their anguished sobbing. The bodies of his daughter and son-in-law were being brought home to allow the children time with their parents before the funerals later in the afternoon.

He watched as the caskets were taken from the rear compartments of the black Cadillac Medalist limousines and borne by two teams of four men into a room at the side of the house. By agreement, everyone else held back while the mortician opened the coffins and prepared the bodies for viewing. He had already applied a special filling paste and skin creams which left no trace of the horrible gunshot wounds on the faces of Mark and Ruth McAndrew.

Charlie and Sophie had begged their grandfather to allow them to see their parents for the last time. He understood they needed closure, but was not prepared to accede to their requests. It was child psychologist Maria Zeigler who'd pointed out the benefits of reuniting the children with their parents, if only for a short time. Zeigler had remained at the Fleming house, spending much of her time smoothing the way for what was to come. She'd talked at length to the kids about how their parents were happy in God's embrace, and how Charlie and Sophie would always carry special memories of them in their hearts.

But she didn't colour everything with a rosy tint. Yes, life was cruel and unfair. Yes, they didn't deserve for this to have happened to them, which didn't mean there wouldn't be other heartaches and disappointments. They had to be ready for the challenges. Be strong and brave and be there for each other, she'd told them.

Zeigler walked behind the children as Fleming guided them towards the coffins. Despite her preparations, what came next was no surprise.

Charlie ran forward, stopping first at his mother's body to stroke her hair, and then moving across to his father. Sophie held back, her little body wracked by shivers; indecision etched in her tear-filled eyes. Finally, she moved, reaching on tiptoes to peer into her mother's coffin.

"Mommy, mommy, please wake up. Talk to me."

Fleming knelt beside her. "She's sleeping, honey. She can't wake up. It's okay to talk to her though. She hears you and is glad that you're safe and well. She understands why you're crying, but she wants you to be happy and to visit her as often as you can, and to tell her all the stories about what you're doing. Let her know you'll do that."

"I will, mommy. I'll come every day....." The voice petered away, consumed by another bout of sobbing.

Charlie put an arm around Sophie's shoulder.

Zeigler watched the youngster bite down on his lip, determined to stifle his own grief while he comforted his sister. He was one of the strongest-willed children she'd ever met. Didn't mean he wasn't hurting bad; he was simply postponing the inevitable.

A third hearse entered the Fleming estate shortly before midday. It had travelled from Glenwood Cemetery where the workers using the mini digger had finished their labours. They had not been preparing graves for the McAndrew couple. That was never part of the plan. They had disinterred the body of Fleming's wife, Samantha, who would now be reburied alongside her daughter and son-in-law in a new family plot at Bailey's Crossroads.

It was also never part of the plan that funerals to Glenwood would go ahead at three o'clock, as publicly announced. There would have been the pretence of a motorcade of principal mourners, but that was intended purely to draw out the killers. Fleming quite simply was not prepared to risk the lives of his grandchildren until the threat was eliminated. He would remain behind with Charlie and Sophie and their Secret Service protection detail while FBI agents laid a false trail.

Fleming had intended to use Glenwood an hour after the advertised time, and then only if an all-clear had been signalled. He had changed his mind after Quinn persuaded him to consider the creation of a new family plot within the estate. It was what Quinn had put forward during their final talk before he'd left to stalk the assassins.

The idea had taken root in Quinn's mind after stumbling across the burial site at the home of Chad Evans. He'd told Fleming about being struck by the appropriateness and serenity of the place, and how it seemed to provide an anchor for those who'd departed. The clincher for Fleming was Quinn's insistence that such a site would give Charlie and Sophie easy access to their parents and grandmother.

The old boy had cried openly to Quinn, admitting it was something he should have done for his wife years ago. The damned job had always come first, he'd said. "Hardly an excuse for not doing the right thing by my family. But it won't happen again," he'd promised.

Quinn arrived at Bailey's Crossroads an hour before the start of the funeral procession. It would be a short two-hundred-yard walk to the prepared graves, with only a handful of invited guests allowed to attend. The other eight justices of the Supreme Court had already visited the house to pay their respects, but would not be part of the cortege. Neither would the large contingent of FBI and Secret Service agents, who had been asked to vacate the area. Fleming wanted an immediate return to normality for the sake of his grandchildren.

Secret Service team leader Sheridan Smith and his quota of two resident agents were allowed to stay, as was Carl Freeman who received a special invitation. The name of Francis Xavier Quinn was the only other guest permitted beyond the front gate.

Quinn had got his twelve hours sleep. He'd showered, shaved and eaten a hearty breakfast at a budget hotel before stepping out to buy a new suit, white shirt and black tie. He already had a sizeable wardrobe, but that was in his RV in a lock-up at Bangor.

A taxi dropped Quinn at the end of the long driveway. The morning's drizzle had given way to bright skies as he walked reluctantly towards the big house, wondering why he'd resisted the urge to grab a train and disappear. His work here was done. Better for everyone if he moved on as soon as possible. He hadn't worked out what the future held, only that he was certain he couldn't go back to what he had been doing previously.

Halfway to the house he knew why he'd come. He lifted his eyes at the sound of running feet and saw Charlie running forward.

"Mr Quinn, Mr Quinn, I knew you'd come!"

The boy launched himself at Quinn, jumping against the new suit and circling his arms around his neck. "Can I stand beside you when we bury mom and dad?"

Quinn was genuinely moved by the show of affection. He squeezed Charlie's back and whispered. "Of course you can, but I think it would be better if you stood beside your grandpa and helped him to get through everything."

"But who's going to help me?"

Quinn felt the tension in Charlie's body and heard the sobs as the youngster finally let go of his emotions.

"Keep going, Charlie. Cry and scream and be

mad at everything that's happened. That's what I'd do. That's what strong men are meant to do."

Several minutes elapsed before Charlie's anguish finally passed. He pushed away from Quinn's shoulders and stared into his face. "You're just saying that. I bet you wouldn't cry."

Quinn broke into a false laugh. "Of course I would. You should see me crying up a storm when things get bad. Bet I could put you to shame when I start."

Charlie giggled. "I'd like to see that." Then he put on a serious face. "Will you be standing close to me if I hold grandpa's hand?"

"You betcha! We're partners, ain't we?"

Unseen by Quinn, the curtains in an upstairs room folded back into place. Thomas Jefferson Fleming had been watching the scene below, grateful once again to the tall young man who'd helped put things right.

Quinn stood in the back yard and took a last drag on the cigarette. It was thirty minutes after the funerals, the first he'd attended since the burial of his great grandfather, Sam Quinn, back in Downpatrick all those years ago. He didn't remember much about it, only that his mother and her sisters had wailed pitifully as the coffin had been lowered into the ground. He'd never got to know his forebear the way he should have. He'd been too young to understand, too innocent to shed tears, and much too naïve to realise the strongest root in the family tree had just withered and died.

This time the significance of saying goodbye

carried much more impact, particularly after watching Charlie, Sophie and old man Fleming struggle through the short ceremony. It was part of the natural process. Letting go in order to move on. So, at one point, Quinn had lifted his eyes skyward and muttered a few words that were long overdue. *Thanks for everything, Da Sam.*

"Thought you were going to give those things up?"

He spun around as Carl Freeman walked up to his side. "Pretty sombre occasion."

"Yeah," Quinn acknowledged. "Glad it's over. Where to now, Agent Freeman? Guess you can write your own ticket after being the hero of the hour?"

"Cut the crap, Quinn. We both know I was riding on your back, getting nowhere unless you were calling the shots. I owe you a lot."

"Bullshit! If we're going to do the mutual admiration dance, you should know that I learned a lot from you. You're quite a guy, Freeman, when you let down what's left of that buzzcut hair, and relax. You shook up quite a storm in this city. You'd have got to the Atwoods without any help from me, and we both know it."

"You know, Quinn, for an intelligent guy you do come out with some nonsense. Will you accept a handshake from someone who knows what really happened?"

Quinn extended an arm. "My pleasure. It's been nice doing business and all that, but you didn't answer the question."

"Which was?"

"What are you going to do next?"

"I gotta track down Montgomery and the people he worked for."

"Good luck with that. Not my concern any more."

"Actually, there's something I've been meaning to ask you. Old Man Fleming told me you figured there was a leak in the FBI. Care to elaborate?"

"I'm guessing you already knew that. Probably put it on the back burner, but now it needs to be dealt with. Are you looking for a sounding board?"

Freeman splayed his arms across the top of the garden fence. "I know an FBI leak is the only thing that makes sense, but I can't figure out who. The list of candidates is very small, and yet none of the suspects makes any sense."

"Who knew about your meetings with Mark McAndrew?"

"I tried to keep a tight rein on information. There was the Director, of course, and also the Executive Assistant Director in charge of the Criminal Investigation Division, and lastly there was Drew Eisler. Those were the only people in the loop, and even then I'm not sure I shared everything equally around them."

"The old need-to-know mentality?"

"Pretty much, which is why I'm baffled."

"What about support staff? Switchboard operators, filing clerks, drivers, or computer geeks?"

"No. Nobody else had a sniff of what we were doing with McAndrew."

Quinn pulled away from the fence. "I've a feeling you've already got a prime suspect. You just won't admit it."

Freeman frowned. "Director Perry has me worried. He's always been a jerk, and I admit I don't like the guy, but I'm gonna need a lot of hard facts before I go down that particular road."

"Seems to me, you don't have a choice."

They were interrupted by Secret Service leader Sheridan Smith. "Sorry to butt in gents. Chief Justice Fleming would like a word with Quinn."

CHAPTER 41

THERE ARE NO shortcuts in a murder manhunt. The FBI has long-established protocols which involve working from the ground up, sifting through minutiae, following leads with due diligence and patience, and resisting the temptation to cut corners. That's what Agent Drew Eisler started out doing the moment he arrived at the underground car park at East 53rd Street in New York's Brooklyn district and looked at the four bodies strewn across the floor.

Protocol number one. Let the forensic guys do their job. Keep everyone back, protect the scene, gather the evidence, and work outwards from there. Thankfully, the crime scientists had arrived an hour before Eisler and were mopping up, figuratively speaking, by the time the FBI agent-in-charge walked forward to get his first up-close glimpse of the victims. He isolated the four forensic workers and made them walk through everything they'd found. There were weapons, spent shell casings, blood splatter, footprints on the dusty floor, and wallets full of Social Security cards, driver licence IDs and miscellaneous items of crunched-up receipts and faded family photographs. More than enough to be getting on with.

That triggered Protocol number two. Identify the bodies, run prints through the system, get teams to home and work addresses, track down known associates, put together their personal histories, and try to figure out what the hell they were doing here.

Protocol number three. Look for potential witnesses, check CCTV cameras, interview nearby residents and car park users, and search a three-block radius in case any incriminating evidence had been dumped.

Only when teams of agents had been assigned to these tasks did Eisler call forward a senior detective, who had been first on the scene. "Was it you who called our offices about the link to Devlin Montgomery?"

"It was. Recognised two of the bodies immediately. They used to work for us. A bad duo and no mistake."

"What where they into?" Eisler asked.

"Anything that involved money, and they didn't care how they went about getting it."

"Did they spread themselves around, or did they contract out to anyone in particular."

The detective scratched at a two-day stubble. "Ran into them a few times over the years. Always boasting about how easy the jobs kept coming to them. Liked to flash the cash in our faces."

"Doesn't answer the question."

"Like I said, they weren't fussy about who they got into bed with. They did tell me once that they'd secured a nice arrangement with some sort of private consortium. The usual stuff, like bodyguarding or lending a bit of muscle when it was needed."

"What was the organisation called?"

"Dunno. Said they dealt only with a flash-Harry type of guy by the name of Devlin Montgomery. Which was why I called you lot, on account of the flyers and all-agency alerts that have been papering our office walls for a few days."

"How come you never remembered the connection before now? Could've saved a lot of trouble if you'd let us know about this sooner." There was an edge to Eisler's voice, one that left the detective in no doubt that he'd fouled up.

"It was a long time ago. Tell the truth I'd forgotten all about this pair until I found them here this afternoon. You must want this Montgomery guy bad?"

Eisler blanked out the question and walked to a corner of the car park. He had a lot of thinking to do. This was a breakthrough, and no mistake, but how many days and nights would be spent chasing it down? He knew how things worked; endless foot-slogging, and interviews, hoping to stumble across the one piece of information that would connect them to Montgomery's location. As it turned out, he couldn't have been more wrong.

"We got a hit on two vehicles!"

Eisler turned towards the voice. It belonged to Jan Moseley, whom he'd brought with him from Lynchburg. "What?"

"A camera at traffic lights on the corner shows a Mercedes and Lincoln Continental driving away from this location at the estimated time of the murders. And get this, the back-seat passenger in one of the vehicles has been identified as Devlin Montgomery."

"You're kidding," Eisler said. "Any luck with the

number plates?"

"Clear as a bell. The Lincoln had false plates, but the Merc was more forthcoming. It's registered to a Tyrell B Linkmeyer, the chairman of a big conglomerate based in Manhattan. Want me to get a team over to his offices?"

Eisler stared off into space. This was not what he was expecting. Was Linkmeyer behind the four murders? Did he meet with Montgomery in an attempt to cover the tracks of his organisation? Who were the other parties to what went down here?

"Sir?"

He focussed his attention back to Moseley. "It's hardly likely that Linkmeyer went straight back to his office, but I'll go there just in case. You concentrate on running down the Lincoln. See if it was picked up at any other camera locations. Something tells me the occupants of that car are a lot more interesting than some weaselly chairman with tenuous links to Montgomery."

Jan Moseley spent most of the afternoon in the Traffic Management Centre office at NYC's Department of Transportation. In a city with America's worst congestion figures, she quickly realised she was looking for the proverbial needle among the snarl-ups and gridlocks that were pretty much a fact of normal life in the five boroughs. Her eyes stung and her head throbbed and she dreamed of being back with her daughter in Washington.

She'd long since tuned out the senior manager who'd waxed lyrical about the city's new wireless network, unsurprisingly tagged with the acronym NYCWIN, which had connected more than ten thousand signalised intersections by fitting them with advanced, solid-state traffic controllers. Ten thousand!

They'd got an early sighting of the Lincoln and Mercedes less than a mile from the shoot-out. Later they picked up a nice piece of action when the Merc was trapped at lights and a man jumped from a rear seat and bolted across the intersection. A zoom revealed the face of Devlin Montgomery. Now we're getting somewhere!

But that was it. Despite another two hours of painstaking screen-watching, the cars had simply vanished. Too many side streets and underground tunnels, the manager offered, aware that his explanations were cutting no ice with the FBI agent.

"That's just great," Moseley said. "What happens now?"

"Guess we keep looking."

"Can we get more bodies in here?"

The manager looked around the room at eight people sitting on stools and staring at screens. "This is our full complement of staff. We had to bring in shift workers on your say-so."

Moseley took the barb on the chin, knowing the guy was right. She was being a pain the ass, which she reckoned was understandable in the circumstances, no matter that it was neither helpful nor productive. She just wanted out of this place.

She got her wish sooner than expected.

Her cellphone buzzed with Eisler's caller ID.

"Jan, drop what you're doing. I've got an address where those two vehicles are holed up."

"You're kidding! How?"

"Got an anonymous tip-off. Round up a full tact team and meet me there." Eisler rattled off directions and cut the connection.

Tyrell B Linkmeyer heard the screech of tyres and dared to hope.

He was sitting on a bare wood chair in the centre of a large open-plan room that served as the office and living quarters of the Iraqi mobsters. It was on the second floor of a converted linen factory, one of three turnkey developments that had gone on the market for a half-million each. He was aware of the location, but this was the first time he'd been inside the property.

Clarissa sat twenty feet away, her clothes torn and her face bloodied by a gratuitous beating that was meant more as a warning to Linkmeyer than a threat to the unfortunate woman. She'd given up computer passwords and bank encryption details almost as soon as they'd tied her to a chair with hints of what they intended to do with her body. The beating was unnecessary, but it was what the Iraqis liked to do.

When Clarissa had finished syphoning and transferring whatever Corporation cash reserves she could find, Linkmeyer knew he'd nothing left to bargain with. He'd tried to persuade the gang leader that the cash was only part of the huge reserves in assets held by the Corporation's myriad companies. It would take time to convert these into some serious money, but not if cash shortages caused a run on shares. Let the money stay in place, he'd argued, until arrangements could be made to sell off stock at a pace calculated to fool Wall Street.

The gang leader made a call to Baghdad. Linkmeyer sweated while the conversation with Asif Morani played out. The outcome was predictable. Morani wasn't willing to hang around for what might he might get. He was happy to settle for what he already had.

Which meant Linkmeyer was disposable. His future was now measured in minutes.

And then came the squeal of tyres. Linkmeyer made a silent plea. *Please God, let it be the FBI.*

Could it really be salvation? He could bargain with the Feds for his life. He had a lot of secrets to put on the table, more than enough to avoid jail, maybe even force them into letting him start up a new venture. And he had an ace in the hole, a guy who'd want to protect his identity at all costs.

One of the Iraqi gunmen rushed to a window and looked down at an enclosed residents' car park. He saw at least twenty men and women spilling from vehicles, each wearing an FBI identification jacket. "We've got company," he said without a trace of fear.

The gang leader smiled. "Today we will go about the work of Allah. Take your positions and let these infidels realise what it is we do in His Blessed Name."

No sooner had he uttered the words than two of the bank of windows on that side of the building were shattered by rapid machine-pistol fire, the rounds ploughing into the ceiling because of their upward trajectory. The cacophony was followed immediately by a series of pops, which signalled the arrival of tear-gas canisters, six in total, which bounced across the room leaving trails of noxious vapour.

Drew Eisler led the first-team assault up fire escape stairs, which were bolted to the right side of the building. A second team of eight agents made their way up similar steps at the opposite side. One man in each group carried a small shaped-charge package, designed to obliterate door locks on a synchronous command. It was a classic military-breach technique, refined by the FBI for use in urban areas.

Before they'd left for the target address, Eisler had warned his agents about what they were facing. "These are dedicated terrorists. They won't surrender and they won't sell their lives cheaply. Make sure you do the same."

As soon as the door blew inwards, Eisler bolted through the opening and dived to his left, his hand squeezing the MP5 trigger while he was still in mid-air. It was a spray-and-pray play that ignored the need to isolate targets. Keep the threat pinned down, find a base to work from, and advance from there. Behind him, other agents were doing the same, as was the group charging through the door at the opposite end of the room.

The FBI contingent wore face masks and body armour, but that's where their advantage ended. The vapour-filled room provided a level playing field, with neither side able to distinguish targets, just blurred shapes, most of which could merely be furniture items. Gunfire became heavy and erratic, the muzzle sparks providing the only targets for the shooters.

Eisler had been careful to remind his teams to aim only to the left and right, and only at a forward distance of thirty yards. They'd divided the room notionally in half to avoid hitting each other with friendly fire, a tactic that would work as long as the Iraqis co-operated by staying away from the middle ground. Freeman was banking on the gas dispersing quickly to provide line-of-sight targeting, but until then his men would keep firing at anything that moved within their segment.

Despite the suddenness and ferocity of the action, the five-man Iraqi team maintained their discipline. The leader had despatched two men to each side of the room while he stood beside a shattered window, gulping air and reserving his energy for the final showdown.

His men fired at an alarming rate, swopping out magazines in an alternating fashion which allowed them to maintain a prolonged barrage. It gradually subsided, as one by one they fell, until finally the noise stopped completely. Almost simultaneously, the gas in the room dissipated, as if someone had used an industrial blower.

The Iraqi locked eyes with Eisler and moved his weapon to cover his enemy's advance. *Allahu Akbar* escaped from his lips in a hoarse intonation that was cut short by a sustained volley from three separate pistols. The Iraqi was catapulted out the window, the concrete rising to meet his dead body.

Eisler pulled off his mask and walked to the centre or the room, looking down at the corpse of an elderly man coiled in a foetal position. If it hadn't been for a dozen red-coloured holes in the expensive designer suit it might have seemed that Tyrell B Linkmeyer was having an afternoon nap.

CHAPTER 42

QUINN WAS CONFLICTED. A big part of him wanted to walk away. The urge to return to Bangor, climb into his RV, and see where the road took him was almost overwhelming. It's what he'd done for most of his life, so why should it be any different now? But it was! Things had changed dramatically since he'd returned from his assignment in Mexico. He was no longer the merciless gun-for-hire who accepted lucrative contracts, killed without compassion, and waited impatiently for the next big score. He knew that now. There had to be something different out there, something which utilised his skills to help people in the way he'd helped to protect Charlie and Sophie.

Staying here was not the answer. Old Man Fleming's tentative offer to turn him into some kind of government agent was fanciful thinking. It demanded commitment and setting down roots and taking orders, all of which had not been part of his DNA for the better part of twenty years. He was a loner. He worked on instinct and the freedom to cut corners without worrying about rule books, or proprieties, or someone looking over his shoulder.

Nonetheless, he had to admit to a certain satisfaction from working with Carl Freeman and seeing the other side of the track. It'd been strange to look at things from a new perspective, stranger still to realise how much commonality there was between the mindset of a perpetrator and a law enforcer. Most men could be one or the other, never both. And yet in under two weeks, he had done just that. He knew which path he wanted to walk in the future.

Which didn't exactly square the circle of his present quandary. He'd think more about it after recharging the batteries. For now he'd simply tell Chief Justice Fleming thanks, but no thanks.

It was a resolution that dissolved within a minute of walking into the old man's study.

A large brown manila envelope was sitting atop Fleming's desk. It was bulky and it had Quinn's name scrawled across it, the cursive writing all but obliterating a rectangular address label that bore the seal of the Office of President of the United States of America. Fleming beckoned Quinn to a seat and pushed the envelope forward.

Quinn grabbed it and bent back the unsealed flap, his hand dipping inside to withdraw the contents. He was surprised by the pristine USA passport, Social Security card, driving licence and a certificate of birth registration document, all of which were in the name of *Francis Xavier Quinn,* an American native born in New York City in 1985! A single sheet of typed paper provided a timeline of a fictitious life, covering university attendance, military service with the Army Rangers, and various civilian jobs within the defence sector.

Quinn's surprise became total shock when he spilled out a small leather wallet. It was an official federal badge, proclaiming the holder to be a special investigator for the Department of Justice. Fleming saw the bewilderment on Quinn's face. "That's a nice catch-all accreditation, which will open a lot of doors, whilst not exactly tying you down to one particular agency."

Quinn shook his head. "Where did you get my photograph for all these identification documents?"

"We've got Special Agent Freeman to thank for that. He used one of your bogus passports to retrieve the image. The FBI lab boys did a nice job of smoothing out the wrinkles, metaphorically speaking, don't you think?"

"How could all this be done in such a short time?"

Fleming waved his hand in a dismissive gesture. "It would surprise you how quickly the wheels of bureaucracy can spin when the right motivation is provided. Let's just say the various departments involved in this were suitably incentivised to do what they were told."

Quinn was lost for words. It was over a minute before he leant forward and fixed Fleming with a suspicious stare. "I don't get it. I could have taken off at any time. I could have failed to stop the threat against Charlie and Sophie. Why go to all this trouble before knowing the outcome?"

"It was quite simple," Fleming said. "There was never any prospect of you taking off, as you call it. I saw how motivated you were to help, not because cutting a deal was expedient, but because you'd clearly undergone a renaissance which precluded you from giving us anything but your total commitment, even to the extent of putting your life on the line for my grandchildren. My offer was never predicated in the success of your endeavours.

The mere fact that you agreed to help, and were forthcoming with your reasons for doing so, was enough for me to set the ball rolling within minutes of shaking your hand on the deal."

"I'm not sure I deserve the faith placed in me. I'm also not sure I can accept what you're offering."

Instead of being puzzled by Quinn's statement, Fleming smiled and nodded at the envelope. "There's still something in there you haven't read."

Quinn upended the package and spilled a single sheet on the desk. It was thick, cream-coloured, document-quality paper, neatly folded in the middle and covered in faint watermarks. Quinn hinged it open, immediately seeing the official Presidential seal in the top centre of the page.. The colour drained from his face as he read through the copperplate-printed text.

I affirm Francis Xavier Quinn to be a true American patriot. He has provided valuable service to his country by carrying out many hazardous and selfless tasks, some of which may have exposed him to the risk of prosecution. This would be unjust reward for the efforts he has expended on our behalf. I therefore decree he is entitled to full immunity and I so stipulate this pardon on behalf of a grateful nation.

Signed
Robert Masterson
President

"What say you now, son?"

"I'm not sure how to react, sir," Quinn said. "I have to be honest with you. I came in here today to tell you I wanted to disappear and find a new life on my own terms. I believed I could not provide the

366

services you'd hoped I could. I was becoming convinced I'm not that kind of person."

"And what about now?"

"This changes everything. It's not the pardon or the new credentials, great though they are. It's the realisation that you and others have faith in me and are willing to take a gamble on someone who frankly doesn't deserve it. I can't walk away from that. I owe it to you to give this a go, and I promise to do all I can to make it work."

"Splendid!" Fleming beamed. "I know you won't let me down."

Quinn lifted the DOJ badge and examined it closely. "How exactly does this work? Who do I report to?"

Fleming shook his head. "Can't answer that because I don't know. The logistics haven't been smoothed out as yet. For the moment you don't have a boss or an office or a place in the system. The general idea is to keep you independent for occasions that might arise and which will require your special input. Could be you'll be operating across a number of agencies, but this is still being worked on. In the meantime, you're on the DOJ official payroll, which means we can start a proper IRS history for you, which in turn means paying taxes, something I suspect hasn't happened beforehand."

Quinn reddened. "Not something that went with my former life. I'd be happy to work for nothing, although the idea of paying taxes and being part of the system appeals to me."

"You won't get rich working for the government," Fleming said. "It's five-thousand-dollars a month before deductions. I need you to use your new credentials to open a bank account so that the salary can be paid. Do this as soon as possible and hand the details to Special Agent Freeman."

"He knows all about this?"

"He helped set it up. Made sure I knew who was due the real credit for neutralising the assassins. You two seemed to have hit it off."

Before Quinn could respond, three urgent raps on the study door ended the conversation.

"Come in."

Carl Freeman entered and offered his apologies. "Sorry for the interruption, sir. It *is* rather urgent."

"We were just talking about you. What's up?"

"Just got word of an FBI shoot-out in New York. Five Iraqi gunmen have been killed, along with the Chairman of a Corporation with direct links to Devlin Montgomery. It appears Montgomery was with this group prior to the incident, but escaped in some sort of kidnap scenario. There's a lot we're still learning about what went down. What can be said is that the net is closing and I'm heading to New York to make sure Montgomery is finally brought in."

"That's great news," Fleming said. "Might I recommend that you take the Justice Department's latest special investigator with you?"

The internal review lasted almost two hours. The FBI was big on convening scrutiny committees when deaths resulted from one of their operations. More so, when potential civilian collateral damage was involved. They liked to think of it as being transparent. Cynics accused them of using the procedure to cover their asses. The truth was often to be found somewhere between the two.

The Director was there as a matter of necessity, so too was the Assistant Director in charge of the Bureau's Criminal Investigation Division. Also present was a member of a little-known Senate federal watchdog committee, and a stenographer, whose job it was to record the session and prepare a written report, which would most likely end up in a sealed file. Unless, of course, the review found reasons for concern about the operation against the Iraqi gunmen. In which case, heads would roll.

Carl Freeman had insisted on being present. He was confident Drew Eisler had done everything by the book, but that didn't mean he wouldn't fall foul of a witch-hunt, if Director Perry wanted to go down that route.

To Freeman's surprise, the review turned out to be little more than a debrief. Forensic probity took a back seat to a collective desire not to find anything untoward. The raid had the potential to reinforce the FBI's reputation for decisive and punitive action against terrorism, provided there were no wrinkles to attract the attention of the media. It seemed everyone in the room was buying into a PR-friendly outcome.

Eisler took them through the events of the afternoon. He'd received an anonymous tip-off direct to his cellphone from someone who'd claimed to know the whereabouts of the gunmen responsible for the shootings in the underground car park. The caller had claimed these were Iraqi terrorists and that they were torturing a man who would die within an hour unless the FBI acted quickly. Eisler didn't have a clue about the identity of the informant, nor how the caller had obtained his private number.

The plan to breach the premises was straight out of the Quantico training manual. Eisler said his primary concern was the safety of his agents, so he hit hard and he hit fast. When they'd arrived at the location, the Mercedes and Lincoln cars were parked out front, which confirmed the veracity of the tip-off. A woman's scream from the second floor told them there was no time to waste.

Eisler said he regretted the death of Linkmeyer. They were awaiting autopsy results on bullets recovered from the body, though he was confident this would show the fatal shots had come from the Iraqis rather than one of his agents. In any event, Eisler said, the risk to the captive being caught in crossfire had to be balanced against the need to protect his men at all costs.

He admitted he hadn't been aware of the presence of the woman. There had been no mention of her in the anonymous phone call. It was only when he'd heard her screams that he'd realised there was at least one other captive on site. She'd been badly beaten about the head and body and had suffered a gunshot wound to her upper arm, but she was still alive, Eisler said with feeling.

"What do we know about her?" Director Perry asked.

"Her name is Clarissa Mae Anderson, long-time private secretary to Linkmeyer," Eisler responded. "She has undergone minor surgery at the George

Washington Memorial and should be available for interview within a few hours. I'd planned to go over there as soon as we finish up here."

"Assuming, of course, that we return you to active duty after we conclude our deliberations?"

"Sorry, sir, didn't intend that to come out the way it did."

"Relax, Agent Eisler. I think we've heard enough to know that your actions were beyond reproach. However, I'm not sure you're the most appropriate person to conduct the interview. We've got to think of the press scrutiny that will follow. Probably best if we keep you well away from the hospital."

Freeman listened intently to the conversation. Perry's willingness to exonerate Eisler had come as something of a surprise, particularly if he had been looking for a scapegoat. It also made sense to distance Eisler from a follow-up interview of a victim of an attack which he'd orchestrated.

Freeman jumped in immediately. "I agree, sir. I'll take charge of the interview along with the DOJ special investigator who travelled down from Washington with me. This is all part of the case he was working on."

Perry looked ready to explode, but thought better of it. Instead, he shook his head in obvious vexation and stormed out of the room.

Quinn, who'd viewed the proceedings behind a two-way mirror in an anteroom, watched Perry leave. Something nagged at the back of his head. Was it an oddity about Perry, or was it because he'd missed the significance of something that was said during the mock enquiry?

CHAPTER 43

CLARISSA MAE Anderson was in a world of trouble. There was no getting away from it. She'd stood beside Linkmeyer in all his dirty dealings, often even acting in his absence to sanction kill orders when people who got in the way of the Corporation had to be silenced. She'd never lost any sleep over those decisions. If she was being honest, she'd enjoyed the buzz of every single one, much like a junkie on the kind of thrill-ride that only a fix will provide.

Linkmeyer's death left her alone to face the rap for a long list of misdeeds. It was not something Clarissa was prepared to do, leastways not without using every bargaining chip at her disposal. She'd learnt that much from Linkmeyer, and she intended to play her hand to the full.

She twisted awkwardly and stared down at the handcuffs which manacled her to the bed. Was this what the rest of her life was going to be like? The idea of rotting away in a federal prison made her shake uncontrollably, a rare moment of self-doubt and pity for a woman who'd always maintained imperious control of her emotions. She chided herself for the momentary weakness, knowing there was still a way out.

She'd dealt with situations like this, albeit in reverse, when she'd sneered at snivelling businessmen begging for deals when they'd nothing left to bargain with. The trick was to know the value of the trade. There was a lot she could divulge; things these people would never uncover or understand without her help. She'd drip-feed them enough to make them drool for more. She knew she could count on their greed for career-making results.

What she hadn't counted on as she ran through her options on a hospital bed in a quarantined room guarded by the FBI was the ferocity of the two men who came to interrogate her. These guys weren't looking to cut deals. They were out for blood.

Quinn and Freeman had spent the previous two hours at the headquarters of the mysterious Corporation. They discovered very little to expand their knowledge of Linkmeyer's empire other than to learn it traded under the elongated title of *The Import and Export Exchange Corporation,* according to an inscribed nameplate mounted on a wall beside an elevator bank inside an opulent Manhattan office block. The other floors of the building were occupied by various companies, none of which appeared to have any connections to the Corporation.

Quinn thought the set-up was distinctly odd, particularly when he looked at the interiors of the main rooms of the Corporation office suite. There were no secretarial stations, no desks for executives or run-of-the-mill employees, no canteen facilities, no stationery store, no computer stations with back-up servers and no filing cabinets. In short, there was no evidence that this was anything other than a luxury apartment. All it needed was a bedroom and a few wardrobes to complete the illusion.

Most of the space was taken up by a large boardroom which appeared to have been created by removing interior dividing walls to make way for a twenty-seater mahogany conference table, a single massive oak and marble desk, and a luxury lounge filled with recliner chairs, book cabinets, coffee tables and expensive accessories which included Persian rugs and intricate statues that looked like they came from a museum.

Leading off the lounge were two doors, one that led to a shower and toilet room, and one which took Quinn into an office that was quite obviously the domain of Clarissa Mae Anderson, the only other person he knew for sure actually worked out of *The Import and Export Exchange Corporation*. Here again the absence of typical office paraphernalia was baffling.

Quinn shook his head. What did these people do here, apart from admiring the Manhattan skyline?

A six-man team of FBI forensic officers was already on site when Quinn and Freeman entered the building. They'd been deployed here to gather evidence after the discovery of Linkmeyer's body, although it didn't appear the agents had much to uncover.

"We've bagged a few laptops and an assortment of paperwork from desks, but truth to tell there's not much else," the lead searcher told Freeman.

"I'm particularly interested in anything to do

with the secretary," Freeman responded. "We're heading to interview her at the hospital and we need some leverage on how she ties into Linkmeyer's affairs."

"Not much to tell. We found a bunch of folders in her desk. There was more than forty of them and they contain short snapshots of companies apparently linked to the Corporation. They should help us produce some kind of flowchart, but they were careful to keep Linkmeyer's name from any of the shareholder lists. On the other hand, Anderson's name appears in most of them as either company secretary or legal executor. That's about the size of it."

"Anything else worth noting," Freeman asked in exasperation.

"Just the usual collection of fingerprints. We'll maybe get more when we root inside the laptops. 'Fraid that'll have to wait until we get back to the lab."

On the drive to the hospital, Freeman vented his frustration by banging the palms of his hand on the steering wheel. "How do we rattle this woman's cage when we know so little about her?"

"We know enough," Quinn replied. "It's patently obvious she's Linkmeyer's confidante. Why else would she have an office adjacent to his, and why is it her name on those company documents? She's a big wheel in this corporation, which explains why she was with Linkmeyer at the shoot-out in the underground garage? The two go together like ham and eggs. Ask me they were probably inseparable, in a business sense at least. Maybe they were banging each other on the side, but that doesn't really matter. What's important is that we know Anderson was at the top of the Corporation tree and is just as culpable for its actions as Linkmeyer himself."

"It still doesn't give us a lot to go on. We'll need more if we're going to get anywhere with her."

Quinn smiled. "She doesn't know that. You're the FBI for heaven's sake. Use a bit of creativity. Make her believe the dots have already been joined."

Freeman showed his shield to Anderson and introduced Quinn, who'd almost forgotten about his shiny new ID until Freeman nodded towards him. The DOJ shield was waved proudly before the two men took up station at either side of the hospital bed.

Freeman got straight to the point. "You will be charged with numerous felonies, including conspiracy to murder, conspiracy to commit fraud, working against the interests of your country, colluding with terrorists, and a whole raft of other charges which my people are still working on. These will be formally put to you at the end of this interview. Before then, you have an opportunity to tell us everything you know, maybe even convince us not to seek the death penalty, which I'm required to do in matters of high treason."

Anderson's wide-eyed stare was enough to know she was taking the words seriously. "Not treason, I would never do anything to harm my country....."

Quinn spoke for the first time. "Don't be so

fucking naïve! What do you imagine we'd call it when you're one of the central characters behind a concerted attempt to undermine the economy of the state? What did you think would happen when you climbed into bed with a bunch of Iraqi terrorists? Despite what the FBI is prepared to offer, I will see to it that you get the chair, with me standing on the other side of the viewing screen. I might even put in a request to pull the switch myself."

It was a deliberate over-the-top threat which left Freeman struggling to keep a poker face as he listened to Quinn's tirade. This was an unrehearsed good-cop-bad-cop approach, which appeared to be having a sobering effect on Anderson."

"Please believe me, I'm not a traitor. Yes, we bought and sold stolen goods, but these were purely financial transactions. The Iraqis were business partners, not terrorists."

Quinn ignored her plea. "Aren't you forgetting all those shady deals that helped to build the Corporation's empire. God knows how many executives you people killed in order to get your hands on their businesses. And don't forget what happened to the McAndrew family. A mother and father murdered and two children put in the crosshairs of assassins, all so that you and Linkmeyer could protect your sordid little secrets."

"No, that was Devlin Montgomery. He acted without the Chairman's permission, which was why we were hunting him down. We tried to put that right before the Iraqis stepped in."

"Explain," Freeman said.

"As I said, the Iraqis were our business

partners. They sourced goods for us in the Middle East and earned a percentage of the profits when we brought them back to the U.S. and disposed of them. The Chairman skimmed off the top and Montgomery ratted him out when he knew he'd been marked for termination."

"What was the meeting at the underground garage about?"

"Montgomery wanted to trade his secrets for a payment of twenty-million. We were meeting to take possession of a USB flash drive which chronicled all our deals. Then out of nowhere the Iraqis showed up. They killed those men at the garage and took us hostage."

"Where's the flash drive now?" asked Freeman.

"Dunno, one of the gunmen put it in his pocket. Guess it's still there."

Freeman looked quizzically at Quinn. "Wasn't in any of the evidence logs. I'll get the morgue to double-check the clothing."

"Yeah, you should do that," Quinn responded before turning his attention to Anderson. "Why did the Iraqis take you hostage?"

"They wanted their money. They forced me to carry out a number of bank transactions to transfer the Corporation's cash into their overseas accounts."

"Did you do what they asked?"

"Of course I did!"

"How much did you transfer?"

"The final amount was sixty-two-million dollars. It wiped the Corporation out. All our businesses will be forced to close within the next twenty-four hours, with the loss of more than a thousand jobs."

Quinn and Freeman exchanged raised-eyebrow glances at the amount of money involved. Freeman took over the questioning. "It's hardly likely you give a rat's ass about employees, so spare us the fake regrets. Who was in charge of the Iraqis? How do we find him?"

Anderson shook her head defiantly. When she spoke it was clear she was regaining a measure of composure. "Not so fast. I can lead you right to his door, but what's in it for me? This is way bigger than you can possibly imagine, which means I'm not giving it up until I get some reassurances."

"You're in no position to make demands," Freeman responded.

"In that case I have nothing more to say until I get a lawyer."

Freeman fought to keep his emotions in check. "Suit yourself, but it's really not that important," he lied. "I'm more interested in you telling us about the FBI agent who was supplying information to Linkmeyer."

"You know about that?"

Freeman's shoulders sagged. He hadn't really known until now. The views he'd shared with Quinn were no longer suspicions or conjecture. There *was* an FBI mole!

He shook aside a growing anger and moved closer to the hospital bed. "Of course, we know about it, but I want to hear everything you know."

"Nothing, nothing. I wasn't aware the Chairman had a link to the FBI. He didn't disclose everything to me. The first I knew was when the Chairman told Montgomery at the garage that he had received a call informing him the FBI had raided the operational plant at Lynchburg early this morning. That's all I know."

"Did Linkmeyer mention the agent's name?"

"No. Even if I'd wanted him to tell me there was no time. It was at that point that the Iraqi gunmen appeared."

Quinn could see Freeman's frustration and decided now was the time to change the subject. "What about Devlin Montgomery? Where is he now?"

"He was in a separate vehicle when we left the car park. He didn't show up at the Iraqis' house and I overheard them saying he'd escaped."

"So, where is he?"

"How would I know?"

"Don't be modest, Clarissa," Quinn said. "There's not a lot you don't know. What about addresses where Montgomery hung out, or places where he could go to, such as safe houses operated by the Corporation within New York?"

"Those were the first places the Chairman had ordered searches on. Montgomery would have known better than to have used any of them."

"Yes, but now that Linkmeyer is dead, those addresses will suddenly have become a lot safer for Montgomery."

CHAPTER 44

DEVLIN MONTGOMERY had already followed Quinn's logic. He'd spent a few hours in a coffee house, listening intently to television news bulletins and checking the CNN app on his smartphone for updates on the day's events in New York. The confirmed death of Linkmeyer and all the Iraqi gunmen had suddenly opened up a new world of possibilities. He was no longer hunted! The FBI didn't concern him, not when he considered how long he'd been on the loose and how ineffective they'd been in trying to run him to ground. Maybe he'd rub their noses in it by taking up residence in Bolivia or Nicaragua or Morocco. There had to be more than twenty countries which had no extradition treaties with the U.S.

What about sending the Feds a postcard when he got to his final destination? *Glad you're not here* would be an appropriate message. The idea appealed to him.

But he needed breathing space. Somewhere to stay off the radar while he planned his way out of the country. The solution presented itself the moment he'd heard of Linkmeyer's death. There was no-one in the Corporation left to worry about, which meant he could use any of their vacant properties without worrying about discovery.

He was now sitting in a small townhouse in Juno Street, just off Continental Avenue in the Forest Hills district, a conveyor-belt suburb, full of terraced housing and people too busy commuting to take any real notice of their neighbours. It was why the Corporation had chosen the area as one of many invisible addresses it used for transacting business away from the limelight, mostly for people who preferred things that way.

Montgomery had simply jemmied the back door and made himself comfortable on a long settee in a front room screened by closed curtains. As was customary, the Corporation kept a well-stocked freezer and a drinks cabinet that would see him through the next three of four days. After that, he was gone.

Pity about having to forget about the do-gooder who'd meddled in things at Bangor. Seeking retribution had been all well and good when he'd run out of options, but now there was a way out and Montgomery intended taking it. Maybe some day he'd come back and finish the job.

He walked into the bathroom and opened the cistern to retrieve a waterproofed package, ripping the cellophane wrapping to reveal a brown-handled Makarov PM, another of the Corporation's 'guest' services. He toggled the pistol's slide magazine and rammed in an eight-round magazine, grateful for the security comfort it provided.

He replaced the cistern lid and walked through to a small kitchen where he rummaged in the freezer, settling for a bag of chicken wings, which he defrosted and cooked in a microwave. After wolfing down the meal he climbed the stairs and collapsed on top of a double bed, not bothering to undress or pull the sheets over the top of his lanky frame. He was asleep within minutes.

There were ten New York addresses on Clarissa Mae Anderson's list of Corporation properties. She'd made it clear she was providing them as a goodwill gesture, something to go on her credit balance when her lawyer faced down the federal prosecutor. In truth, she knew they'd find the information eventually from records at her office, so why not store up a bit of advance collateral?

She'd also offered unprompted info on the existence of other Corporation addresses in numerous states and cities. The scale of the enterprise was mind-boggling, which was why she was confident of cutting a deal, she'd told Freeman.

"Can you believe the smugness of that bitch?" The question was directed at Quinn who was hunched over a computer in a room at the Bureau's NYC Field Office.

Quinn ignored the comment, guessing it was more rhetorical than an attempt to elicit a response. He was scrolling through Google Maps, calling up each of the addresses, studying the areas around them, and trying to put himself into Montgomery's head. There were six apartment block listings, not ideal if you wanted to avoid running into other tenants, so he dismissed these immediately. Montgomery would opt for somewhere more isolated. Two of the remaining four addresses looked promising, in that they were separate-entrance, second-floor bedsits above retail premises. Nothing to worry about nosy neighbours in either location.

Then there were two townhouses, each crammed into narrow streets at opposite ends of the city, and each giving out the appearance of typical student accommodation. He chalked them down as distinct possibilities, if only because the constant toing and froing of academia tended to provide a certain amount of anonymity in the midst of their tendency for partying over the need for study and research.

Quinn printed out street-level views of all ten locations and handed them to Freeman. "We have to check these out tonight. I'm guessing Montgomery will lie low for a few days but we can't ignore the possibility that he's just looking for a one-nighter before he moves on."

"That's assuming he hasn't already done so," Freeman offered.

"Could be, but look at it from his point of view. Not that many hours ago he was kidnapped by a bunch of merciless Iraqis. His prospects at that point were zero until he somehow managed to escape. There's no way he could've just jumped on a plane, not with the dragnet the FBI has thrown around the city, nor could he risk hopping onto a bus or train. Give it a few days and the heat starts to cool, which would allow him to change his appearance and maybe get an acquaintance to provide a lift to a town or city where the search will be less intensive. That's what I'd do in his situation."

Freeman looked through the address print-outs. "You're very thorough when it comes to researching people and places. We usually work on the basis of heading straight to the location and sizing things up at ground level when we get there."

"Works okay when there's only one site to worry about," Quinn conceded. "However, this is a multi-target operation which will require a bit of prioritisation."

"Don't see how it's any different," Freeman responded. "There's no imperative to carry out simultaneous searches since there's no-one left to convey a tip-off to Montgomery. I'll get five teams of agents to visit each location. That's two addresses per team, which means we should wrap this up within a few hours."

Quinn frowned. He couldn't fault Freeman's logic but the FBI man's plan omitted one crucial element. Quinn wanted Montgomery for himself. It didn't matter whether it took all night and most of the next day; the important thing was that he was determined to be the one who stared down the barrel at the man who'd ordered the assassination of two innocent children.

Freeman read his thoughts. "Forget it Quinn! We don't have time to do this ourselves. If Montgomery is at any of these locations we find him as quickly as possible and we close the book."

"I have to be part of this," Quinn pleaded. "The least you can do is reserve two of the addresses for a repeat of our double act when we took down the snipers. That's a one-in-five chance, not great odds we'll hit paydirt, but a whole lot better than sitting here waiting for reports to filter in."

"Agreed," Freeman said. "Pick us out two spots and I'll despatch agents to the others."

Quinn used his multi-purpose lock pick to gain silent access to a door beside a kebab shop which was still doing a roaring take-out trade at two o'clock in the morning. None of the sidewalk customers paid any heed to two darkly-dressed gents who appeared to be fumbling their keys after returning home from a night-out. Once inside, Quinn led the way up rickety stairs while Freeman kept his Glock trained at the dim landing above them.

Despite their attempts at stealth, the wooden risers creaked harshly under the slow advance, a noise that would normally wake the heaviest sleeper, if not for the accompanying din coming from the downstairs fast-food establishment. Quite how anyone would want to live above such a racket was beyond Quinn, until he considered that beggars, or in this case a fugitive, couldn't be choosers.

It took them less than five minutes to clear the rooms. There was a single bedroom, a bathroom, a cramped TV lounge, and a kitchen cum dining room. All tastefully decorated, but minus one important thing. There was no inhabitant, nor no indication that anyone had been in residence for at least several weeks.

Back in the car, Freeman took a succession of calls on his satphone, all from the FBI teams at the first of their target locations, and all reporting that they too had drawn blanks. "Looks like the possibilities just narrowed dramatically by fifty per cent." He told Quinn.

"The odds are still the same as we started. Five properties remaining means our second location still carries a twenty per cent chance that we'll hit paydirt."

Freeman squirmed in his seat. "You're twisting the math to suit your own selfish ends. When this operation started, there was a one-in-ten chance of locating Montgomery. Now it's a one-in-five....."

"See what I mean," Quinn scoffed. "When I went to school in the backwoods of Ireland we were taught that one-in-five was twenty per cent, when expressed as a decimal. I knew you'd agree when you had a chance to work it out scientifically."

Both men started laughing and were still grinning when Freeman steered the Ford Expedition off Continental Avenue into Juno Street, a two-lane thoroughfare that was dotted with trees and cramped with parked cars. Freeman found a gap by mounting the sidewalk and nudging gently against a trash can. He cut the engine and turned to Quinn. "I never asked your logic in picking the two addresses for us."

"What makes you think it wasn't just a random selection?"

"Because I know you don't do spontaneous. Everything has to be looked at six ways from Sunday before you come to a decision. So, spill it."

"You're partly right," Quinn said. "I immediately ruled out the apartments because they're too obvious, not enough privacy. I was banking on the retail bedsits, but figured I'd need to spread my bets. Which was why I plumped for one bedsit and one town house."

"Yes, but why did you choose the ones you did?"

"The bedsits were a mental toss of a coin. The address on this street was simply a matter of my Irish roots."

"Care to explain?"

"I was intrigued by the name, which reminded me of that great Irish play *Juno and the Paycock* by Sean O'Casey. Went to see it several times at the Abbey Theatre in Dublin."

"Never heard of it," Freeman said with sincerity.

"And to think they used to say the Irish were heathens? You Yanks have a lot of catching up to do when it comes to literary works of art."

"Just hang on there a minute, buster," Freeman chided. "What about Arthur Millar or Tennessee Williams or James Goldman? And don't forget, you're a born-again Yank yourself, just like the rest of us."

"I'll grant you that," Quinn said, "but doesn't take away from the fact that Ireland is the land of Saints and Scholars. I rest my case."

Both men turned off the banter when they climbed from the SUV and surveyed the street. They knew from the print-out maps that the address they were looking for was about a hundred yards away on the opposite side. It was a small bungalow, which meant they would have to split up to cover the front and rear.

It was sheer bad luck that Devlin Montgomery was at that moment looking through an upstairs window.

He'd slept soundly for eight hours until his out-of-sync body clock brought him back to consciousness. It was the middle of the night and he cursed at the long day that lay ahead. He grabbed the Makarov from a bedside table and was heading for the door when an engine sound drifted from the street below. He created a two-inch gap in the curtains, almost recoiling in shock when the blacked-out Expedition mounted the kerb and came to a stop. Only law enforcement agencies were permitted to use those kinds of vehicles!

Montgomery waited a moment to watch what was happening. He saw two men alight from the car and reach inside their jackets for what appeared to be weapons. Because of the distance and the lack of street lighting, he couldn't be sure. But there was no doubting the body language of the two figures making their way towards his location from the opposite sidewalk. His attention centred on the taller of the two men. He was wiry and muscly at the same time, and carried himself with an air of authority, just as his men had described the interloper at Bangor. Could it really be him?

Montgomery sprinted out of the room, down the stairs and through the kitchen to the rear of the house. He stepped cautiously through the damaged door and tiptoed his way across an overgrown lawn to a fence. He had no idea where it led to, but now was not the time for doubt. He needed to put distance between himself and his pursuers.

Just as he was about to climb the fence, he changed his mind. He shuffled across to a large bush, settling himself behind its protective screen, and trained his pistol at the centre of the rear door. He had a score to settle!

CHAPTER 45

QUINN REACHED the rear of the house and leaned against the gable wall. Visibility was poor because of a watery moon and the absence of light spillage from adjacent properties. He made out the dark shape of a fence and thornbush at the bottom of a small garden, but little else came into focus. He cursed for forgetting to bring the image-intensifier scope which would have made short work of cutting through the gloom. Too late for maybes now.

He leaned forward and whispered into a lapel mic. "Ready when you are."

He'd left Freeman at the front door with the anti-lock gadget and the honour of going first. The plan was for Quinn to cover a possible rear exit, while the FBI man made the initial breach. Another typical example, Quinn reckoned, of him drawing the short straw.

A soft creaking noise set Quinn's senses on full alert. It was like a hinge in need of oil, and it was coming from the direction of the rear door. He aimed his Glock and edged away from the wall to get a better line of sight. The door moved a fraction of an inch before settling into a swaying motion in tempo with a breeze which rustled the grass as it rolled across the lawn.

"Wait one," Quinn said urgently into the mic. "I've got movement. The rear door is open."

"Anyone there?"

"Can't see. Going for a closer look. Our bird may have already flown the coop."

Quinn angled his way forward, reaching the doorstep within five long strides, his finger already tightening on the Glock's trigger. There was no-one there, certainly not immediately behind the glass-panelled frame, or in the short hallway that led away from it. He nudged against the door and was about to walk through when a warning light seared across his brain.

It came from the depths of time, all the way back to his Ranger training. It had been drilled and redrilled, until it became a part of all recruits. *Watch your six!*

Quinn had almost forsaken it. Almost, but not quite. He dived forward just as the first three shots peppered the point where he'd been standing a millisecond before, sending a shower of glass fragments over his body as he wriggled to face the danger. He saw a figure running towards him, the muzzle flashes from a small pistol illuminating the snarling face of a man he recognised from countless photographs. Devlin Montgomery!

It's almost impossible for untrained individuals to ignore multiple incoming rounds aimed directly at them. Not so for a trained Special Forces operative. Quinn lay on his back and calmly squeezed off two rounds, knowing they'd struck centre mass even before the charging figure shuddered to a stop. The sound of two additional rounds came from behind Quinn. He didn't need to look up to know Freeman had breached the front door and was lending a hand.

Both men stared out at the attacker, now kneeling oddly among the garden weeds, his head drooped on his chest, his hands flopped by the sides, and the white sclera of his eyes highlighted against the dark background.

Quinn and Freeman walked forward, holding torches under the barrels of their pistols. Three paces away they knew there was no longer any threat. Devlin Montgomery was dead. Quinn touched a finger against the corpse and stood back to let it fall.

"I don't get it," Freeman said. "If he was already clear of the house, why wait around for a shoot-out?"

"Guess we'll never know," Quinn shrugged. "Could be he was tired of running or maybe he figured he could take us. Either way, I'm not sorry he decided to make a stand."

Drew Eisler couldn't keep the excitement from his face as he burst into the room where Quinn and Freeman were seated behind a table laden with coffee and sandwiches. "Is it true? Did you get Montgomery?"

"Yes, we got him," Freeman said, nodding at the coffee pot. "Not quite a champagne celebration but it's hitting the mark."

"Mind if I join you?"

"It's as much your party as anybody's, Drew. Couldn't have wrapped it up without you."

Eisler poured a cup and stretched on a chair opposite Quinn. "I know we didn't exactly hit it off at the outset, but I guess I oughta thank you for what you did. This is the Bureau's biggest ever result, so I'll hope you'll accept my apologies."

"Not necessary," Quinn mumbled.

Freeman sensed the tension and decided to move things along. "Let's put the attaboys aside for a moment. We still have one outstanding mess to clear up. Sooner or later I'm going to have to confront Director Perry about being Linkmeyer's mole. All I've got is a heap of conjecture, but I can't let things sit the way they are."

Eisler choked on a mouthful of coffee. "What's this about a mole?"

"Couldn't tell you my suspicions until now, Drew. It all seemed very tentative until the Anderson woman confirmed it."

"She told you who the mole was?"

"No, she didn't have a name, but she did know that someone from the FBI was feeding Linkmeyer a lot of sensitive information."

"What makes you think it's Director Perry?"

"Wish I could answer that in a way that makes sense. Didn't you wonder why he went so easy on you at the internal review of the Iraqi shooting. I reckon he was relieved that Linkmeyer was dead, which meant there was nobody left to make the connection to him. He wouldn't have factored Anderson into the equation, so he was content not to rake up too much ground when you give your report. This also goes right back to the start when somebody tipped off Linkmeyer, and therefore Montgomery, that we were running an off-the-books operation with the help of Mark McAndrew."

Eisler leaned back and puffed out his cheeks. "It did surprise me that Perry was not his usual objectionable self at the review, but c'mon Carl, you don't have enough to start throwing accusations at the Director. It could mean your shield if you're wrong about this."

"I can't sit on it," Freeman exploded. "We'll soon have a sworn affidavit from Anderson pointing to an FBI insider, which means I can be accused of dereliction of duty, or aiding and abetting corruption, if I don't do something. I intend to demand that Perry steps down and provides us with access to all his bank and phone records. An innocent man couldn't refuse such a perfectly reasonable request."

Eisler turned back to Quinn. "Tell him this is folly. If he goes up against Perry, he'll lose."

"I agree," Quinn said.

"Et tu, Brute." Freeman looked daggers at Quinn.

"No, boss, we can't both be wrong," Eisler interjected. "If you won't listen to me, at least take Quinn's opinion on board. You've always respected what he's had to say until now."

"Okay," Freeman responded, still staring at Quinn. "Tell me why you think I shouldn't go after Perry?"

"Because I think he's innocent. Director Perry is not your mole."

The room fell silent for several minutes while the FBI men looked at each other in puzzlement and waited for Quinn to continue. The newly-minted DOJ Special Investigator was not relishing what he was about to say, so he refilled his coffee mug while he gathered his thoughts. This would hurt Freeman badly, not something Quinn wanted to do.

Finally he spoke. "There were never more than four suspects for the mole, and two are sitting in this room. I've already discounted the Director, for reasons which will become obvious, and the same can be said of you Carl. That leaves just the Assistant Director and Agent Eisler. From what I've gathered in the short time spent on this operation, the AD has largely been kept out of the picture, particularly when key moments were triggered, which makes me believe he also couldn't be the traitor."

Eisler jumped up. "What the fuck are you saying? You accusing me of being the mole? I oughta tear your fucking head off!"

Quinn was unperturbed. "Why don't you sit back down and I'll explain it to you. If you can prove me wrong, I'll be the first to admit it, but you won't know what I've got unless you shut up and listen."

Freeman reached out and touched Eisler's sleeve. "Sit down, Drew, and let's get this nonsense out of the way." Then he turned to Quinn. "You'd better be damned sure about where you're going."

"As sure as I've been about anything," Quinn said. "It all boils down to box-ticking. Montgomery went after the McAndrew family because he'd learned about the lawyer's collusion with the FBI. Eisler was one of only four people who knew about it. That's a tick right there."

"The same could be said of all four names you mentioned," Freeman countered.

"Yes," Quinn agreed, "but let's see who ticks the rest of the boxes. The next point of interest was the raid on the distribution warehouse at Lynchburg. Before your team moved in, there was feverish activity to clear the place, including the arrival of three container trucks to ship the goods. That tells me they were tipped off about the raid, albeit with very little time to do anything about it. As far as I'm aware, only you and Agent Eisler knew in advance about the operation. Someone made a call, which means there's another tick against Eisler's name."

"Freeman held up a hand. "Actually, I did inform Director Perry about the intention to check out the Lynchburg address. I didn't go into specifics, but he would have gleaned enough to make a call to Linkmeyer."

"I guess he could've, except for one damning piece of follow-up information," Quinn stated. "We learned from the interview with Linkmeyer's secretary that within several hours of what happened at Lynchburg, her boss had been informed by his FBI mole that everything had been confiscated. You told me yourself that you'd not divulged the outcome of the operation to Director Perry, which means the only box to get ticked this time is Eisler's."

"This is fairy-tale stuff," Eisler shouted. "You're adding two and two together and coming up with the biggest load of bollocks I've ever heard."

"Try this for size," Quinn responded. "That tip-off you received about the location of the Iraqi gunmen was a helluva break. I kept asking myself who would do it, what would they stand to gain, and - most important of all - how did they get your personal cellphone number? And bear in mind, you just happened to be on your own at the time after volunteering to check Linkmeyer's office while the rest of your team were left to run down other leads. Did you go to Linkmeyer's office to make sure there were no trails leading back to you? Maybe you wanted to see if he had an address for the Iraqis pinned on his noticeboard or, most likely, you already knew the address because of your prior dealings with the Corporation. The boxes keep on getting ticked."

Eisler turned to Freeman. "I swear to God, Carl, this is all bullshit. He's trying to force square pegs into round holes. C'mon, you know me better than anyone."

Freeman's reply crackled with emotion. "Jeez, Drew, this doesn't look good. Tell me you didn't do this."

Quinn interrupted before Eisler had a chance to respond. "I've still got two more items to put on the table. The first concerns the attack on the Iraqi house. The review panel seemed to think it was a textbook operation, designed to protect the lives of the agents taking part. A cynic might surmise Eisler wanted a bullet storm in the hope that Linkmeyer was eliminated in the crossfire. Then we have the mysterious case of the missing USB flash drive, which still hasn't turned up. I'm betting Eisler here snaffled it during the confusion in the aftermath of the gunfight. He needed to know what was on it, certainly to ensure there was no incriminating evidence against himself. Who knows, he might still have it stashed away somewhere. I guess a search of his car and home will answer that particular question."

Eisler's face had lost all colour. He sat staring at

the table, his hands joined together in what looked like a white-knuckled prayer. He gulped heavily in preparation for verbalising an explanation, which when it came out was little more than the disjointed mumblings of a man who already knew there was no way of justifying what he'd done. "Carl, I'm....I'm so sorry....it was never meant to get this far....I tried to stop.....they had their clutches in me.

Freeman turned and settled his gaze somewhere on a hazy horizon beyond the small office window. "Stow it, Drew. You can't make this right. This was naked, unadulterated treason from someone who swore to uphold the Constitution and protect the interests of America against all its enemies, foreign and domestic. You were supposed to be my friend and confidante. That's what hurts the most."

"I'd give anything to turn back the clock. Honestly, Carl, I would."

Freeman frowned and switched to a formal tone. "Too late for that, Agent Eisler. Surrender your shield and weapon. Remain seated until I make formal arrangements for you to be taken into custody."

Quinn wanted no part of what was to follow. He got to his feet and walked out of the room.

CHAPTER 46
Florida – six weeks later

THE NOON SUN burned at Quinn's back as he pounded the holiday promenade along the edge of Old Tampa Bay. Not the coolest time of day for a punishing ten-mile run which consisted of mild jogging, building to rhythmical 15mph runs, and crescendoing to Usain Bolt one-hundred-yard dashes. The combination helped prevent a build-up of lactic acid whilst giving muscles the kind of workout he required. Each session ended with thirty minutes of push-ups and squats before returning to his RV, which was parked at a rented site beside a shorefront hotel.

It was a daily regimen he'd been following for the past three weeks, satisfied that his fitness levels were back on a par with his peak as an eighteen-year-old recruit at the end of his basic Army training. Probably a slight exaggeration, he conceded.

He'd arrived in Florida after a meandering trip down the eastern seaboard, stopping off at places like Philadelphia, Richmond, Charlestown and Jacksonville. After picking up the RV from the garage at Bangor, he'd simply pointed it south and kept driving.

Before leaving, he'd spent two days at Chief Justice Fleming's house, playing ball with Charlie and accompanying Sophie on trips to some of Washington's most upmarket boutiques. Psychologist Marie Zeigler was still in residence, something Quinn hoped would develop into a long-term arrangement, for the kids' sake. He had to admit he also liked having her around.

Fleming had insisted on Quinn making regular future visits. The old boy had hinted at retiring from the bench to devote his remaining years to the grandchildren. At one point he'd even asked Quinn to 'bodyguard' the kids during a well-earned holiday to Disney World when things settled down. It had been easy for Quinn to agree.

The final call before the road trip saw Quinn waiting anxiously in a Washington coffee shop for the arrival of Special Agent Carl Freeman. It had been over a week since the two men had talked, leaving Quinn to wonder what kind of reception he'd get. Freeman looked like he'd aged ten years when he eventually sauntered in and pulled up a seat at Quinn's table.

"Are we good?" Quinn had asked tentatively.

"Not your fault things went as pear-shaped as they did, although I would've appreciated a heads-up before you dropped the bombshell about Drew Eisler."

"Sorry about that. I hadn't fully worked it out until that moment. There was something about the way Eisler beamed over Montgomery's death that made me realise my suspicions were correct. Must have been hard for you to take."

"You know, Quinn, you were always a master of understatement, not to mention being a royal pain in the ass." It had been said without rancour. "Of course, it was hard. I went through the Academy with Drew, and stood shoulder to shoulder with him throughout our entire careers. Counted him as my best friend. More fool me."

"Don't beat yourself up. He was a clever manipulator. Mind me asking what he had to say for himself?"

"Nothing you probably wouldn't have guessed. Money and blackmail, two of the three most common motives for law-breaking. In case you're wondering, the other one is sex, which was not a factor in Eisler's case. It seems he was working a drugs-bust case about ten years ago and came across a stash of cash that he helped himself to. It was only five grand, for fuck's sake, but Eisler claimed he needed the money to help with his daughter's university education. It was just sitting there in a drawer, begging to be taken, according to him. So, on the spur of the moment, that's what he did. The money was never missed, mainly because the drugs haul ran into several million, which meant the Bureau's attention was focussed entirely on patting itself on the back for a job well done. Strangely, the men who were arrested at the time never mentioned it in subsequent court appearances, but we can now guess why."

"I'm all ears," Quinn said.

"According to Eisler there was a hidden camera in the room and it caught what went down. Turns out, the building - and the drugs operation - was owned by the Corporation, though of course their name was lost in a mire of shell companies."

"I can guess the rest," Quinn interrupted. "The Corporation showed the video to Eisler and got themselves an FBI inside man."

"Nailed it in one," Freeman agreed. "It was none other than Linkmeyer who made the approach personally. Said all he wanted in exchange for his silence was to be kept informed about any investigations into the Corporation or its myriad businesses. Eisler claims he tried to ensure most of what he passed on was low-level stuff, nothing that amounted to much, until the Mark McAndrew business came along."

"How did he justify what he did there? It was his tip-off that led directly to the murders of an innocent couple. And what about the kids? The bastard was willing to let that play out rather than give us an early heads-up on the Corporation."

Freeman's eyes narrowed. "No getting away from the fact that it was Eisler who started the ball rolling. His excuse was that he told Linkmeyer about our collaboration with McAndrew for the express purpose of getting the Lynchburg warehouse cleared out. Seems Linkmeyer didn't think it was important at the time, at least not until Eisler made a second call shortly before we moved in. It was too late by then, which was why everything was still in place when we made our raid. According to Eisler, he could never foresee a hit being taken against McAndrew when all that was needed was to remove evidence from the warehouse."

"Bollocks!" Quinn's raised voice drew attention from other coffee house patrons. He ignored them. "Did he really think he was working for a bunch of saints? Montgomery might have jumped the gun by killing the lawyer and his wife, but did Eisler honestly believe Linkmeyer wouldn't have eventually gotten around to it? Far as I'm concerned, Eisler might as well have pulled the trigger himself. I hope he rots."

There was a tinge of sadness in Freeman's response. "Guess that's gonna happen. He's staring at a twenty-to-life in Leavenworth. Don't get me wrong, he deserves it, but it could've been different if he'd approached me with his money problems. I know it's not easy for parents, particularly on a government salary, but why didn't he come to me? I'd have tried to help out."

"Wouldn't have happened," Quinn said with conviction. "Most people find it hard to reach out for help, particularly where money is concerned. This was not a tragic sequence of events that befell Eisler; there was always a dark side to his soul. We have a saying back in Ireland: *You can take a man out of the bog, but you can't take the bog out of a man*."

Freeman simply nodded in agreement.

"So, what else has been happening since I left?" Quinn asked, trying to lighten the mood.

Freeman spent a few minutes bringing Quinn up to date. Linkmeyer's secretary, Clarissa Mae Anderson, had cut a 5 to 10 deal for co-operating in unravelling the Corporation's full workings; and the State Department had agreed to return a number of artefacts to the Museum of Baghdad. Oh, and Director Perry was back to his obnoxious best, though Freeman seemed to welcome the return of the status quo.

The two had warmly embraced before Quinn left, wondering if their paths would cross again.

Somehow, he'd felt it was inevitable.

And here he was in Tampa, doing the whole touristy bit. Straw sunhat, garish shorts and tee, flip-flops and mirrored sunglasses. Coffee and cocktails in the afternoon, entertainment shows at night. He was loving every minute of his first R & R in years. Provided it came to an end soon!

He was exiting the RV shortly after seven o'clock in the morning when his cellphone vibrated. He liberated it from a back pocket and studied an incoming text.

URGENT. Parcel awaiting collection at Tampa Post Office. Ask for box number 2215.

Forty minutes later, Quinn was back in the RV after a taxi ride to the postal depot. The package turned out to be a strongly-sealed A4 envelope, which sat unopened on the breakfast table while he speculated on the contents. Might as well get it over with, he decided, lifting his combat knife and slipping it under the flap. A single piece of paper was all that was inside.

There were no logos or seals or address labels. No introduction, no signature, no contact details. Nothing except a typed page of instructions.

Report to McDill Air Force Base at Tampa at 1100 hours this day. Bring no identification or personal effects. You will report to the duty hut for onward journey to Camp Victory Army Base in Baghdad aboard a Boeing C-108. You are to give your name as Michael Tate, but do not divulge mission details to anyone. On arrival at Camp Victory you will be met by Captain Ellis Cheadle who will supply any items you require for the advancement of your mission. You will meet with one Asif Morani, a long-term supplier of goods to the late Tyrell B Linkmeyer, and advise the subject that his business deals, both current and in the future, are now terminated. Mr Morani is to be made aware this is a permanent arrangement.

A 72-hour window has been allocated for your mission. Return to Camp Victory within this timeframe, or advise Captain Cheadle of any difficulties. In any event, do not seek return trip to the United States until the objective has been completed.

Destroy this message as soon as read and understood.

Quinn smiled at the official speak for wet work. They wanted Morani killed, so why not just say so? He'd told Chief Justice Fleming he was out of the assassination business, and he'd meant it. An exception would have to be made in this case. He knew that. Something told him there would probably be other exceptions. But he'd cross those bridges when he came to them.

END

Printed in Poland
by Amazon Fulfillment
Poland Sp. z o.o., Wrocław

53976878R00231